Play at Soul's Edge

Sophia Amador

ALFORD MARR PRESS
Seattle, Washington

First print edition: October 2016
ISBN: 978-1-943881-02-4

Cover by Christian Fuenfhausen
Published by Alford Marr Press
www.alfordmarr.com

Contents

Prologue

 *Elisa*

THREE CONCENTRIC DIAMONDS slashed the wall, spray-painted in glittering black strokes. A symbol Elisa had come to know all too well. Her lip throbbed with remembered pain, and she almost turned back. After all, it was kind of stupid to risk her life—or more—for the truth, wasn't it?

She stood at the end of a long, unfamiliar corridor. She rarely visited this part of the school. Half the ceiling fluorescents had gone dark and the rest flickered a sickly, pale pink. Shattered glass glinted in the corners. Her fingernails burrowed into her palms, and when she unclenched her hand, three tiny crescents glistened with pinpoints of sweat.

In the wavering light, Cesar stood ramrod-straight before the metal double doors that led to the basement, impeccably dressed in a sleeveless white linen tunic and perfectly pressed khakis. Long braids hung below his shoulders and brushed his muscular arms. He glared at Elisa as she approached.

"You can't go in there." He stepped in front of the door.

"Adrian told me to come." She didn't even blink at the lie. Not anymore.

"What evidence do I have of that?"

She swallowed, but she had to go on. She had to know what was really happening. It was time to draw upon all the tricks she had unwillingly learned these past six months since the start of senior year. "You know who I am, right? Who I am to Adrian?"

She lifted her chin. "He wouldn't want you to go against his orders."

He eyed her for a few long moments. Then he stepped aside, his face expressionless.

She slipped inside before he could change his mind. Her legs were shaky, and she clung to the railing for balance, placing her feet carefully on the metal stairs. She stopped short on the landing. Voices rose from below. In the dim basement, a dozen people stood in a rough semi-circle around a girl with her head bowed so only her dark, close-cropped hair was visible. On a raised platform at one end of the room, lounging in a black armchair, sat Adrian. His bangs fell over his face, and the faint light reflected off his glasses.

"So, you no longer want to be a courier for me, Keisha?" Adrian's voice was soft. "In that case, you're no longer of any use to me." He glanced at the boy leaning against the back wall and nodded once. "Rory."

"Aww, not my new bestie," Rory mocked. He strode forward, reaching into his jacket. He gripped Keisha's collar, slammed her shoulder hard with his elbow, and pinned her against the wall. She stared defiantly up at him. Light glinted off a long blade.

Elisa snuck down another step.

1

 *Elisa*

LUNCH WITH ELISA'S FRIENDS could be a dangerous event. She never knew whether she was risking her life simply by eating a peanut butter sandwich. And it wasn't even that she was allergic or anything.

It was the beginning of senior year. She was zoning out a little. Not too much, but just enough to annoy her friends. And anyone who annoyed Sumiko better watch out. She was like a laser-targeted rifle aimed at the tiniest character flaw her friends might let slip.

Elisa sat at their usual table in the Rockton High courtyard, holding a piece of waxed paper up to the sun. Heat shimmered across the wide stretch of concrete and up the decrepit walls of the old building, hazing the air above the long rows of dingy orange tables packed with students eating lunch. Elisa meant to pay attention to what Sumiko was saying, but the pattern of creases in the paper right before her eyes was more beautiful than a kaleidoscope, a golden sun-fired tracery of a million branches, and it felt like she could see the secrets of the future if she only examined it closely enough. It was the exact color of Ben Lancaster's hair when it shone in the sun. She smiled and stretched the wrapping across her knuckles. A few crumbs fell onto her lap.

The buzzing drone of conversation swished over her ears. The fresh whole-grain bread in her sandwich blended perfectly with that rich peanut butter scent. She inhaled deeply, and her stomach growled.

"Hey. Hey!" Sumiko grabbed the waxed paper out of her hand and crumpled it on the table. They had been friends since second grade, when they rescued a cat from a group of boys who'd been chasing it, but sometimes Elisa could swear Sumiko thought she was her gym coach. It didn't help that she was a brown belt in karate and believed every expression of affection required a punch for emphasis.

Elisa blinked. "Did you say something, Sumiko?" She picked up the ball of waxed paper and smoothed it out.

Sumiko snorted, and Chloe flipped her perfectly flat-ironed blonde hair over her shoulder. "Don't bother! She's off in her own world as usual," Chloe said.

A loud babbling from the courtyard overrode the background conversations. A tall, skinny kid staggered between the lunch tables, tossing his scraggly dark hair. Kids rolled their eyes and jeered, but he ignored them. The waxed paper in Elisa's hand crinkled, and his gaze zeroed in on her food.

"Peanut butter! My favorite!" He lurched sideways, lost his footing, and sat down hard on the pavement in front of the three girls. He sniggered and flopped his head back and forth.

Chloe braced her hands against the table, poised for flight. "Who's that creep?"

"Pete Waddell." Sumiko slid to the side of the bench. "He's high on something."

The kid crawled closer and licked the ground near their table.

"Yuck!" Chloe recoiled.

Pete banged his head on the ground in an uneven tempo.

The slam of his skull against the hard surface echoed in Elisa's brain. She knew what it felt like when someone rammed your head into a wall. Even if they said it was for your own good. Her guts twisted and she jumped up. "Stop it! You're going to hurt yourself."

"Just ignore him, Elisa," Chloe stage-whispered.

He kept pounding his face on the pavement. A trail of blood oozed down his cheek. A girl shrieked and people abandoned half-eaten pudding cups on their tables. Someone's lunch meat landed —*splat*—on the asphalt.

Shaking off Chloe's grip, Elisa squatted beside Pete and put a hand on his shoulder. His muscles jerked spasmodically, tensing and going limp in an erratic rhythm.

"Shhh," she said. "You need to stop or you'll hurt yourself."

"Quit being mean!" the kid whined in a voice that sounded far younger than he appeared. "Wha'd I ever do to you?" He stuck a thumb in his mouth and started to cry. "Pete's sad."

"Sad people shouldn't hurt themselves," Elisa told him.

"Yes ma'am!" Pete bared all his teeth in a childish grin. Then he tried to stand up and fell over, giggling. He flailed his arms and almost knocked her over. She jumped out of the way.

Sumiko tugged at her arm. "Elisa, watch out."

"He needs help." Elisa pulled away. "He's going to smash his head open."

"I'll call security," Sumiko said.

Rockton High's finest was already on the way. Pudgy Mr. Thompson, the part-time security guard, scurried across the courtyard. Like most Rockton High support staff, he wasn't exactly a paragon of excellence. Due to the budget crisis, everyone had been given pink slips and only some of them had been re-hired. Thompson spent most of his time in his office on the district's sluggish internet searching for another job.

"All right, what's going on here?" His face shone scarlet. One of his uniform buttons had popped open, exposing a ratty white undershirt pulled taut over his belly.

Sumiko took charge as usual. "Pete needs a doctor. I think he's OD'ing."

"I'll call the police." Thompson pulled out a beat-up phone and punched a couple of buttons.

Pete wrapped his arms around his knees and rocked back and forth. Elisa squatted next to him again. He sucked loudly on his thumb, the slurping audible from a dozen feet away. A ring of kids had gathered, staring and pointing cell phones at him. The hubbub of conversation got louder. Adrian Salas, a tall boy Elisa knew from math class, pushed his glasses up his nose and shifted his load of books to the other arm. He glanced at her and looked away swiftly. The boy next to him stood on tiptoe to whisper something in his ear.

Thompson mumbled into his phone. Elisa carefully peeled open the fingers of Pete's free hand. His fingernails had cut into his skin, and he was bleeding.

"Mr. Thompson, don't you think he should go to the hospital?" Sumiko jabbed her fists onto her hips.

"I'm calling 911." Thompson backed away, unconsciously gripping his baton. Facing down Sumiko could make anyone nervous. He said to Elisa, "Now step back, young lady."

Before she could move, a kid with unevenly-cut ginger hair burst into the circle. The voices of the crowd faded again into the background chatter, and she blushed furiously. It was Ben Lancaster. He knelt on the ground beside Pete, brows lowered in a scowl. He didn't even glance toward the girls.

"You okay, Pete?" The only response was more giggles as Pete decided to roll around on the ground. Ben's scowl deepened. "Let's go, man. I know a safe place."

"Hey," said Thompson, "you need to wait for the police."

Ben glared. "911 takes forever these days. The clinic's only three blocks away."

He picked up the semi-conscious kid and tried to sling him over his shoulder in a fireman's carry. Ben's legs bent, and he struggled to straighten under the kid's weight.

Adrian stepped forward, light glinting off his glasses, a humble, half-apologetic smile on his face. "Need some help?"

The two of them made a chair with their arms and draped Pete's arms around their shoulders. Pete slumped in their hold, emitting occasional baby sounds.

"Now, wait a minute, you two, you're violating school rules," Thompson protested. He gripped Adrian's forearm. The bland smile faded, and Adrian shot him a long, cool glance from behind his glasses. Thompson jerked back as if burned. He cleared his throat and lifted his baton, but by then Ben and Adrian had already trotted halfway across the courtyard with Pete suspended between them. Thompson moseyed half-heartedly after them, wiping his forehead. It was too hot for a chase.

Sumiko yanked on Elisa's arm and led her back to the table. "Ugh. You've got blood on you."

Elisa rubbed the rusty stains on her hands. "I guess."

Sumiko rolled her eyes. "Why do you always get involved?"

"He was going to hurt himself!"

"Don't worry. I've got it." She pulled a neatly-folded bundle of paper towels out of her lunch bag and wiped Elisa's hands with quick, efficient strokes.

The excited chatter died away, and kids went back to their interrupted conversations. Elisa wondered if Pete would be okay. Drug overdoses, students bringing knives or guns to school—it had become too common at Rockton High lately. People didn't care anymore. They'd gotten used to it, although Ben was the opposite of unconcerned. He'd built up quite a reputation for fighting at the slightest excuse, sassing the teachers, ignoring all the rules. But he'd looked so fine marching to Pete's rescue. It gave Elisa a little thrill.

OK, maybe she was far too stuck on him.

She had first met Ben in middle school. It was five years ago, the year after her father left. That was a bad year; her mother became even more bitter and grouchy, her prayers louder and more frequent. She only talked to Elisa about how she was going to the devil and about money—or more precisely, the lack of it. Her older brother had moved out, and Elisa had never felt so alone. One day in school some of the football players were harassing her, and Ben had—

Elisa's memory was interrupted by a thud as Sumiko's binder smacked her on the head.

"Ow!" she said, rubbing her ear.

"You're welcome."

Sumiko scrutinized Elisa more closely. "You're not just red-faced because of being stupid around Pete. Don't tell me you still have that crush on Ben Lancaster. That delinquent isn't worth your time. He didn't win any points with Thompson today."

She seemed even more annoyed than usual. A bad sign. It usually meant she was hatching some plot to "improve" Elisa's life.

"He's not a delinquent," Elisa said, still kneading her scalp.

"Didn't Ben get suspended for fighting a couple of weeks ago?" Chloe adjusted the opalescent blue frames of her glasses.

"What happened?" Elisa asked.

"Just the usual." Sumiko rolled her eyes. "He and that loser Mario Fonseca got into it right in front of the principal's office. Brilliant."

"It's not fair that he got in trouble today. Ben was just trying to help. I wonder what's wrong with Pete."

Sumiko shrugged. "Druggie. OD. What else?"

"Don't you think it's weird, Sumiko?"

"Drugs always make kids act weird. Let's talk about something more important: your love life."

"Stop it." Elisa took a bite of her sandwich. "I just think Ben is cute."

Chloe frowned. "Ewww, he's not cute at all, and he's constantly in trouble. Just last week—"

"Shut up!" Sumiko said.

"Hey, I'm on your side! Just trying to help Elisa get over her stupid crush."

"Ben's not a bad person," Sumiko said. "He's just—I was thinking it's time for Elisa to find *another* guy to like. Someone who's not always getting into fights." She stopped to scan the lunchtime crowd. The circle of kids, still gathered in tight knots, was gossiping about what had happened with Pete.

"I got it! Why not Adrian Salas? Senior class president, straight-A student. He'd keep you out of trouble." She poked Elisa's side. "And he's awfully cute. Built, too."

Elisa remembered Adrian striding across the courtyard to help Ben. He'd lifted Pete like he weighed nothing.

"Mmm," said Chloe. "Those glasses make him look like too much of a nerd. But he's got nice hair," she conceded. "Dresses well, too." She smirked. "I bet it would feel nice to run your hands through that thick brown hair."

Elisa frowned and licked some jelly off her finger. "I think my fingers would make his hair too sticky."

"I know what it is," said Chloe with a simper. "You miss that bad-boy spark you see in Ben."

"Besides, why would anyone be interested in me?"

"What are you talking about?" asked Chloe in mock surprise. "You may be quiet, but you've got the assets every guy wants." She cupped her own breasts.

Elisa shook her head so her hair covered her face to hide her embarrassment. Though she had come to it late, her body had recently started to develop in ways that drew attention she wasn't altogether sure she wanted.

"Yeah," said Sumiko. "From what I hear, there isn't a single guy—or girl"—she eyed Chloe—"who doesn't think you're hot."

Chloe made an exaggerated "O" with her mouth. "Hot is right!" She winked, and Elisa concentrated on her sandwich as if it were the most interesting thing in the world. She adored her friends, but the constant sexual innuendoes could get a little old.

"Anyway," said Sumiko, "I just think you should broaden your horizons. You've had that crush forever." She wiped up some crumbs from the table with a napkin. "Really, you could have anyone. I think you should give it a try. It's just dating; it's not a permanent thing. Hey, who knows? Maybe it would make Ben jealous," she said with a grin.

Elisa groaned. "Both of you, shut up! You're not running my love life and that's final!"

2

 *Ben*

HUMID, STALE AIR pressed down onto the streets around Rockton High. Sweat from the unconscious burden on Ben's shoulder soaked into his shirt. He hobbled the last block to the clinic. He'd insisted Adrian return to school before the bell rang, and his classmate had been only too willing to avoid an unexcused absence. Ben's record was already too spotty for more truancy to matter.

Teachers didn't like it when you missed class or didn't get your homework done. They called it a "bad attitude," even if the reason was that you'd been up until 3 AM at the clinic, keeping a homeless man who'd been nearly beaten to death hydrated through the night. No, he'd just been wasting time on "unproductive" members of society again.

Homework was useless anyway. Still, the stupid grades mattered. He heaved Pete higher up on his back and increased his pace. Maybe if he was super-efficient today he could get it done.

He shook his head. Who was he kidding? He was going to be working in the clinic all night.

Pete whimpered a little. Ben scowled.

The Lancaster Free Clinic operated out of a ramshackle old house squeezed between two high-rise apartment buildings. Ben struggled up the chipped cement steps. Pete might have appeared skinny, but he was heavier than he looked. Ben got him into one of the examination rooms and went to find his father.

Dr. Lancaster examined the boy, who hadn't regained consciousness. "Looks like a narcotics overdose. I need to take a blood sample, but I'm pretty sure I know what he's on." He adjusted the IV. "There's a new drug out on the streets. I've been seeing more cases lately. I don't know much about it, but I treated a kid who said it makes you feel like everything you wish for will come true." He smoothed back Pete's dark hair, lying in matted tufts on the pillow. "But an overdose can cause mental regression, brain damage. Childish behavior."

"Can you help him?" asked Ben.

His father shrugged. "I don't know. Sometimes they behave normally for a while, then have flashbacks and think they're children again." He replaced his stethoscope in the breast pocket of his lab coat. "The drug's more addictive than heroin. Only takes maybe two, three doses before you're hooked."

"Aren't the cops doing anything?"

"I'm sure, but from what I hear, no one even knows where it's manufactured, or how it's being smuggled into the country."

Ben clenched his fists. "I've got a good idea who's mixed up in it." He imagined himself planting a fist in Mario Fonseca's grinning face. He could practically hear the satisfying crunch of bone.

"Son, you shouldn't get involved. Leave it to the police."

"Right, Dad. While more cases like this happen." The least he could do was beat the hell out of the bastard he knew was dealing drugs, along with the rest of his scummy friends. That might end up being the only way he could make a difference.

◈ Mario

The droning voice of Chief Keef's latest rap single battered the crowd at the private lounge at headquarters and rammed into the gaps between shouted conversations. Bodies writhed and bumped in the smoky air.

Mario Fonseca leaned against a wall, a can of beer in one hand and a careless half-smirk on his face. His gaze flicked from one group to another, and then to the shadows at the end of the room, where the Captain lounged in an armchair on a raised platform overlooking the hall. Gloom obscured his face, but that didn't stop the half-nervous, half-admiring glances from his audience. A crowd clustered around his feet. Beside the armchair, a tall, thin kid with straight black hair bent close to the shadowy figure's ear, then slipped into the crowd. Rory Fong. Mario straightened, noting where he had disappeared to.

"Lonnie," he said in a low voice, "go check up on Rory."

Lonnie wiped his nose, sniffed, and licked the back of his hand. "Do I hafta?"

"Look, dipshit, you're the one begging to get in. I don't give a fuck whether you—or anyone—just get ganked. Now, you in or out, you lazy motherfucker?"

Muttering to himself, Lonnie skulked away.

Mario took a swig of his beer and shook his head. It was important to keep tabs on Rory. The Captain's second-in-command was sneaky and seemed to know everything. Wherever he went, you knew the Captain had an interest, and Rory had been heading out on more errands lately. Something must be going down.

Mario chugged the rest of the beer, scanning the room. In the center of the dance floor, perched on six-inch rose-colored heels, he spotted Kim Lugo. A pert ass in a tiny pleated coral skirt waggled and twisted above her slim legs, and he found himself staring at the smooth skin between her thighs, wondering if the skirt would wiggle out of the way during one of her turns. He imagined himself sliding a hand inside the shimmering fabric to cup the warm flesh beneath.

Kim stopped dancing, and Mario raised his eyes to her face. The metal spike in her nose quivered as she stared, pale brows drawn together, at the man in the armchair. The Captain spoke briefly to his entourage, then glided to his feet. A statuesque blonde at his side extended a hand, and he stroked her hand with long fingers. The two slipped out a door behind the chair.

Two red spots blossomed on Kim's cheeks. She lifted a glass of golden liquid to her lips and tossed it back, her frizzy platinum ponytails trembling. A few drops fell from the glass and rolled into the chains dangling between her full breasts.

"Hey, Kim!" Mario's deep voice rose over the noise of the crowd. He grinned and patted the couch beside him. Kim tossed her hair. He tipped his head to one side and mimed lighting a pipe. She hesitated, threw one glance over her shoulder at the empty armchair, then shrugged and strutted over, the pleated skirt wiggling back and forth.

"What th' fuck you want, Mario?" She collapsed onto the couch.

"Is it wrong to wanna spend time with a pretty girl?" He put a hand on her thigh, slipping a finger underneath her skirt.

She slapped it away. "Keep your hands off," she warned. "Where's your shit?"

Laughing, he lit the pipe and handed it to her. She closed her eyes and took a long drag. She had big lungs for such a tiny girl.

Mario said, "I saw what happened. That bitch Tina chasing after the Captain?"

"You think I give a fuck?"

He held out his hands defensively. "Hey, I just thought you might wanna make it with a guy who appreciates you. Someone who thinks you're really hot."

"Fuck that," she said, her voice hard.

He shrugged. They passed the pipe back and forth in silence for a few minutes and she slumped lower in the seat, her legs falling apart. Her lowered lashes grew damp.

He leaned into her and teased at her skirt again, his fingers caressing the warmth between her thighs. This time she didn't slap his hand away, but writhed slowly, her eyes still closed. He placed his palm on her belly, then slid it lower, and she half-arched, baring her throat. A moan escaped her lips. He grabbed her head and slammed their mouths together.

She tasted of Jack Daniels and smoke. He yanked at the metal ring on the zipper of her pink leather vest, exposing more of her large, soft breasts. Her head fell back, and she groaned. Breathing heavily, he squeezed her breasts hard. They were soft under his hands, and the contrast between his dark, calloused skin and the pale, yielding flesh under his fingers made his jeans far too tight.

He could smell sweat, perfume, and alcohol wafting from her skin, and it aroused him. He pulled her closer.

She sat up so suddenly the top of her head banged into his chin. "Fuck you, Mario! I'm not putting out for you!" She stood, zipped up her vest and flounced away.

He watched the rhythmic swing of her hips until she disappeared in the crowd.

Fucking bitch thought she was too good for him. She'd change her tune soon enough. They all would. Maybe no one knew yet what was going down, but everything was about to change at Rockton High.

Keisha

Keisha Huston strode through the Rockton Eleventh Precinct bullpen to Captain Truong's office. She tugged at her sweat-soaked uniform collar. The emergency call had come at the end of a double shift, and she was exhausted. Overhead fans spun in the late afternoon sun, disturbing clouds of dust motes that winked in the humid air. They had been supposed to get air conditioning for the office, but budget cuts had delayed the installation.

Keisha knocked on the captain's door. She scowled when she saw Vince Devore sitting in one of Truong's straight-backed chairs. He'd shaved off his beard: a bad sign. Even at twenty-five, Vince could pass for a middle-school student with his short stature and face like a twelve-year-old's carved out of fine mahogany. Vince was also one of the best martial artists she knew. If he'd been called from outside the precinct, it was going to be a rough assignment.

Truong's office was crammed with gunmetal-gray file cabinets. Drawers hung half-open and files were balanced sideways on top of each. Against the back wall, an ancient radiator dripped rusty liquid onto the utilitarian green linoleum.

Truong's eyes twinkled at Keisha. How he managed to keep his air of sunny benevolence in a district ravaged by cutbacks and rumored corruption was one of life's enduring mysteries, but she wouldn't complain. You couldn't ask for a better boss.

"Thanks so much for coming, Officer Huston. I know you're on overtime, so I'll make this brief. I'm sure you've heard about the new drug that's flooding the streets. We just got a report today of an overdose at Rockton High. We have intel that a high school gang may be involved, so I want you two to go undercover."

Keisha groaned inwardly. Not again. Just because she only stood four foot ten, she always got the "infiltrate the high school" assignments.

Vince grinned. "Another canceled undercover police program revamped for modern times? Precinct Eleven ain't got no creativity."

Keisha rolled her eyes. "Good to see you again too, Devore."

He wagged his finger at Truong. "I'm only working with this skinny-ass bitch if you swear to me on a stack of Bibles she got rid of her cats."

Keisha bristled. "What've you got against cats? They're smarter, prettier, and better with a weapon than most babyface cops I know."

Truong smiled. "Glad to see you two still have a great working relationship. You're going to need it. This is going to be a tough one. Rockton High seems to be the latest source of this shit. They call it 'Rapture' or 'slip' and it's bad. Crime's up by over seventy percent in the affected areas; emergency rooms are overflowing." He pushed a report across his desk. "Read it and weep."

Vince folded his arms. "Guess that's why you're sending in the big boys." He shot a glance at Keisha. "And, uh, cats."

 ## *Elisa*

Elisa peeked over the edge of her math book. Tangled brown bangs flopped over Adrian's nerdy glasses as he concentrated on a problem on the other side of the classroom.

When he'd been elected class president, people had been shocked. She'd heard the jealous whispers. "The principal stuffed the ballot box because he didn't want someone with more suspensions than honors credits to win."

But she hadn't been surprised. Despite being quiet, Adrian always seemed to be surrounded by a crowd. When he did speak in class, a silence followed his words, as though no one wanted to disrespect him with an interruption. She'd never seen anyone so competitive, so driven to win at any cost.

She and Adrian had competed for the top spot in honors math ever since she could remember. Boys sometimes got upset when she outscored them in math and science, since girls weren't supposed to do that. Not Adrian. He had always been outwardly polite, but... there was something she couldn't put her finger on. Last year, he had hated it when the two of them both got perfect math scores all year. He actually told the teacher that she needed to make the tests harder. Elisa was pretty good at math, despite being clueless in other areas. When she kept up even with the more challenging tests, Adrian seemed to brood.

His mood didn't change until the end of the year, when she broke her arm just before the final, and had to take a make-up test without the opportunity for extra credit. It allowed Adrian to secure the top spot. She remembered his face at the end-of-school ceremony. He had flashed her the oddest expression of, well, glee. But how could that be? No one could have predicted the strange events that culminated in her falling off that ladder in the gym.

As if he'd become aware of her thoughts, Adrian raised his head and met her eyes across the classroom. His eyes crinkled at the corners. She reddened and bent to her work.

It was all Sumiko's fault. When she got an idea in her head, she wouldn't let go until she'd pounded it into everyone else's.

After class, Adrian fell into step beside Elisa. He flashed her a shy smile. "May I ask you something?"

Her shoulders tensed, but she nodded.

"I was wondering if you'd like to get together after school to study. I've been looking for a homework partner in math."

She was unable to hide her disbelief. "I can't imagine how I could help you."

"I think we could learn from each other." His voice was polite, even gracious.

She muttered, "Maybe some other time."

He held her gaze a moment too long before walking away. She caught herself staring at his back.

No. No way. It wasn't like he appealed to her the same way Ben did.

Although her unrequited crush was getting old. And let's face it, she wanted to go out with someone. After all those years under her mother's unrelenting rules, now was her chance. It might not be so bad to date someone quiet and well-behaved. Her big brother would have approved. He had taken her aside one day before he left and wagged a finger in her face.

"Don't end up like your mother, pregnant before she got out of high school. I want you only to date polite boys, you hear?" He glared down at her, obviously trying to appear imposing and mature. He was six years older than her and she adored him, but in those days she had been too busy trying to make sure he didn't know it.

She scoffed. "Carlos, I'm only eleven. I'm not planning on dating any time soon."

"You never know, with all the lowlifes around here. Even better, you should wait till you get married before you sleep with anyone."

"Sleep with—what? Carlos!" She giggled, rolling her eyes. "What are you talking about?"

"If I were the one taking care of my little sister, I'd want to make sure you have a good life."

She laughed and hugged him. "How can I go wrong when I have you?"

He scowled. "Are you listening to me? What if I'm not around?"

"You'll always be around!"

"Just be good, okay?"

"I'm always good, Carlos."

Elisa blinked away tears. She still missed him. He was the only person who'd ever really loved her. Her mother didn't have any love left in her. She'd been raised Catholic, had rebelled violently in high school and gone so far as to turn a few tricks. Her parents had kicked her out on the street. She'd gotten pregnant with Carlos at sixteen, but then had found Jesus and become extremely religious—the harsh, fire-and-brimstone kind of religion. She'd beaten Elisa with a strap when she wasn't obedient. Carlos had shielded her from the worst of it, but when he left it got brutal. Elisa hadn't been allowed even to date until she turned sixteen. Kind of ridiculous in this day and age, but what could she do? At least now her mother was gone most of the time at religious retreats.

Elisa didn't want to make Carlos unhappy, even if he wasn't around to see what she did.

She shook her head and rushed off to her locker. It was no good being sad about Carlos. Besides, she had happier things to think about—she was going to learn a new job at the bakery that afternoon. Mrs. Rojas was going to let her roll out the filo dough. She could already smell the sugar-scented air in the big kitchen, feel the cool, soft flour-and-butter mixture under her fingertips.

Sumiko was waiting at her locker. "I saw Adrian speaking to you upstairs. What did he want?"

"Nothing," she said, twirling her combination lock. No way would she give in to Sumiko's ridiculous plans. "He wanted to do some homework together, and I said no. He certainly doesn't need any help since he's the top student in the school."

Sumiko put her hands on her hips. "You said no?"

Elisa decided the best defense was to babble. "I mean, if he wanted to learn how to cook, I know something about that, and I could show him some of the dishes I've made—"

"You idiot!" interrupted Sumiko. "He was asking you out, not trying to get help on his homework!"

"It's not like he asked me to a movie!"

Sumiko's face was stern. "Next time," she said, "you say yes, understood?"

Elisa bit her lip. Maybe she'd missed her chance. Adrian was awfully cute, and maybe she'd hurt his feelings. She wouldn't reject him next time, especially since it would keep Sumiko off her case.

Of course, it took a while until Adrian asked her out again.

Later that week, he approached her at her locker, arms full of books. He'd said more to her in the past couple of days than he had in their entire high school career. Was he up to something? Or was it Sumiko? "You like acting, right? Ms. Littleton wants to start a drama club. She's asked me to be president, and I was wondering if you'd be interested."

A drama club? Now that was bizarre. "What would we do?"

Adrian stepped closer. He was much taller than her, and his skin was smooth, stretched taut over high cheekbones, long and abundant lashes encircling dark brown eyes. "She just got a grant from some foundation or other, and it's not enough money to actually produce any plays, but she thought we could read a few together, and maybe attend one or two at the Third Avenue Theater."

He was standing so near she could feel the heat of his body. She usually tried not to pay attention to looks, but when he stood this close it was obvious he was built, in a sleek, understated sort of way. He smelled good, too. And those dark eyes were what romance writers would call "liquid-center chocolate"—simply delicious.

She licked her lips. After all, Ben wasn't interested. Anyway, she had to follow Sumiko's advice before she got even more annoyed. Next time she might arrange for something truly weird, like a date at a shooting range or something. "Sure! It sounds... very educational. Should I bake brownies or something?"

He smiled at her, and she imagined a whole bowlful of warm, melted chocolate batter. "Awesome. And brownies would be delicious." He slid a book out of his stack and flipped it open. "I found a book of Shakespeare plays. Would you like to try a dramatic reading of *Othello* tomorrow after school?"

Her jaw dropped. Was he asking her out to read some stuffy old play together? Could her instincts about him have been wrong? He radiated the puppy-dog innocence of a nerd, not the driven intensity of an academic competitor. Maybe she owed him a chance. Why shouldn't she go out with someone smart and hard-working?

What harm could it do?

3

 *Elisa*

ELISA WAS RUNNING LATE for lunch with her friends. She zipped back and forth through the crowded corridors, imagining she was a ping-pong ball bouncing her way around knots of chattering students. As she rounded a corner near the courtyard exit, she missed a bounce and crashed into someone.

Her books scattered to the floor. A reek of mingled sweat and cologne washed over her. "I'm so sorry!" she said by reflex.

Ron Hundley's glare pierced her from beneath stringy black hair. "Watch where the fuck you going, bitch!" He kicked her binder and books, hard, and stomped away. The binder crunched open on the floor, homework spraying out a trail of lined paper. Her Econ textbook soared in a high, wide arc before slamming into the wall and fluttering limply to the floor in three pieces.

"It was an accident, and I said I was sorry!" she shouted at his back. The textbook had been kicked so hard its binding had split. She was going to have to tape it back together. She hoped the school wouldn't charge her for it.

Why did she always crash into people? Elisa, the human bumper car. Ben had called her that in middle school; luckily, he'd never told anyone.

It was the day she'd first noticed him. She'd been scuttling along the hallway, hunched over her binder, hugging the dark brown walls, hoping to remain invisible in her faded, too-tight clothes.

Up ahead, some boys from the football team were hanging out by their lockers. One of them muttered something about "ugly" as Elisa slunk past, pretending to ignore them.

"Why can't that freak stop wearing purple flowers and orange polyester?"

"Maybe she thinks she's sexy." The boys guffawed.

Her cheeks burned and she scurried faster.

One of the football players shouted, "Stop it, freak!" He elbowed her and knocked her books to the floor. "Oops!" he cried, and all his friends laughed.

She tried to pick everything up, only to trip over a leg stuck casually in her way, sending her sprawling to the floor.

There was a commotion behind her, and then Ben Lancaster, scowling, charged past. Pale and freckled, wiry arms pumping, a full head shorter than any of her tormentors, he didn't say a word, just planted his fist straight into the tallest one's grinning face.

Elisa shrank back from the disconnected shouts and sounds of fists landing on flesh with odd, hollow slaps, and pressed herself against the wall. One of the football players grabbed Ben from behind while another kicked his legs out from under him. He hit the ground hard, but bounced up in a moment, blocking and punching. Soon, one of the football players was curled up on the floor, then another.

When the biggest boy lay on the floor groaning, the rest of them slunk away, nursing their injuries.

"You okay?" Ben asked, the frown still creasing his forehead.

She wasn't used to people talking to her so gently. Unable to speak, she stared into his pale blue eyes. She noticed his eyelashes, so long, so close to her face...

She shook her head. It had been from crash to crush, but now it was time to get over him already, because no matter how different Ben was from guys like Ron Hundley, he was never going to be interested in her the way she wanted. She gathered up the dirty, torn remains of her homework, jammed them into her binder, and walked into the courtyard.

The late fall air tasted crisp and dry on the back of her throat. The leaves on the oak trees glowed bright yellow edged with brown. Darker leaves crunched underfoot on the asphalt, filling the air with their spicy scent.

She plumped down on the metal seat next to Sumiko and Chloe and rubbed her shin where a bruise was forming. Sumiko frowned. "Are you all right?"

"I'm fine." She brushed her hair out of her face. "But Ron Hundley is a jerk!"

Sumiko's face darkened. "Elisa, you should watch out. He's got a really bad reputation."

"It was an accident!"

"You should be careful," Chloe said. "Haven't you heard? He's a member of Tenebras."

"A member of what?" Elisa asked, rooting in her disheveled backpack for her lunch. Of course she knew who they were. How could she not have heard about the biggest gang in the school? But it made her friends happy to think they could educate her.

Sumiko rolled her eyes. "You really are an innocent. Don't you know about them?" She lowered her voice. "They control most of the drug sales around the neighborhood. And who knows what else they're into."

"At my aunt's shop," Chloe said, "she has to pay them protection money every month so she doesn't get robbed." She bent her head, eyes gleaming with the anticipation of sharing a particularly juicy piece of gossip. "And they say that all the top gang members have tattoos somewhere on their body showing their rank."

"What?" Elisa had never heard that bit. "Creepy."

"Yeah," Chloe continued, her eyes bright with excitement. "Watch the next time Hundley opens his mouth. You'll see his gang marking on his tongue."

"Gross." Elisa wrinkled her nose.

Sumiko shook her head. "Stop it, Chloe."

Undeterred, Chloe whispered, "Membership is supposed to be secret, but some of these guys like to brag. That's why Hundley has his gang tattoo on his tongue, so he can show off." She leaned closer. "But no one knows who their leader is."

"Chloe, shut up with the rumors. You're making it up."

"It's all absolutely true, I swear. I knew a girl who dated one of their members. She said not to tell anyone on pain of death!" Chloe whispered in a dramatic voice.

Sumiko rolled her eyes, but Elisa was fascinated.

"They call their leader 'the Captain,'" Chloe said, "and they say he's been running the gang since he was twelve. They say that even though he's only a high school student, he's already lost count of the number of people he's had killed." She narrowed her eyes as she imparted this bit of scandal.

"And this is a student in *our* high school?" Elisa shivered.

"Lots of the kids in this school are members. You'd be surprised."

Both girls raised their heads as someone approached. Sumiko dropped one eyelid in a brief wink. Elisa twisted in her seat. It was Adrian, backpack slung over one shoulder, black polo shirt tucked into tight jeans. "Hey, Elisa."

"H-hi, Adrian." She hoped the heat in her cheeks was not obviously visible. She forced herself to glance away from the smooth skin outlining his collarbones above the open neck of his shirt.

"I hope you haven't forgotten drama club this afternoon."

"I never forget my lines," she said. "Plus, I made a surprise."

He grinned, and it transformed his face. She wanted to keep doing things that made him smile. "See you then." He walked away, his long legs filling out those close-fitting designer jeans.

Sumiko waved her hand in front of Elisa's eyes, breaking her gaze. She grinned. "So you do like him after all."

Elisa shrugged, ignoring the flush rising in her cheeks. She took another bite of her forgotten sandwich. Sumiko scrutinized her face. "Don't you think he's hot?" she asked.

Chloe sniffed, her nose in the air.

Elisa smiled, glancing down at her hands. "Well," she said softly, "yeah."

Room 325 was a small, empty third-floor classroom toward the back of the school, overlooking a gas station and a row of auto body shops. The final bell rang, and Elisa sat down at one of the desks to wait for Adrian.

Three shadows fell on the pebbled glass pane and two faded away. A moment later, Adrian came in. His clothes were crisp and perfectly arrayed as always, but his hair was a little messy, bangs falling over his forehead. Elisa remembered Chloe's comments and wondered what it would be like to brush it back from his face, to run her fingers through those dark curls, to feel their warmth against her skin.

"I hope I'm not late." He touched her shoulder casually. A tingle spread from his fingers all the way down her arm.

She had to think of something clever to say. "Yup, I already ate up all the Shakespeare. It was delicious. Tasted like brownies." She patted her stomach. "See? All gone." Oops. Not really clever.

But Adrian laughed and sat next to her, sliding the two desks closer together. Their shoulders brushed and her heart raced. She peeked out of the corner of her eye at his profile. "Is Shakespeare as tasty as brownies?" he said, his hands paging gracefully through the book.

"There's a lot of drama around chocolate these days." Elisa pulled a foil-wrapped package out of her backpack, keeping her eyes away from his face. Otherwise, she was going to turn altogether too red. "Stage brownies," she announced, folding back the foil.

"Tasty," he said, popping a morsel in his mouth. He picked up another piece and held it to her lips. She opened her mouth, and her tongue brushed across his fingertips. They were sweet and smooth and warm. Her face got so hot she couldn't think straight.

"Uh-oh." Was Adrian staring at her lips?

"What?"

He reached out slowly, touched a finger to her mouth, ran it delicately over her lower lip. She sat, unable to move. Without taking his eyes from hers, he held up his finger, paused, and then, very deliberately, licked it.

His tongue circled his lips.

"Wha—"

"You had chocolate on your mouth. I just wanted to make sure it didn't interfere with your reading your part."

Elisa closed her eyes and swallowed, trying to get her heartbeat under control. She was not ready for this. She sucked at flirting, as her friends were always eager to inform her.

Behind her closed lids, Carlos frowned at her. "Boys only want one thing. You need to be a good girl."

Her mother's voice echoed in her head. "Men don't like women who are too forward." Elisa squeezed her eyes further shut.

Adrian cleared his throat. "We should get started on *Othello*."

She opened her eyes. He paged through the book, his expression serious and brisk.

Of course. She must have been imagining all the innuendos. He just thought the brownies were tasty, that was it. Not flirting after all.

"You and your friends looked like you were having a fairly intense conversation at lunch." He found the page he was searching for and pressed the book open at the binding. His fingers were long and slender, tipped by the long, clean ovals of his nails. Elisa focused on the pages.

"Not really," she said. "They were just talking about gangs in our high school."

He arched one eyebrow. It drew attention to his thickly-lashed brown eyes. She shook herself. Concentrate on what he's saying, not his *eyebrows* for goodness' sake.

He rested his cheek on his knuckles. "That's kind of a strange topic, isn't it?"

"I crashed into Ron Hundley and they were warning me about him."

"Ah, the notorious Hundley. I hope he didn't give you any trouble."

"Adrian, do you think there's gangs here at Rockton?"

He ran a hand through his hair and considered her, eyes intent behind his glasses. "I'm pretty sure there's some in every high school."

"Do you know anyone who's a gang member? Are they really as dangerous as people say?"

He scoffed. "I doubt it. Gangs are just a reaction to society's rules. Let's face it, teenagers are basically powerless; we don't have the rights adults take for granted." His voice was soft and deep as velvet. "We're supposed to be legal adults at eighteen, but we can't enter bars; we can't even rent cars until we're twenty-five. We're essentially second-class citizens."

"But Hundley—" She shuddered. "He looks like he'd be capable of anything."

He shrugged. "He just wants to scare people with that tough-guy act."

"But what they say about gangs is kind of scary."

"Adults are threatened by kids. We're stronger and better looking." Adrian's gaze dropped briefly below her neckline and returned to her eyes. "We're full of energy and we're in their faces." His smile widened. "Of course they focus on the negative. They want us to be afraid of each other."

"That almost sounds like you're in favor of gangs."

"Of course not—they're illegal." His expression grew stern. "But I don't think they're as bad as the press they get." He shifted in his seat. "Now, should we get to work?"

They read Desdemona's and Othello's lines for a while and Elisa managed—mostly—to keep her mind on the play. When Adrian announced they'd done enough for the day, she blinked at the time.

"I didn't realize you knew so much about Shakespeare."

He gave her a neutral glance. "I find his work intellectually stimulating."

She stifled a giggle at his comment. She couldn't tell if he was putting her on. "Is English your favorite subject?"

He shook his head, and a lock of hair fell in his eyes. "No, chemistry."

"That's mine too!" She bounced in her seat. "Well, actually, biochemistry. There's got to be a ton of interesting discoveries just waiting to be made about the human body." She was babbling again, like Sumiko and Chloe always warned her.

Adrian smiled. "Yes, there's plenty of money to be made in pharmaceuticals. I'm not going to stay poor all my life like most of the kids around here." His cell phone beeped. "I'm sorry—I need to get to my internship."

"You're an intern?" she blurted.

"I'm a lab assistant. Nothing special. But it helps my family pay the bills."

After he left, she sat for a moment in the empty classroom as it got darker outside. Adrian was definitely flirting. But why did he stop? Was it because she didn't know how to flirt back?

She heard her mother's voice again. "Don't get a swelled head, a plain girl like you." Elisa wrinkled her nose. The last time she went on a date with someone her friends suggested it didn't turn out well.

She traced circles with her finger on the desk. When Sumiko had first launched her at Adrian, she'd frankly thought he was boring. Even though she couldn't seem to stop herself from following rules didn't mean she wanted to date someone who felt the same way. Ben was exciting because she never knew what he might do next.

Except ask her out.

Now Adrian was unpredictable in a completely different way. Elisa rubbed her lips slowly. What *had* he meant with those brownies? Was he really interested in her? And there had been something in their conversation about gangs that bothered her, some kind of odd light in his eyes as they talked.

A shiver went over her entire body. She wanted to see him again.

 ## Adrian

Multiple alarms blared, strobes flashed, and bars slammed into place when Adrian walked through the security gate at Schwartz Pharmaceuticals.

"Oops! Sorry about that." The security guard jumped up and ran to one of the terminals. "The alarm company was running a few tests this afternoon and forgot to turn off analysis mode. Just let me fix it for you."

Adrian waited patiently for the system to be reset. Schwartz Pharmaceuticals was housed in a dilapidated whitewashed building at the edge of town near the bypass. The monthly charge for security monitoring was higher than the property lease.

When the opening for the internship had first been posted, Adrian had gone all out to get the job. It was an opportunity rarely offered to students from their neighborhood. Rockton High had a decades-long rep as "low-performing," and companies usually didn't want to waste time and resources on the illiterate delinquents they imagined filled the school.

But when he actually arrived to start his internship, nothing had turned out the way he hoped. He had been called into his boss's office and told his concepts were "too far out," and that he would do better to focus on not making everyone else look bad.

It didn't matter. The company had turned out to serve other purposes for him.

Adrian carefully adjusted his heavy black glasses as the high-resolution camera over the door scanned his face. He didn't need glasses, but they helped solidify his image as a nonthreatening, bookish nerd as well as serving as a constant reminder to stay in character. He smoothed his face into a bland expression, tinged with just a hint of puppy-dog eagerness, and waited for the door to click open.

Inside, ventilation fans whirred but the lab was still permeated by the smell of acetone and sulfuric acid. Adrian rounded a corner and heard a racket in one of the side corridors. Another student intern, the chief scientist's diminutive nephew, Jim, waved a broom around wildly. He was supposed to be sweeping the office, but he'd left piles of dust and rubbish untouched in every corner.

Jim lifted the broom and banged it against the wall like he was beating a drum set. "Here's the quadruple platinum rapper Jimmy Big dropping another shit-rattling mixtape."

His equally tiny sister, Mira, came around the corner and wagged her dark pigtails, frowning. "Jim, Uncle Eric's gonna get mad you're not sweeping up."

Jim had been hired as a lab assistant by his uncle. However, after several accidents and a pile of broken glassware, the CEO had demoted him to errand boy and janitor.

"I'm too important to sweep." He struck a pose, tipping a pair of mirrored sunglasses down onto his nose. "C-c-c-cause I'm the king of bling, we might just get hit with a RICO or anything..."

Mira snorted. "Don't quit your day job. You don't even scan."

Jim pouted. "Aw, you're just not cool." He spotted Adrian at the end of the corridor and yelled, "Hey, Adrian, whatcha think, man?"

Adrian fixed a polite smile on his face. "Well, rap serves an important societal purpose—"

Jim blew a raspberry. "Shit. You don't have an ounce of cool in your body, man." He swiveled and ran down the hall, whooping like an air raid siren. "Nerd alert! Nerd alert!"

Behind him, Mira rolled her eyes. Adrian kept the smile, now slightly stiff, steady on his face. He didn't want to lose this job. His life depended on it.

 *Elisa*

Sumiko was waiting at Elisa's locker the next morning. "So, how'd it go?"

Elisa pulled out her physics book. Fluorescent light from the ceiling fixture flashed across the glossy binding and she tipped the book back and forth, admiring the patterns. "How'd what go?"

"Your date! With Adrian!"

"Not exactly a date. We read a play together."

Sumiko wedged her arm on the wall in front of Elisa's nose. "What did you talk about?"

"We read a lot of cool lines from *Othello*. Did you know that many of our everyday expressions came from there? Like 'wearing your heart on your sleeve'? And—Ow!" She rubbed her side where Sumiko had poked her hard in the ribs.

"No, you idiot, I mean what did you *talk* about. You can't just have nerded on about some play for the whole time—not even *you* would do that."

"The play was the whole point of getting together!"

"You didn't talk about anything personal?"

"Not really." Elisa slammed her locker shut. "Well—I did lick his fingers."

"You what?" Sumiko's jaw dropped. "You are going to tell me everything, right now!"

"He texted me this morning. He wants to take me to the Fall Festival Fair next Saturday."

The bell rang then, so she avoided the rest of Sumiko's interrogation. By the time lunch period rolled around she was starving. It was too wet and rainy to eat outside, so everyone crammed themselves into the cafeteria. Why that place always reeked of overcooked gym socks and old vomit Elisa still hadn't figured out. Maybe they marinated the socks in those tall vats in the back.

"Uh oh," said Chloe, "I hope Mario and Ben don't get into it in here."

Elisa dumped her books on the table. At the far end of the cafeteria, Ben faced off with a tall, brawny kid.

"That would make Ben's third fight in a month. He'll get suspended again for sure."

"Who's the other guy?" Elisa squinted. They were too far away for her to see clearly. She was a little nearsighted, but her mother said they couldn't afford glasses. She'd gotten a pair last year through a free program, but she'd stupidly lost them and wouldn't be eligible for another until next year.

"Mario Fonseca. He and Ben have it in for each other, as usual." Sumiko shook her head. "Boys."

"I hope Ben doesn't get hurt."

Sumiko grunted. "Don't worry. As many fights as he gets into, he's got a cast-iron head."

Elisa got in the cafeteria line. As she handed her lunch ticket to the cashier, Adrian came up behind her. "May I carry your tray, Elisa?"

She almost dropped her entire lunch. No one had ever said anything like that to her before. "Carry—? Sure!"

Adrian moved in quickly and managed to snag it before it fell from her hands. Milk sloshed over the rim of her glass, pooling along the edge of the tray and dissolving the blobs of ketchup she'd already spilled. "Sorry!"

"No problem," Adrian said. He tugged a couple of extra napkins from the dispenser and mopped up the spill with a single swipe. He lobbed the red- and white-smeared napkins into the compost. Her tray gleamed shiny and new. "Where are you sitting?" His gaze roamed over the crowd and settled on Sumiko and Chloe in animated discussion.

"Don't you usually sit with your friends?" Elisa asked.

"I can do what I want," Adrian replied, indifferent. He held both trays with one hand and lightly steered her elbow with the other. A tingling jolted her where his fingers made contact with her skin. His grip was unexpectedly warm and firm. "Besides, I needed to know if you got my text."

"I'm sorry. The bell rang before I could answer." What an idiotic excuse.

"All you have to do is say yes now," he murmured in her ear. His breath tickled her skin, and he tightened his hold on her arm. "Please?"

Several girls at a nearby table gaped at them, whispering. She wondered if they thought he was hot. Sumiko would never let her live it down if she said no. Besides, the way he said please was kind of irresistible. "Y-yes," she squeaked.

He released her and a brilliant smile spread over his face. His eyes crinkled, and she felt like she did when the bakery oven opened and that rich cookie smell poured out. It made up for feeling a little cornered.

Besides, maybe it would be fun.

"What's up, ladies?" Adrian asked as they approached the table.

Sumiko gestured in welcome at the empty seats. "Be my guest, Adrian. How was the drama club meeting?"

He grinned. "Elisa's pretty talented."

Elisa blushed and took a bite of meat. She chewed it thoughtfully, momentarily distracted from the conversation as she tried to figure out what kind of meat it was. Could it be buffalo? She'd heard it was becoming a common source of protein in some areas. She imagined what life must have been like when herds of buffalo roamed the plains, so numerous that they were the main source of meat for humans.

A hard jab in the shins brought her back to the lunch table. Sumiko scowled.

"Yes?" Elisa hazarded, giving the bright smile she often used to cover such moments of inattention.

"I was asking what you thought of the other club members."

She avoided glancing at Adrian. "Actually, it seems Adrian and I are the only members."

"What?" asked Chloe. "How can it be a club with only two members?" She snorted. "Sounds more like a date to me."

Adrian chuckled. "Elisa and I were the only ones who passed the entrance exam."

"A drama club with an entrance exam?" asked Sumiko. "That's weird."

The commotion on the other side of the room got louder. The fight between Mario and Ben, averted earlier, had re-started.

Mario knocked Ben to the floor and said something with a sneer. Ben, his face red, leapt up and decked Mario. Elisa stopped eating, her eyes on the fight. Everyone else was watching, too, except Adrian, who continued to eat his lunch.

"Adrian, are you really going to ignore those guys?" asked Chloe.

He shrugged. "Displays of brute force don't interest me."

Elisa blushed and averted her eyes from the fight. Ben and Mario *were* kind of brutish, punching each other that way. She snuck a glance at one of Adrian's long, slender hands, and couldn't imagine it balled into a fist. No, a hand like that was made for something else, something far more graceful. She could imagine him playing the piano, running his fingers over a stringed instrument... or a woman's skin. She imagined those hands stroking her cheeks, sliding down to caress her throat, fingers resting gently on her pulse point. She swallowed, closed her eyes, and those long, delicate fingers slipped around her neck, pressing her against the wall. She gasped and met his dark eyes inches from hers, something unspeakable in their depths. His hands tightened around her throat. She tried to pull his fingers away, but they were so strong. She couldn't breathe. His eyes bored into hers, his expression suddenly full of regret and sadness. Her vision started to darken.

She shook herself and focused on the table in front of her. Why would she have such an odd little daydream about a nerd like Adrian? Crazy.

Adrian was still talking. "Deadly force is far more effective when used subtly and with finesse."

Elisa blinked, and the other girls nodded.

What had just happened?

4

 *Elisa*

HER MOTHER WOULD have spent a full hour insulting Elisa about her preparations for her night out with Adrian if she hadn't been at her retreat. Although she had finally given permission for Elisa to date this year, it wasn't without plenty of snide remarks about shameful behavior.

Elisa smoothed a flowered skirt over tan stockings. She had topped her black silk blouse with a fitted red sweater since it was chilly—plus the sweater hid the small mended patch on one shoulder.

She didn't have spare money for clothes; her mother's spotty income covered food and rent and not much more. But she'd discovered that if she took the bus to the Goodwill in the wealthy suburbs to the north of town, she could find plenty of inexpensive, quality clothing. The rich didn't seem to mind getting rid of clothes as soon as they got tired of them, well before they wore out.

The doorbell rang. Adrian, all in black, leaned against the wall, eyes half-lidded, hair tousled. He held a bouquet of deep red roses. Something about his movements made her think of the YouTube documentary on panthers she'd seen last week.

"Elisa, you look stunning."

"Hi!" she said, blushing and trying to cover it up by acting cheerful. "Oh my God, they're gorgeous! Thanks!" She took the flowers and breathed in deeply. "Mmm, they smell wonderful! I love flowers, but no one's ever given me roses before. Thank you so much!" A slow smile curled Adrian's lips. "Please come on in."

She left him in the living room and banged open cabinet doors in the kitchen, searching for a vase to put the flowers in. She imagined how he would see her apartment: beige walls streaked with water stains from the leaking toilet upstairs, utilitarian brown curtains covering tiny windows, a vinyl-upholstered armchair patched with duct tape. Her mother didn't care much about decorating, although Elisa tried to keep everything as clean as she could.

"Who else lives here?" Adrian propped his elbows on the kitchen counter. She hadn't noticed him entering the room.

"My mother," she said. "She's at a retreat right now. My dad left a few years ago. My brother used to live with us until he ran away."

Adrian's voice was gentle. "I'm so sorry. Oh." He tapped one of the rose leaves. "My apologies are needed here as well." He cupped a hand around a petal.

"What?"

He tilted his hand to show her a spider crawling on his palm. "I didn't see him there. Please forgive me for bringing unwanted visitors into your home."

"It doesn't matter," she said, but he had already returned to the living room. He unlatched the window and laid the back of his hand flat against the sill. The spider scurried off his palm and onto the outer sill. He waited until it had vanished into the darkness, then quietly closed and latched the window.

"There. All taken care of."

"Thanks! That was nice of you." Wow. He wouldn't even kill a spider? She'd never known a guy like that. Even Carlos swatted any bugs that got into their house.

"Is that your brother over there?" Carlos' photos were arranged on a side table.

Her nails bit into her palms. The more she thought about Carlos, the more she heard his warning voice. He collected stupid old-fashioned sayings, maybe from the old ladies at church. "Going on a date? Remember, he won't buy the cow if he gets the milk for free."

Adrian squatted in front of Carlos's photos. Elisa followed reluctantly. She hadn't ever had a guy inside the apartment. But surely Carlos would have approved of someone like Adrian.

"He looks like you."

She followed Adrian's gaze to the picture. That wasn't what people usually said. "His hair is a different color."

Adrian straightened. "No. I mean his eyes are kind, like yours."

She ducked her head so her hair fell over her face. "He was kind. Very good to me."

Adrian must have noticed her discomfort. "Come," he said, holding out his hand. "Let's go."

They walked downstairs together. Adrian bent to open the passenger door of a low-slung, bright yellow car.

She hung back. They were going to ride in that tiny thing? "What kind of car is that?" she asked. What a stupid question.

"It's a Lotus Elan. If gods lived on earth, it's what they would drive." He smiled.

She had to squat to slide into the seat. Adrian closed the door with a soft click. It didn't even sound like a regular car door. The seats were upholstered in supple tan leather. She ran her fingers over them—luxuriously soft. A faint smell of gasoline tickled her nose.

Adrian got in the driver's side and started the engine. The smell of gasoline intensified, and the engine reverberated.

"Aren't sports cars expensive?"

"Not this one. It's a 1969 model that I bought for nothing at a junkyard auction. A friend of mine restored it for me." He ran his fingers lovingly over the polished wood dashboard.

She had never ridden with someone who drove like Adrian. He wove in and out of traffic, accelerating and decelerating rapidly. She felt like she was sitting about two inches above the road, and the car registered every bump. She squeezed the handgrip so hard her knuckles went white.

Adrian asked, "What's wrong?" He nearly sideswiped a Honda and slipped into a miniscule gap between a BMW and a beat-up SUV.

She gulped at the truck towering over them. "Nothing."

"I don't like other cars getting in my way." He overtook the SUV, darted back into the lane and accelerated through a yellow light.

"Don't you get a lot of tickets?" She expected to see flashing lights behind them at any moment.

"No." He shifted gears smoothly and they shot forward. "I have a radar detector and naturally fast reflexes."

She clutched the handle more tightly.

He put one hand on her arm. "Trust me. I'll get you there safely." He ran a red light and cut off another car. The other driver honked furiously. She stared out the front windshield.

"I can tone it down for you if you want." His voice held a hint of mockery.

"No," she said, despite feeling that all her muscles had turned to jelly. "I'm fine."

She didn't want to check the speedometer, but couldn't resist a peek. The little needle was creeping towards eighty-five. And it wasn't kilometers. A car pulled into their lane and Adrian jammed on the brakes. She was thrown forward into the seat belt.

Like a cross between bumper cars and a roller coaster. The image made her smile. Another driver honked at them. "I think you're making the other drivers angry."

"We'll be out of their way soon enough."

Despite her fear of imminent death, Elisa felt a secret, shameful thrill. They were breaking all the rules and getting away with it. Her bones felt like they had melted, her lungs expanding with fast, hot breaths, her skin bathed in sparks.

She glanced at Adrian out of the corner of her eye. She'd always thought of him as a model student, polite and dutiful. His profile was serene, dark eyes flicking over the road, one hand resting on the wheel, the other wrapped around the stick shift. There was much more than the harmless nerd inside him, something powerful and almost—deadly. Part of her wanted to run away, but he was starting to fascinate her. To draw her in with the gravitational pull of a black hole.

 *Keisha*

Keisha pored over the stack of reports and scribbled another note on a beat-up yellow pad. Vince was cleaning his pistol, rubbing a silk cloth over the firing pin.

"You still studying for your homework assignment?"

"Shut up," Keisha said without heat, making another notation. "You know we'll have to memorize all this background before we go in—it'll be too dangerous to keep notes around."

"I've already memorized my part. Have you looked at the list of sites where they've made Rapture arrests?"

A crease appeared in the middle of Keisha's forehead. She pulled out a diagram from the yellow pad. "They keep moving them around, of course, but I plotted everything we've got on a map of the city to see if they clustered anywhere. Here."

Vince bent over the map and whistled. "Good work. I didn't see that pattern. That would suggest we might want to focus our search on the east side."

Keisha shrugged. "Maybe." She tossed a report to him. "Did you see the latest mortality figures from Donald Hospital?"

Vince glanced at the numbers. "Shit. It's getting worse. A lot worse."

 Elisa

The carnival had transformed the vacant lot in back of the mall into a mass of lights, sounds and smells. Straw lay scattered over the ground and its warm, earthy scent reminded Elisa of a long-ago field trip to a farm just outside of town. People laughed and shouted, and off-key carnival music blared from tinny speakers. The smell of popcorn and cotton candy hung in the night air.

She loved the sensory overload of places like this. Adrian took one of her hands in his, his grip warm. She had never held hands with anyone in public before. How could such a simple touch make her body feel like it was buzzing, her skin sparking all over like the lights on the carnival machines?

She imagined Carlos walking beside her, frowning. "Didn't I tell you to be good?"

"It's just holding hands," she protested.

Adrian's hold was comforting and secure. Carlos coughed. "I suppose he seems like a gentleman," he said grudgingly.

They walked along a row of game booths, where chattering groups threw balls at small targets, tried to drop objects in arrays of glasses, or tossed hoops over stuffed animals. When she stopped for the third time to watch, Adrian nudged her.

"Do you want one of those prizes?"

She wasn't used to having money to play these games, and she assumed Adrian didn't have much either. "I just like to watch."

"I've got plenty of money tonight," he said. "I'd like to treat you to whatever you want."

She lifted a shoulder. "If you don't mind wasting it, sure."

At the counter, the middle-aged, paunchy operator called, "Five dollars for three shots; knock down three targets and you get the choice of our top prizes." He pointed at a row of huge stuffed dogs.

Adrian handed over a five. The small target disks were battered, a few bent to the side. He sighted along the air rifle and squeezed the trigger without taking much time to aim. The shot struck the center of one of the targets with a loud clang.

The paunchy man raised his eyebrows and bellowed, "Great shot. Congratulations. Can you do as well the second time?"

Adrian ignored him and fired off another shot, downing a second target. The man congratulated him again, and Adrian whispered in Elisa's ear, "Watch what he's doing with his left hand."

The man fiddled with something underneath the counter. Adrian murmured, "He just locked the targets." He pointed with his chin at the row of disks, and indeed, they had stopped quivering in the breeze.

"What—" she whispered, "those crooks!"

Adrian's eyes narrowed and a feline grin appeared on his face. "Go over to the other side and ask him if that large blue dog is one of the prizes."

The stuffed toy stood at the very end of the row. Puzzled, she obeyed. "Mister?" she asked, stretching over the counter. "Is that one of the prizes we can get?"

"Eh, little lady?" he asked. "You betcha. Any of them, you could bring home tonight." His eyes strayed to her neckline.

She heard a loud clang. Adrian had taken the third shot, knocking down yet another target. The man's brows knotted. Adrian smiled mildly.

"Congratulations, young man. You're our first winner of the night," the man said with a tight smile. "Which prize would you like?"

"The young lady will choose," Adrian replied.

She pointed at the large blue dog.

The man untied it, his mouth taut. Adrian thanked him graciously.

He chuckled as they left the booth.

"What did you do?" she asked, balancing the giant stuffed animal.

"I just evened the odds a bit."

"But how?"

"While you distracted him, I took my knife and cut the cord that held the targets in place." An amused, superior half-smile floated onto his lips. "Just making the game fair." He stopped, his eye caught by something or someone on the other side of the field, and his face stilled and became serious. He lifted a hand in acknowledgment.

"Elisa, I've got to run a quick errand. Do you mind waiting for me?" He scanned the nearby booths. A red banner flapped above a gray tent. The banner stretched in the wind, revealing heavily curlicued letters: "Fortune Telling."

"How would you like to know your future?" he asked.

Inside, the tent was dimly lit and the air stuffy with incense. Adrian steered her to where a gray-haired woman sat behind a small table. He laid down a twenty dollar bill.

"That'll be ten dollars, young man."

"Keep the change. Just give her a good fortune." To Elisa, he said, "I'll be back in less than fifteen minutes." He scooped up the large stuffed dog. "I'll take this back to the car so you don't have to carry it around." The tent flap stirred behind him on a quick flurry of cool air.

"Please go right in, miss." The woman gestured at a dark red curtain in the rear. "Madame will see you now."

Elisa pushed the fabric aside. This part of the tent was even gloomier and more heavily fragranced than the waiting area. A woman sat at the far end behind a table draped in black cloth. Unevenly cut black hair framed her face, and a white bandanna wrapped her head. A crystal ball rested on a small stand on the table, a single straight-backed chair before it.

"Come in, come in, don't just stand there."

The woman took a pipe out of her mouth and placed it on a stand. Dark, shrewd eyes narrowed as Elisa approached. "So you've come for your fortune, eh?" She grinned, exposing stained teeth. "What would you like to know? No, don't tell me. You want to know about *love*. All the young girls do." She bent forward. With her left hand she rapidly flicked a number of elaborately painted cards out onto the table.

Then she stopped and her eyes widened. She barked, "Give me your hand!"

"What?" Elisa rubbed sweating palms on her thighs.

"Your hand, girl, so I can read your palm," she snapped.

She bent over Elisa's hand, muttering to herself. "Well. I don't see this too often." She stroked one line on Elisa's palm with a dark, calloused finger and cackled. "You are one of the fortunate few who will meet your soul mate in this lifetime. In fact—" She drew the hand closer to her beaky nose. "You have already met him." She leered. "Did you come in with your boyfriend? I see you and your soul mate married, with not one or two but four children in your future."

Elisa's mouth fell open. She couldn't imagine Adrian as a father. The woman scrutinized her palm again. "But wait—I see dark times ahead for you and your young man. Over the next year, very dark times—and again, about another decade in the future. A shadow crosses your path, and it will be the same one both times." She frowned. "Your life will be in danger."

Her eyes had dilated in the murky light, her earlier bravado gone. "I don't give this warning very often, but I must ask you to be extremely cautious. The shadow stands very close to you now."

Elisa marveled at the quality of the woman's act. She was really terrifying. "What should I do?"

"Your boyfriend," she whispered, "must stay away from the shadow, the temptation of the mask. The shadow has two faces, and both are deadly." Her eyes bored into Elisa. "He holds his hand out to you now, but it will all be up to you; you are the one who must be strong…"

Elisa pushed back her chair, breaking into a cold sweat at the utter conviction in the fortune teller's words.

Voices sounded in the outer room. The curtain was drawn back and cool air brushed Elisa. The woman's eyes lifted to meet the visitor. She blanched further. "No," she whispered. "It has him…"

Adrian walked into the room, smiling. "Did you have an interesting visit, Elisa?" he asked. "Did you predict a wonderful future for the two of us, madam?"

The woman's mouth seemed stuck for a moment. "Yes, yes," she croaked. "An excellent future. Good evening." She turned her back.

Adrian held out his hand. "Come. Let's go." He seemed very pleased with something.

"Did you see your friend?" Elisa lifted the tent flap.

"Yes. And how was your fortune?"

She shivered. "It was a bit… strange. Kind of scary, actually. At first she sounded normal, all this stuff about soul mates, but then she got a little weird, telling me my life was in danger."

Adrian snorted. "The usual twaddle. Beware the dark stranger, isn't that usually it?"

"Not quite," she said. "She told me—and you—to beware a shadow."

"Sounds ridiculous. Besides, what's wrong with shadows?"

5

 *Vince*

VINCE TOSSED HIS THIRD empty coffee cup on the floor of the squad car, watching through the tinted windshield as Lonnie exchanged rubber-banded baggies for crumpled-up cash on the corner across from the Fair. Vince donned his oversized mirrored shades. When he shaved off his beard and dyed his hair, seasoned detectives had been unable to pick him out of a lineup, but since he was about to go undercover it paid to be careful.

When the boy was distracted, Vince jumped out. Lonnie saw him coming and took off, but he was out of luck that night. Before he got half a block he tripped over an uneven patch of cement, and Vince was on him, one heavy black boot pinning Lonnie's skull to the sidewalk.

Vince wrestled Lonnie's skinny arms behind him and tightened the pair of handcuffs. "You are going down, punk. I got enough evidence to lock you up for years."

"I ain't done nothing," Lonnie whined. "I'm innocent! Police brutality! Folks got video cameras on you, man."

Vince laughed. "Bring on the video cameras. What're they gonna see? A decorated officer pulling scum off the streets, legally and without *too* much violence." He yanked on Lonnie's wrists. "Although, I gotta admit, in your case, violence is tempting. You know what most folks think of you dealing slip, right? The news is filled with slipheads bleeding their brains out in back alleys, and folks are scared it's gonna be their kids next." He shook Lonnie, none too gently. "They'll probably cheer, seeing a dealer get a little roughed up."

"Ain't done nothing," Lonnie repeated.

Vince dug his fingers into one of Lonnie's pockets and pulled out a wad of cash. "This is nothing, huh?"

"You need a warrant to search my pockets," Lonnie recited.

"Not if you're under arrest. And this?" He waved a baggie of white powder in Lonnie's face.

"That's not mine! You planted it on me!"

"Yeah, right. Every jury in the country will believe that." Vince shook his head. "Listen, kid. Your luck isn't looking good right now, but maybe I can help you. You know we're not really after you. We just want to get this shit off the streets. We're after the boss, the man known as the Captain."

Lonnie squeezed his eyes shut and shook his head like a dog. "I don't know anyone like that."

Vince put more weight on his boot. "Tell me who the Captain is. You wanna get locked up? Is that what you want? I can let you go. Just tell me who, or where, the Captain is and I'll let you go."

"I don't know, I don't know, I don't know," Lonnie whined.

Vince grunted and heaved the kid up and into the back of his squad car. It was no good trying to get any of these losers to talk. They were all terrified of the Captain. Plus they knew Tenebras always paid the bail for kids that didn't snitch. Lonnie would be out on the street selling more bags within days.

 *Elisa*

On their way to the Ferris wheel, four men came out of an alley and flanked them. Elisa stiffened. Adrian took a half step forward, guarding her.

The man in the lead spoke to Adrian, his face hard and closed. "I'm afraid I'm going to have to ask you to leave the Fair."

Adrian raised his eyebrows. "Really? May I ask why?" he asked mildly.

"I'm Evan Merrill, the general manager of the Fair, and we have the right to deny access to anyone for any reason. Please step this way." The three other men closed ranks behind him. Two were large and burly, and all were hostile.

"Mr. Merrill, I suggest that you not go through with this." There was no anger in Adrian's voice, but it rang with an odd certainty. "You'll regret it if you do."

Merrill's face hardened further. "I'll have to insist that you leave. Now, will you come quietly or will we have to carry you out of here?" The other men edged closer. Elisa clutched Adrian's arm.

He placed a hand on hers. "Don't worry. It's time to go anyway."

She let out her breath, relieved that Adrian's face was placid, without a trace of anger or hostility. They were escorted to an exit gate in silence.

At Adrian's car, his eyes sparkled. "Well. That was quite an experience."

"Was it because of what happened at the booth?"

"Probably. Surprising they'd target me. Not very polite, was it?"

His car gleamed under the halogen lights. He helped her into the seat. "I'm sorry, but I need to make a phone call. Do you mind?"

"Go ahead." He pulled out his cell phone and she watched through the windshield. His face was composed; she wondered what he was saying. After a few minutes he slid into the driver's seat.

"I've got a favorite spot I'd like to take you to. It's a long drive, but worth it. The road winds a little, but the view is spectacular."

She hesitated. "I get a little carsick on winding roads."

"What you're not saying is: the way I drive, you're sure to lose that fine hot dog dinner." His lips twitched. "Don't worry. I'll keep it slow for you."

It took about an hour. He kept his word, driving almost as sedately as a normal person. Finally he turned left, crested a small rise, and there it was—the entire city spread out before them.

Jewels of orange and white were strung against a black velvet night, lines of living light crisscrossing the darkness below. Overhead, stars flickered in their heavy, dark dome.

Adrian helped Elisa out, and they sat on a large, flat rock. An icy breeze blew in their faces, and goose bumps rose on her arms. Adrian spread out his coat for her.

He took her cold hand in his warm one. His touch was electrifying and comforting at the same time. She followed his gaze out over the city. Far below and to their right, she noticed something odd.

"It looks like something's on fire over there." She squinted and wished once again for the glasses she had lost.

Tiny points of flame flickered over a square marked by a miniscule glowing wheel. "I think it's the Fair!" The flames appeared to leap and gather, and as she squinted harder, she could pick out other landmarks.

Adrian gave an indifferent shrug. "Who knows?" He touched her arm. "I have something important to tell you."

She tore her eyes away from the display.

"Do you know you're gorgeous?"

Her cheeks heated. "That's a nice thing to say, but—"

"The color of your hair—it's the exact color of the last trace of sunset. Those eyes are like the morning after a storm. And your face..." He cupped both hands around her cheeks. "Your face is perfection. As though you were crafted by a master artist."

A rush of heat shot through her. A chill breeze threaded its way through her hair and she shivered. Adrian slid closer and enveloped her in his arms. She relaxed against his chest; it was firm and solid and radiated warmth. She had never been so physically close to a man before, unless you counted that disastrous date with Jeremy Brunswick last year, and she didn't think he really counted. Adrian's arms and chest were hard and muscular; his flesh felt dense and altogether alien. Even the scent of him was unlike anything she'd encountered before, the clean scent of his skin mingling with the spicy aroma of a soap she didn't recognize. He gathered her in under his chin and rubbed his cheek against her hair. Her face brushed against his shirt; the fabric was soft and smooth.

His hand encircled the nape of her neck, warm beneath her hair. His lips brushed her forehead, and she found herself shaking. Was he going to kiss her? She wasn't ready.

Carlos had warned, "Never kiss on the first date."

She'd promised him she'd be good, sworn she would never be like their mother. She should pull away, make some snide comment to break the mood. Like she should have before Jeremy slobbered all over her.

But instead, she snuggled closer to Adrian, even tipping her head back, letting the smooth, cool skin of his jawline rub against her face. She felt the soft pressure of his lips against her mouth, and froze. She had no idea how to kiss. She pressed her closed lips against his, while a fountain of sparks burst from every part of her body.

He pulled back a moment, giving her time to catch her breath. She relaxed, but he teased her mouth with small kisses, stroking and caressing. His fingers brushed her skin, and with his thumb he eased her lips open. He matched his mouth to hers, his lips softer than the silk of his shirt. He tasted extraordinary, like peppermint and high-tension wires, the flavor generating a sensation that engulfed Elisa's body in a wave of fire. His tongue sunk inside her and she welcomed him in, electricity shooting down to her breasts and below.

If this was what kissing was like, no wonder so many people raved about it. How could she have lived this long and never known? He released her, and she found herself straining toward him, seeking the heat of his mouth, the silk of his tongue. She had never dared feel this way before. He made a sound deep in his throat, and she collapsed against him.

He held her, breathing fast, his heart thumping against her cheek, his hand stroking her ever so gently.

They sat together, gazing out over the city. Off in the distance, fire engine sirens blared. But they were faint and far away, and she barely heard them over the drumming of her heart.

6

 *Elisa*

"Elisa!" Chloe's voice carried across the courtyard as she ran down the school steps. "Oh my God, I'm so glad you're okay!" Elisa ducked out of the way with the ease of long practice at evading Chloe's full-body hugs.

"What's wrong?"

"Didn't you see the news yesterday?"

"I got home late on Saturday, and spent Sunday catching up on homework." Elisa swung her backpack over the other shoulder. "What happened?"

"There was a huge fire at the Fall Festival Fair." Chloe's eyes were big. "All sorts of trailers and equipment burned down. A bunch of people had to go to the hospital. One guy died! And it turned out they were dealing drugs out there. The police made a bunch of arrests and they shut down the entire Fair."

So it *was* a fire. And someone died? Elisa shivered. She hadn't even been thinking about it all weekend. To be honest, she'd spent the entire time replaying Adrian's kiss in her head and wondering if he'd kiss her again. Could she possibly be shallower? "That's awful! We didn't see anything like that. It was pretty quiet. I guess we got lucky they threw us out."

"What? Who threw you out? Why?"

"Slow down! I'll tell you and Sumiko everything at lunch."

"No!" Chloe grabbed her around the shoulders, hard. "You're going to tell me everything, now!"

Elisa pushed her away. "Adrian discovered a rigged booth, and he somehow got around it. I guess that made them mad, because not too much later, the Fair manager came up to us with three goons and told us we had to leave."

"The Fair manager? What was his name?"

"Evan something."

"Evan Merrill?" Chloe pulled her cell phone out of her pocket. "Yeah, that was the guy that was killed! The police found drugs in his trailer. They think he was the ringleader of a drug cartel." Her fingers flew over the phone. "You actually *met* the guy that night? Scary!"

"He's dead?" Elisa wrapped her arms around her stomach. "He didn't seem like a drug dealer at all." She paused, suddenly wondering exactly *what* a drug dealer would be like.

"What else did he say?"

"Not much. He just ordered us to leave." She thought back over the confrontation. "At first I was afraid Adrian would get upset. He said something a little strange—at least I thought it was weird at the time."

"What? What did he say?"

"Something like, 'You'll regret this.' It sounded all ominous. I was worried there might be a fight."

"Yeah?"

"But Adrian was really mature about the whole situation." Elisa tilted her head. "Not like some other people at this school."

"You really like him, don't you? Did he kiss you?"

Elisa blushed but didn't say anything. Her body felt light, as though it were bread slowly rising in a warm oven.

"I'll take that as a yes."

Elisa had to say something to distract Chloe. She did *not* want to be describing her kiss right here in school. "I was always kind of hoping that I could be with—" Her voice faded. "With Ben," she whispered. "But Adrian—he's always doing these little things for me, like holding doors open. I didn't know people did that anymore."

"Ha! Chivalry is not dead!"

"When he looks at me, I feel strange inside. When he held my hand, I didn't want to let go. He said I was beautiful."

Chloe's expression softened. "That just means he has eyes. Of course you're beautiful."

The bell rang, and Chloe started. "Shit! I'm late for my test! Tell me everything at lunch!" She streaked off down the hall.

Elisa's first class had been temporarily moved to a new location since the regular classroom had gotten flooded. Apparently the school roof had some major leaks, but, of course, the budget didn't stretch to fixing them. It didn't cost as much to move students around. So she ended up late, running to the new room in one of the far wings. She wasn't as familiar with this part of the school, so she had to check the room numbers as she ran. She stopped to catch her breath in front of a girls' bathroom.

This was an older, run-down wing. The building was so big, it was rumored that even the principal didn't know where all the rooms were. Certainly the maintenance staff regularly got lost. It didn't look like they knew their way here. Many of the windows were cracked, and leaks had left faded stains on the walls.

Elisa needed to use the bathroom, so she pushed open the marked-up door. It smelled even worse than the one she usually used. Black spray paint crisscrossed the walls. Her shoes stuck to the floor, and a pile of used pads lay scattered against one wall.

A hand grabbed her shoulder. Two girls, one blonde, one brunette, stood in a little nook she hadn't seen at first.

"What the fuck you think you're doing?" The shorter, blonde girl bared her teeth, a metal spike glittering in her nose, and her two high ponytails of frizzy pale hair quivered.

The dark-haired girl backed her up. Short, spiky brown hair topped a thin face, and her eyes glinted beneath thick eyeliner.

Elisa's heart battered her chest. She should step up to them and stare them down. They didn't own the place. But instead she offered a weak smile and tried to be placating. "I really need to use the bathroom."

The blonde grunted. "Right. Invade our territory, try to pretend you're innocent. That ain't gonna work, bitch." She raised her fist. "We gonna show you why you should stay the fuck out."

"I just wanted to use the bathroom. If you want me to go, I'll go." Elisa edged backwards toward the door.

The girl hissed. "Don't think you gonna get away, bitch. Debra, get behind her."

"Kim, let her go. It's not worth it."

"She's gotta be punished."

"We don't need any more trouble."

"Shut up!" Kim shrieked as she rounded on Debra. "Who's gonna know?"

Before Elisa could move, Kim grabbed a handful of her hair and punched her in the face. The reek of alcohol gusted over Elisa and bright pain flared in her mouth. She tasted blood.

She needed to do something. Say something. Fight back. Elisa lifted her hand. But all she could remember was her mother shrieking, the same smell of alcohol on her breath. "Don't move! Don't talk! Good girls shouldn't fight." Instead of attacking, Elisa froze. Her mother screamed in her face, that horrible alcoholic stench filling her brain.

Kim laughed, and shoved her so hard she fell to the floor. "Stupid little bitch. Can't even fight. Lessee, what next?"

The brunette tugged at Kim's arm. "That's enough! Just let her go."

Kim shrugged her off. "I'm only starting."

Elisa gathered her legs under her. No matter what her mother said, she was going to fight back.

The bathroom door crashed against the wall, and the whole room shook. A tall guy appeared in the doorway, arms bulging with muscle under a denim vest. The one who'd been fighting with Ben in the lunchroom.

"Mario!" gasped Kim. "You ain't s'posed to be here!"

"I heard you two bitches all the way down the hall." He took in the scene: Elisa kneeling on the floor, blood on her face, and Kim's fierce grip on her hair. "Having some fun when nobody's watching?"

He took two quick steps forward and slammed his fist hard into Kim's jaw. She was thrown violently against the wall, landing with a smack and sliding down into the dirty pads. Debra, wheeling around, tried to attack Mario from behind, but he swung his arm almost casually to the side and knocked her into the other wall, where she lay stunned. Kim struggled to lift herself up on her elbows. Blood streamed from her lips.

"You bastard! The Captain's gonna get you!" she spat, wiping her mouth with her fist. "I'm his... *princess*, and you can't hurt me! He'll kill you!"

"As if the Captain would do anything for a shithead like you. What's wrong with you? Are you too drunk or too stupid to remember our orders?"

He rounded on Elisa. "And you, dumbass, are you really stupid enough to enter our territory without permission?"

She pressed her elbows into her sides. "I'm sorry. I didn't know."

He rolled his eyes. "What's with all the dipshit idiots today? All right." He grabbed Elisa roughly by the arm and dragged her to the door. "Time for a lesson, bitch. See that mark?" He pointed to a symbol, three concentric diamonds sprayed on the door with black paint. "That means it's Tenebras territory and you should stay out. You know who we are, right?"

Elisa nodded, not trusting her voice.

"Good." Mario propped himself against the wall, one hand on his hip. "We own this school. You stay out of our way, you'll be okay. But if you cross us..." He drew his finger across his throat. "Get it?"

Terrified, Elisa nodded again.

"Get the fuck out of here." He folded his arms. "Keep your mouth shut or you'll be in a fuckload of trouble."

"I won't say a word to anyone," she promised. She dusted off her clothes, grabbed her backpack, and ran into the hall.

She decided it would be better to skip class and go directly to the health center.

"What happened to you, dear?" the volunteer asked as she examined Elisa's mouth and teeth for damage.

"I ran into a bathroom door," she explained, eyes downcast.

The woman lifted an eyebrow. But she swabbed Elisa's face and daubed disinfectant on her cut lip. "There. No permanent harm done. Just some lacerations and a little bruising. You'll have to be careful what you eat for a couple of days, but you should heal quickly." She unlocked a medicine cabinet and shook two acetaminophen tablets into her hand.

"Here." She filled a paper cup with water from the sink. "Take these for the pain and swelling." Elisa obediently swallowed the pills. "Do you have more at home?"

Elisa shook her head. Her mother didn't believe in medicine. The woman opened another drawer. She poured a few tablets into a tiny cardboard pillbox. "You can take two more every four to six hours."

Elisa nodded her thanks and slipped away to class. The halls were uncharacteristically silent, only a few students with hall passes ambling through. As she rounded a corner near her classroom, a boy loomed out of a hallway.

She jumped backwards, still shell-shocked from her experience. Then she recognized him. "Ben! You startled me."

"I saw you in the hall bleeding, and that bastard Fonseca leaving from the same direction." He eyed the bandage on her chin. "Did he hurt you?"

Just what she needed, more people involved in her problems. "No, he didn't do anything. I just, uh, ran into a bathroom door and hurt my mouth." She pointed at the bandage. "It didn't really hurt, but I went to the health center." She didn't meet his eyes. She was a terrible liar.

"You ran into a bathroom door with your *mouth*?"

"Yeah," she mumbled. "I wasn't looking where I was going." She gave an embarrassed laugh that sounded fake even to her.

Ben crossed his arms over his chest. "All right. But if Fonseca or anybody else bothers you, you let me know, right?"

He stepped away from the wall to let her pass. Something terrifying lurked in his eyes.

 ## Ben

Ben frowned. Something was off about Elisa's story. That bastard Mario Fonseca always seemed to be around whenever something bad was going down. But because of his connections, he got away with everything. Ben seemed to be the only one who noticed Fonseca's crap.

The other day, Ben had been coming home from the store, striding along mostly deserted streets on the sleepy Sunday afternoon. Out of the corner of his eye he saw a flash of movement. Fonseca and Ron Hundley were sneaking into the bushes near an apartment building. Ben crossed the street to follow them, but by the time he reached the building, they were gone. He prowled around the area for a few more minutes, but couldn't find any trace of them, so finally he gave up and went home. All at once, he realized it had been Elisa's apartment building.

When he'd seen Fonseca coming out of the corridor after Elisa had been injured, he'd been surprised at the incredible blaze of anger that had risen in his chest. Was the bastard targeting Elisa in some way? The next time he saw Fonseca, he was going to goddamn well piece him. Just for the hell of it.

Elisa's face stayed in his mind. Irritated, he shrugged it off. She was an acquaintance, nothing more. He didn't have time to get interested in girls right now; he was busy writing scholarship applications so he could get the hell out of this lousy neighborhood. He needed to stay focused.

 *Elisa*

Adrian was waiting for Elisa at her locker after school. Something leaped in her chest when she saw him leaning against the wall.

"Hi!" she said cheerily.

His eyes narrowed when he saw the bandage on her chin. "What happened to you?"

"Oh, it's nothing." She was getting tired of her own story by now. "I ran into a bathroom door."

"Really?"

"Nobody seems to believe me," she said with an annoyed expression.

"It *is* a rather lame excuse." Adrian smiled at her exasperation. But to her relief, he didn't pursue it further. "I wanted to ask you if you'd like to go out to dinner on Friday."

She pulled her books out of her backpack and shoved them into her locker. Her friends had advised her at lunchtime to tell Adrian she was busy the next time he asked her out, so he didn't think she was easy.

Sumiko had said, hand on her hip, "Girl, you don't want to look like you're thirsting."

Chloe added, "No one likes a girl who's always available. No matter how horndogs you are, you gotta play it cool."

"Both of you, shut up! You're disgusting!"

Elisa slammed the locker shut. Now that Adrian was standing here asking her, she found the idea of playing such a game repulsive. But it was hard to go against Sumiko's advice.

"I'm sorry," she said, "but I'm busy. I've got to, uh, do homework, you see, and it's a really long assignment."

He leaned into her, his face inches from hers. "Homework?" he whispered. "Really?" He was standing so close, too close. That gorgeous face filled Elisa's vision and she smelled his spicy cologne, and all she wanted was to fall into his arms and ravish his mouth. Her legs felt weak, and her eyes fluttered.

No. Not in the middle of the hallway in broad daylight.

She swallowed. What were they talking about again?

He straightened, smirking. "I suppose it's no problem. We'll just have to see what we can do about your... homework. I'll come by your apartment and pick you up at six."

"What?" Hadn't she said no?

Heading off, he called over his shoulder, "And don't forget drama club on Wednesday!"

 Mario

Mario sat half-dozing in the back row of English class, ignoring the teacher going on about subordinate clauses. He yawned ostentatiously. Contrary to popular belief, he wasn't stupid. He just had an utter lack of interest in anything that didn't translate into immediate advantage on the streets. All he needed to know about language was how to trash talk his opponents in a fight.

A freshman entered the class and timidly handed the teacher a note. Mario found it hard to believe he could have ever been that young.

The teacher read it. "Mario Fonseca," she said, "you are to go to the principal's office at once." She clearly disapproved of him and his behavior, but frankly, Mario felt the same about her. To him, it was a mark of achievement to be a thorn in the side of the school administration.

Mario got up with a swagger. One of his friends in the back row muttered, and Mario retorted, "Don't get jealous that I'm so important the principal asks my advice now." His friend sniggered.

The tiny freshman escorted him to the principal's office without saying a word. Mario spent the walk looming over the kid and enjoying his obvious terror. He wondered idly what transgression he had been caught at this time. There were so many it was hard to keep track.

But when the door opened and Mario walked in, the person sitting behind the principal's desk was not old man Robson, but Adrian Salas. He lounged in the high-backed leather chair, a faint smile on his face. He had removed his glasses, and his expression of serene arrogance was very different from that of the quiet, straight-A student his teachers knew. An aura of power and command seemed to surround him. Mario glanced over his shoulder to see Cesar Peralta closing the door and Rory Fong leaning against the wall.

Mario swallowed. This wasn't good. Mario had never been summoned to the office this way before. He rarely even met with Adrian outside of gang territory, and if he did, he was supposed to pretend he didn't know him. They were expected to move in completely different social circles, where Adrian would never associate with the likes of him. But now, the mask was off, and Adrian was in his other persona, that of the feared "Captain" of Tenebras, the absolute ruler of one of the most powerful gangs in the city, and the man who held Mario's and many other lives in the palm of his hand. Although Mario had utterly no concerns about Robson's opinion of him, it was a completely different story with

Adrian. His heart raced. Could Adrian have learned what he was doing? Mario had heard all the stories of people who'd crossed him and never been seen again. The space between his shoulder blades prickled as he stood with his back to Peralta and Fong, both of whom were very good with a knife.

He approached the desk. "You wanted to see me?" he asked, schooling the tone of his voice to deference.

"Yes." Adrian's voice was composed, giving no clue as to the state of his mind. "Please sit down, Mario."

As Mario settled himself, Adrian spoke with his trademark politeness. "Thank you for coming. I have a few questions for you."

Sweat broke out on Mario's forehead and he forced himself to appear calm. "Yeah, sure."

"I understand you had an... encounter with Elisa Gallardo yesterday morning."

Mario was puzzled. He didn't recognize the name, and he cast his memory over what had happened that morning but drew a blank. Adrian's eyes narrowed. He tossed a small photograph in front of Mario. "This girl."

Mario picked up the photo. The girl's face was angled toward the camera, gazing over her shoulder and laughing. She had huge, dark eyes, and masses of auburn hair falling over her shoulder. His heart chilled. It was the girl he had met in the bathroom yesterday, the girl Kim and Debra had been beating up. What was Adrian's interest in the fight? Had Kim made good on her threat to tattle to Adrian? It would be surprising if Adrian cared; he never had before when Mario or one of the other Blades disciplined lower-ranking members of the gang. Or was this girl really a rival gang member encroaching on their territory, rather than the innocent civilian he had taken her for? In that case, he would be in big trouble.

He took a deep breath, and tried to order the events in his mind so he could describe them.

"OK. I heard a racket coming from the bathroom on the first floor at the far end of building three, so I went to check it out. I saw Kim and Debra beating up this girl, who said she had walked into the bathroom by accident. I told them to stop." He took a breath. Adrian's face continued to be neutral. "In my opinion, Kim was just looking for someone to have some fun with. She was too wasted to remember your orders. This girl was just clueless and had walked in by mistake. She didn't even recognize our mark on the door. I showed it to her, warned her to keep her mouth shut, and she left. I gave Kim and Debra a little lesson; then I left."

"My sources tell me the girl was bleeding from the mouth when she left the bathroom. Did you have anything to do with that?"

Mario gaped, confused at Adrian's interest in this detail. "Me? No. Kim punched her and was roughing her up, that's all. I didn't touch her." Adrian's eyes bored into his. The silence in the room stretched out and became uncomfortable, but Mario didn't dare break it. He wasn't quite sure what was going on, but he had been in Tenebras long enough to realize that his life was at risk.

But he was telling the truth. Adrian sometimes appeared to have an uncanny ability to read people's faces, extracting their emotions and even their inmost thoughts from the slightest movements of their facial muscles. Mario swallowed again, convulsively, but kept his face impassive. He was innocent of whatever Adrian suspected with the girl. But did Adrian know about Mario's other plans? A bead of sweat formed on his forehead and rolled down the side of his face. If Adrian suspected what Mario had been doing on the side, he would surely order him killed.

"I see." Adrian finally broke the silence. "Thanks for your information." He propped his elbow on the armrest. "I have new orders for you. This girl, Elisa Gallardo, is to be placed on the list of individuals under our protection. Do you understand?" Mario struggled to keep his face neutral. "Make an announcement at the next meeting."

Mario nodded, still a little mystified. There were a number of people under the gang's protection for various reasons, due to ransom payments, deals, or other purposes that suited Adrian's often convoluted plans. He knew Adrian wouldn't want to hear questions about his orders, so he simply stood up. He kept himself from breathing a sigh of relief. Adrian hadn't said anything, so surely he didn't suspect. Mario was still alive, wasn't he?

As he was about to open the door, Adrian's quiet voice stopped him. "Oh, and Mario? What about your other task?"

Mario paused, hand on the door, relaxed and grinning now. "That's all been taken care of. Everything done as you ordered."

After Adrian dismissed him and Mario was walking back to his classroom, a sly grin spread over his face. There was a new spring in his step. He would be dead by now if Adrian knew. He must be getting away with it.

But what was going on with Elisa Gallardo? Why would Adrian place her under their protection? Was he fucking her? Adrian never cared what happened to his fuck-toys. He'd never put any of them under the gang's protection before. And this Elisa— she seemed too clueless to be doing anything of value to them.

He shrugged. He didn't give a shit. He remembered the girl's face in the bathroom as she lay on the floor, her hair in Kim's grasp. Whatever was going on, it was clear Kim was in big trouble. But after what Kim had done to him—fuck her. She was gonna be in a world of hurt soon. Very soon.

7

 *Elisa*

ELISA PLOPPED DOWN beside Sumiko at their usual lunch table in the cafeteria. "I'm glad to see that you've healed completely from your *accident* earlier this week," Sumiko said.

Elisa flushed. Nobody ever believed her stories. It was a good thing she never had anything major to hide. "I told you it wasn't a big deal." She bent her head and rooted around in her bag. Sumiko snorted.

Chloe arrived, scowling and out of breath, and dumped her backpack on the table with a loud thump. "Why do the teachers in this school think they have to set a new world record for homework? We're seniors. They know we need to be working on our college applications."

"Wow! You're both in bad moods today. Cheer up!"

Sumiko grimaced. "Why? Because the weather is so delightful?" She waved at the window where a cold rain was sleeting heavily down.

Chloe rolled her eyes. "No, Elisa is happy because she's finally seeing someone. And whose fault is that? Sumiko?"

"What can I say? I'm good," Sumiko said smugly over a bite of hamburger.

"So now we're stuck with her boyfriend." Chloe got out her lunch. "And speaking of boyfriends, I hear you have a date tonight. Are you going to tell us about it?"

"Adrian asked me out for dinner. We're going to a restaurant."

"Yeah, tell me again why you didn't say no? After all my advice?" Sumiko scowled.

"I did say no!" Elisa protested. "But somehow... he thought I said yes." She couldn't help a tiny smile. Everything always felt a little out of control with Adrian; was there something wrong with her that she found it kind of exciting?

Sumiko shook her head. "Either you ignored my advice again or Adrian's a controlling bastard." she said darkly. Then she straightened. "I suppose it doesn't matter, since he still seems to be interested. So, which restaurant is he taking you to?"

"He said it was called something like La Seagull or something like that." Elisa pulled out a plastic container of peanut butter and some crackers.

Chloe's jaw dropped. "*La Cigale*?" she asked. "He's taking you to the fanciest French restaurant in town?"

"I don't know about fancy. I guess it's French."

"Where does he get his money? Is he from a rich family?" Chloe grabbed her arm. "That place costs more than a couple hundred dollars a person!"

Elisa gulped. That couldn't be true, could it? "He has a part-time job." At least, that's what he'd told her when she expressed concern about the cost.

"Some part-time job," Sumiko commented dryly. "I know mine doesn't pay well enough to treat people to dinner at fancy restaurants." She lowered her brows. "How could he possibly—"

Elisa stopped spreading the peanut butter, knife poised over the last cracker. They were right. How could he afford it? She'd never been to a fancy restaurant before and it hadn't occurred to her how insanely expensive it might be. "Maybe I should ask him to take me to McDonalds instead. I don't want him to waste money on me."

Chloe groaned. "Elisa, you're being clueless again. Nobody takes anyone out for a romantic date to McDonalds."

"No," Sumiko said. "You don't want to insult him. He obviously wants to do something special for you. You have to go along with it."

The first bell rang, and Sumiko stuffed the last of her burger in her mouth. "I doubt he'll be able to afford to take you to places that nice very often. Enjoy it while it lasts!" She balled her trash into a pile and dumped it on her lunch tray. "Gotta go—test in math. See you later!"

Chloe hoisted her backpack with a grunt. "The forecast says it'll clear up later tonight. You should have a nice night. And the moon is full." She called over her shoulder: "Make sure he takes you to some romantic spot."

When Adrian knocked on Elisa's door that evening, he was wearing a charcoal gray wool suit over a white linen shirt and dark maroon tie, and it transformed him. He was no longer merely an attractive teenager; he was a man, exuding power and elegance. The stylishly tailored suit outlined his long limbs and subtly emphasized the grace and beauty of his body, setting off his narrow face with its high cheekbones, full lips, and shock of thick brown hair. Elisa's cheeks heated and she almost stumbled as she stepped aside to let him enter.

He chuckled deep in his throat as he steadied her with one strong hand. His body was hard and solid, and she found herself clinging to him.

"Careful," he murmured, his voice like dark chocolate. "You don't want to fall."

Too late. She had already fallen. She gazed up at his dark, dark eyes. Thrills chased through her body at his touch, alternating hot and cold, as though she was burning up with fever. She'd gone on dates with classmates before, but this was something completely different.

There was an energy about him, a deep vibrating power like she had once felt when she placed her bare foot on the train tracks at the far south of town. Dangerous. Risky. She should run away.

He was definitely not the quiet, intellectual classmate she had once thought he was. Like his wild and unrestrained driving, she could sense something equally hazardous lurking beneath his calm smile.

He was everything her mother had warned her about, the day she first bled. "Now you're a woman. That means you're vulnerable." His hair tumbled over his eyes, eyes traveling up and down her body as though he were starving and she was the only food he wanted to eat.

No one had ever looked at Elisa like that before. She smoothed her hands down her dress self-consciously. It was of a simple cut, but the soft jersey clung to her body in a way that enhanced its contours, subtly flattering her figure. With its demure neckline, long sleeves and full mid-calf-length skirt, it was suitable for formal events, but someone had once told her it was sexy.

"Elisa, you look spectacular in that dress." The resonance in his voice made her shiver. Her head swam, and she swayed. Did she want to fall so he would catch her?

She heard Carlos' voice. "You need to go outside, now, or you're going to do something you'll regret for the rest of your life."

What did he mean? Her face was flushed, and her clothing felt far too constricting.

"Get a grip on yourself, girl. You look like a bitch in heat." Her mother's voice was harsh.

She stuffed her feelings down, hard, and tried a polite smile. "Thank you. Should we go now?"

Adrian was still holding her arm, power vibrating in his muscles. With his other hand, he traced a fiery line across her eyebrows and down her cheek. She caught a whiff of his scent, something spicy and wild that made the fine hairs on the back of her neck stand up. "Yes," he whispered. "Let's go."

He drove fast but smoothly to the restaurant. As they traveled north, apartments faded to single-family houses. The houses gradually got bigger and nicer, and the yards more manicured until they arrived at a fancy shopping district Elisa had never visited. A parking spot opened up just in front of the entrance as they arrived, and Adrian pulled in smoothly.

The woman who checked their reservation was dressed more elegantly than a supermodel on TV. Exquisitely made-up, her dark hair wound into an elaborate knot on her head, she led them to a table for two in a private nook, where a waiter in a tuxedo pulled out a chair for Elisa. Awkward and unsure, she sat down too soon, but the waiter handled it gracefully. The long fall of the tablecloth brushed against her knees, and she lifted it nervously, afraid she might pull it off the table and make a scene.

Everything was too classy for a poor kid from Rockton. She was sure in a moment one of those elegant waiters would find her out, and they would be evicted from the restaurant. She touched one of the three differently-shaped forks in the place setting. What if she used the wrong one?

Adrian was from her own neighborhood, and he was as poor as she was; why did he appear so at ease in this high-class environment? He whispered in her ear. "What is it, Elisa?"

"I don't know how to use all this."

"Just relax. This isn't a test. The restaurant exists to serve its customers."

She didn't even recognize most of the items on the menu, so Adrian ordered. He chose a caviar appetizer and a main course of roast lobster with chanterelle mushrooms. When he spoke to the waiter, he sounded as though he did it every day, even ordering from the wine list.

She turned down the wine, not wanting to mention they were underage in front of the waiter. It was time for another nervous whisper. "Aren't you going to get in trouble asking for wine?"

He laid a warm hand over hers and her fingers fluttered involuntarily like the wings of a butterfly. "You are such an innocent." Why did everyone say that to her? "They won't object at a restaurant of this caliber."

After the perfectly prepared lobster served with mushrooms so tender and flavorful they burst in her mouth, they had passion fruit and mango napoleon for dessert. She couldn't help moaning with pleasure as she forked up the creamy mango custard layered with delicate puff pastry.

Adrian smiled at her obvious delight. "I'd like to take you to another favorite spot of mine."

About to eagerly agree, Elisa remembered her friends' advice and mumbled, "Maybe I should get home."

"Mmm, just for a little while? It would mean a lot to me."

Why was it so hard to say no to him? Her heart was beating so fast. The thought of going somewhere with him, alone, made a current buzz through her veins. She should say no. But he was gazing at her with such a sweet face, so vulnerable and hopeful, that for once even Carlos seemed satisfied.

"I think he's a gentleman, Elisa. You can go. But be careful."

True to the forecast, the clouds had disappeared. The sky blazed with a luminous full moon and a heavy dusting of brilliant stars. Adrian drove carefully, holding Elisa's hand when he wasn't shifting.

They parked on a quiet hillside overlooking the reservoir. The dark, still water reflected the stars and blended with the city lights far below. Tall trees ringed the meadow. When Elisa rolled down her window, the spicy scent of fall leaves mingled with the richer aroma of wildflowers and grasses. The air was cool and moist after the day's rain. "Thank you, Adrian, for that amazing dinner."

"It was my pleasure. I don't think I've enjoyed a meal more in a very long time." He picked up her hand, brushed it across his lips. "You are fascinating."

She was glad the light was low in the car. Someone hadn't gotten her mother's memo. "I'm nothing special."

"You're completely wrong. You are beyond special. Please don't tell me again that you still don't realize your own beauty." He caressed her cheek with the back of his knuckles, and unconsciously, she lifted her face to his touch.

He stroked her hair back from her face. "Your hair—that color is like nothing else in the world, glowing like a flame. Your eyes are the color of the sky after a thunderstorm. And your lips..." He shook his head. "Your lips are softer and more delicate than the petals of a rose. You have such power to overwhelm me with your gentleness." He touched the base of his neck. "When I look at you, I'm reminded of what it's like to feel... deeply, what it's like to care for another human being, more than anything else in the world."

She fiddled with her sleeve. "Adrian, you are a poet."

He took her face in his hands and brought it to his. When his face was inches away, she closed her eyes.

His lips were warm as he caressed her with his mouth. He slipped one hand behind her head, running his fingers through her hair. His other hand moved around her back, pulling her closer, his body warm against hers. The expensive fabric of his suit brushed against her skin like warm silk, and she inhaled his clean, sweet scent. His lips opened, and he softly kissed each side of her mouth; his tongue licked her lips and glided inside. Heat rose through her body like warm water and she pressed herself against him. His arms tightened around her. She could feel the blood pulsing through her veins, alive in her fingertips, her face, her lips, every place where her skin was touching his; she felt lighter than air and anchored only by his arms.

 *Ben*

Ben checked the far corner of the cafeteria where Sumiko, Chloe, and Elisa normally sat. To his surprise, there was a fourth person sitting at their table. His eyes widened as he recognized Adrian Salas, class nerd and senior class president. What was he doing at Elisa's table? Adrian laughed at something one of the other girls said and slipped his arm around Elisa. Rather than pulling away, Elisa smiled up at him and sank into his embrace.

Red hazed Ben's vision, and before he knew it, he was standing in front of their table.

"Hey, Ben," Sumiko asked, "what's up?"

"Hello, Ben," Elisa sang out, far too happy for his liking.

Adrian's expression was mild, but Ben detected a glint of triumph and possessiveness in his eyes, half-hidden behind his lenses. Ben wanted nothing more than to punch those glasses off his face, to wipe the faint smirk off his mouth, but he took a deep breath. He had to get it under control.

Ben ran a hand through his hair, making it stick out in all directions. "Elisa, could I speak to you for a moment?"

"Sure," she said cheerfully, standing up. Adrian let his arm slip away from her, capturing one of her hands in his and giving it a small squeeze.

Ben's temper flared again, but he tamped it down as he and Elisa stepped away from the table. "What is it, Ben? Has something happened?"

"Huh? No, it's nothing."

"You look so upset."

"No, I just had a problem last period and got to the cafeteria late." He put a hand to the back of his neck and hesitated.

"Then what's wrong?"

"Elisa," he blurted out, "would you like to go to the Halloween Ball with me?" He stopped short, surprised at himself. Hadn't he been certain he didn't want to get involved with anyone senior year? He couldn't read the expression on Elisa's face. He didn't want to give her false hopes. "I mean, just as friends," he stuttered.

Elisa's shoulders drooped a little. "I'm sorry, Ben. I would have very much enjoyed going to the dance with you—as friends." She reached out her hand and then drew it back. "But Adrian has already asked me—and I said yes. Maybe some other time?"

He couldn't speak for a minute. Then he saw she was getting uncomfortable and roused himself. "Sure, Elisa. That's okay." He stood frozen, a cold wave washing over him as she returned to the table.

He didn't move, oblivious to the crowds of students passing by. He was still staring at the back of Elisa's head when he felt a sudden, hard shove.

"Hey!" he snarled at Sumiko, who had stood up when he wasn't looking. "What was that for?"

"Stop staring at her, idiot!" She put her hands on her hips. "Who said he wasn't interested in anyone, hmm?"

"I—" Ben stopped himself. "I'm *not* interested in anyone," he insisted. "And of course Elisa can date anyone she likes." He caught his breath. "Just not—him."

"Why not? Adrian's a good person, and he treats her right, Ben."

Unlike you. "There's something off about him. I don't trust him. He's… dangerous. I don't feel Elisa's safe around him."

Sumiko scoffed. "Ben, that's the most ridiculous thing I've ever heard. The only danger here is the green-eyed monster rearing its head. Adrian has only been kind and gentle with Elisa." She crossed her arms over her chest. "Since you didn't ask her out, you have no right to object to her going out with someone else."

He rubbed his forehead. "You're right. I won't bother her anymore. I better get back in line for lunch."

8

 *Adrian*

ADRIAN STRETCHED HIS ARMS above his head. He was relaxing in the study in his headquarters, an older building in the business district that he had bought and renovated with profits from his activities. The study was a large, windowless room on the second floor, lined with bookshelves. It was securely located in the center of the building, easily defended in the event of attack, and comfortably furnished.

It was late at night, but Adrian typically needed little sleep. He reclined with a book in an overstuffed armchair in front of a crackling fire, his feet up on an ottoman. A glass of wine rested on a teak end table beside his chair. He spent most of his time away from school here rather than in his aunt's cramped and dingy apartment under her disapproving glower. He knew she was relieved that he was gone much of the time as well. She had never seen him as anything other than an inconvenience: another mouth to feed, another drag on her time. The few times he did show up, she never even bothered to ask where he had been.

It was better here. He sipped his wine. It was an excellent vintage, and it was pleasant to be relaxing here with the dancing warmth of an open fire on his face and arms, so pleasant to watch the flames lick at the fresh, dry wood and slowly consume it.

There was a tap at the door. Adrian swung to face it, eyes going to the display on the small hand unit on the end table. He glanced at the information on the screen and released the lock.

The door opened and Debra entered. Clinging to her leg was a small blonde girl of about four or five. Debra jerked to a stop when she spotted Adrian.

"Oh, Captain—I'm so sorry! I didn't realize you were still here." She gestured apologetically toward the dining table at the other end of the study. "I was just going to clear the dinner dishes."

Adrian inclined his head. "By all means, Debra. Please go ahead."

The child let go of Debra's leg and stared at Adrian, her thumb in her mouth, her eyes wide. A huge, dark bruise discolored one puffy eye and half her face.

He frowned. "What happened to her face?"

Debra stacked the plates and glasses on a tray. She shot a glance at the little girl and her face darkened. "It was my mom's new boyfriend. He came home drunk and my mom was passed out again."

"What happened?" Adrian asked again.

Debra's face reddened and her hands clenched at her sides. "I guess—he wanted my mom, but she wouldn't wake up, so he went into my sister's room, and—" She trailed off. "I heard Lily scream, and I ran into the room. He was on top of her. I grabbed the desk lamp and hit him on the head. It knocked him out, and I took Lily and came here." She swallowed. "I talked to Cesar, and he said she could stay here tonight, and I should ask you in the morning for permission for her to stay longer."

Adrian's face remained impassive. The child clung to her sister's leg. "This isn't an orphanage, Debra."

"Please, Captain." Debra's voice wavered. "She can stay with me; she won't be any trouble. I can do both night and day shifts to pay for her being here."

"And you think a child would be safe here?" He raised an eyebrow, thinking of the drug-fueled parties that took place in the lounge downstairs.

"It's safer than my mom's." Debra drew a deep, shuddering breath. "I'd make it up to you. I swear it."

It might serve his purposes to grant her request, he mused. There were plenty of available bedrooms, the use of which he granted to those he favored. Debra had demonstrated her loyalty to him when she came forward to inform on Kim after the incident with Elisa in the bathroom. A favor such as this could bind her more securely to him at relatively little cost. On the other hand, it wouldn't do for him to get a reputation for being charitable. He'd have to make sure he extracted payment from her in a very visible way. He was still mulling over his revenge on Kim for her actions that day; perhaps he could involve Debra in her punishment.

He considered the little girl again. "You'd have to keep her locked in your room or with you at all times. I don't want children wandering around."

"Of course, Captain." Debra nodded eagerly. "I promise she won't be any trouble to you. You won't even know she's here."

Adrian gave her a long, level stare. Finally, he leaned back in the chair, picking up his book. "All right. I'll allow it on a trial basis."

Debra hugged her sister with one arm. "Thank you! I can't tell you how much I appreciate it."

"I'll expect to be repaid, completely, no matter what the cost," Adrian said softly. He allowed a hint of menace to creep into his tone. His dark eyes met hers and she nodded fiercely in understanding. They both knew what it meant to be indebted to him. If she was willing to pay that price, so much the better. He could always find a use for desperately loyal foot soldiers.

Then he lowered his eyes to his book, and the girls scurried out without further comment.

A few minutes later, five rapid knocks sounded in a rhythmic pattern. "Enter," Adrian called, unlocking the door with the remote. Cesar slipped into the room, his face expressionless.

"I've been following the girl as you ordered. Tonight, I scared off a couple of creeps planning to ambush her on the street downtown. She wasn't disturbed and didn't even notice them."

Adrian's eyes hardened. "Who were they?"

"Probably just addicts looking for their next fix. I doubt they even knew of her connection to us. They don't belong to the Third Street gang."

Adrian rested his chin in his hand and pondered.

"I recorded the incident, if you want further details."

"Good." Adrian shifted in his chair. "Send one copy to me, and another to Rory with a note that he is to identify the attackers and produce a report on their connections and potential motivations."

"Yes, Captain."

Adrian settled back into his armchair and picked up his glass. "Thank you, Cesar. That is all."

Cesar took a few steps toward the door, then stopped. "Captain, if you want to keep this girl safe, it might be easier if you brought her into our organization."

"No." He set his glass down on the table with a snap. "She is to stay unaware of us and our purpose." His voice dropped nearly to a whisper. "That is an order."

"Of course, Captain."

After Cesar left, Adrian stared into the dancing flames for a long time. It was unlikely the attack on Elisa was a deliberate strike by one of his enemies. However, Cesar's recommendation was logical. Bring Elisa fully into the gang, place her directly under their protection, and drill her in the security techniques everyone else followed—that would make it much easier to protect her.

This incident wasn't directed against him—yet. However, as soon as their connection became more broadly known, it was inevitable that further attacks on her would follow, as his enemies sought to gain leverage.

As he deliberated, there was a tapping on the door. "Enter," he called.

The door opened and Rory sauntered in. He wore a white Oxford button-down shirt over faded denims. He hitched his hip up onto the armrest of a chair, regarding his long-time ally with a wide grin on his face.

"So," he drawled, "I hear you have a new interest."

"And if I do?"

"Isn't it a bad time to get distracted, Captain?"

Adrian gazed into the fire. "I'm not distracted."

"You see something you want and you reach out for it, same as always. Don't you think it might be a risk, especially now?"

"She serves a purpose in my plans. That's all you need to know."

"I know what you're using her for, but why put her officially under your protection? Why spare so much manpower to guard her?" Rory's smile was wider than usual. "Sounds like she's something more than another one of your tools. Why should it matter whether she lives or dies?"

"That's enough, Rory." Adrian's voice was quiet but held a deadly edge. "It's my decision where to seek entertainment."

"Entertainment? Is that all it is?"

Adrian picked up his glass and sipped, still gazing into the fire. "Why would it be anything else?"

"This one is different. She's not in the gang; you're hiding your true identity from her. You've never done that before." Rory tilted his head so his fine hair fell over his forehead. "What have you always said about attachments?"

Adrian looked him directly in the eyes and held his gaze. "Attachments, Rory? Do you really want to go there?"

Rory swallowed. His face had gone pale. No doubt he was wondering how much Adrian knew about his little secret. About the attachment in Rory's life.

And more importantly— what Adrian was going to do about it.

Adrian let him stew for a few moments, and then he shrugged. "She caught my fancy; that's all. Why should I limit myself? In any event, I will not have my decisions questioned or gossiped over. I want you to make it clear to everyone that I won't tolerate any discussion about this matter." He rested his head on the back of the chair and crossed his arms. "The usual consequences will apply. Do I make myself clear?" His voice was soft, but Rory would hear the steel undertone.

"Of course, Captain." Rory slid off the armrest. "But what about next week? Won't there be a big risk to her—" He stopped abruptly at the expression on Adrian's face. "Sorry." He left without another word.

Robson

Principal Robson walked slowly up the main flight of stairs at the front of the school. He was burly and still muscular despite his age, and his head was crowned with thick white hair. His knees protested as he climbed. It stuck in his craw every time he had to grovel to a person—a student!—who should have no authority over him whatsoever. In the twenty-five years he had been principal, Robson had never before encountered anyone brazen enough to challenge him. Until now.

He growled to himself. At least it would be coming to an end soon, when Adrian Salas left high school.

Robson had been one of the gang's agents for more than three years. Ever since the day when he'd gotten that phone call threatening to expose his daughter. She'd thought no one knew her secret, that she'd had an abortion before she married her deeply religious husband. She had begged Robson to keep it quiet, and so he had given in to the blackmail. Since then he had carried out all the gang's orders and served as their local coordinator, as they moved their primary base and main headquarters to the campus of Rockton High. Payments had appeared in his bank account, and everything had been carefully documented.

So now they owned him, holding not just his daughter's secrets in their hands, but plenty of his own.

The one promise the boy—whom he'd been forced to call "Captain"—had made was that at the end of his senior year, the gang would move its headquarters elsewhere and Robson would be allowed to retire, his silence the only further price to pay. Four years of hell, of being an accessory to crimes he didn't even want to think about, and finally the end was in sight.

He nodded to the student on guard outside the door to the former teachers' lounge. "I have important information for the Captain. He'll want to see me immediately."

The student sniffed, but entered the room at once to relay the message. In a minute he returned and swung the door open.

The teachers' lounge was spacious and comfortable. It was located in one of the older parts of the building, but had been maintained reasonably well over the years. The wainscoting and crown molding gracing the once-elegant room echoed bygone days of larger school district budgets, when education was believed by the state government to be a priority and teaching was a respected profession. The floor-to-ceiling wood-mullioned windows offered the best view from the school, overlooking the neighborhood park.

At one end of the room sat Adrian Salas, at his ease in an antique wing-back armchair upholstered in white satin. About two dozen members of his gang sat or stood around his chair. In the center of the room, facing Adrian, a younger blond boy was kneeling, wrists bound behind his back, his face pale and terrified, and a bright red welt rising on one cheek. Robson grimaced. Although he had made his peace, mostly, with his own complicity in Adrian's crimes, the youth seemed to enjoy rubbing his servitude in his face, forcing him to witness scenes of intimidation, torture, and even threats of murder. The scowl on Robson's face deepened.

He ignored all the others, walked straight up to Adrian and said, "I have important information for your ears alone, Captain."

Adrian gave him a level stare, then gestured peremptorily with his head. At once, the gang members began filing out of the room. One jerked the bound student to his feet and made him follow.

When the door had closed behind them and the two of them were alone in the room, Robson said, "Police Chief Davenport called me this morning."

Adrian said nothing; he only raised a brow in inquiry.

"He said that the drug trafficking and gang activity in this area is getting out of hand, and he's had orders directly from the mayor to do something about it. They're especially concerned about this new drug that's been appearing on the streets." He beetled his thick white brows at Adrian. "So he's sending a team of undercover agents to the school on an infiltration mission. He informed me that I was to be the sole contact to minimize the possibility of leaks."

"Is that so?" Adrian rested his chin in his hand. "And have you received any information on these undercover agents?"

"Yes. I have their names and descriptions here, as well as the schedule of their arrival. They're adults who can pass for teenagers, experienced undercover cops from other jurisdictions."

Adrian held out his hand for the information. He unfolded the piece of paper and ran his eye over the names. "Keisha Huston and Vince Devore. Very interesting. Have they informed you when they'll send more information?"

"No. This was the final exchange."

"They'll undoubtedly attempt to infiltrate that notorious gang that's rumored to have operations at Rockton High." Adrian's eyes flashed with amusement. "We'll just have to make sure we—

facilitate their work," he said softly. "Thank you, Robson. As always, your cooperation makes my work so much easier."

The old man scowled.

The part that bothered him the most was not the crimes. It was the loss of control over his own school, the way he had to bow to Adrian, the fact that if the crimes came to light, it would be Robson, not Adrian, who would go to jail.

And if what he'd heard was about to happen next week went down—

He gritted his teeth, aware that Adrian, as always, was amused by his reaction.

9

 *Kim*

KIM CROUCHED ON THE FLOOR of the basement furnace room beside the other members of Tenebras, waiting for the Captain to come down the stairs. The room echoed with taunts and sneers, but she avoided the eyes of the scrawny kid tied to a classroom chair in front of the furnace. His arms and legs had been strapped to the chair with zip ties that cut into his pale flesh. She knew why the meeting had been called, and she wanted to distance herself from the unlucky captive as much as possible.

Hulking equipment of unknown vintage surrounded the room. The antique furnace glowed dimly around the iron door in its squat belly, and the reek of sour iron pervaded the air. Two bare bulbs hung from twisted wires nailed to the rafters amongst a maze of pipes, drains, and loose clusters of wire. The largest of the pipes was wrapped with insulating tape stained with decades of rust. The painted cement floor slanted downward toward the recessed drain at the low end of the room.

About twenty of the gang members stood against the walls, mostly male except for three or four girls. Their jeering stopped when Adrian appeared on the landing. He was not wearing his glasses, and a small smile played about his lips.

Kim waited in her customary position on the floor beside the Captain's chair. Watching Adrian walk down the stairs sent a shiver through her, as it did every time.

The first time she had seen him take command of a meeting, his physical beauty had struck her like a knife in the heart. The large, expressive eyes surrounded by impossibly thick, long lashes; that deep, resonant voice that spoke so politely of torture and death; his lean, sculpted torso and utterly graceful movements—between one breath and the next she had known what she wanted.

From that moment on, she had set herself to catch his attention in the most brazen way possible. She knew she had an attractive body, lithe and well endowed. She shivered as she recalled the day she had finally caught his eye. How well she remembered that night, the night he had brought her to his room at headquarters. She had expected him to be like all the others, the men who tore her clothes, grabbed her breasts, pressed sloppy mouths reeking of whisky or smoke to her lips, and then took her roughly, taking their pleasure eagerly and tossing her aside until the next time.

But instead he had been a gentleman. He spoke to her politely. He asked her permission, unbuttoned her shirt slowly, his eyes smoldering and a dark smile on his expressive face. He touched his lips, sweeter than honey, to hers, entered her mouth tenderly with his warm tongue. He teased her, stroked her with his long fingers until she thought she would die from the torment and wonder of it.

Sex had always been a tedious task for her, something she did to get things she wanted, pleasurable mostly in that it finally gave her a small power over others. But that night with Adrian had been a revelation.

She had been so desperate for him that she trembled, for once in her life unable to speak, as he bent over her, finally naked, his hair brushing her face when he lowered his mouth to hers. His body was even more impossibly gorgeous than she had imagined, his well-muscled, tanned chest like that of a god, his beautiful eyes alight with lust.

At last he had taken her, and in that moment she was lost, her body clenching in waves of agonized passion, in a pleasure more intense than she had dreamed possible. In the end, as he collapsed on her, he gently sought out her mouth and kissed her again.

That night she had lost her heart to the worst man possible. She had heard all the stories whispered about Adrian: he had utterly no morals; he cared for nothing and no one besides himself; at the very most he might toy with her, use her for his pleasure. That had, to her horror, in one deadly instant, become her only goal in life.

The sight of him, a glimpse of the curve of his throat, a single gesture with a graceful hand—any of these made her violently fascinated, weak and trembling at her core, all her resolve seared away in a single instant. She was helplessly, hopelessly attracted to him; like a moth to a flame, she would go to him knowing full well it would bring her only pain and death.

She still held that one golden night in her memory, precious and unrecoverable, as the one crowning moment of her life when everything had been worthwhile, when she was not Kim Lugo, trash from a lousy neighborhood, but a princess, a treasure, taken by a king.

They had had sex again since that night, but it had never been the same. He had never again shown her that gentle, caring side. Instead, he had been indifferent, or even worse, playful, a devilish smile dancing on his lips, as he whispered commands in her ear that she must follow regardless of pain or cost.

She did everything he asked of her, obeying the least of his whims to the letter, never voicing the despair that filled her heart and mind. If she were caught, he would not care in the slightest when they took her to jail. And, she thought in hopeless anguish, she would be loyal to him even there, and would not let his name pass her lips as they sentenced her.

And now... he had let her know her part in his plans, let her know exactly what he thought of her, what was going to happen to her... and the worst of it, not even by his own hand. She could have borne it if it had been at his hands.

But no. She bowed her head. She was nothing now. Less than nothing. A tear squeezed out of her eye. All because of that girl.

She ground her teeth. She wouldn't let it go. Kim Lugo didn't just take shit. Even if it killed her, she would get her revenge.

 ## Mario

Mario examined the small slip of paper and painfully decoded the message with his little codebook. He hated this part of the job. So easy to get one letter wrong and mess up the whole thing. Tongue between his teeth, a stub of a pencil in his hand, he peered at the codebook and back at the message several times.

What a waste of time. Who the hell was going to find that piece of paper anyway? Why did it need to be in code? But it was the Captain's orders. Mario didn't really understand why. Not that it mattered.

You did it the way the Captain wanted, or you didn't survive long.

Finally he finished. "Shit," he said. "It's tonight."

School had been dismissed hours ago, and it would soon be dark. The sky was overcast and it was cold enough that Mario's fingers were clumsy as he manipulated the stubby pencil. He and Ron Hundley had been hanging out behind the school, smoking. Nobody ever came to the back lot; it was known to be their territory.

Hundley grimaced. "It's Wednesday. We never have to go on Wednesday. It's always Friday or the weekend."

"Stop wiping your ass, Hundley. It's time for our delivery."

Hundley ran a hand through his greasy black hair. "Shut the fuck up. I'm coming."

Hundley's battered old Chevy waited at the far end of the school lot. Mario sneered. He'd prefer to take his Harley, but they had to take the shipment in the trunk, so they needed a car. Mario hated being cooped up inside a metal box. Especially Hundley's old piece of shit, stinking of stale tobacco smoke and rancid burgers.

He sat in the passenger seat, the window rolled all the way down, drumming his fingers impatiently on the door handle as Hundley coaxed the old claptrap into life.

Hundley grinned evilly at him as he pulled out of the lot. "What's the problem, Fonseca? You look like you're in heat or something."

"Your car smells like a shithole." Mario popped open the glove box and wrinkled his nose at the mess inside. "I can't believe you reuse condoms, you cheap bastard."

"Hey. They're expensive, especially when you go through them as fast as I do."

Mario rooted through the pile. "What's this? Used toilet paper? Fuck."

"Get your fucking hands off my shit. Funny you're complaining, seeing that rathole you live in. I'd rather live in a sewer than your dingy-ass apartment."

"Shut your hole." Mario held up a crumpled fast-food bag. Something was written on one side and Mario smoothed it out. It read "Britny." He peered into the bag. "Shit. No wonder your car reeks. Half a month-old burger covered in mold."

Hundley made a grab for it but Mario tossed it out the window. "Hey! That was my dinner!"

"You didn't even buy it. You jacked it from this chick Britny."

"You don't know shit. Maybe she's my girl."

Mario snickered. "Even one of your slutty hos ain't giving you a moldy burger. Bet you fished it out of a trash can."

"You're just jealous because none of the ladies give you gifts."

"I know what kinda 'gifts' those 'ladies' give you."

Hundley suddenly hit the brakes and Mario was thrown forward in the seatbelt.

"What the fuck—" Mario fell silent. Up ahead a lone patrol car cruised leisurely past.

Hundley slowed to within the speed limit, but the squad car didn't turn around. Mario returned to leaning out the window and glaring. With no more incidents, they drove through the city streets and onto a frontage road in the industrial section until they got to their destination, the parking lot of a nondescript, windowless white building with a faded sign. Hundley pulled around to the back, past an overflowing dumpster and into a garbage-strewn lot.

Mario got out while Hundley left the car idling. It was a routine job, but Mario kept a sharp eye out for anyone who might be following them or loitering around. The back lot was deserted. At the back door, he pressed the button and waited, making sure his face was visible through the peephole in the center of the scuffed, dented door.

It only took a few minutes before the door was opened by a thin, pasty-faced kid holding a laundry bag. Mario didn't bother with greetings. He nodded and hoisted the bag onto his shoulders. The door slammed behind him.

Hundley already had the trunk open and waiting. Mario tossed the heavy bag in.

Then they were back on the road heading to their next stop. Mario leaned out the open window again. It hadn't taken him long to figure out that it was Adrian's new girlfriend who lived in the apartment they'd been using. But what was confusing was why. What kind of game was Adrian playing?

Adrian thought of people only as tools to be used for his own purposes. Hell, the only reason Tenebras existed was to serve

Adrian Salas's ambitions. It bothered Mario sometimes, but in the past he had always shrugged it off. What else could someone like him do? Besides, he had once thought it was too late. He had thrown in his lot with Adrian, and no one left Adrian's service alive.

Mario had to admit he had done well for himself since he joined the gang. It had enabled him to get out of a number of scrapes. Adrian made sure the gang members took care of one another, and Adrian's connections with the cops and school administration guaranteed that, if caught, Mario always got away with a slap on the wrist. And the financial rewards were far better than he could get with a regular job.

But it was getting far too difficult to continue to obey Adrian's every whim. Now, though, if—when—Mario's plans came to fruition, everything would change.

Hundley parked a block away from their destination. The two of them scanned up and down the street; there were no pedestrians visible. Mario hoisted the laundry bag across his shoulders. They walked across the parking lot and overgrown side yard of a beat-up four-story apartment building. Their target was behind it on the next block.

Mario pulled out a key and slipped it into the lock. He eased the door open and checked the hallway.

After the door to the girl's apartment had shut behind them, they relaxed. The place was unoccupied as it always was during the times listed on the coded messages.

The apartment was shabby, not much better than Mario's own home. But it was significantly cleaner than the dump where he, his three younger half-brothers and two half-sisters crashed with their mom. She never bothered to clean up after her binges on drugs or liquor. But it had been the only roof over Mario's head until he joined Tenebras and had instantly taken a big step upwards in street cred, as well as gaining access to the gang headquarters for nights when the screaming and stink became unbearable.

Mario dumped the bag open in front of the huge stuffed blue dog, out of place in the corner of the living room. Hundley flipped the dog around and unzipped the back, then rooted around in the stuffing. He emerged with a small packet, showed it to Mario, and stuffed it in his jacket pocket.

The two of them took several small, soft-sided packages wrapped up in butcher paper and twine out of the bigger cloth bag and buried them deep within the stuffed dog. When the bag was empty, Mario rolled it up and shoved it into the dog as well. Hundley adjusted the stuffing to cover the new objects within the dog, and zipped up the back. The two of them replaced the animal in its corner. Mario gave the apartment a once-over to make sure they were leaving it as they had found it. Then they silently slipped out the door and down the hall.

As they stepped out the back door, a shadow emerged from the bushes and confronted them.

10

 *Ben*

"WHAT ARE YOU TWO assholes doing hanging around Elisa's apartment?" Ben Lancaster came forward into the light cast by the fixture by the door, fists raised.

Hundley and Mario exchanged a glance. "Go," said Mario. "I'll take care of this fuckwad." Hundley nodded and took off running.

Ben ignored him, focusing on Mario. "I said, what are you doing in Elisa's building?"

"Who?" asked Mario, grinning.

"Don't give me that crap, Fonseca. I saw you hanging around her a couple of weeks ago. And I've seen you here before. Tell me what you're doing or I'll pound your face in."

"You and who else?" sneered Mario. He made a show of glancing around the street, his grin mocking. "I'll wipe the ground with your fucking ass."

"What're you doing with Elisa?"

Mario tried a blank look. "Dunno who the fuck you're talking about. Ron's got a friend in this building. We were visiting him, that's all."

Ben snorted. "Sure he does."

"It don't matter, cause I'm gonna fucking kill you." With the speed of a cobra striking, Mario darted forward and led off with a hard, fast uppercut.

Ben blocked and threw a roundhouse punch at Mario's jaw. "Ha! I'd like to see you try!" He threw a flurry of punches, fast and furious and hard.

Mario, panting, danced out of reach, feinted, blocked, and then returned a barrage of blows and kicks. Ben felt rage swelling, the rage that had been building up ever since he had watched that kid Pete regress to infancy and then slowly recover in his father's clinic, since he had heard about the new drug—that was the rage he funneled into his fists, attacking Mario with everything he had. His fury was like a creature deep within him. He hammered on Mario, crushing him to the ground, moving faster and harder than ever before. He might not be able to stop the drug, but he could protect all the innocents on the street from Mario here and now.

Mario fell to the ground, limp. Even though he had stopped fighting, Ben continued beating him, raging in fury. He couldn't stop smashing his fists into the bastard's face and gut.

It wasn't until he noticed Mario's head lolling at a crazy angle that he came to his senses. It was as though the rage had been turned off like a spigot. Ben dropped to his knees and closed his eyes. What had he become? He was acting like a crazy monster, beating an unconscious man. He had always been a fair fighter, not someone who would attack someone already down. He had become unhinged.

Ben heard a grunt and opened his eyes. Mario had dragged himself to his feet, blood pouring out of his nose, clothes torn. His teeth were bared, and in his hand he held a wicked-looking knife.

"You bastard," Mario snarled. "I'm gonna nail your ass for good." He raised the knife.

Ben knew he should defend himself, but something in him seemed to have snapped. He felt dizzy, weak. He sat on the ground, waiting for Mario to stab him.

There was a blur of movement, almost too fast for him to see. A tiny, dark-skinned girl appeared in front of him, kicked the knife out of Mario's hand, and took Mario in a headlock before either of them could move. The girl couldn't have been more than four and a half feet tall. She had tightly curled black hair, black velvet eyes, and despite the pink Hello Kitty shirt she was wearing, the fiercest expression Ben had ever seen on a human being before.

"All right, what's going on here?" her voice rang out.

Ben could only stare, dazed, at this apparition. "Who are you?"

She tightened her grip on Mario to keep him immobilized. "Keisha Huston. Pleased to meet you. I think I've seen you around school."

Ben laughed. It was all so incongruous. "I'm Ben Lancaster, and that jackass you're holding is Mario Fonseca."

Mario glared. "Get the fuck off me, bitch."

Keisha shook her head. "Not until I know why you were coming at this guy with a knife. Looked like you were about to kill him."

Mario struggled ferociously in Keisha's grip for another few seconds, then gave up, wheezing. "That shithead tried to kill me."

"Is that true?" Keisha asked Ben.

"Yeah. But he deserved it. I caught him breaking and entering."

"No way, you liar!" shouted Mario. "Check the fucking apartment for all I care."

Keisha's nostrils flared. "Why don't you each tell your story?" She tightened her hold on Mario. "If I let you go, will you calm down and talk?"

The muscles in Mario's neck tensed. "Yeah."

Keisha released her headlock. Mario sprang free and jumped backwards, dropping into a crouch, his head flipping back and forth between Keisha and Ben.

"Now," she said, hands on her hips, "what's going on here?"

"Dumb idea, letting me go, bitch. Matter of fact," Mario said, a nasty grin appearing on his battered face, "I'm gonna take your fucking ass down hard."

94

A siren snarled off in the distance, coming closer, and Mario cursed. All at once, he spun and took off, rounding the corner and disappearing.

Ben and Keisha were left standing in the empty yard, glaring at each other.

Ben was the first to recover. He straightened and offered his hand with a smile. "Wow. Where'd you learn moves like that? I don't think I've ever seen such a great kick." He absently rubbed the back of his head. It was wet. When he pulled his hand back, it was stained red.

"You're bleeding," Keisha said. "We better get you to a hospital."

"As it happens," said Ben with a grin, "I was just going there. Going home, that is."

In an examination room of the Lancaster Free Clinic, Keisha sat on a folding chair while Dr. Lancaster bandaged Ben's injuries. He winced as his father daubed antiseptic on another one of his wounds.

His father said cheerfully, "I told you to stay away from Mario. How many times have I had to patch you up because of him?"

Ben glowered.

"If you hadn't come and saved my son's butt, I might have an even bigger mess to clean up." Dr. Lancaster nodded at Keisha. "Did you really kick a knife out of that guy's hand?"

Keisha shrugged. "Lucky shot."

"Lucky my ass," said Ben. "It was a great move. Where'd you learn it?"

Her eyes shifted to the ceiling. "Here and there. I've studied martial arts for a while."

"Hmm." Dr. Lancaster shot a piercing glance at her, but continued to work on Ben's injuries. "How old are you?"

"I'm a senior," said Keisha. She changed the subject. "Did you say that kid was a gang member?"

"Yeah," said Ben. "He's a member of Tenebras. You've heard of them, right?"

"I just transferred in today. I don't know much about Rockton."

"They're the biggest gang in the school. That asshole is responsible for more shit than any ten average criminals. Drugs, robbery, you name it."

She aimed a brilliant, fascinated smile at him. Ben had never seen anyone like her before, and he found a goofy grin spreading across his face. The fact that she was half his size but packed a wallop bigger than guys three times bigger than her was just another thing that made her intriguing. "Anything else you wanna know?"

 *Elisa*

Adrian deftly maneuvered the little car into a halfway-legal parking spot just a bit too close to a fire hydrant. When Elisa pointed it out to him, he only smiled.

"Don't worry about it. There's no one writing tickets on this street at this time of night."

He opened the car door and helped her out. It was a cold, crisp late October night, and a crescent moon oversaw fitful wisps of clouds. The night air smelled like winter, and Elisa shivered. Adrian draped an arm around her. He smelled like roasted chestnuts fresh off the bonfire, and she inhaled deeply as he pressed her into his shoulder. His fingers tangled in her hair and left fiery trails over the back of her neck. She lifted her face up to his. Then his lips connected with hers, her eyes closed, and her body roared like a furnace, vanquishing the chill of the night.

At her apartment door, she paused on the threshold and sniffed deeply several times. Something was very wrong.

"What is it?" Adrian asked.

She tiptoed to the hall closet door and flung it open. "Someone's been in my apartment!" she cried, twisting her head from side to side and sniffing some more.

"What makes you think that?"

"I can smell them," she said, wrinkling my nose.

Adrian kissed her on the tip of her nose. "You're so cute when you do that. Are you a bloodhound? What makes you think you can smell someone's trail?" He went to the living room window and checked behind the curtains. "No broken glass, no signs of forced entry. I don't think you have to worry." He poked his head in the bedroom. "Nothing here either."

"I don't know. This guy smells like sweat and some kind of cheap cologne. I've smelled that combination before. Here in the apartment, once before, and—" she put a finger to her mouth. "I know I've smelled it somewhere else, but I can't remember where." She squinted. "Can't you smell it?"

Obligingly, he sniffed, but shook his head. "I'm sorry, I don't smell anything unusual." Then a lazy smile crossed his face and he teased, "Except for that wasabi and cumin bean dip you made yesterday."

She made a face at him. "Don't be silly, Adrian. I can't smell that one at all anymore."

He laughed and playfully took her face in his hands. "Can you smell me?" He brushed his lips over her nose and kissed her again, trailing across her cheek and down her throat. She closed her eyes and almost forgot to breathe.

Gasping, she put her hands on his chest to push him away. "You don't believe me, do you?"

"Elisa," he said, taking both her hands in his and steering her to sit down on the couch, "let's look at the evidence. Are there any signs of forced entry? Is anything missing?"

"That doesn't matter!" she cried. "Why don't you believe me?"

He reclined on the couch and ran his hands through his hair. "I—" he said and then stopped. His confident smile faded. Wrinkles gathered on his forehead and he stared at her, the skin around his eyes bunching.

She'd never seen him like that. "Are you okay?"

"I'm sorry." He grimaced. "I think I pulled a muscle at the gym today." His face smoothed out and his voice gentled. "I wanted to say I do believe you. I'm sorry for doubting you."

She reached up and hugged him, but he still seemed distracted. "I don't see anything missing," she said.

The pictures of Carlos were undisturbed, and they were of the most value to her. She glanced around one more time, but before she could say anything, Adrian's hands went to either side of her head. "So it's settled, then. Let's not talk about this anymore," he murmured. "I have a better use for that fine mouth of yours." He fisted his hands in her hair, tilting the bones of her jaw back with his thumbs, skimming her mouth with his lips over and over until the most delicate areas of her skin quivered and sparks of pleasure fired in her core. She arched into his kiss, straining to meet his lips and tongue, and this time, she forgot everything as the world went away.

 Adrian

Driving away from Elisa's apartment, Adrian rubbed the back of his neck. He felt extremely strange. And it was perplexing enough in itself that he would articulate to himself the word "feel." He hadn't allowed himself to feel for years. Emotion got in the way of doing what needed to be done. Even a moment of weakness could be fatal. It almost had been, that one night. Afterwards, as he had staggered away, bleeding and terrified, darting and weaving from shadow to shadow, he had sworn to himself: never again.

But this was worse than simple emotion. He felt... distress. It was becoming distasteful to lie to Elisa, to use her the way he used everyone around him.

He had never felt this way before.

Everything about her fascinated him. The expression of bliss on her face whenever she ate sweets, her absurd compassion, the way she twirled her hair around her index finger just like Adrian's sister used to, how she cried every time she read a romance novel. She was so different from everyone he had known, unbelievably innocent. How could she have lived so long and remained so untouched? It made him want to touch her all over, to lay his tracks through fresh-fallen snow. He wanted to explore that unblemished skin, pale beneath his fingers, softer than silk against his mouth.

Foolish.

She was foolish.

She was beautiful.

He wanted her, but not just as a conquest. He wanted something more. Much more.

But for only the second time in his life, Adrian Salas had no idea how to get what he wanted.

11

 *Lonnie*

LONNIE GRUMBLED TO HIMSELF as he slunk through the bushes on the way to his target. This was a boring and stupid job. Hadn't he done enough of these to demonstrate how skillful and clever he was? When was he going to be given a chance to earn real money? He gave a quick glance to his left and right. The streets were quiet in the thin early afternoon sunlight.

"It's a fucking easy job," Mario had told him, "but you gotta obey orders exactly, and make sure no one sees you."

"I got it, I got it," Lonnie said. "But—"

Mario's eyes were flinty. "Shut the fuck up. No questions. Now get on it. It's gotta be done by three today."

There was a rustle nearby and Lonnie held his breath, hand moving to the knife at his belt. He peered into the shadows behind the leaves surrounding him, caught a glimpse of movement, and froze.

"Lonnie!" came a whispered voice from behind a particularly leafy cluster of branches. "Is that you?" A figure squeezed out from under a branch and sidled up to him.

"Kim?" asked Lonnie, his mouth falling open. "Whatcha doing here?" He immediately straightened and threw his shoulders back. Kim was super hot, and hung out with all the top-ranking members of Tenebras. Way out of his league. How did she even know his name?

She stood very close, her skin dappled by shadow. She smiled, and a quiver went through his body. She had a killer smile. Not to mention boobs that didn't quit. "Mario told me to catch up with you and give you some new orders."

"Oh yeah?" Maybe this job wasn't so bad if someone like Kim got sent after him.

Kim drew her shoulders together so the cleft between her breasts deepened. "Mario said to tell you that girl's not under our protection anymore. So if you want to trash her apartment, have some fun, go ahead."

Lonnie tore his eyes away from Kim's cleavage. "Huh? Orders were not to touch anything."

Kim frowned. "Things have changed. Besides, why do you care? You know what I heard her say, last time she was with the Captain?"

"What?"

"She tried to get him to stop moving slip. Said she was tired of all the 'illegal' crap he was doing." Her fingers made air quotes around the word.

Lonnie squinted. "No fucking shit?"

"Biggest haul we've ever made, and she's fucking trying to get us to give up all that cash. Pinching off *your* cut."

"What the fuck she up to?"

"Dumbass bitch," Kim spat. "Anyway, that's the word. I gotta go." She squeezed through the branches and was gone.

Lonnie squinted after her. What should he do? Now he had two different sets of orders. He didn't dare trash the apartment or do anything obvious. The orders said to clean everything out, leave it all apparently untouched. But maybe he could do something to get even. Make that girl pay.

He hesitated in the quiet living room after emptying the contents of the stuffed blue dog into his trash bag. A row of canisters standing on the tidy kitchen counter caught his eye. Perfect.

He pulled out a packet of white powder and carefully emptied it into the tin marked "Sugar."

 Keisha

The first bell rang, and Keisha checked up and down the third floor hall. No one in sight. She unlocked a nondescript door and slipped inside. It was a windowless supply closet, but it was private.

It had been a frustrating couple of days. She had heard plenty of rumors about gang operations at Rockton High, but nothing other than hearsay.

Principal Robson had given her the names of a few kids he thought might be gang members. Ben Lancaster was at the top of the list.

A key rattled in the lock, and Vince Devore slipped inside. The tattoos on his arms rippled as he closed the door.

"Hey. What's up?" Keisha asked. "Any leads?"

"Not much, but I did make contact with Lancaster and Fonseca." Vince rubbed his jaw. "A couple of hot-headed assholes with short fuses."

Keisha tugged at her Hello Kitty necklace. "Lancaster's the only one I've been able to get to open up even a little."

"This is the tightest I've ever seen a school sealed up. The entire student body's scared—no, terrified—of Tenebras."

Something meowed from behind a stack of boxes at the back of the room. Keisha immediately cleared her throat.

"I thought I smelled tuna fish," Vince groaned. "Don't tell me you 'rescued' another stray cat, Keisha. That's completely unprofessional in the middle of an operation."

"I didn't have any choice! She was so thin." She sent him a half-pleading, half-threatening glance.

"You're gonna blow our cover, if Robson finds out you're violating school rules by allowing animals into the building. Maybe you'll even get expelled from high school." He winked.

"Shut up," Keisha snapped. "Let's get back to work."

"All right, all right, if you say so," he grumbled, shaking his head. He sat on an open box of filler paper. "I got more info here." He tossed her a small notebook. "The lieutenants of the gang are called Blades."

"Any word on if the leader, the Captain, is a student or an adult?"

"Rumor says he's a student, but shit, the extent of his reported activities scares me. He's gotta be an adult. A student would've been awfully young when the gang first appeared." He scratched his head. "There's a lot of talk about Rapture, and how fast it's spreading. Rumor says that Tenebras is controlling the distribution, but other rumors say that they don't have the organization to peddle hard drugs." He shook his head. "I'm not sure what to believe. The gang actually has what you might call PR agents spreading disinformation."

"Kind of sophisticated for a high school gang."

"Makes me think there are adults behind it. I've sent a request for a check of departmental records of organized crime in this neighborhood to see if I can scope something out."

"Heard anything?"

"Not yet. We're down two officers in our division. But Rapture's spreading faster than expected, so there was no way we could've just sat back on this one." He scratched under his muscle shirt. "We're in a precarious spot. This Captain, whoever he is, is extremely well-organized, and from our intelligence, highly dangerous."

 *Adrian*

In another room at the opposite end of the school, Adrian sat behind a desk, wearing headphones, listening to the two cops' conversation. Cesar and Rory sat in front of the desk, waiting for him to finish. The corners of Adrian's mouth crooked upward slightly as Vince pronounced him "highly dangerous." He removed the headset and placed it on the desk.

"Cesar. Perfect placement with the new bugs," he said. "Signal strength is five by five. And it looks like they really are untraceable."

Cesar's voice was stern. "Good. That means Robson didn't try to double-cross us and give us the wrong room."

"He doesn't dare defy us at this point." Adrian reclined in his chair. "No chance of it."

Rory grinned. "He belongs to you completely, Captain. Ain't that fine?" He scratched an ear. "How long are you gonna let these cops run loose?"

Adrian shrugged. "They won't find anything we don't give them. But I think it's time to spring our little trap." He rested his chin on his knuckles. "Cesar, carry out the plan we discussed last week. Don't forget the changes I made yesterday. I want it to come to fruition on the night of the Halloween Ball."

Cesar nodded. "I'm on it."

"Captain?" Rory said. "You've been keeping everybody busy lately with all these sudden changes to our operations. Might I ask if—"

"It's your job to keep everyone in line." Adrian's voice was cold. "My orders are to be obeyed without question. Is that clear?"

Rory dropped his eyes. "Of course."

"Do we have any preliminary reports on profits from the new operation?"

"They'll be ready tonight," Cesar responded. "Looks like all lines are up by over 300%."

"Excellent. Rory, I want you to make contact with Keisha Huston as we discussed."

They nodded and rose. As they reached the door, Adrian spoke again. "One more thing. Bring Kim Lugo here at once."

Rory raised his eyebrows. "What did the bitch do now?"

Adrian gave him a level stare.

"Sorry," Rory said, lifting his hands. "I'll get her right away."

The two left the room. Adrian shifted in his chair. It was irritating to have to deal with Kim, but necessary. His network of informants had been buzzing even more than usual lately.

His mind circled back, as it so often did these days, to Elisa, with her flood of thick auburn hair, her smooth skin and extravagant curves, her hesitant and soft voice that could turn to steel at unexpected moments. Simply thinking about her felt like traveling in unknown territory.

He had been putting her in danger.

Thoughtlessly.

It had never mattered to him before if he put any of his chess pieces at risk. If they survived, they became stronger. He had helped them to grow. If they failed—well, there were always others to lure in and put to use.

He had learned on that long-ago day that it was a terrible weakness to care for another living being, that it brought nothing but unbearable pain. He had sworn he would never make that mistake again.

But now... all of a sudden, it occurred to him that a human life might be irreplaceable.

12

 *Elisa*

SUMIKO GRABBED Elisa's arm. "What do you mean, you're not going to the Halloween Ball in costume? You have to!"

"Sumiko, my mom hates Halloween. I've never worn a costume in my life. I'm only going this year because, well, you know."

"Are you serious?" Chloe asked. "It's not like it's a religious event. Besides, isn't your mom out of town?"

Elisa squirmed. How could she tell them it was against one of her mother's Rules? And although she didn't really believe in those rules anymore, it was hard to get away from ideas that had been beaten into her head all her life. "The whole Halloween thing is kind of creepy, isn't it? All those skulls and witches and bad things. Reminders of death."

Sumiko and Chloe exchanged a glance.

And Hell, Elisa thought but didn't say. She didn't believe in Hell any more, but sometimes Halloween gave her nightmares. She remembered the revival tent her mother had taken her to when she was just a little girl.

"Imagine," the preacher had bellowed, his amplified voice echoing across the tent. "Have you ever brought your hand a little too close to a fire? You remember how it burned, how your skin heated up and turned red, maybe even blistered. Maybe you put some ointment on it but it still hurt. The painful scalding seemed to linger inside your hand long after the fire was gone.

"Now imagine the heat of the hottest bonfire you can think of. Then imagine yourself in the center of that fire, not only your hand but your entire body, your skin peeling off your flesh. Now imagine that ten times, a hundred times, a thousand times worse.

"If you commit a sin, disobey God, *that* is what you are dooming yourself to.

"Hell. Yes, you will go to Hell. You will roast in hellfire, not for a year, not for a thousand years, but for eternity. Eternity! In the most vicious, corroding, burning pain you could ever possibly imagine."

She shuddered, remembering the lesson her mother had given her that evening. Elisa's skin had blistered and bubbled as her flesh roasted in the fire. She put her hands behind her back. It had taken a long time to heal and she could still see some of the scars.

Chloe was still chattering about how much fun it was to dress up.

Sumiko peered closely at Elisa. "Are you okay?"

Anger bubbled up inside Elisa. It was time she stopped letting her mother's rules dictate her life. She was different now. She was an adult.

"I'll do it," she announced.

"You'll go in costume?" Chloe asked.

"Yeah. Adrian said it was up to me whether or not we dress up." Feeling reckless, she said to Sumiko, "What should we go as? What's a typical Halloween thing we could dress up as?"

Warm arms slipped around her from behind.

"Adrian!" She twisted around to return his hug. "We were just talking about costumes for the Halloween Ball. Want to dress up?"

A smile spread across his face. "I'd love to. Got any ideas?"

Chloe jumped up and down. "Ooh, I have the perfect costume idea for you two!" She elbowed Sumiko in the ribs. "Want to get together and do some sewing at my place today?" She whispered in Sumiko's ear and both girls doubled over in laughter.

107

Elisa ignored them and bent to pick up some books from the bottom of her locker. "Oh, Adrian, are you free after school today? I wanted to show you something."

"I'm sorry. I'm helping one of the teachers tutor elementary school kids this afternoon."

Sumiko shook her head, still grinning. "I don't see how you get all your homework done with all the volunteer work you do."

"I enjoy helping others. And as you probably know, it doesn't hurt to have plenty of charity work on your college applications to compete with all those private school kids." With a squeeze of Elisa's hand and a wave, he headed off down the hall.

Sumiko watched Adrian disappear down the corridor. "You sure got lucky, Elisa. Adrian seems too good to be true."

 Mario

The furnace cast a dull reddish glow over the gang members' faces, outlining them in shadows. Adrian descended the steps to the basement. At the final landing, his gaze passed over the group neutrally. Their faces all lifted to follow him, like plants to the sun.

Mario's nostrils pinched together. The bastard knew he cut a striking figure on the stairs. Adrian strode with poise across the room as though unaware of all the eyes on him. In an alcove at the end of the room, a large black armchair stood on an elevated platform. Adrian lowered himself into it, resting one elbow on an armrest.

At his motion, Kim rose from the floor at his feet. Her long blonde hair flowed down her back, and her eyes were heavily made up. She wore a halter top and tight shorts that exposed a great deal of her soft flesh.

Underneath the makeup, her face was pale and her forehead creased. She pasted an attempt at a seductive smile on her lips and tried to slide onto Adrian's lap.

Adrian had sometimes allowed this behavior. But today, he appeared indifferent—no, angry. He disentangled her arms from his neck none too gently.

"Kim. Off," he commanded.

She instantly let go and slid off his lap. "I'm sorry, Captain." She crept to the side of the room, hunched her shoulders and twisted her shaking hands together. Mario wondered for a moment what could possibly have put her in such a state.

The others in the room shifted restlessly as Adrian reclined in his seat and raised one finger. At his command, two burly kids walked to the back and hauled in a chair that they set down before Adrian. A thin, pasty-faced boy had been strapped to it, and he lifted his head, staring at Adrian with defiance mingled with terror.

Mario sucked in his breath; it was Lonnie. He wondered how the kid could have made a mistake big enough to land him on Adrian's shit list so soon after joining the gang. He almost felt sorry for the poor kid. Soon all that defiance would be gone.

"Lonnie," Adrian said softly. "You disobeyed my direct orders. What do you have to say for yourself?"

The boy tossed tangled brown hair back from his face. "Lies. All lies, Captain. They were spread by my enemies—" He glared at Kim where she crouched against the wall. "I would never have gone against your orders."

"Really?" Adrian asked. "Cesar, tell them what you found."

Mario noted a slight tightening of Adrian's fingers, and realized that Adrian was uncharacteristically furious. As usual, none of his emotion showed on his face. What had Lonnie done? And how was Kim connected?

Cesar stepped forward, dreads swinging against his chest. "You scum," he spat. "You were trusted with a sensitive delivery. Instead of doing your job, you stole from us. On top of that, you endangered someone we were contracted to protect."

Lonnie fidgeted. His eyes dropped.

"Captain," he whispered. "Please, you have to understand, there's gotta be a mistake..." His voice faded into a hopeless whimper.

Adrian stood and paced towards the squirming captive. "Did you really think I wouldn't find out?" His lip curled. "I had to personally retrieve the stolen product. And clean up your mess. Really, Lonnie? Sugar?" He shook his head slowly. "How unimaginative."

Sweat slid down Lonnie's forehead.

"Normally," Adrian said, "disloyalty is punishable by death. But there are things far worse than an easy death." Lonnie lifted his eyes to him in fear and rising alarm.

Adrian swung his left hand out from behind his back. He held a syringe. He lifted it point upwards and squeezed so one drop of clear liquid oozed from the tip.

"Do you know what this is, Lonnie?"

There was utter silence in the room.

"Rapture," Adrian murmured. "The ultimate drug. Once you get started, there's no turning back." His voice was low and melodic. "You are consumed by desire for it from the moment you get up in the morning till the minute you go to bed at night." His voice dropped even lower. "You become a slave to the drug. Or... to the person who controls its supply."

Adrian glanced at the silent group. "We now control the entire supply of Rapture to this city. Imagine the power that gives us."

Lonnie licked his lips. Adrian's right hand came up, and Mario saw he held a knife. With a lightning-fast movement, he spun it and slashed across Lonnie's neck and shoulder.

The boy gasped. He hadn't even had time to flinch. Mario had frequently seen demonstrations of Adrian's inhumanly fast reflexes. All the Blades knew never to get suckered into a knife fight with him. He could cut you before you even knew he had moved. But this must have been the first time this kid had seen it.

Lonnie peered down at his chest, breathing heavily, no doubt expecting to see Adrian's knife buried in his heart.

But all Adrian had done was slice his clothing. A piece of his shirt fell to the ground, exposing his right shoulder. A thin red line crossed his skin, oozing small drops of bright red blood. With another lightning-fast move Adrian brought his left hand, still holding the syringe, to the boy's shoulder. Another second and he had injected the full dose into one of his veins.

The boy stiffened as the drug hit him, eyes rolling back in his head. Adrian watched dispassionately as the drug took effect. Lonnie slumped in his bonds. His eyes opened, hazy and languid.

He laughed. "This—is punishment? I've never felt better in my life." He threw his head back with a brash glare that encompassed everyone in the room.

Adrian tossed the syringe casually on the floor. "You say that now, my friend, but wait until your supply is cut off and your only chance for more is in my hands.

"Your body, heart, and soul now belong to me," Adrian whispered. "I have been merciful and allowed you to live—this time. But should you, in the future, disobey the least of my commands, I shall make sure you endure agony beyond the fires of Hell."

Mario shifted from foot to foot, avoiding glancing at Lonnie. He jolted when he heard his name. "Mario," Adrian ordered, "take our prisoner back to his cell for the next few days. Make sure he gets a regular fix for three days. Then—" He waved a hand. "Withhold it for two."

"Yes, Captain," said Mario. He jerked his head at two kids in the back of the room. They hoisted the chair with its captive, now slumped with his eyes closed, writhing in pleasure, no longer aware of his surroundings or his fate.

It was impressive that the stuff could make him completely unafraid. Maybe taking just a small amount could be useful, if

Mario wanted to hide something from Adrian. He'd just have to be careful not to get hooked. He could skim a tiny bit off the bricks he handled. No one would notice since he, unlike Lonnie, knew enough to alter the records before they went to Cesar.

He fingered the baggie in his jeans. If he could hide his emotions from Adrian's scrutiny, it would change everything.

Adrian

Adrian strode away from the meeting, making sure his face remained impassive. When had it become so complicated? The realization that Elisa could have been endangered by his own people had lit a conflagration of rage within him that he could barely contain. Lonnie's punishment suited one who had tried to addict an innocent to Rapture.

It was one of his few codes. No innocents were to be hurt. Those who chose to buy drugs, to lead a life of crime, to attack Adrian or those he protected—they were no longer innocent. When he dealt out punishment, he prided himself on his neutrality, his ability to dispense his own form of justice.

He couldn't remember feeling this kind of fury, not for a very long time.

He shook his head. He didn't have time for speculation. Mario was hiding something, he was certain of it. Adrian had almost called him out in the meeting, forced him to confess. But he had too many other tasks to do today. He could always take care of Mario later.

He had extracted a detailed confession from Kim and let her know to expect punishment. Of course, the knowledge that he had been done with her had been sufficient for now. Her devastation had been visible on her face. Pain of the heart could be far worse than physical pain.

Then he had to arrange to keep Elisa out of her apartment while he searched it. He was not going to leave sensitive tasks to underlings again. He found the tainted sugar and replaced it, checking carefully to make sure the apartment was clean. Then he had to arrange an excuse that would convince Elisa to change her locks.

It used to be that everything went smoothly, as smooth and cold as the stroke of a knife. As it had since the day, so long ago, he had made the decision to live for one thing only.

It was so much easier to shut away the pain, to focus on that single task. Revenge. He hadn't been more than seven years old when he started his hunt in earnest. It took two years to track down his first target.

But once he found him, it had been smooth, smooth like butter, like the tenderest of meat.

The money he had squirreled away, the deals he had set up, pretending to be a courier for a mysterious adult—all had gone off without a hitch.

No one believed a nine-year-old could plan like an adult, could commit crimes like an adult. It made it all so simple. He could do what he wanted practically beneath their eyes, and they never suspected. The few times he had been caught, it had been easy to pretend he was innocent, while his accusers searched in vain for the adult who had "used" him.

Curious about their consistent disbelief in his machinations, he had once arranged an IQ test for himself. The shocked expression on the psychologist's face had been intriguing. She had checked her answer key twice.

"He's reached the ceiling on this test; I need to administer a second one to determine your son's true score," she told the drug addict he had bribed to pose as his mother.

When the results came back, an avid gleam appeared in the psychologist's eyes. "I've never seen a score like this before.

According to the statistics, it's reached by only one in a hundred thousand children. We don't use this terminology anymore, but you could say his physical age is nine while his mental age is eighteen."

Walking away from the psychologist's office, he knew he had been wise to stay anonymous. He still remembered her fervent attempts to convince his 'mother' to have him return for more testing.

He was a freak.

Maybe his life could have been different. Maybe he could have been a scientist, someone who made discoveries that could change the world.

He snorted. Unlikely. He had seen what happened to children who were too smart, even if they had the support of their parents. Especially in their poor neighborhood. There were no programs for the "gifted" in their area. The smart kids in his school were made fun of, or beat up. Even though part of him longed to be nothing more than a bookish nerd who spent all his time in the library instead of running the streets, Adrian knew that was foolish.

Besides, he had a job to do. There had been four of them. He was going to hunt them down one by one.

The man's eyes had rolled from side to side as Adrian held the knife to his throat. "What's going on? You just a kid. What are you, nine? Listen, kid, untie me. Let me go. You don't wanna do this."

Adrian's hand tightened on the knife. A drop of blood oozed from the man's skin. "Her name was Beth, did you know that?" he whispered. "Beth. She loved music and games."

"Who? What you talking about? I swear, I ain't done nothing."

"Beth," he whispered one more time. His hand shook, and for a moment he almost turned away. He almost made a different choice.

But then he drew the knife across the bastard's throat.

13

 *Elisa*

ADRIAN AND ELISA STOOD outside the main doors of the gym, shivering in the icy air, waiting for the Halloween Ball to start.

Sumiko and Chloe had gone all out, dressing them as Bonnie and Clyde. Adrian wore a slick vintage 30s gangster suit, and Elisa a 30s-style jumper in black satin, with the tiniest of slit skirts.

Elisa fingered her low-cut neckline. Sumiko and Chloe had knotted a saucy red tie around her throat, pointing straight to her cleavage, and put a red velvet garter way up her thigh. She had never worn anything that exposed so much of her body before, and it made her hyperaware of parts of her anatomy she'd spent years being instructed by her mother to ignore.

She caught Adrian staring at her décolleté and self-consciously dropped her arm. Her face grew warm. He winked at her and dipped his head to lightly graze her cleavage with his lips.

His touch sent a shiver through her body. Not that her legs weren't already dotted with goosebumps, in the skimpy skirt that barely covered her ass.

She had almost refused to wear it when Sumiko and Chloe had unveiled the costume that afternoon.

"Come on," Sumiko insisted. "Don't you want to look sexy for Adrian?"

Elisa glanced over her shoulder at herself in the mirror. "Sexy, maybe, but practically naked? It looks like you were hoarding every square inch of fabric like it was gold." Although, she had to admit, she liked the way her legs stretched so long and elegant from the tiny skirt to the strappy black heels.

Chloe pouted. "Aw, we worked so hard on these costumes. Don't tell me you're going to throw away all our work."

Elisa had to give in, though not without hearing her mother's voice again. "Shameless hussy! Halloween belongs to the devil, and now you will too!"

"Shut up!" Elisa said to her. "Everything you told me about Halloween was a lie. It's time for me to start my own life!"

And she had strutted out of Chloe's apartment on those stiletto heels.

A cold gust snapped at the hem of her skirt, and she shivered. Adrian draped his striped jacket over her, and she huddled into the warm silk lining.

At last, their group reached the head of the line. They were swept into the gym, now transformed into a murky cave of thumping, bruising music lit by occasional strobe flashes. Adrian led her onto the dance floor.

He tilted up the brim of his fedora with the barrel of his gun. "Not bad, eh?" The striped suit outlined his lean body perfectly, making him every inch the Depression-era gangster.

His glance slid coolly down her tight skirt, over the red velvet garter encircling her thigh like a warm hand. His gaze seared her bare skin like a laser, leaving a fiery trail over the exposed swell of her breasts.

Amazing how clothes could change everything about a person.

Elisa's hair trailed over her naked shoulders, and she tossed her head so her heated curls stroked her skin. The rough bodice of the dress rubbed her nipples and they hardened.

She could see why her mother said costumes were the work of the devil. Wearing the tight, slinky outfit, her lips outlined in a crimson pout, she felt wild and daring, a little like an actual 1930s gun moll. What rebellious and sinful desires had Bonnie indulged when she followed Clyde away from her safe Kansas life?

Elisa's own life was so tightly constrained—her mother had ruled her every thought and action for so long.

Had Bonnie felt this kind of heady freedom, this spark of forbidden excitement, when she left it all behind?

Adrian moved out of the darkness, shadows playing over the planes of his face. Casually, he slid one spaghetti strap off Elisa's shoulder with the barrel of the gun.

It was a game.

But it made her feel sexy. Excited.

She tingled all over. His eyes raked across her like they were stripping her bare.

"You know," he whispered, his lips grazing her ear, "Bonnie was quite the innocent until Clyde drew her into his criminal life. But then she eagerly embraced his wicked ways. He corrupted her completely. Would you do that for me, if I were a man like that? Forsake your morals, live the outlaw life?"

She sucked in a breath.

"Think of it: utter freedom. No rules. They went where they chose to go, in stolen cars, caroused brazenly in luxury hotels. If they wanted something"—he snapped his fingers—"they took it.

"Anyone who crossed them died." He mimed pulling a trigger.

Elisa inhaled, licked her lips. It was just play. Not real.

"To Clyde, taking a life meant nothing. Killing was only another tool to get what he wanted."

Adrian's acting ability was superb; Elisa was enthralled. Even though she shouldn't be.

"Yet she followed him." His voice was low, sparking across her brain with that taste of the forbidden, vibrating over her naked shoulders, his words lapping at her exposed throat. "Would you do that for me?"

Caught up in his illicit fantasy, she nodded, breathless, playacting, as thrills pierced her over and over. "I'd follow you anywhere, Adrian," she whispered. "Do whatever you asked."

He smiled, and it was a dark, dark smile. "Good."

 Keisha

Keisha pushed her way through the crowd of students dancing, posing, and shouting in the badly-lit gym. The outfit she wore was ill-fitting, and the cheap material rubbed her skin raw in several places, especially the garters at the top of the fishnet stockings. She was having a hard time concentrating on her targets.

She had caught sight of Mario earlier and had shoved her way after him in the darkness. But by the time she pushed through the gyrating bodies, he was gone. She'd lost Ben Lancaster as well. It didn't improve her mood.

She finally decided to take a break. It was quieter behind the gym, by the drinking fountain, away from the music and shouting. Keisha relaxed against a wall, half-hidden behind some potted plants, and drank a soda, allowing her energy to gradually return.

As she was about to return to the ball, she heard whispers and froze.

"The rap?" muttered someone down the hall.

"Big haul tonight."

She listened intently as they talked, her heart beating against her ribs. This was it. A real lead at last.

By the time she emerged, they were gone. She strolled to the far end of the corridor and pulled out her phone.

No one was around. "Vince? I think we can get a warrant for the Tenebras headquarters tonight. I got a tip on a Rapture delivery. I just need to verify it. Maybe we can finally get enough to shut those bastards down."

 ## Ben

Ben paced the halls behind the gym, ignoring the muffled throbbing of the bass. He still wasn't sure why he had come to the dance, without a date, without a costume. Catching a glimpse of Elisa dancing with Adrian was enough. He'd had to leave the gym to be alone for a while.

He rounded a corner and saw Cesar Peralta and Mario Fonseca talking at the very end of a long hallway. Cesar passed something to Mario, and the two of them split off in opposite directions.

Ben stared after them. He knew Cesar was one of Adrian Salas's best friends; the two were always together. He had seen them talking only a few minutes ago. After Adrian had spoken at length to Cesar, he had nodded and trotted off.

Could Cesar be connected with Tenebras? He was obviously doing some sort of business with Mario, a high-ranking member of the gang. If Cesar was Tenebras, then surely Adrian must be too.

Straight-A, squeaky-clean, student body president Adrian Salas was in Tenebras.

Ben's spirits suddenly lifted. All he had to do was prove it, and tell Elisa about the connection. Surely she would see that Adrian was no good for her. Chin high, he tiptoed down the hall, following in Cesar's wake.

 ## Elisa

The music throbbed in Elisa's skull, wild and wicked. It slammed all rational thought out of her and left her swinging in the darkness, whirling in Adrian's hands.

Adrian knew how to lead. His skill made Elisa feel like she could dance, too. Even as she tottered on her stiletto heels, he twirled and carried her through the music. When the song ended, she found herself in a deep dip, one leg pointing into the air. She gazed straight into his eyes, grateful that his arms were keeping her from an inevitable, humiliating crash onto the floor.

She relaxed completely and allowed him to reel her into the next dance. The strobes spun around her head, flashing and outlining a press of bodies all around them, and nothing was certain in the dark world except Adrian and his strength and confidence, his completely secure grasp as he poured her boneless body from one step to the next.

It was exhilarating. She felt overheated and excited and strangely graceful.

Like a totally different person.

She *was* a different person.

Elisa was free of her mother. She was done with her.

She shouted in Adrian's ear. "I'm thirsty." Laughing, she led the way to the punch table and scooped herself a brimming ladle of bright orange liquid.

"Not that one, Elisa." Adrian touched her arm. "You want the punch at the other table."

"Why?" She glanced at the cup.

"That one's spiked. Someone put vodka in it."

She frowned. "I know what spiked means." Tonight she wasn't naïve, rule-following Elisa. "I want some anyway," she declared.

Adrian looked shocked, then amused. He poured out half the cup and replaced it with punch from the other bowl. "You don't want to have too much your first time."

"What? Why not?"

He slanted her a wicked grin. "I want your first experience breaking the rules to be pleasant, so you'll do it again." He handed her the cup with a flourish.

She raised it to him in salute and gulped it straight down. Dancing had made her thirsty, and she didn't taste anything odd about the punch.

He raised his eyebrows at her but said nothing.

"That felt good," she announced. She stuck her empty cup in Adrian's hand and poked his chest. "I want more."

Laughing, he filled her cup from the other bowl. "I think that was enough."

She swayed in mock outrage. "What!" She slid her toy gun out of its thigh holster and pointed it at him. "Give me some more, now!"

He pushed the barrel of her gun aside. "It's not a good idea to get in the habit of pointing even a toy gun at anyone... unless you mean to shoot them."

"Hey." She tried to get around Adrian to reach the punch bowl, but her shoes had become difficult to balance on. He caught her before she could tip over completely.

"What would Bonnie do?" she asked, struggling up out of his arms. "She would have another cup."

Adrian's arms gripped her like velvet-covered iron. "She would do what Clyde told her to," he murmured in her ear.

Elisa giggled and hung on his neck. "Aw, don't you want to get me drunk and have your way with me?"

"I don't need to get you drunk to have my way with you. Besides, I would want you to *remember*." He tugged her back to the dance floor.

The music shifted to another slow dance. Adrian's hands stroked up her back and tangled in her hair. "I find your hair irresistible," he murmured. "So thick, and long, and lush."

She rested her cheek against his chest. "I want to dance with you all night."

His chest vibrated as he chuckled. "I don't mind. I can't go home tonight, anyway."

"What? Why not?"

His fingers, resting on her bare back, tightened. "My aunt told me not to."

"What happened?" She knew he didn't get along with his aunt very well, but he was so close-mouthed about his family that she had no idea if his parents were even alive.

He shook his head. "It doesn't matter."

"Of course it matters!" she declared, indignant for him. "And I have an extra couch," she said, greatly daring. "My mother will be at her retreat for another couple of months, so you can sleep at my place."

"Are you sure?"

"Of course. Of course you can stay with me. You can stay any time." She buried her face in his shirt. The fabric was soft against her skin, and his scent lingered on it. Her mother and Carlos would never have allowed her to let a boy stay in their apartment overnight. But she was done listening to them.

Adrian stroked her hair again and kissed her forehead. "Thank you," he whispered. "You don't know how much that means to me."

"You don't even need to ask, Adrian. I'd like my home to be yours." She stopped. Surely that was coming on too strong. That almost sounded like a declaration of... something serious. And it was far too early to be serious.

But his gaze was strange and warm. "Elisa," he said softly. "I've been alone for a very long time. I haven't had a home for so long." He drew her in to his chest again. "Not since..." He broke off, and his voice changed. It became rougher than she had ever heard— broken, almost hesitant. For a moment, it seemed like he was no longer perfectly confident, cool, and utterly in control.

"Elisa, you make me feel things I haven't felt since I did have a home. I want to tell you something I have never told anyone else. About my family." He paused, and she made an encouraging noise. "When I was five—"

Before he could finish, the crowd of dancers parted, and Ben was shoved hard toward them. He fell against Elisa, and she lost her balance. In a flash, Adrian grabbed her and stopped her from falling.

"Be careful!" he hissed at Ben in a low, dangerous voice.

Ben stepped back, his face red. He hesitated for a long beat, glancing at Elisa as if he were about to say something. Then he whirled away and disappeared into the crowd.

"You were saying?" Elisa prompted, hoping to get Adrian back into a confessional mood.

Adrian shrugged. "Nothing important, really. Why don't we just enjoy the music for a while?" He seized two fistfuls of her hair, drew her close, and crushed his mouth against hers. His lips pressed warm and demanding on hers; her heart drubbed against his. His tongue burst past her lips and swept fast and deep into her.

14

 *Elisa*

ELISA SASHAYED OUT of the overheated gym into the cold, clear midnight air. The stiletto heels were tough to balance on, and she leaned heavily on Adrian. He held her in a secure grip and playfully stroked the bare skin of her shoulders. It felt brazen and delicious, like he was asserting his ownership of her in public, and she tipped her head against his chest.

Whenever her mother saw a young couple on the street with their arms wrapped around each other, she would always shake her head. "How shameful! I know you'll never do something so disgusting."

Remembering, Elisa put both arms around Adrian and rubbed against him. It gave her a forbidden thrill. His chest was firm underneath the suit, and she reveled in the play of his muscles flexing around her.

They reached his tiny sports car, and she pouted. "Your car isn't very good to snuggle in."

Adrian raised an eyebrow. "Why don't we take another, then?" He scanned the parking lot, strode to a gleaming older Plymouth Valiant, and began to fiddle with the lock.

She giggled, disbelieving, as he popped open the door. "Adrian, you're not actually stealing a car!"

"This one has a wide bench seat. Perfect for snuggling." He lifted her, still protesting feebly, into the front.

Her bare legs tingled against the soft nap of the velveteen as she tried to decide what to say. Her heart pounded. This couldn't be happening. A game was one thing, but actually breaking the law...?

He slid into the driver's seat and reached under the dashboard. "Ah. Easy to hotwire."

The engine started. He backed out of the parking space and she finally found her voice. "Adrian! I can't believe this."

He grinned. "I don't think I've ever seen your eyes so wide." He patted the seat beside him. "Slide over. One of the advantages of an automatic transmission—I can use my right arm for something better than shifting."

She fitted herself into the curl of his arm, her entire body sparking with a blend of terror and exhilaration. "You can't—I mean, this isn't—oh, Adrian!"

They turned onto the main road and Adrian accelerated with his usual verve. She clutched his leg and squeezed her eyes shut.

He chuckled. "It's almost more fun watching you than driving."

She cracked open one eye. "Nooo! Watch the road!" she cried. Visions of being arrested in the hospital flashed in front of her eyes. "Adrian, put it back. Put the car back, please."

He slowed at once and made a U-turn. "Whatever you say, Elisa. But I have to admit," he confessed with an impish grin, "this is Rory's car. We're not really stealing. I texted him, and he won't mind if I borrow it."

She gaped. "What?" She swung at him with her tiny beaded purse. "You let me think—"

He shot her a puppy-dog glance from under his fedora. "I'm sorry. I couldn't resist teasing you. I'll put it back. And I'll be good now."

She collapsed against him, relief flooding her body. Then she said, "No. I've changed my mind. I like this car better than yours. Let's keep it."

His jaw dropped in mock chagrin. "Better than my Lotus? Ouch. You're better at revenge than I thought."

She grinned, feeling wild again. "Let's take this baby out on the open road."

Elisa's eyes flew open. It was the middle of the night. A blue glow streamed underneath her bedroom door. Her pulse raced as she thought of those alien abduction stories in the tabloids.

As she woke more fully, she realized there was a rational explanation. She had her first houseguest ever, sleeping in the living room. A houseguest who had made her drink about a gallon of water after they got back from the dance.

Adrian had insisted the couch was comfortable enough for him. They had said a chaste good night. No, she had not been disappointed; she had definitely not hoped he would try something. Not at all.

She drew on her robe and eased open the bedroom door. The couch was empty, blankets thrown back from the cushions, and Adrian's laptop was sitting open on the coffee table—the source of the blue glow. The front door was ajar, and she heard a murmur of conversation from the hallway. Who was he talking to at three in the morning?

The laptop had a couple of browser windows open. She bent closer to check the website and recognized the logo: the Common Application for college admissions. Although she used the site often herself, she didn't recognize the page he was on: the teacher recommendation page. She skimmed it and saw phrases such as, "most brilliant student I've had in twenty years of teaching," "truly altruistic and always helping others," and "natural leader." The letter was partially completed, the cursor blinking in the text field. At the bottom was a teacher's digital signature.

That was odd. This section of the website was supposed to be password-protected, accessible only by teachers.

She clicked on one of the other windows. It was the College Board site, open to a page listing Adrian's results for the SAT. "Congratulations! Out of the nearly two million US students who took the Scholastic Aptitude Test (SAT) this year, you are one of only 273 who received a perfect score."

She knew he was smart, but she had never known anyone who got a perfect score on the SAT before. He hadn't even told her about it.

Wait. What was she doing? She shouldn't spy on Adrian this way. She put all the windows back the way she had found them. If he wanted to tell her his SAT score, he would. He must have a perfectly reasonable explanation for why he was on the teacher recommendation page.

And what did it matter, anyway? She crept back into her room. Her bed was cold. She lay awake, staring at the ceiling, still lit with that pale blue glow. She rolled over and punched her pillow. She twisted from side to side, then jumped out of bed.

Adrian was working at the computer when she came out of her bedroom.

"Hey," she said.

"Hey yourself." He closed his laptop. "You can't sleep either?"

A sliver of moon shone through the curtains and made his skin glow. "No. I missed you."

Brazenly, she pushed his computer aside and sat on his lap. He laughed a little. "Someone still a bit buzzed?"

"No. As a matter of fact I'm not nearly drunk enough. Can we get something to drink? Or even better," she announced recklessly, "how about some weed?"

Adrian looked alarmed. "Now Elisa, let's take this one step at a time."

"If you don't know where to get any weed, I bet Ben does. Let's go find him."

She tried to get up, but Adrian locked his arms firmly around her waist. "You're not going out in the middle of the night. You're staying right here."

"I'm done with being a good girl," she said. "If we're staying here, I want to go to bed."

He threw her a bemused glance. "Elisa—"

She jumped off his lap and grabbed his hand. Then she tugged him into the bedroom.

"Elisa, I told myself I wouldn't make any moves on you tonight, but if you make any, I'm not going to be able to stop you. I can't resist you."

She climbed into bed and patted the pillow.

"Let me rub your back. It might help you get to sleep." He began to rub small circles all over her shoulders. She relaxed as his strong fingers worked on the knots in her back and neck. She rolled closer to him. He stretched out full-length on the bed and pressed himself against her. Heat radiated from beneath his thin shirt.

"Mmmm," he murmured. "This feels good. You're so warm." His hands moved from her back to her hair, stroking her scalp. He rolled her over, bringing her face toward his, then drew his face to hers and his lips brushed the delicate skin at her throat. Tingles pricked up and down her spine.

She tangled her fingers in his thick, soft hair and ran her hands over his warm shoulders. She bared her throat and neck to him, yearning for his lips to travel her heated skin.

"Adrian," she whispered, "I'm scared."

He pulled her head to his ever so gently, and his lips grazed her ear. "Elisa, sweetheart, don't be. I'll stop whenever you want. Do you want me to stop?"

The voices of her mother and brother were silent, at last. For once, she heard none of the chatter and scolding that filled her days and clogged her nights. It was her decision, hers and hers alone.

"No," she whispered back, sliding her hands over his torso, silver in the moonlight. The muscles of his back rippled, silk over warm iron. "No. Don't stop."

"Are you sure?" Adrian's voice was low and oddly hesitant. The bed shifted under his weight. Shadows and moonlight played across his face and Elisa couldn't read his expression.

"I'm sure," she whispered. "I want to do this."

"Elisa, before we keep going, you should know—I'm not the man you think I am."

Her heart beat faster. She knew, had always known somewhere deep within her, that he was dangerous. That he had a dark secret. That he wasn't the type of boy Carlos would have wanted for her. "I don't care."

"I've done terrible things." His voice was almost inaudible.

She didn't want to hear him say it. Not now. "So have I!" she said recklessly before he could go on. "I cheated on a science quiz in seventh grade. And once—" She stumbled over the words. She had never admitted this to anyone. "Once I wanted this little heart-shaped aquamarine pendant. I wanted it so much. I stayed up every night to pray, on my knees for hours. Can you believe it? For some stupid little meaningless bit of jewelry. I kept going to Penney's to stare at it and dream.

"Then one day I was in the store when a dog got inside. He was running up and down the aisles, barking and wagging his tail, knocking over displays. Everyone was shouting or chasing after that dog. I—I just grabbed the necklace and ran. No one came after me." She swallowed. She felt better just saying it out loud. "But I didn't go back inside that store for years."

"Elisa, I—" He sounded a little choked up.

"No! I'm sure you're going to say that you've done something far worse. But it doesn't matter. Don't you see? My mother always said I was going to get punished, no matter how small my sins were. And I believed her. I've spent my whole life hating myself and being afraid." She buried her face in his chest. "I don't want to be afraid anymore. Please, Adrian... let me not have to worry about being good. I want to be free, and I want to be with you."

He was silent for a long moment. "You're making it hard for me."

"Why?"

"Because I want you so very much. But I also want to do what's right for you." He gave a harsh laugh. "And unlike you, I'm not accustomed to stopping myself from doing the wrong thing."

She traced the well-defined lines of his biceps with her fingers and rubbed her face against his shoulder. "Then let's forget about the world, and right and wrong, and just be together."

He let out a long breath and stirred in the dimness. She lifted her face to his. His tongue darted out to circle his mouth, and she caught a glimmer of moonlight on his lush lower lip.

His features were shadowed by moonlight, his hair in disarray. He drew nearer, closer and closer, only an inch away, less.

Then he tangled his hands in her hair and smashed his lips into hers. She let out a small cry, but it was muffled by the heat of his flesh. His tongue searched deep inside her, stroking the roof of her mouth back and forth in an erotic dance. She gripped the sheet, and her body thrashed in his hold.

Adrian covered her mouth with his, his lips caressing hers over and over. But this time she tasted something different in his kiss, something fierce and full of longing. It was as though he needed something from her this time, something only she could give him.

He stroked his thumbs along her cheekbones, and she quivered at the careless power in his grip. "I want you," he said. "I've never wanted anything like I want you."

"I'm here."

He gave a dark chuckle. "You're in the lion's den and you willingly give yourself to me? I would say you're foolish, but I think you already know." His eyes glinted in the dimness. "You've put yourself in my hands. There's no escape."

His hands brushed long, slow strokes of heat down her sides and she quaked at the barely contained force in his muscles. His teeth nipped at her earlobe, and her body shook. His lips skimmed over her cheek and swept down her throat, like fire licking over paper, burning, consuming, flashing. Her body broke out in flame.

His mouth was scalding. Lightning zigzagged across her skin and his kiss poured molten moonlight down her spine. She was in too deep; this was too dangerous for her, but the spark of the forbidden had caught her and she couldn't turn back.

His fingers spread across her neckline, tugging her loose nightgown off her shoulders. Cool air splashed over her bare breasts. No one had touched her like this before, no one had ever felt how soft she was, how her breasts were a pillow made for a head to rest on: his head, only his, her own secret locked away all her life, now bared to him, given to him, shared.

She arched into his touch. She wanted his hands on her; she longed to drag her hair across his skin, to match skin to skin in an agony of delight. She had never known anything like this, had never experienced this urgency, this craving, this yearning for closeness to another human being.

He drew away; she whimpered and reached for him. "Patience," he whispered. With a single, long, languid movement he shed his nightshirt and stood naked before her, a shadow outlined in moonlit silver. She could not see his face, but she knew his expression was dark and sensual; her gaze dropped lower but all she could see was darkness pooling between his legs.

The bed dipped under his weight and he pressed himself against her belly, stripping her nightgown from her body like flame takes wood from iron. Their bodies glided against each other, tongues of fire licking and twirling. She wanted him like paper wants to burn, desiring nothing more than to be utterly consumed, losing all rationality under his deadly touch.

His hands and mouth trailed along her torso and across her flat belly, fingers and tongue playing with the hair below. She gasped, clutching him, crying out as a gush of pleasure shot from her core. He dragged his tongue through her curls, circled the area below no one had ever touched, licked her with that incendiary tongue until she was about to explode.

"Trust me," he whispered. Amusement flooded into his voice. "Of course, you don't have any other choice."

She shuddered, a wreck of sensation, the fever at her core flaring across her body. His tongue probed deeper, curled into her, slid out, warm and wet and delicately circling.

He paused and leaned away with a lopsided smirk.

"No!" she cried. "Please, don't stop!"

He laughed and slid his torso along her legs; his mouth stroked up her thighs until his head nestled between her legs, his tongue lapping at her folds. Shaking, she ran her fingers through his soft thick hair. She was a throbbing mess of heat and need, reduced to inarticulate groans. His circling tongue paused and he gave a single lick to the heart of her sex.

She screamed.

Finally, finally, he kissed and caressed exactly where she wanted him, where she needed him, stroking with his long silken tongue, more, more, the unbearable tension rising to a peak until she couldn't hold it any longer and her body exploded: she was his; she belonged to him, utterly and completely. She would do anything, go into any darkness for him and for him alone. She cried out and clutched him, convulsing over and over until she gradually quieted, easing into long, lingering streamers of pleasure, his tongue lazily stroking her with slow caresses of utter bliss.

After a few sweet minutes just lying together, he twined his arms around her, slid along her body, and very gently kissed her throat; something hard and hot pushed against her core. He shifted and reached underneath himself, his palm flat against her, his finger probing inside, deeper, deeper, reaching through the waves of pleasure until she felt a sudden, burning pain.

She gave a sharp cry.

"Shhh," he whispered, "I'm stretching you so it won't hurt. Relax." Trembling, she let herself enfold his fingers; but it burned, and she cried out; he murmured to her, and she relaxed. He moved deeper; she felt pain where she had never sensed anything before, and then his fingers were caressing, stroking, and once again a wave of pleasure began to mount in her.

He lifted himself away from her, and she heard a crinkling noise.

"Mmm?"

"Just getting a condom, my sweet." He returned and kissed each of her nipples, flicking his pointed tongue across the tips and tracing rings around each, his mouth fiery across her skin. His teeth grazed her lips, something salty and strange on his tongue. He rubbed his long and toned body against her, her soft flesh molding to his ridges of muscle, skin to skin, from her breasts to her belly to the soles of her feet, and back to her aching core.

He straddled her legs, his shadow stretching tall above her, and she felt him at her entrance. She tensed. "I'll be gentle," he said. "May I?" he asked with infinite tenderness.

"Yes," she said, breathing deeply. Her hands sprawled over his broad, firm, smooth back, and she shivered at the potency in his eyes, at the barely constrained danger they emanated.

Then he slipped inside her, excruciatingly slowly, filling her, stretching her beyond belief, and she burned and gasped.

"Relax," he whispered. She felt the tightness in a ring of pain, until at last her muscles loosened. As she breathed, she realized it didn't hurt as much as she had feared; it was bearable, it was worth it, it was satisfying, it was wonderful.

He began to move, slowly, slowly, like a groundswell of the ocean, like the tide surging; heavy, undulating waves washed over her as he thrust, plunging in and drawing out in an ancient rhythm. His arms tightened around her, and at last they were close, as close as two people could be, one within the other, dancing the dance of passion and completion.

And at last she saw him, this tightly controlled man who never made a move without calculation, surrendering himself to his own sensations. He threw his head back, thrusting deep into her, and released in shuddering waves; he held her as though he would never let her go, collapsing over her, his breathing harsh and fast against her ear.

He sought out her mouth with his, and she drank him in, sealing her lips against his.

They lay together, skin against skin, heart against heart, as their heat slowed and cooled, embers glowing, fire banked by the long shore.

Enfolded by his warmth, in the ringing silence, with no voice but his echoing in her ears, she slept.

 ## Keisha

Keisha kicked aside the used syringes on the precinct steps. It was precisely 8 AM on the morning of All Souls Day. The desk sergeant didn't meet her eyes as she strode past him into the bullpen. All her colleagues appeared to be exceedingly busy at their desks, conspicuously not glancing in her direction. The path to Captain Truong's office had never seemed so long.

Truong's head was bent, only his fine black hair visible as he scratched away at some paperwork.

"Sir," she said stiffly. "I apologize for the events of last night. I—"

"Lieutenant Huston." He held up his hand to stop her. "Please sit down. I want you to hear the details from me, because I was there. We've got an informant somewhere, so I decided I'd handle it myself to make sure it stayed unleaked. I don't want you to blame yourself. None of us expected the target address to be a safe house for battered women and not the gang headquarters."

Keisha's lips tightened.

"All those terrified young girls... One girl—she couldn't have been more than sixteen, a tiny blonde—had bruises all over her face and arms, two black eyes, cut up lips. Broken collarbone, arm in a sling." He glanced up at the far corner of the ceiling. "She spat in my face."

"I'm sorry."

He shrugged. "We'll be taking some flack. From the press, from some elected officials, no doubt. I think the department's going to be facing a lawsuit. The woman who ran the place came out and tore into me. Kept repeating that we had just compromised the safety of all the women and children there."

He let Keisha take it in. "Somebody planned this out very carefully. They set us up so we would raid the wrong place."

"But—how?" asked Keisha.

Truong's nostrils flared. "It was a perfectly baited trap. They lured us in—and snapped it shut on us last night." His fingers curled into a fist on his desk. "I don't need to tell you that we need to take down whoever is making us run in circles for their amusement."

"The 'Captain' of Tenebras?"

"Maybe. One thing is definite. We're not dealing with just a high school gang. This is a full-blown organized crime syndicate, and I'm certain the leaders are adults. We're trying to find who could be capable of running an operation of this magnitude. We've contacted the federal Drug Enforcement Agency for help."

He pinned Keisha with his glare. "I need you to find out more. We're getting pressure from above. I want you to solve this. Solve it now, and I don't really care how you do it. Find out who's running the gang at Rockton High. Find this 'Captain.'"

15

 *Adrian*

ADRIAN OPENED HIS EYES in the early morning darkness of Elisa's apartment. He lay curled around her, face buried in her sweet-smelling hair. Her breathing was peaceful and even. His internal clock told him it was around five in the morning. He never needed much sleep, and usually rose early, using the time to work and plan for the day. His adversaries were behind from the moment they got up. He had never given a lover the pleasure of waking up beside him.

But today—today would be different.

He smiled into the darkness. The night had been fulfilling in more ways than one.

Cesar had called him during the night with the coded responses that indicated their headquarters' location was safe for now, and more cops had been made to look like incompetent fools.

He brought his lips to the back of Elisa's head and kissed her. She murmured in her sleep. Adrian remembered her sweet body lying under his, her eager, inexperienced kisses. She had been so responsive, so delightfully enthusiastic about following his lead.

Elisa had whispered, "I love you," and for the first time, Adrian had felt an odd twinge at those words. He had heard them many times before from so many people, and they had previously only shown him that yet another soul had fallen under his control.

Control.

Power.

For so long, nothing had mattered more than bringing as many people as possible under his dominion, expanding his own influence and wealth by whatever means necessary.

But now, for the first time, he wondered if there was something more.

Last night had been overwhelming. Terrifying. Completely different from anything he had felt in his life. When they made love, Elisa had held him as though she would never let him go. It had been her first time, so he was not surprised that she was so emotionally affected. But his own reaction disturbed him like nothing had for many years.

He had thought himself incapable of feeling certain emotions, had thought they had been burned out of him long ago. He had accepted that state, even welcomed it; emotions only limited his actions, hindered his rational, linear progression towards his goals.

But now, with Elisa warm in his arms, he wondered. A part of him he had thought long dead was coming to life again. Although it was intensely painful, he did not want it to stop. The way a person with nerve damage welcomes the pain of pins and needles as the signal of awakening life, so did this agony remind him of another Adrian Salas, of the child he had been a lifetime ago, when he had once been loved, before everything changed.

He still remembered bits and pieces from his early life. His mother was warm and beautiful, with long curly hair that he could grab in his small fists, soft hair that tickled his skin when she bent over him. How comfortable and secure it was to be held in her arms, and how sweetly she sang to him. She smelled like flowers, and her voice itself was like a melody.

She played games with him, reading and counting games. She had been so proud of him. She cut up his meat, and he counted the pieces and laughed. She clapped her hands and he spun in a circle, jumped up and down to the rhythm.

But so much was gone. What was left was vague, as though a gauzy curtain had been drawn over it.

Everything afterwards had been seared into his memory in sharp focus.

Sharp, cold focus.

He had been five years old. He was at home watching television after dinner with his parents and older sister when four intruders burst into their house. He remembered glancing up from the TV, uncomprehending, as they entered the living room.

"All right!" one shouted. "Everybody down and don't move!" The boy Adrian froze, staring at what he realized was a gun.

His father, tall, dark-haired and imposing, stood up slowly. "What is the meaning of this?"

The leader pointed his gun at him. "Shut up and get down on the floor!"

It happened in what seemed like an instant. His father, enraged, charged the guy and knocked him to the ground. But one of the others must have fired. The shot was so loud, the young boy felt it in his eardrums and mouth more than he heard it, and the echoes rang in his head, muting the sound of the television. His father crumpled to the floor, and blood oozed from beneath his shirt.

His mother screamed. She was crying, shrieking in panic and fear. One of the others slapped her face. "Shut up, bitch!" But she seemed unable to stop. His sister sobbed and wailed, adding to the din.

"Shut up or I'll shoot you all!" someone shouted.

The young boy, crouching motionless on the floor, wanted to urge his mother and sister to please be quiet; couldn't they see what was going to happen?

And then it did. Two more gunshots made the boy's ears ring even more. His mother and sister collapsed on the floor. Blood spurted from his mother's thigh and spread across the pitted hardwood floor.

"Come on! Tie him up and let's go." One of them pulled out a couple of zip ties and locked the boy's wrists to the arm of a heavy wooden chair. They pounded up the stairs.

He heard them stomping and cursing upstairs for what seemed like hours. Eventually, there were more thumps on the stairs; they ran downstairs and were gone.

He learned later that it had all been a mistake: their neighbor had been involved in a drug deal, and had kept cash in his mattress. Somehow their house had been mistaken for his. His family had been shot over nothing.

Adrian stood there, chained to the arm of the chair, listening to the footsteps die away. And then it was silent in the living room that had once held the three people he loved most in his life. In the silence, he gradually became aware that his mother was still alive. She was whimpering and gasping.

"Mommy," he called, but she did not respond, just continued with tiny moans and cries of pain. Blood seeped from her wound. 911, he thought, he had to call 911. The telephone was on the kitchen counter. He began dragging the heavy chair, slowly, in that direction. The sharp plastic hurt his wrists, but he kept on going.

After a very long time he reached the kitchen. He saw the telephone, just above his eye level, on the counter. But he couldn't reach it. He tried lifting his bound hands, over and over again, but he was just not strong enough. He tried to reach the phone with his head, push the buttons with his nose or mouth, but he was just a little too short. He collapsed over the chair arm. His eyes stung with tears.

Then he told himself he must not cry, and the tears dried up. He tried to slide his hands out of the zip ties, but they were clamped over his wrists too tightly.

He thought of going out the kitchen door to get help, but he couldn't reach the doorknob. He thought of flicking the light switch on and off to signal a neighbor, but it was also out of reach. He shouted for help, but no one came.

So he methodically attempted once more to slip his hands out of the zip ties. He worked and worked at it for a long time, as the whimpers and cries from the living room gradually became fainter and fainter until they stopped altogether.

When they finally found five-year-old Adrian the next morning, still handcuffed to the chair in the kitchen, the soft skin of his wrists was so battered it looked like raw meat. The chair arm was covered in blood.

Much later, they told him his family was dead, but he didn't cry. He never cried again.

Adrian buried his nose in Elisa's waterfall of wavy hair, spread across the pillow. To think it had once been all a whim. He had long thought Elisa was attractive, with her lush curves and luminous skin. He had been drawn to her quick, sharp wit. But for so long she had been a rival, nothing more. She had nothing he wanted. As a rule, he stayed away from the more straitlaced girls. Why waste his valuable time convincing someone to give him what was freely available from so many others?

But something had changed at the beginning of the school year. Despite her prim wardrobe and innocent mannerisms, Elisa had begun to exude an unconscious sensuality. He found himself noticing the flash of sunlight over her mass of auburn curls, the swing of her slender hips, the swell of her breasts beneath her demure blouses. Every time she walked by she had stirred him.

It no longer seemed a waste to spend time with her.

Most people were boring; their motivations were selfish, straightforward, and transparent. They were so easy to manipulate. So easy to predict. To twist.

But Elisa kept surprising him. Intriguing him. Her sudden turn to what she thought was the dark side was a prime example. He wasn't sure whether to be amused or worried.

And there was something about her that kept bringing up odd feelings within him, flashes of memory from long ago that he had thought well sealed.

His mother had been a kind, sweet person.

He frowned and shifted in the bed, curling himself more tightly around Elisa as she slept.

In the past, he had always felt a vague letdown after he slept with someone, a feeling that somehow, they had not measured up. He had always assumed that he simply grew bored quickly with his lovers. But his feelings for Elisa had, if anything, become more intense after last night.

He had found himself wanting to pleasure her, to give her joy, to make her first experience one of wonder, not merely to gratify his own ego, but for her. And now all he wanted was to repeat the occasion, to build on it, over and over again. For the first time in his life, sex had been more than a performance, more than merely a giving and taking of pleasure. It had transcended all of these and had taken his thoughts and emotions in entirely new directions. He had found himself considering what would be best for another human being besides himself. As she lay in his arms, he struggled with the strange and unknown feeling that he wanted to share everything he had with another person.

He lifted his face up to the first light of dawn and found himself smiling. Why should he deny himself this new joy? He had always gotten whatever he wanted, whatever the cost. Why should he not get what he wanted now?

But it would be dangerous. For the first time a chill swept through him at the thought of danger. Not to himself; he had lived with risk for so long it no longer mattered. But Elisa would be plunged into ever greater peril from both his enemies and his own subordinates.

A fierce conviction welled up in him. He would protect her at any cost. At all costs. Those who even attempted to hurt her would be punished. He would burn, maim, kill, do utterly anything to keep her safe, regardless of the consequences.

His train of thought halted, his fury abruptly quenched.

Would she want him to?

Ordinarily, he would simply manipulate or force anyone who disagreed with him into wanting exactly what he wanted. But he did not want to manipulate Elisa.

He wanted her to know him. To know his true self, down to the core. To love the person he actually was. As an equal. A partner.

Was it even possible?

Could she love his true self?

Of course, he could go legit. Assuming he could get out from under the arrangements he had made with some very bad, very powerful people.

He had always known that with sufficient capital and connections, he could rack up profits while staying on the reputable side of the law, something that would not have been possible had he remained a poor child from the slums of Rockton. His lips twisted briefly. Despite the constant media blather about rags to riches stories, the so-called American dream was a myth perpetuated by the rich to keep the poor docile. In reality, the poor had no chance to move up unless they broke the rules. Adrian had no choice. He had to make the decisions he had. He hadn't wanted to deal drugs at first. But what other choice did a powerless boy have?

How did Balzac put it? "Behind every great fortune lies a great crime." With wealth one could buy legitimacy and respectability. He could list the stories of the great American entrepreneurs, all their sordid pasts, the subtle and blatant cheating, deceit, even murder that had been committed, and how it was all washed clean by the flood of wealth. He would follow in their illustrious footsteps.

He had once planned to first complete his Ivy League college education. There he would gain the legitimate business connections that would catapult him to the top of the business world. And there, he had long assumed that he would find a daughter of a rich, powerful family, woo her, marry her, and make himself indispensable to the rulers of the family, insinuating or threatening his way to an executive position in the family business. It would be the fastest way to acquire control over billions.

Elisa slept peacefully beside him in the morning light. Her face, in repose, was exquisite—burnished lashes laying dark gold filigree across her cheeks, delicate breaths parting her lips rosy in the sunrise.

It would be boring, after all. Too easy, to marry into money. How much more challenging, more satisfying, to build that huge fortune all on his own, pitting only his wits and cunning against the business world. Why should he tie himself to an inferior, waste time and energy manipulating them? How infinitely preferable it would be to make his choice of companion based on his own desires, on intellectual compatibility, on beauty—on love.

He stroked Elisa's cheek. She murmured something unintelligible.

He rolled over and stared at the ceiling. He had deliberately created a particular persona for himself as leader of Tenebras, his only goal to exercise control over the violent and aggressive members of his gang. He had built up and nurtured that persona to be a figure of fear and dread, larger than life, almost supernatural in his abilities and inclinations. As Machiavelli had said, it was better to be feared than loved.

But what could he do now, if he wanted to be loved after all? What would be her reaction when she found out that her boyfriend was actually the dreaded "Captain" of Tenebras? Could she accept it?

And could he get free from his entanglements? Or would they kill him—and Elisa?

 ## *Elisa*

She woke up warm.

That never happened. She usually awakened curled up in a tight ball, freezing beneath the covers. For some reason she could never get warm in the early mornings. But today, she was enfolded in Adrian's arms. His heat surrounded her, and the deep, slow beating of his heart thumped against her cheek. Elisa's face was pressed to the muscles of his bare chest, her fingers tangled in his messy hair, his curls soft against her skin.

She was completely naked, lying in bed with a dangerous man.

She tingled all over. She was a little sore in an unusual place, but even that simply made her vibrate like a tuning fork. Then she noticed something else. She always awoke with her mother's or Carlos's voice in her ears, scolding her about all the things she had done wrong the day before.

Today there was silence.

Last night she had violated just about every rule she had been brought up with. She had given her virginity away. And to someone who admitted he was hiding something. But instead of guilt, she felt only exhilaration. Adrian's dark secret intrigued and thrilled her. Rationally, she should be afraid. But deep in her heart, something sang with joy.

16

 *Elisa*

THE BED DIPPED and creaked, and Adrian fitted himself around
Elisa. He nuzzled his mouth into the back of her neck. His lips
traced the delicate skin just under her hairline, sending tingling
streaks across her bare shoulders and throat. She wasn't used to
sleeping in the nude; the sheets rubbed the soft hair along her
pubic bone. All the sensations bombarding her felt odd. Erotic. A
word she normally never used.

"Mmmm," he said. His lips vibrated against the fine hairs at
the nape of her neck. "It's more wonderful than I could've
imagined, waking up in bed beside you. We'll have to do this more
often."

It might be nice to stay in bed and explore these new
experiences. But she wasn't sure exactly how she felt. Warm and
happy, yes. Thrilled, yes. But also a little embarrassed and not at all
ready for a morning-after talk.

So she jumped out of bed. "Dibs on the shower!" This was the
first time she'd ever been completely naked when she got out from
under the covers. "Brr!" She shivered and ran into the bathroom.

"I'd call foul, but that is one fine ass you're shaking as you
monopolize the facilities," he called. She laughed and locked the
door.

By the time she finished showering she had gathered enough
courage to leave the bathroom and face him again. She slid open
the door and smelled the unmistakable scent of something rich and

savory frying. She found Adrian in the kitchen, leaning casually against the stove, a spatula in his hand. He was completely dressed and as elegant and immaculate as ever. Four eggs, their glossy yolks bubbling, were sizzling in her largest skillet, and several slices of bacon were spattering away in her second-largest. Her stomach rumbled.

She leaned against the doorjamb. "Wow, you cook, too?"

"One of my many secrets." He flipped the bacon over with a pair of tongs.

Her insides clenched. She didn't want to hear his secrets. Not today, not so soon. For some reason, she remembered her flight of fantasy in the cafeteria, when he had threaded his fingers around her neck and squeezed, absolutely no expression in his eyes.

"How do you like your eggs?" he asked.

"It's no secret I like them sunny side up," she said. "Although I do have a fondness for over easy on alternate Thursdays."

"Sunny side up it is." He tipped the skillet, spooned hot melted butter over the yolks. His movements were sure and practiced. "How are you feeling?" he asked after a short silence.

She glanced away. "I'm fine, Adrian. I feel terrific." She wasn't lying, but she couldn't bear to think about it in detail right now. It was just too much. He had swept into her life the way he drove, fast and aggressive, thrilling and illicit, and changed so many things. Part of her wanted to rush after him, to follow wherever he led, but another part needed to jam on the brakes.

He arched a brow at her non-response but didn't probe further. She puttered around, getting out knives and forks. Bread popped out from the toaster, and Adrian slid the eggs and bacon onto a couple of her chipped plates.

He set the dishes on the rickety card table. "Breakfast is served."

She sat across from him, avoiding his eyes, and stared at her food instead. The egg yolks gleamed golden in the morning light, the lacy brown edges of the whites bubbling gently. The bacon lay drained on a paper towel, completely crispy, not charred or soggy anywhere. It smelled mouthwatering and her stomach growled in anticipation. She picked up a slice of bacon with thumb and forefinger, crunched it between her teeth, and had to close her eyes at the roasty, rich flavor that suffused her mouth. It was so utterly satisfying she moaned a little.

He chuckled. "The way to a woman's heart."

"...is through her mouth?"

His eyes were hooded. "As well as other places. I don't think I've ever seen lips so glistening and tasty as yours." He licked a crumb off one of his. Then he deliberately swept his pointed tongue from corner to corner of his mouth, making her remember exactly what he had done with it last night.

Elisa blushed. Wasn't she supposed to stop doing that, now that she was a woman and no longer innocent? Now that she was a rule-breaker, a fallen soul? She swirled a piece of buttered wheat toast in the yolk and scooped it into her mouth to cover up any trace of embarrassment. Bad girls weren't supposed to be ashamed, were they?

Toast. Wait. "I didn't think I had any fresh bread left. Nor any eggs."

Adrian inclined his head but said nothing. She ran to the refrigerator and yanked it open.

Her shelves were bursting with fresh produce, leafy red and green kale sticking out from the crisper drawer, two dozen eggs nestled neatly in their cups in the refrigerator door, butter and cream and six pomegranates perched on the top shelf, and just beneath them a net bag of mandarin oranges with green leaves still attached.

She gaped at Adrian out the pass-through window. "What happened?"

"I guess if I said magic you wouldn't believe me."

She scowled at him.

"Too bad you're not more gullible. It's easier when people believe everything I say." His voice was lazy and amused.

She lowered her brows, and he rotated his hands palm upwards with a mock sigh. "All right. I was up early and ordered some groceries. Paying you back for your kindness giving me a home for the night."

"You didn't need to do that."

"I don't *need* to do anything. I do whatever I choose. And today, I chose to give you a gift."

It would have been rude of her to protest any further. "Thank you." She opened another cupboard and sucked in her breath. "My favorite organic pastry flour!" There were not one but three bags of the sinfully expensive flour she adored baking with because it felt like silk under her fingers.

Her guts twisted. How much did this all cost? "Adrian, I—"

Suddenly she was afraid, so afraid that something terrible would happen if he told her. She closed the cupboard. "This is terrific!" she said brightly. "Thank you so much!"

Adrian set down his fork. "Aren't you going to—"

She panicked. "No, I don't need to know." She pushed her chair back from the table. "Besides, we have to get ready for school, don't we?"

"Elisa, listen—"

"No!" She jumped up and put her fingers in her ears. "I'm not listening, la, la, la, la..." She backed away toward the bedroom. "Too busy loading my books into my school bag, la, la, la."

He shook his head, laughing. "All right. Have it your way."

His cell phone rang. He glanced at the number on the front and his smile faded, but he put the phone to his ear. "Yes."

So much authority compressed into one single syllable. Elisa grabbed the doorframe to steady herself, realizing she was trembling.

There was a short silence. "On my way," Adrian said curtly. He rose from the table. "I'm sorry, I need to go. See you at school?"

"I'll walk you downstairs," she said, her heart still beating rapidly.

It was a chilly, overcast morning. Adrian took her in his arms and kissed her. His lips lingered on hers, warm and sweet as butter and honey. "Elisa," he said softly, cupping her face in his hands, "what happened last night meant a lot to me. I'm sorry to have to leave so soon. Forgive me?"

He zoomed away from the curb with his usual abandon. Where he was going, what he was doing, she didn't want to know. She felt those long fingers around her throat once again and she heard the fortuneteller's voice creaking. "You are in danger. The shadow has him..."

 ## Ben

The alarm clock rang, and Ben reached up to silence it. He dragged himself out of bed. The dance the night before had been miserable.

He skipped breakfast, saying a quick goodbye to his father. Then he was out on the street in the chill air, running to Elisa's apartment building. He didn't know yet what he would say, but somehow he would convince her of the danger Adrian posed.

He skidded to a stop as he rounded the corner onto Elisa's block. To his horror, he realized that Adrian and Elisa were embracing on the sidewalk outside her front door. They parted, and Elisa waved cheerily to Adrian as he strode to a car parked at the curb and sped off.

Ben's entire body tensed. Had the bastard actually spent the night with Elisa?

His feet carried him forward; he ran to Elisa as she stood there on the sidewalk, not even wearing a jacket, seemingly oblivious to the early-morning cold, still gazing after the car.

"Elisa," he gasped, coming to a stop a few feet away.

She whirled, the fear in her eyes becoming relief when she recognized him. "Ben," she said. Her voice sounded even warmer and more lovely than usual. "What are you doing here so early in the morning?"

"I—needed to talk to you about something important," he said, still out of breath.

Then he stopped. He couldn't help himself. "Was that Adrian Salas I saw driving away just now?" He couldn't keep an angry note out of his voice.

To his chagrin, Elisa blushed at his words. "Yes, it was," she said very quickly, not meeting his eyes. "His aunt wouldn't let him in the house last night, so he asked if he could sleep on my couch, and I said yes." Her face grew bright red, and she wrung her hands together.

Ben shook his head. Something more than Adrian innocently sleeping on her couch last night had happened. "Elisa," he began, "Salas really isn't good for you. He's just not safe."

Elisa switched from embarrassment to defensiveness. "What? What do you mean? Adrian is a kind, good person."

"He's just playing the role of squeaky clean straight-A student. I think he's involved in some bad things," Ben said.

Elisa shook her head. "What are you talking about?"

"He's got gang connections. With Tenebras." Ben wanted to shake her. His evidence was sketchy, but he had to get her away from Adrian at any cost.

Elisa shook her head, but Ben saw the flicker of doubt in her eyes. "You're so obsessed with Tenebras, Ben. You see everything as a conspiracy with that gang behind it."

"Because it's true! I've seen him brawling! I've seen his friends talking to gang members," Ben burst out. "Don't you see, Elisa? Tenebras is behind the spread of Rapture. Haven't you seen all the new addicts on the streets? Our clinic's beds are filled with overdose cases."

"Yes, I agree it's terrible." Elisa was shouting as well. "But Adrian has nothing to do with it! How can you even say that?"

"Come on!" Ben stuck his hands in his pockets to keep himself from grabbing her. "How does he get the money for that fancy car, to take you out to all those expensive restaurants?"

Elisa stiffened. "Adrian has a part-time job."

"Do the math, Elisa! You're supposed to be the genius. How many hours a week would he have to work at minimum wage to afford to take you out every week?"

"How do you know how often he takes me out? Have you been spying on me?" She put her hands on her hips.

"No! I've just been trying to watch out for you!"

"You don't have the right to choose *my* boyfriend. I like Adrian, and I'm going to continue to go out with him no matter what. Now, leave me alone so I can get ready for school." She spun around and flounced back into her apartment building.

Ben stood alone on the sidewalk, cursing himself. What had happened to reasonable argument? He'd yelled at her and jeopardized their friendship. Angry at himself, he jammed his fists into his pockets and slouched away.

 ## Rory

Rory Fong stood in the shadows of the unkempt vegetation around the old apartment building. He had watched the argument with great interest. So, Ben thought Adrian was connected with Tenebras. That could be very useful information. Rory put his head to one side as he considered what he should do with it. He collected information about Adrian as well as about everybody else, and he was judicious about how he chose to use or reveal that information. It was the most valuable commodity in his world.

The question of Adrian's relationship with Elisa—now *that* was interesting. Most of what Adrian did, even for his own entertainment, served dual purposes, cementing his control over his gang or furthering various plans to increase Tenebras's influence or profits. Rory knew how Adrian treated most women he'd had sexual relationships with, and there were some key differences with Elisa. Nevertheless, he had some difficulty believing that Adrian could really have what others might consider a normal relationship with anyone.

He knew Adrian's attitude about attachments. "It's a mistake to make yourself vulnerable, Rory," he had once told him. They had been relaxing in Adrian's study after a particularly successful operation. Adrian rarely drank hard liquor, but this particular haul had included a rare bottle of aged Chivas Regal scotch. Adrian hadn't been able to resist the exclusive, numbered bottle.

Adrian had been unusually loquacious that evening, dispensing advice and dropping hints of secret knowledge until Rory had been practically salivating for more of his favorite commodity. Adrian's eyes glinted with reflected firelight as he showed more emotion than Rory had ever seen.

"Attachments are dangerous," said Adrian.

"What about Tina? She's one fine woman. Seems like you might have some feelings for her."

"Feelings?" Adrian scoffed. "If I did, it would only turn out badly for me—not to mention her."

"Really? I think she likes you, Captain."

"They all like me." His fingers caressed his glass, swirled the amber liquid within. "It serves my purposes."

A shiver passed through Rory.

"We have no need for weaknesses like that." Adrian's eyes glittered, and he pinned Rory with a dark glance. "Don't you agree?"

It was only afterward that Rory had wondered.

Did Adrian suspect his secret?

Had the whole evening been a setup?

Rory had been so careful in all his furtive and increasingly desperate searches through the foster care system. He could have sworn he had never left any evidence, had never let *her* name cross his lips where Adrian might find out.

He still hadn't found her. He had no idea where Sierra had ended up after she went into the system. And Adrian had never given any sign he knew of Rory's... attachment.

Rory shivered. If what he suspected now was true, it would be easy to displease Adrian over Elisa Gallardo. He did not want to be added to the list of people who had disappeared. He had gotten to where he was, and kept his position as Adrian's top lieutenant, by carefully anticipating and attending to his every need and desire.

Still, if he could gain leverage over Adrian—it could be extremely lucrative.

He thought again about Sierra.

In more ways than one.

17

 *Keisha*

KEISHA OPENED ANOTHER CAN of cat food and plopped it into the last of the four bowls under the kitchen table. Miranda rubbed against her legs on her way to the food, Goon Squad mewed, and Cease-and-Desist turned up his nose at the food.

Keisha swiped a hand across her forehead. Ever since the Halloween debacle, it had become increasingly difficult for her to go about her undercover work. The department's progress was too slow. Truong himself had hinted it was time to break a few rules.

She opened the refrigerator and rooted through Tupperware containers filled with moldy leftovers. When she was on a case, she tended to forget that she, like her cats, needed to eat. She swayed for a minute, dizzy, then shook herself. She didn't have time to eat or sleep. She had been up all night working on her crime board, trying to put more pieces together. She was out of coffee, so she went to the bathroom and took a No-Doz.

On the way to school on the bus, she finalized the new ideas she'd worked on all night. In the supply closet, Vince Devore was waiting for her. "Got an anonymous tip that looks interesting."

"Another? We've already wasted a boatload of time checking too many of them out. Nothing."

"This one's different. There's a local company, Schwartz Pharmaceuticals, that synthesizes industrial chemicals. Their lab's less than five miles from here, in the warehouse district. Small company, been in business about ten years, on shaky financial ground."

Keisha glanced up from her notes, her interest piqued. "You think they might be looking for additional sources of revenue?"

"The owner, Alfred Schwartz, seems shady. Long hair, snarky personality, makes no secret he was a former hippie who experimented with psychedelics. He's got two drug busts from his college days, and has published anonymously at recreational drug sites, including a long biographical piece on Owsley."

Keisha snorted at the mention of the underground chemist who mass-produced LSD in the sixties. "That would definitely shoot Schwartz up my list. I wonder if we could get someone undercover."

"I'll see if the department has the budget for that." Vince shook his head.

"What about someone already on the inside?"

"I got some of the employee files." He rifled through his backpack, handed a stack of manila folders to her.

"Good. I'll work on it." It could dovetail well with her plans.

"Hey, you feeling okay?" He squinted at her.

"Huh? As good as can be expected."

"You seem a little manic today."

"Shut up! I'm fine." She forced a smile. He could be a little too perceptive. Better not to go into detail about what she was thinking. Vince was a good cop, but he had a tendency to quote regulations to her at the wrong time.

Later that day, after remedial algebra, Keisha flipped through the files. Robson had given her the backgrounds of a few students who interned at local companies. Not that she'd told him the extent of her plans. It was all up to her now.

She glanced at the photo stapled to the form. The boy seemed vaguely familiar, one of the quiet kids she hadn't paid much attention to. His eyes were mild behind rectangular glasses; unruly brown bangs fell in his face. One of the forgettable nerds you saw in every high school, obviously not a gang member and equally obviously inconsequential in the high school social hierarchy.

Of course, it went against all standard procedures to bring students in on a police operation. But it seemed like only the kids knew what was going on. And it was worth it, if it meant saving lives. Truong's latest report traced over a hundred crimes to Rapture in the past week alone.

She studied the student carefully. Someone she could give just enough information to get him on board. Someone unimportant who could blend into the background.

Perfect.

Adrian sat across the desk from Keisha outside the principal's office, obediently sorting through the photographs she had brought. The admin had gone home for the day and they were alone in the narrow foyer with nicotine-stained walls. Adrian tapped a picture of a paunchy middle-aged man with long dark blond hair pulled back into a messy ponytail. Mild, watery eyes peered out from under a receding hairline. "This is Alfred Schwartz, the company owner," Adrian said. "He used to be a scientist, but now he's mostly an administrator."

"Is it true he's a former hippie?"

Adrian nodded. "He makes no secret of his past. When he was in school, he dabbled in many different drugs. Led kind of a dissipated life. But now he seems to have settled down. Although," he mused, "he's easily distractible and sometimes appears confused. Maybe a bit of brain damage from all the psychedelics."

Keisha made a note on a pad of paper. One of the fluorescent panels in the ceiling flickered and went dark.

Adrian picked up the next photograph. Curly, uncombed dark hair surrounded a long face topped with penetrating eyes. Behind him, two young kids peeked around a doorjamb. "Eric Holman is the chief scientist. He's somewhat of a character as well. Schwartz is always scolding him for wearing open-toed shoes while handling chemicals. These two are his niece and nephew, Mira and Jim. They do janitorial work around the lab." He set the photo down. "Holman has kind of a cavalier attitude toward safety. He often makes fun of the rules we're supposed to follow."

"Do you think he or Schwartz could be synthesizing illegal chemicals?"

"I've never seen any evidence of it. But then I don't have access to many of the secured areas of the lab." His eyes were sharp behind his glasses. "You think they're behind the synthesis of Rapture."

It was a statement, not a question, although Keisha hadn't said anything about the purpose of their mission to Rockton. She had to admit the kid was smart. "I can't comment on an ongoing investigation," she said, glancing up at the clock on the wall. "Now, how often do you work and what do you do?"

"Part-time after school, three days a week. I wash the glassware, run the centrifuges, errands like that."

"I saw you were listed as a co-author on a paper written by Holman and Schwartz last year."

Adrian nodded. "They added me because I made a few small contributions to the research."

"What was the paper about?"

"Neurotransmitter potentials in inhibitory neural synapses and latent class-II modifications."

"Which means what?"

Adrian shrugged. "It's an academic publication with no real-world applications. A bit of incremental research in a vanishingly narrow specialty, intended for nothing more than to enhance the reputation of the first author among the six people who can understand it."

Off in the distance, someone slammed a locker shut. "So it's not important work, nor could it be connected with the synthesis of a chemical like Rapture?"

He stared at her, his face shocked. "Of course not."

 Adrian

In the chilly early morning air, Adrian sauntered toward one of the back entrances to the school. Mario was waiting exactly where Adrian had told him to be. He stepped forward on cue.

"Hey, Sa—Adrian. You'll have the product ready by the end of the day, right?" Mario's words sounded stilted, but that didn't matter. It was the content that counted.

"Don't worry about it, Mario. It's all taken care of." Adrian's voice was clear and carried in the cold, still winter air.

Mario scowled but didn't miss his final line. "Good. Don't forget the meeting after school today." With that, he moved off as scripted, leaving Adrian alone in the quiet passage. He pretended to text, waiting to see if Elisa, who he knew was standing just around the corner, would approach him.

When nothing happened after a few minutes, he slid his phone back in his pocket and went off to class.

The bell tinkled when Adrian opened the door to the Apricot Apron.

He had been looking forward to picking up Elisa from work all day. The bakery always smelled so rich and satisfying, odors of cinnamon and caramel, chocolate and fresh-baked bread wafting out into the air.

The tiny, wrinkled woman behind the cash register beamed at him, one hand brushing her salt-and-pepper cap of hair.

"Why, hello there, Adrian. Are you here to take my sweetest employee away?" Her eyelashes dipped in what could have been flirtatiousness if she were half a century younger.

He ran fingers through tousled hair, adjusted his glasses and flashed her a shy, crooked smile. "It's good to see you, Mrs. Rojas. Is her shift over yet?"

She dropped one eyelid in a wink and called over her shoulder into the kitchen. "Did you put the maple blackberry scones in the oven, Elisa, dear?"

"Almost done, Mrs. Rojas." Elisa slid a tray into the stainless steel oven. Her glossy hair was bound up in a white net, and her creamy skin stood out against the brown fabric of her shirt. A white cotton apron, streaked with chocolate and raspberry smears, was wrapped tightly around her slender waist, emphasizing her figure. She shook a few strands of hair out of her eyes and wiped a hand on her apron. A wispy line of white powder arched across one cheekbone. "I'm just dusting the last batch with powdered sugar now." She stood on tiptoes to set the temperature.

Mrs. Rojas ushered Adrian into the back room. "You have a visitor, dear." Her hip just grazed his leg as they passed through the narrow door. Her cheeks flamed.

Elisa teased him that he encouraged Marisol Rojas too much in her little crush, but everything went so much more smoothly when he bestowed just a tiny bit of attention on her. It was all innocent, of course. The poor woman probably hadn't got it on in two decades.

"She'll be ready for you in a minute, Adrian. Our Elisa, she's so smart. Did you know she figured out a way to get better texture in our buttermilk biscuits? Now they're so flaky the customers can't get enough of them." She patted Elisa's arm. "What was it, folding and pinching the dough by hand and changing the temperature by fifty degrees did what?"

"It allowed the Maillard reaction to proceed more efficiently and the gluten chains in the dough to set up. Baking is really just chemistry."

Mrs. Rojas pinched Adrian's cheek. "Chemistry! Did you hear that? And did you know that our little Elisa wants to be a chemist?" She shook her head. "All that baking talent, wasted in some lab." She wagged a finger at Adrian. "You make sure to talk her out of it, you hear?"

She untied her apron and bustled back to the cash register. "You two take some time together, I'm off to the bank with the deposits. I'll lock the door."

She winked at Adrian. The bakery door chimed as she left.

Alone in the wide kitchen lined with trays of crisp, flaky scones and succulent dark chocolate squares topped with fresh raspberries, Adrian reached for Elisa. "It smells wonderful in here."

"I just put some scones in the oven. No, wait, don't touch me—"

He had already enveloped Elisa and her messy apron in a close embrace. His fingers trailed over her exposed arms, and he pulled her head in to lie against his chest. "The scones smell good too." He buried his nose in her hair, one hand stroking down her back and dipping just a little too far over her softly rounded ass.

She tried to pull away, but his arms encircled her like steel. "You'll get powdered sugar all over your clothes," she warned.

It was too late. His black silk shirt was dusted with white.

"Do I look like I care?" He cupped her face in his hands. "I've missed you."

"It's been like what, six hours since I saw you last?" She drew away from him and put floury hands on her hips.

"Feels more like forever," he said, feeling an unexpected pang at her expression. She was upset, deeply upset, about his activities. He didn't want to manipulate her, but maybe just a little would be necessary.

He couldn't bear to lose her.

"Do you really like being covered in powdered sugar?" she asked.

He glanced down at his speckled sleeves and got a gleam in his eye. "Hmmm. Never thought about it before, but it does sound tasty." He ran the tip of his tongue slowly and deliberately across his lips and backed her against the bulletin board, just out of sight of the front door. He ran one finger down her pearly throat, savoring the quiver of her skin beneath his touch. He wanted her. He wanted her more than he had ever wanted anything before.

She swallowed, obviously steeling herself.

He waited.

"Adrian. You're a member, aren't you."

"A member? Of what?" he drawled, the picture of nonchalance. He unbuttoned the top of her blouse and stroked her soft skin. He hooked one finger under her apron and ran it back and forth over the warm silk of her breast. "Let's see. What if we took everything off of you except this apron and rolled you in sugar?"

Elisa's lips parted and her breathing quickened. But she took hold of his wrists and held them. "That gang. Tenebras. I saw you talking to them. I heard what you said to them." Her nostrils flared. She took a step forward and stood toe to toe with him. "Don't lie to me!"

He leaned back and put some space between them, studying her face. This was the critical moment. He had to persuade her. He had to.

He kept his voice sincere and soothing. "I apologize for misleading you." He took a deep breath and his voice became sad. "But I was so afraid I would lose you if you knew, and I couldn't bear that."

She froze, conflicting emotions passing across her face like clouds in a high storm. Her expression softened. "Adrian, I—you have to explain."

"I promise I'll explain everything. I'll tell you the whole truth. There's a reason behind everything I did." He ran a finger down her cheek. "Everything," he whispered against her ear. He flattened himself against her, body to body, length to length, and her pulse accelerated.

They drew apart, and she wet her lips and drew her arms together, unconsciously deepening the valley between her breasts.

His heart leapt in his chest. She was wavering. Now was the time to go straight to the primal urges, the deep-seated desires he had been the first to waken in her.

There was nothing like sexual arousal to sweep away rationality—or doubt.

To his surprise, he felt something odd. Unpleasant. Did he want to manipulate the woman he cared for like this?

It was *wrong*.

He shook his head. He had never used that word except in derision before.

He pushed away the tiny voice.

"So you admit you're a gang member?" Elisa's eyes were wide.

He couldn't lose her. He wouldn't.

He moved closer, his eyes holding hers prisoner. He tipped his head and allowed his eyes to swirl and darken with lust, noting her tiny intake of breath, her deepening flush.

"And if I am?" He shrugged. "You already knew I wasn't the good boy I appear to be," he whispered, lowering his lips to hers. He kissed the left side of her mouth, then the right. She trembled under his touch, but made no move to push him away. Instead, she arched her back and lifted her hips into his.

"I'm not a good person, Elisa. But maybe being good isn't everything, is it?" He brushed his fingers over her nipples, feeling them harden under the rough fabric of the apron. "What did being good ever do for you?" He ran his fingers over the scar on her hand.

She jerked her hand back as if burned. "Nothing." Her eyes glittered up at him. She lay back against the wall and bared her neck to him, panting, every part of her body softening and opening.

He took her lips in his, driving his tongue deep into her mouth. Hesitant at first, she kissed him back, her tongue curling gently under his as he took command of her body.

"So sweet," he murmured. "I'm going to lick you all over, starting with here—" He leaned in and glided his tongue along her cheek, across her lips, and down her throat. "And here." His lips hovered at her ear. "You already have powdered sugar inside the shell of your ear," he whispered.

Her breathing was quick. "Mrs. Rojas will come back any second."

"No, she won't. She always takes exactly forty-five minutes to make the deposits. That's plenty of time." He was so hungry for her he could barely stand it. With a single pull, he untied the bow at the back of her apron and slid her blouse off her shoulders. Her bare flesh was rosy in the sweet warm air of the kitchen, and the black lace bra just barely contained the swell of her generous breasts.

Her lips were swollen, lush and shiny as sugared cherries. She gazed up at him, those once-innocent eyes dark with lust. A smirk crooked the corner of his mouth. "You knew from the beginning I would corrupt you, Elisa," he said. "Admit it. It's why you said yes to me in the first place."

She bit her lip and said nothing. Then she reached out and grabbed his shirt with eager hands.

He unfastened her bra with one hand and let the softness of her breasts spring free. She stood bare-chested and wanton in the middle of the stainless steel kitchen, a blush spreading across her cheeks and down her throat as he undressed her, peeling the layers of fabric away from her body languorously, taking his time to caress every inch of her exposed flesh.

Slowly, teasingly, he kissed his way across her satin skin and sucked one nipple into his mouth. She rocked her hips into his. His mouth feasted on her milky expanse of skin.

"Now you're going to let me have you right here, in the middle of your employer's kitchen, precisely because you know you shouldn't."

Elisa drew in her breath and her gaze transformed to molten gold. She lifted her face up to his, something unspeakable and wanton clouding her eyes. "Do whatever you want with me."

18

 *Adrian*

THERE WAS A POUNDING on the bakery door.

Elisa stood up so fast her head banged into Adrian's chin. Her face burned bright red, her eyes wide.

"Ignore it," he said.

She shook her head. She was already throwing on her clothes with trembling hands. "No, no, I have to—we shouldn't be doing this, it's a health code violation." She looked around frantically, found her shirt and buttoned it up.

Adrian leaned against the wall and watched, amused.

The hammering continued. "Hey!" called a voice from outside. "I need to pick up my order."

Elisa tied her apron. "Do I look okay?" she asked Adrian.

He gave her a slow once-over from head to toe. "Perfect."

She blushed, and then ran to the front. The bell jingled. "I'm so sorry, sir, please come in."

"What's wrong with you?" a male voice whined. "I was waiting for five minutes."

Adrian walked to the front counter and gave one of his charming smiles to the customer. "Why don't you let me ring you up while Elisa gets your order, sir?"

"After that poor service, you should give me a discount," the man huffed. "I should report you to your manager," he shouted at Elisa, who was running around in the back gathering his order.

Adrian took the man's credit card and ran his fingers over the raised letters on the front, memorizing them. "I'll need to see a picture ID, please." His eyes raked over the man's face, and he smiled, a bit too pleasantly. "All finished, sir."

Elisa handed a full bag to the man. After he left, a line creased her forehead. "I hope he's not too mad," she said. "I don't want to lose Mrs. Rojas a customer."

Adrian bestowed a dark smile on her. "You have nothing to worry about."

His cell phone buzzed and he frowned. His thumbs flicked over the keyboard. "I'm sorry, Elisa, there's an emergency I have to deal with." He drew her close and kissed her gently on the forehead. "Forgive me? And we're still on for tonight, aren't we? This new club is supposed to be the hottest thing."

She knit her brow. "It's too expensive. Those downtown clubs are for rich kids, not us."

He kissed the top of her head. "Why shouldn't we have whatever we want?"

"Adrian—"

"I have money tonight."

"You always have money," she said, frowning.

"Come on, it'll be fun."

 Elisa

Elisa walked home from the bakery, her shoulders in knots. It got dark early this time of year in Rockton, and a chill rain had begun to fall, raising a damp odor of gasoline and oil from the asphalt. She wrapped her rain jacket more tightly around her body.

How could she go out with a gang member? It went against everything she had been brought up to value.

But the thought of breaking up with Adrian was even worse.

An all-too-familiar dark Plymouth Valiant pulled up beside her in the gloom, wipers swishing. The window rolled down. "Hey, darling," Rory called to her. "Let me give you a ride home."

She only hesitated a moment. She was cold, and he was Adrian's best friend, wasn't he?

He had the heater on full, and her tense muscles eased in the sudden warmth. She reclined against the velveteen headrest. Rory grinned. "Kind of a bad night, isn't it?" He pulled out into traffic. "You look a little tense. Is there anything wrong?"

She stiffened. "Nothing. Nothing's wrong."

"Have it your way." They stopped at a red light. He palmed the steering wheel and took out a joint. "Do you mind? I've had a stressful week too."

She shrugged. She'd be a hypocrite if she scolded someone about breaking the law when her boyfriend had just admitted he was a gang member. She twisted to face the window.

His lighter flared, and a tangy, burning scent filled the car.

"What's it feel like?" she asked suddenly.

"What?" he asked, exhaling.

"Smoking." She gestured at his joint.

His eyes crinkled almost shut and his mouth stretched in a wide grin. "It feels awesome, so relaxing. And hey, no stumbling around like with whiskey."

If she was now the girlfriend of a gang member, she should do something reckless. "Can I have a hit?"

His mouth dropped open in an O of surprise. "Why Elisa, don't you know that's illegal?"

She scowled. "Don't be an idiot. Let me try."

"You do look twitchy. Maybe it'll help you relax."

He watched, grinning, as she awkwardly sucked on the joint and coughed. The smoke was harsh and burned all the way down her throat. "You have to hold it in your lungs to get the full effect," he said.

Elisa coughed some more. "I don't feel anything." *Other than a sore throat.*

He laughed and pulled out a paper bag wrapped around a bottle. "If you're going to be bad, might as well go all the way. You'll certainly feel it if you have a little of this."

She took a swig right from the mouth of the bottle.

"Oh, someone's gonna enjoy that party tonight."

Adrian

A cold splatter of rain dimpled the puddles tucked between uneven sidewalk slabs on the gloomy side street. Adrian skirted the pools of light cast by streetlamps and strode towards a flickering red neon sign that spelled out "BAR." He pulled open the heavy door and breathed in a damp, warm lungful of stale smoke and cheap beer.

Passing a few silent patrons, Adrian ambled past the bar stools that had worn holes into the linoleum and slid into a booth at the very back. Two minutes after his order was taken, a tall man with blond hair tucked into a black raincoat dropped into the seat across from him.

Adrian tilted his head in greeting and continued sipping his whisky. "Schwartz."

"Grant's Scotch, double, on the rocks," Schwartz said to the waitress who appeared to take his order. He waited until she had disappeared through the swinging door. "We want you to step up your levels of distribution."

Adrian took a sip from his glass and set it down on the Formica table with a clink. "I don't want my operation to become overextended. I've been thinking of cutting back."

"You don't have a choice in the matter."

Adrian raised one brow. "Oh? I agreed to work with you as a partner, not a subordinate."

Schwartz stared down his long nose. "I'm not so sure that's the case anymore."

"I'm an independent operator," Adrian said coolly. "You need me, not the other way around."

"But you see, we finally have what we need to bring the brilliant Adrian Salas under our control. Permanently." His smile was cruel.

Adrian scoffed, but he didn't take his eyes off Schwartz. "No one controls me."

"Leverage." Schwartz tossed a photo across the table. "Perhaps you've heard of the word?"

Adrian's eyes dipped to the photo. It was Elisa at the door of her apartment building, clearly taken that very morning. His heart began to pound, but he kept his face impassive. He forced his eyes away from the image and back to Schwartz.

"So? You should know me better than that."

"We now have a way to reach her anytime, anywhere. To snuff out her life from a distance. You will be unable to protect her."

Adrian's hands clenched under the table. "She is nothing to me."

"We want you to double the amount of product you move starting next month."

"You don't want me as an enemy."

Schwartz stood. He sneered down at Adrian. "You are so arrogant. Remember, you are only a boy. And now you've gotten in over your head. I suggest you do the intelligent thing and obey us." His nostrils flared. "Think on it carefully. Do you really want to pay the price?"

Schwartz strode out of the bar. The door slammed behind him, a swirl of cold damp air in his wake.

Alone at the table, Adrian stared fixedly at the far wall, turning his glass in his hands.

He had selfishly only considered the effect Elisa had on *him*.

It hadn't occurred to him that he would draw her into his darkness, that the gravitational pull of his black hole would overwhelm her bright star. But he should have known. What a blind and selfish idiot he had been.

He didn't know the nature of the threat Schwartz was making. Some slow-acting poison? An agent within his own gang? But it didn't matter.

It was his fault. He was the one who had placed her at risk.

His chest heaved. His fingers clenched slowly on his shot glass. No. He couldn't let her be harmed.

No matter what.

The Traitor's Kiss was the newest—and hottest—club in downtown Rockton. The line snaked halfway around the block, and two huge bouncers stood at the wide doors checking IDs.

Adrian sauntered to the front of the line and was waved in. Inside it was all dark elegance and decadent ambience, antique mirrors lining the walls and pounding music pulsing across the dance floor. Adrian made his way through the gyrating crowd to the VIP lounge at the back.

There, the beat was more muted. Bodies writhed in the dim light, draped over brocaded divans scattered across the plush carpet. Rory sat in the far corner on a settee, and beside him, slumped in a boneless pile, lay Elisa.

Adrian strode across the room. "What's wrong with her?" he snarled through clenched teeth.

Hearing his voice, Elisa's head jerked up and she raised her arms. "Adrian," she slurred, "C'mere." She giggled. "Oh you are a beautif—beautiful man." She shook her head. "It's too bad, too bad." Tears dripped down her cheeks.

Adrian's eyes flashed. "You were supposed to take care of her."

"He did take care of me," insisted Elisa, snuffling. "He showed me everything."

Rory blinked rapidly. "You told me to give her what she wanted. I was just fol— doing what you said."

Adrian grabbed Rory's lapels. "You bastard," he hissed.

Rory's eyes widened at Adrian's uncharacteristic display of anger. "It's true!" He raised his hands defensively. "She wanted it. She asked for a toke, and I tried to say no but she kept on asking." He glanced at Elisa for confirmation.

"Thass' right," Elisa said, nodding vigorously, almost falling off the couch in another fit of giggles. Adrian caught her before she struck the ground. He peeled back one of her eyelids.

"This is much more than just a toke."

"Well," Rory appeared only partially abashed. "She wanted something to drink to cool her throat. And after that she wanted more of a buzz."

"So you've just been pouring drugs into her all evening?" Adrian's voice was icy now, the calm tone all his subordinates knew and feared.

"I was just trying to make her happy like you said."

Adrian's grip tightened on the limp and giggling Elisa in his arms. His nostrils flared. Was Rory the traitor? Was this a scene staged for his benefit?

Rory avoided eye contact. "You've been with girls this wasted before. I didn't think it would matter. She's having a good time. Besides, she said she needed something to take the edge off."

Adrian's hands clenched. The chemicals coursing through Elisa's body had taken something away from her, had taken that bright spark that was quintessentially Elisa.

But what had Adrian taken from her?

He had taken her innocence, exposed her to death threats, and involved her in the drug scene that had claimed so many casualties.

He, himself, had been the direct cause of many of those casualties.

He had always told himself that dealers were only providing people what they wanted, that it was an individual choice to ingest chemicals, to seek an elusive pleasure or escape from a miserable life.

But *he* had been the one who had made Elisa unhappy. He had struck against the moral code she had lived by all her life. It was too much.

And now, choosing to intoxicate herself would make her doubly vulnerable. If Schwartz had something on her, if Rory or another of his trusted lieutenants was an agent for him, Elisa would need to be strong. Sharp. At her best.

It was Adrian's fault. Again. A knife twisted in his gut, drenching him with intense regret. It had been a very long time since he had felt anything so extreme.

His hands and arms had been bandaged and he had been left sitting in a small room scattered with cheap plastic toys. The social worker had gone into another office to make a phone call, but he snuck after her to listen.

"Hello, may I speak with Victoria Salas?" the social worker said into the speakerphone.

"Speaking," came a clipped voice from the phone.

"Ms. Salas, this is Nancy Wilson from Rockton Social Services. I want to let you know that I'm very sorry about the loss of your brother Armando."

There was silence on the other end of the line for a moment. "Let me assure you, your concern is misplaced. As I told the police yesterday, I haven't been in touch with my brother for years, not since he married that trollop. I'm not going to pretend to grieve for him."

"…I understand, Ms. Salas. However, there are a few things we'd like to discuss with you."

Silence.

"Ms. Salas?"

"Yes, I heard you. Listen, I'm about to leave for an important appointment, and I spoke to the police at length already. Can't you talk with them?"

"Ms. Salas, I'm afraid there are some matters I need to discuss with you. As you are aware, your brother's wife and daughter have also passed away."

The voice on the other end of the line sounded impatient. "I told you, I never had contact with his wife, and I've never met his daughter. I'm sorry about all this, but I can't be late for this appointment."

"Ms. Salas, please don't hang up. You see, his five-year-old son survived, and you are next-of-kin."

More silence. "I didn't even know he had a son."

"Yes, he did. His name is Adrian, and he is going to need a home."

This time the silence stretched out for a long while. "If you're asking what I think you are, I'm afraid that's not possible. I'm about to take a position that will require a lot of travel, and I won't be able to take care of a child."

"Ms. Salas, I'm sorry, but as the next-of-kin, you are now the legal guardian of your nephew. If you wish to put him up for adoption, you may, but at this point he is your responsibility until the paperwork goes through."

"What?" The voice rose. "I can't take care of a child! This is ridiculous, to foist this sudden duty on me without so much as a warning!"

"Ms. Salas, I'm very sorry, but can't you please think of the child?"

Agitated breathing was audible on the other end of the line.

"He's in the Rockton Social Services office right now, but we are unable to provide further care, and it would be very helpful if you could pick him up this afternoon."

"Impossible." There was the sound of pages flipping. "I've checked my calendar, and I can't pick him up before Wednesday. What did you say the address was again?"

Adrian crept away, back to the room where he had been waiting. He sat again in the little chair, rested his bandaged arms on the scuffed Formica table, and laid his head in his arms.

"He's a beautiful child," Nancy said to her colleague when she thought he wasn't listening.

"I know. With those gorgeous eyes, that thick hair, and so well-behaved, obviously intelligent." The colleague clicked her tongue. "So tragic."

"I'm hoping once the aunt sees him, she'll change her mind about keeping him. It would be a shame for him to go into the system." Nancy shot a sidelong glance at her colleague. "It always worries me when an exceptionally beautiful child goes into foster care. Sometimes they seem to bring out the worst in people."

The other woman tightened her lips. "Nancy, you shouldn't be talking like that. I'm sure he'll be fine."

When Nancy spoke again, she sounded tired. "I know I shouldn't say anything, but after what happened to little Sierra Mayes, I..."

"You can't keep beating yourself up about her. That couple had an impeccable record as foster parents. No one could have predicted what happened."

Nancy rested her head on the back of her chair. "I know. I just wish..." Then she shook her head. "I can't help worrying about what might be. About what the future might hold for that little guy."

She glanced at the boy in the waiting room. He was trying to play with a toy dollhouse. There was a cheap plastic doll family inside. The boy's hand crept forward. He picked up the mother doll and stared into her painted face, his eyes round, turning her slowly back and forth, running his fingers through her hair.

One little hand rubbed his eyes, but he didn't cry.

19

 *Adrian*

ADRIAN CARRIED ELISA in his arms and Rory lagged behind. The corridor leading to the private rooms was dimly lit by wall sconces placed at long intervals. A faint scent of incense wafted through the hall, and the thumping music sounded far away. Elisa's eyes were closed, her face flushed. Her pores had opened and her sweet scent tickled Adrian's nose. He tucked her head into his chest and her thick, long hair straggled over his hands and forearms.

Rory unlocked one of the rooms.

"Guard the door," Adrian ordered, his face stern.

Rory nodded, his pulse visible in his throat. Adrian twisted away from him. He would deal with him later. Let him wait—and worry.

Adrian entered the room, shouldering the door closed, and placed Elisa on the bed. Her head lolled to one side, and he brushed a few strands of hair away from her face. He tucked her hair behind her ears and ran his fingers through her damp locks. She murmured in her sleep and rolled into his touch. He opened the first few buttons of her blouse to make her more comfortable, his fingers brushing over the rosy skin at her throat and neckline.

She was beautiful even unconscious, her delicate lashes folded over her cheeks, her lips lush and sweet as berries.

Rory was right, he thought with sudden bitterness. He had slept with girls nearly this inebriated before. Of course, they had always been more than willing. He made sure of it, finding the idea of compelling any woman into bed with him distasteful.

But he had thought little of them beyond satisfying his own desires.

He rose from the bed abruptly. His former behavior repulsed him. The idea of desiring anyone other than Elisa seemed ludicrous now. And even the suggestion of making love to her while she was in this condition was deeply upsetting.

He carefully folded back the sheets and slid her legs underneath the blanket. He took off her shoes one at a time and kissed her bare toes. They wiggled under his touch, and he chuckled. He folded the blankets over her and tucked her in.

He sat by the side of the bed. Normally he would have been out and about his business by now, leaving someone behind to guard Elisa while he accomplished more important tasks.

But now nothing seemed more pressing than staying by her side to protect her.

He dropped his head into his hands. What would his mother have said? After all, hadn't it been a drug deal gone wrong that had taken her from him?

He rubbed a hand over his chest, the sudden heaviness strange and overwhelming.

How ironic it was, now that he was finally ready to make different choices, for the first time someone was thwarting his will. He had never thought Schwartz could gain a hold over him. He had always assumed he was the one using the man and his contacts. Because he could think rings around them all.

He had been so blind.

Now, however, he needed to reorient all his priorities. If it wasn't already too late. Adrian took a deep breath and ran his hand through his hair. He would change everything, but under his own terms.

He could still play the necessary roles. He could still make them fear him. Long enough to give him room to maneuver.

He took out his phone, sent a brief text to Cesar, a few longer ones to others.

Then he leaned his head against the wall for a few minutes, lost in thought. At last he strode to the door and opened it.

Rory, still on guard in the hall, bounced to attention. His face was pale. Behind him, Cesar hovered, lips pressed together.

"Rory." Adrian's face was completely emotionless. It showed nothing of what was in his heart.

Rage. Unreasoning, towering rage—at Schwartz, at Rory, at all those who might seek to hurt the one woman who had changed everything.

But Rory knew him well. He swallowed at the expression of icy calm on Adrian's face. "Yes, Captain."

"Do you recall how I said that anyone who allowed Elisa Gallardo to come to harm would be punished?"

Rory's fine hair fell in his eyes. "Yes," he whispered.

"Cesar."

Moisture beaded on Rory's forehead. Adrian nodded casually to Cesar, who took one of Rory's hands. "You're trembling, Rory."

"I'm sorry, Captain."

There was no one else in the corridor. Cesar lifted Rory's hand, and with a single swift motion bent a finger back sharply. The snap was audible even above the beat of the music.

Rory shrieked and all the blood drained from his face. His uninjured hand clenched.

"You're fortunate," Adrian murmured. "Your punishment will heal. But if even the slightest harm comes to Elisa under your watch in the future, I won't be so forgiving. Understood?"

Rory's breath came raggedly as he nursed his injured hand. Cesar stepped back, his face impassive.

"Do you understand, Rory?"

Cesar reached for Rory's hand again.

Rory hissed and drew his arm back with a jerk. He found his voice. "Y-yes, Captain, I understand. It won't happen again. I swear."

"Make sure of that." Adrian turned away, his face indifferent. "You're free to go. Get that injury taken care of."

"Yes, Captain. Thank you, Captain." The last words came out on a whine of pain.

"After that," Adrian said, "call a meeting for tomorrow morning. I've decided it's time to take our operation to the next level. Everything is going so well that I convinced our suppliers that we could double or even triple our volume."

 ## *Mario*

Across the street from the club, Mario waited in a black sedan. The windshield wipers swished, beads of lighted raindrops twirling and sliding across the glass.

Such a boring job. He reached into his pocket, pulled out a glassine envelope, and tipped a small amount of white powder onto the web of skin between his thumb and index finger. He pinched one nostril shut and brought his loosely closed fist to his nose.

Sniff.

The powder stung his nose, but by snorting it he avoided the risk of addiction. He straightened, enthusiasm for his task returning.

He was doing all right. The new wads of cash—and, best of all, his powerful new contacts—were putting him on the fast track to success. And the stuff was so soothing. He was ice cold now. There was no way anyone could detect traitorous emotions from him.

No way would Adrian ever know. Mario was safe now. He was on his way to being more powerful than ever, more powerful even than Adrian.

His phone rang.

His new phone.

"Yes, sir?" He listened closely for a few moments. "Of course, sir. Right away."

 *Adrian*

The early morning light streamed through a gap in Elisa's bedroom curtains, and Adrian got up to adjust them so the light wouldn't fall on her face. But at his movement, Elisa opened her eyes and squinted up at him.

"What—?" she asked. She shaded her eyes with her hand, her features contorted. "Ughh."

Adrian sat beside her on the bed and stroked her hair back. "I brought you home last night. How are you feeling?"

She shook her head and winced at the movement. The sight of her so pale and ill roused strange feelings in his chest. She shouldn't be in such a condition.

No one should be.

He tipped a couple of Alka-Seltzer tablets into a large glass of water. "Here. Drink this; it'll help."

She reached out a shaking hand, and he propped her up and placed a couple of pillows behind her head. She clasped the fizzing glass in her hands and stared into the bubbles, then took a slow sip, grimacing.

"The most important thing is to drink plenty of fluids; you're dehydrated and liquid will help flush out your system."

Her hands shook a little. "The room is wiggling around."

He wrapped an arm around her and held her tightly. "Keep drinking and it will settle you. I've got a mango smoothie for you in the refrigerator. That'll get your blood sugar up. Remember, plenty of liquids."

After a while, color returned to her cheeks and she sagged against the pillows. He took the empty glass from her hand and she rested her cheek against his thigh. "Thank you."

He shook his head. "Thanking me is the last thing you should be doing."

"I feel…" she whispered, "so awful."

He stroked one hand gently over her forehead. "You'll promise me, won't you, that you won't take any more drugs?"

She grimaced. "Aren't you being a hypocrite?"

He smiled. "I prefer to say that I've had a revelation and a change of heart."

Her eyes widened. "You're going to give it up? I mean, the gang?"

He combed his fingers through her hair a moment. What could he tell her? "As soon as I can."

"And you'll stop lying to me?"

He didn't want to lie to her.

But he had to. Not only would the truth drive her to more poor decisions, but there was Schwartz to worry about.

It was just for a little while. Just till he could get things straightened out. And maybe he could minimize the damage. Not lie to her directly. Just… twist the truth slightly.

He cupped both hands around her face. "It turns out that a lot of the stories about Tenebras are just that: stories. They want to build up a scary reputation, so they spread rumors."

Elisa shook her head. "Come on. What about all the violence?"

"I won't say it doesn't happen," Adrian continued in his most reasonable and soft voice. "But Tenebras mostly spreads rumors to scare people and keep them in line."

A thought struck her and she drew away from him, stiffening. "You're not—you're not one of those—'Blades', are you?"

"No. No, I promise you, Elisa, I am not one of the Blades." He pressed her head to his chest and stroked her hair. "So can you possibly forgive me?"

"I—I don't know," she mumbled with her face pressed into his shirt. "Are you really sure they're not as bad as everyone says?"

"Absolutely," he said. "And when I go to college, I'm leaving all this behind me." He took her head in both hands, sincerity shining in his eyes. "I hope I can make you proud of me, Elisa."

He bent his head and kissed her along her jawline and down her neck. She twined her arms around his shoulders. As they kissed, longer and deeper, he gently lowered her down on the bed.

"Shhh," he said. "Rest now."

Every word he said had seemed to twist within him. But it was necessary. Just for a little while longer, until he could figure out how to deal with his problems.

He would kill Schwartz, and everyone involved in the development and synthesis of Rapture. It was no longer just for himself. It was a public service. Look at all the deaths they had been responsible for.

Once they were all taken care of, he would leave the gang. He would start a new life with Elisa. She would never need to know what he had done.

And then he realized.

He was going to have to tell her everything. He was going to have to stop lying.

And that meant he couldn't kill Schwartz.

He was going to have to figure out something different. A way to stop them that did not involve cold-blooded killing.

But could Elisa possibly forgive his past? An icy chill struck his chest. What if, when he told her the truth, she rejected him?

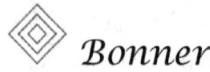 *Bonner*

It was late, and Hyman Bonner was tired. The security guard yawned and shuffled his feet under the desk. Night shift at the security gate to Schwartz Pharmaceuticals was unbelievably boring. He scanned the bank of video monitors, checking for activity. Nothing.

The front doors slid open, and Bonner came to attention. He glanced at the verification unit on his desk. At the ID displayed, he stiffened.

"Good evening, Mr. Salas," he said, avoiding the intern's eyes.

Adrian nodded, a pleasant smile on his face. "Good evening, Mr. Bonner," he said, and passed through the central doors.

Bonner stared after him, sweat breaking out on his forehead. Then he swiveled to the bank of monitors and carefully deleted the last few minutes of video. He pivoted his chair to the computer that stored all entries to the building. Carefully, his big fingers clumsy on the keyboard, he typed in a sequence of keys that would erase the last ID verification. Then he painstakingly checked his work a second time.

He swiped a hand across his face. He was in so much trouble.

It had started with only the smallest of thefts from the lab. Nothing anyone would miss. Hey, the company only paid him minimum wage, so it wasn't his fault he needed to supplement his income. Liquor and cigarettes were expensive.

But somehow the mild-seeming student intern had found out. One night, a few months ago, Adrian had invited him out for a beer after work.

Adrian had delicately hinted about the thefts, and listened intently to Bonner's woes, his face full of sympathy and concern. "Have you ever considered taking on a second job?" he asked softly as Bonner finished another beer. Bonner belched in satisfaction, thumping the mug down on the scarred table.

"Who'd hire me?" He shrugged. "I don't even have a degree."

"I can think of a job for which you're perfectly suited," Adrian murmured.

"Yeah? What?"

"I have something I need some help with. And it doesn't require a degree. What I need is someone discreet and absolutely trustworthy."

So it had begun. At first, it had been fairly simple. Adrian paid him cash to ignore certain of his late night entrances. Bonner was nervous, but Adrian explained it was all perfectly innocuous. He was working hard on a project. As a student, he wasn't allowed to work overtime, and he really needed to spend the extra hours in the lab without anyone knowing. That had seemed fine—at first.

But then Adrian had begun to bring non-employees to the lab at night, and asked for more security codes.

Now, Bonner was in way too deep. If he was ever caught, he would go to jail. Not to mention some of the things he had seen—things that indicated there was much more going on at Schwartz Pharmaceuticals than he had ever suspected.

He was afraid that sooner or later, someone would think Hyman Bonner had seen too much.

 ## Adrian

Adrian noted Bonner's distress, but the night guard seemed under control. Adrian's careful planning was paying off. He walked into the synthesis lab and put on a lab coat. 1:30 AM. He had a long night of work ahead of him.

He went straight to the computer and typed "schwartz." When queried for the password, he paused a moment, musing, then typed in a string of characters.

The screen remained blank for an instant.

Then it displayed the login message, and he smiled.

He pulled up several documents and log files of previous experiments. He paused briefly as he came to a directory containing drafts of the paper Keisha had mentioned earlier. The research for that paper had been performed almost entirely by him. Schwartz and Holman had led him through the work, encouraged him to work with the chemicals that would lead to more addictive precursors. They had promised him that the credentials the purely academic research would generate would lead to a better future, help him get into top colleges.

But when it came time to get it published, Holman had insisted that they put his name first as the senior scientist. Adrian shrugged. That hurt his pride, but the smart move was to let the slight pass. And indeed, it ended up better that no one knew of his hand in the work.

That research did indeed have a connection to Rapture. The cops were too stupid to understand the chemistry, but the reagents described in that piece of research were precursors for Rapture. After the work was completed, Schwartz had half-jokingly proposed that they use it to prop up the faltering sales of his company.

Adrian, seeking to expand his influence, had offered his services as a distributor. It had all happened very quickly after that. Schwartz had many contacts in the drug subculture, shady dealers and slimy lawyers who were more than willing to provide extra-legal services for inflated prices. Adrian had found that his own gang had rapidly become overextended with the influx of demand for the new drug.

Overly eager to increase his own power and wealth, he had struck deals with people he shouldn't have.

Schwartz was at the top of that list.

And now... Adrian stared at the blinking cursor on the screen. Were his mistakes impossible to fix?

He pulled up a shell script from his own directory, keyed in several file names, and set the script running.

Leaning back, he watched as his program ran and text flashed on the screen. The system-level script continued with its work, inserting some files, deleting others, and adjusting modification times so that several timestamps were set back by a few months.

A set of emails appeared, and Adrian frowned, pausing the output and scrolling back to read them more carefully. He pulled up the attached news article and studied the comments.

His eyes widened, and pain and fury coursed through him.

20

 *Elisa*

CURLED UP ON HER COUCH with her laptop, Elisa read her half-finished essay one more time and grimaced. It sounded dull and pedestrian. How was she ever going to get into a good college if she couldn't even write a coherent essay? All her ideas sounded so trivial. But she didn't want to get into the depths of her family difficulties—not in a college essay that strangers would read.

"What's wrong?" Adrian murmured in her ear. "Not going well?" His breath danced lightly over her earlobe.

Pushing the laptop away, she slid her hands along his forearms and slipped her fingers into his.

Adrian had been working on his laptop at the other end of the room. They had gotten in the habit of spending evenings together in her apartment three or four nights a week, since her mother was gone for so long. She wasn't really sure why he had switched from wanting to go out to clubs and fancy restaurants to insisting that they stay at home and hang out together, but she wasn't complaining. Being alone with Adrian was more fun than she'd ever had in her life, no matter what they did.

He had decided she needed to learn self-defense. It was silly; he was being overprotective. But she couldn't deny she found his protectiveness a little sweet. Every few nights, despite her protests, he taught her simple hand-to-hand combat and the basics of defending herself from attackers, right there in her living room. He had even taken her to a firing range to teach her how to shoot.

"Adrian, I don't want to learn how to use a gun! I never want to hurt another person."

"Even if they attack you first?"

"Maybe I should turn the other cheek."

But Adrian was insistent. She supposed it was the world he lived in, where guns and knives were part of everyday life. She ended up going along with it. Adrian could be very persuasive.

Plus she had to secretly admit that self-defense practice was surprisingly erotic. Especially when he pinned her against the ground or the wall, his powerful body pressed against hers, his scent in her nostrils, his arm wrapped around her throat. Was she a bad person to love it when he overpowered her with his casual strength, when he wrapped his long fingers around her neck?

"Now, you do remember how to get out of a headlock, Elisa, don't you?" His arms enveloped her, warm steel and satin, and she inhaled deeply just so she could breathe in his scent. His hair brushed against the back of her neck, his deep voice vibrating along her skin. He held her so securely, his muscles like heated iron, always exactly at the limit of what might hurt her. Such control. Such potency. Oddly, she felt safe rather than threatened. She trusted him on some primal level, even though she knew he was dangerous.

Maybe she was crazy.

Her mind went blank. She clumsily swiveled to one side and swiped ineffectually at his balls.

He sighed. "No. That's not going to work. And then he'll just attack you like this." A flurry of strikes came at her face; his leg looped around hers and she was thrown flat on her back on the couch, his torso heavy across her hips, his leg draped casually over her, his face only inches away from hers, hair falling in his eyes.

A tiny smirk curled her mouth. She deliberately licked her lips and cocked her head. He stared at her for an instant.

"You'll be the death of me, Elisa. I came here to work and somehow you always entice me into bed."

"*I* entice *you*?" She rolled her eyes. "Somehow I think it's the other way around."

"Let's finish your essay, and then we'll get to work on more enticing." His grin was cocky as he stood up. He reached over and handed her the laptop.

She groaned but opened it up. "I can't seem to get this essay right." She frowned at the screen. "It sounds so boring. I wonder if I'll even get accepted anywhere."

He sat down so his hip pressed against hers. "Let me see."

She moved the laptop away from him. "No. It's too embarrassing."

A playful light entered his eyes. "I could help you with it."

"It's supposed to be my own work."

"You surely don't think all those rich kids with ten-thousand-dollar admissions counselors take that seriously?"

"Adrian, please don't get started on that. You know it's important to me to play by the rules."

"But Elisa, you're deliberately putting yourself at a disadvantage. Haven't you heard about legacy preferences and other advantages for the rich at the Ivy League schools?" He stroked her hair, fingers combing her scalp. "It's well documented. If you give a large enough donation to Yale, you get in automatically. If you're on the polo team, you can get into Harvard as an athlete regardless of your scores. How many poor kids play polo in high school? Despite the lies the college admissions officers tell, there's a systematic bias in this country to only admit the elite. I'm not making it up." His voice started to vibrate.

"I know. I know." She smoothed her hands over his face. "I read a couple of articles about it. But it wouldn't feel right if I got in using any of those tricks."

"Don't you want to go to college with me?"

"I just want to get in fair and square."

"Don't you understand that there is no 'fair and square'? If you don't play the game, you simply won't get in." He took her hand in his, brushed his lips over it. It tingled unreasonably. "I'll miss you."

She drew her hand away. Adrian planned on getting into Harvard, and had already submitted his early-action application. He would be hearing from them by the middle of December, but he seemed to be confident that he would be one of the eight percent admitted to the most elite school in the United States.

Worse, he had hinted that he had somehow done something to make certain that he would be admitted, and that he could do the same for her. What disturbed her most was that she was tempted. She knew that a good college education was the only way she'd have a chance to become a biochemist. And she needed a full ride. Her mother had told her there was no money for college. She was supposed to go to work after high school. Although she enjoyed her part-time job at the bakery, she didn't want to work there for the rest of her life. She wanted to learn biochemistry, to put her ideas into practice, and it was depressing to think certain doors might be closed to her simply because she didn't come from a family with money.

Ever since Adrian had admitted to her that he was a gang member, that he was doing something involving synthesizing illegal drugs, he had been letting slip all these hints about other illicit operations he was involved in.

He delighted in breaking the law and defying moral codes. It made him feel that he was putting something over on all those people who had more than he did. He hated the fact that he was a mere high school student, and a poor one at that. He craved status and power, and would do anything to get what he wanted.

Now he wanted Elisa. But what did she want?

She lifted her head. "I'll apply to Harvard, and to a couple other Ivy League schools, even though I don't think I have a chance. But I don't want to go there, really. I want to go to MIT, to study biochemistry." She admired the research of one of the professors there. He was conducting groundbreaking studies on disease and aging, and she wanted to be a part of it. But it was so difficult to get admitted.

"Of course I'd rather you came to Harvard with me. But MIT isn't so far away. We could get an apartment together." His eagerness made her want to cry. Realistically, what were the chances they would end up at universities in the same city? If she even got in anywhere she could afford.

She didn't want to spend any more time on those kinds of thoughts.

She lowered her gaze. "If I get in, we can think about it."

His hand crept around hers. "You could live with me even if you didn't. I'd be happy to pay for an apartment for both of us."

Could she just stay with him, living off his ill-gotten gains? She shook her head. "I want to be with you, Adrian, but I need to be in school. Working is really important to me. I don't want to just be your arm candy."

He gathered her hand in both of his. They were warm and all-encompassing. Hers felt small and cold. "Of course, and it matters to me that you want to use your brain." He caressed her hand, and a glint appeared in his eyes. "You have to let me help you. Just to even the playing field, nothing more," he said. "I promise I won't give you an unfair advantage."

She pulled away. "No."

"Are you sure?" he teased, a wicked sparkle in his eyes.

"I'm positive. And I don't want you to do something and not tell me. Promise me you won't do anything to help me, even to 'level the playing field'. Promise," she insisted.

He pouted. "All right, if you say so, I'll be good."

She shook her head at the mock-sorrowful expression on his face, slammed the laptop shut and slid onto his lap, plunging her hands under the silk of his shirt, feeling his abs ripple beneath her fingers. "Come on," she said. "Let me show you I'm not *all* good."

A smirk twisted his lips. "Now, that's more like it."

 ## Keisha

Keisha fell into step with Ben as he walked home from school one chilly November afternoon. He'd stuffed his hands in his pockets against the cold, and he had deep circles under his eyes.

"Hey," she said.

He gave her a sidelong glance but did not change his expression. "Hey."

"You look like things aren't going so well."

"The clinic's been swamped with overdose cases. I've been up late every night this past week helping out my dad."

Keisha prided herself on her judgment of people. All her instincts told her that despite Ben's history of delinquency, he wasn't a gang member. His father ran the local free clinic, and he obviously cared about the suffering of others. She just couldn't see him being involved in the manufacture or sale of Rapture. Involving a minor went against police procedure, of course. But she had already gone so far off the rulebook.

"Ben," she said. "How much do you want to help stop the spread of Rapture?"

 ## Elisa

Elisa slammed her locker shut with extra force. Far too many tests in a single day. To top it off, it was sleeting and gray, which meant a cold, windy walk home. She whirled away from the wall. Someone was standing right behind her.

"Oh! Sorry—" she began before she recognized him. "Adrian!"

He gave her a slow, lazy smile, lashes lowered beneath his glasses. He put one hand on the wall by her face and brought his lips to her ear. "I have a present for you."

Her annoyance faded as she drank in the warmth of his body. He had one hand behind his back and a huge grin on his face. With a flourish, he brought out a bouquet of lilies, waxy and white with deep red throats, topped with a narrow box.

They smelled fantastic, luxurious and heady; their rich scent made her nostrils tingle. "But—what's the occasion?"

He laughed. "Do I need an occasion to give the special woman in my life a present? It's the two-month anniversary of our first date, Elisa." He brushed his lips over the top of her head.

She felt like such a jerk. Weren't boys supposed to be the ones who forgot anniversaries? "I'm sorry," she mumbled. "I didn't get you anything."

"Never mind," he said. "Why don't you open the box?"

She glanced around the crowded school corridor. "Right here?"

With a laugh, he bent, slipped one arm around her and scooped her up. She stiffened and squeaked as he trotted down the hall. He shouldered open one of the classroom doors and carried her over the threshold. Once they were alone, he combed his fingers through her hair and kissed her deeply.

She finally pulled back, gasping. His eyes were lidded as he drew away. "Open it," he commanded.

She laid the lilies on the desk and unwrapped the box, removing the tissue paper to reveal a long envelope. Sliding her finger under the flap, she removed a glossy brochure and a printed cardboard slip. "What—what is this?" She flipped the brochure over. The Atlantis Hotel, a resort in Nassau.

He laughed at the baffled expression on her face. "I'm taking you on a vacation to the Bahamas."

"W-what do you mean? When?"

"This weekend," he said. "Do you like your present?"

The brochure dangled from her fingers. "Don't we have school?"

He stroked one finger along her cheek. "You'll only have to miss one day. I already got us both passports. We'll leave Thursday night and return Sunday night. First class airline tickets. That'll give us three full days in a warm and sunny paradise. We'll get away from all this dark and cold." He moved closer. "What do you say?"

"It sounds wonderful," she said doubtfully, "but I've never been on an airplane before."

He bent his head to hers. "You are going to love it."

21

 *Elisa*

ELISA CLUTCHED THE ENVELOPE and the lilies to her chest as she ran down the stairs to her next class. Such an extravagant gift. She had never heard of going to the Bahamas for a *weekend*. It was romantic that he wanted to celebrate their two-month anniversary, but the scale of the gift terrified her. It was the sort of thing you'd do for a honeymoon.

Maybe.

If you were rich.

Just how much money did Adrian have? Spending money on a few fancy dinners was one thing, but a vacation like this had to cost thousands of dollars. How much was Tenebras paying him? She shivered.

"Hey!" Sumiko called as she stepped into Elisa's path. "What's been up with you lately? We haven't seen you anywhere."

"We've missed you," said Chloe.

"I've been in school every day. What's to miss?"

"You're always eating lunch alone with Adrian these days and neglecting your friends," Sumiko said.

A wave of guilt washed over Elisa. "I'm sorry. We're both so busy with school it seems there isn't really much time to spend together."

Sumiko scrutinized her face. "What's wrong? You look so distracted and worried." Her eyes fell on the lilies. "And what's this? Flowers? Nice!"

Elisa lifted the bouquet and gazed at it as though puzzled. "Adrian gave them to me for our two-month anniversary."

Both girls grinned widely at that. "Aww, that's sweet," said Sumiko. "He's so romantic, isn't he?"

"But what's wrong?" pressed Chloe. "Why aren't you smiling?"

Elisa stared at them blankly. What could she say? Adrian had warned her of the importance of keeping his membership in Tenebras a secret. Obviously she couldn't tell them that he had invited her on a wildly extravagant vacation. But she could tell them he wanted to go away with her for the weekend. As a matter of fact, she had to let them know, or they would wonder where she was.

She bit her lip, and her eyes shifted back and forth. "Adrian invited me to go away over the weekend, and I'm a bit nervous about that."

"But why?" Chloe demanded. She lowered her voice. "Going away for the weekend sounds fun! Who wouldn't want to be alone with someone as hot as Adrian all weekend? I mean, it's not like your mom's gonna know."

Elisa was sure that her face was becoming redder than the throats of the lilies. She still felt a little guilty about not following Carlos's wishes that she wait until marriage. Although she was a legal adult now and entitled to make her own decisions, everything had ended up being far more complicated than she had ever imagined.

Sumiko said, "I think it's sweet that he's thinking of two months with you as an anniversary, and that he wants to take you somewhere. Where is he taking you, by the way?"

"Well," she began, frantically trying to think of a trip that didn't sound too expensive, "he has a friend with a camper, and we're going to borrow it and go up into the mountains." She twirled a strand of hair around her finger, ashamed that she was lying to her own best friends.

"Camping in the middle of winter?" asked Sumiko, a line appearing in the middle of her forehead. "I hope that camper has a good heater."

 ## Rory

Rory rested against the basement wall, watching the gang meeting through slitted eyes. Adrian lounged in his chair, his chin propped on his fist, listening to a stumbling report from one of the newer members. The furnace rumbled to life and the murky light in the room brightened slightly. The blond kid was stuttering, and the crowd shifted, bored.

Rory wondered when Adrian would order the kid to shut up. He was usually less than tolerant, but today he seemed to be in a very relaxed and genial mood.

Finally, the kid stumbled to a stop.

"All right. Give your figures to Cesar after the meeting," Adrian said. He tapped a finger on his armrest. "I'll give you one more chance. Of course, you're aware of the consequences should you fail again." His voice was light and pleasant.

The blond let out his breath in relief. "Y-yes, Captain. Th-thank you." He wiped his face with his sleeve. "I-I promise I'll do better."

Adrian nodded to Cesar. "Nothing more on the agenda?" He glanced over the crowd. "I'll be away on personal business this weekend. In my absence, Cesar will be in charge. You will obey him as you would me. I'll receive a direct report upon my return and will deal with any insubordination personally." Cesar, standing at Adrian's side, nodded in his impassive way.

Rory watched the others' faces to see how they would take the news. Adrian rarely left his headquarters, preferring to keep personal contact with his subordinates. Rory doubted a few days' absence would make a significant difference in Adrian's hold over the gang; they were too terrified of him to attempt anything in his absence, and Cesar was a good choice as proxy. He was completely ruthless. He would not hesitate to threaten anyone he deemed disloyal to Adrian or mete out any punishment he found necessary to maintain Adrian's rule of terror.

Still, Rory mused, it was interesting that Adrian had decided that something was so important that it was worth taking time away from his operation during this critical period. The distribution of Rapture was going extremely well from a financial standpoint; however, Tenebras's success in this area was already attracting wolves in the form of rival gangs trying to muscle in on their territory, dealers being roughed up and having their product stolen, agents attempting to infiltrate their supply lines, and of course the cops from multiple jurisdictions swarming all over the district like ants looking for a source of sugar. Cesar, though loyal, did not have Adrian's genius for planning and strategy, his flexible and wide-ranging ability to react instantly and brilliantly to any situation. It was a tactical error for Adrian to leave the field of battle at this time.

Adrian's expression gave little away, as always. But Rory could detect a new softness in his face. The Captain—was *happy*. He had never seen Adrian happy before. Intent, triumphant, pleased with a well-conceived and executed plan, yes, but never happy. This emotion was distracting him from his work; and the nature of that work required his entire concentration and delicate touch on the controls at all times. Otherwise, it could all come tumbling down, and would bring many other people down with it, Rory included. Adrian's new love interest was a weakness. Elisa Gallardo posed a threat to all of Tenebras.

Removing the threat without incurring Adrian's wrath would be extremely tricky. Adrian was relentless in pursuit of revenge.

But even though it would be difficult, Rory knew it had to be done.

 # Adrian

Adrian got out of the limo and reached in to help Elisa exit. They were catching a flight out of JFK. A uniformed porter put their suitcases on a cart and trundled them off in the direction of the first-class ticket counter.

Adrian placed his hand under Elisa's elbow to steer her in the right direction. She was trying to peer everywhere at once, eyes wide at her first glimpse of an international airport.

They moved through security rapidly in the area reserved for first class passengers. The TSA agents were polite and friendly. Adrian returned their comments with equal courtesy, satisfied. It only took money to be treated with the respect he deserved.

Once on the plane, they were seated in two roomy, high-backed seats with a full recline, upholstered in royal blue. They formed a semi-private compartment. The very attentive, neatly-coifed blonde flight attendant chatted with them, fetched pillows and blankets, and served them each a glass of wine before takeoff. Meanwhile, the economy passengers stood in a long line, shuffled from foot to foot, struggled with their bags and were scolded by the staff for the size of their carry-ons.

Elisa held the glass of wine with a sweaty hand. "What should I do with this?"

"You're expected to drink it. To do otherwise would be rude." He lifted his glass in a silent toast to her and drained it.

"But," she whispered in his ear, "neither of us is 21."

"Shhh." Adrian put a finger to his lips. "Don't let them know."

Elisa, her eyes darting back and forth, slowly brought the glass to her lips and sipped.

The whine of the engines rose. The plane taxied out, and the flight attendant retrieved their empty glasses. Adrian reclined his seat. Elisa stared out the window at the baggage handlers driving by on carts. Her nervousness had eased after her glass of wine. Adrian took her hand in his and caressed her fingers.

 ## Elisa

It was like being in a different world, strange and unreal. The buzz of the engines, the odd vibrations in the seat, the molded beige plastic covers everywhere. The cabin lights dimmed when they reached cruising altitude, and Adrian helped Elisa recline her seat all the way back until it was flat as a narrow bed. All around them, the cabin occupants settled for the night. Elisa was too agitated to even think of sleeping, the taste of the wine lingering in her mouth, her head swirling with peculiar sensations.

Adrian lifted her blanket and crawled over the armrest between their two seats.

"What are you doing?" she hissed. The flatbed seat was barely big enough for one.

"I want to cuddle."

She glanced nervously at the darkened aisle. They had privacy only as long as no one walked past. Their bodies were jammed together under the blanket, and she could feel every inch of his body against hers.

His scent poured into her, and she inhaled more deeply. His face was only inches from hers, his lips glistening in the dim light. He hovered over her, hands entwined in the fabric of her blouse. She traced the lines of his features, his thickly fringed eyes, the curve of his eyebrows, his mouth, and found herself hesitating. He bent toward her, and his hair brushed her cheek.

How was it that she wanted him so much? Desire rippled like fever across her skin. His lips skimmed hers, velvet over fire; he laid down small open-mouthed kisses from the corner of her mouth to her ear, and her skin flickered like kindling.

Then his hands tilted her head to his, forcing her neck to arch back, bending her to his desires. He kissed her again and again, his tongue sinking into her mouth in a slow and intense rhythm.

With one finger, he sketched a line of flame along her throat and circled her breast. His hands worked at the buttons of her shirt, and a chill breeze grazed her skin.

Coming to her senses, she pulled away. "What are you doing? We're in public here."

"So?" he whispered in her ear, his breath teasing the nape of her neck like a gust of hellfire. "No one can see us."

"What about the flight attendant?" she whispered back. "It's got to be illegal to make out on an airplane."

"Of course it is. However…" He unhooked her bra. "I slipped her a few hundred-dollar bills. She'll leave us alone." He drew back briefly. "And we're going to do much more than make out."

His hands snuck behind her back, pulled off her bra and tossed it on the floor.

The cool air hit her bare breasts and she grasped at the threads of her resistance. "What if someone sees us?"

"So? They'll just be jealous because we're such a sexy couple." He bent his head to lie on her heart, his hair feathering over her skin. Her nipples ached.

She couldn't believe what they were doing. She needed to tell him to stop. This was just wrong. She didn't want to have public sex.

His fingers dawdled down her bare torso, teasing and dancing, and she gasped, even though she tried to be silent, aware of all the people sitting only a few feet away in the dim cabin. He gripped her ass hard, his fingers digging into her flesh.

"Do you really want me to stop?" Leisurely, he licked a line from between her breasts down to her belly button. He plunged both hands into the gap between her legs. Arousal pooled like lava in her core. His fingers slipped into her panties, and she was lost.

She lay on the rough fabric of the airplane seat, half-undressed under the blanket, both ashamed and thrilled. Adrian's expert fingers stroked her between her legs and spread her lips apart so he could reach more deeply inside her, an intimate caress that drowned her in sensation. She groaned.

"You like it after all," he murmured. He took her mouth in his, his tongue probing her at the same time as his fingers entered her. She curled and twisted under his touch and let him take utter control of her. She was his, she would do anything for him; it didn't matter; she would do whatever he wanted, even though she knew it was wrong, knew that he had done so many things that were wrong. But everything about him aroused her incredibly and now, at this moment, she would not think or judge; she simply belonged to him.

22

 *Adrian*

THE AIR WAS SOFT and warm as they stepped off the plane in the stillness at the Nassau Airport. It was almost shocking after the cold sleet they had left behind in Rockton. The air felt gentle, like a loving caress over smooth skin.

Adrian trailed his fingers over Elisa's bare shoulders, observing her first visit to a tropical island. Clusters of orchids and calatheas lined the terminal hallways, open to the outside air. Elisa's eyes widened at the sight, and her mouth went slack. She ran to the railing, gazed out into the sunlight, and stroked one waxy petal. Two tiny dark birds swooped in front of her and landed at her feet, pecked at crumbs on the floor, and darted away. She flinched and jumped backwards with a small yelp, a huge grin on her face.

Adrian marveled at the fact that he could take such joy in another person's delight.

It was extraordinary how his thoughts turned to Elisa all the time now. When she was with him, he was fascinated by her smallest gesture or facial expression. When she wasn't, he found himself thinking about her, desiring her, wanting, needing to do something to make her react to him. He wanted to tell her everything, share his entire dangerous, secret life with her. The habits he had built over a lifetime of lying and hiding were being stripped away. It should have been frightening, but instead, it was exhilarating.

With that odd sensitivity he had developed around Elisa, he knew that something was bothering her. As he drove their rental car out of the lot, he said, "Elisa, please tell me what's upsetting you."

She glanced away from him, out the window, and twisted a lock of hair around one finger. "What you—we—did last night on the plane? That was wrong."

"Why? It was fun. And I thought you enjoyed it."

"You deliberately manipulated me into doing something I didn't want to do."

He stopped, taken aback, to consider her words. It simply had not occurred to him to ask her permission. He had desired her, and so he had taken her. That was how he led his life; he took what he wanted, and everyone around him scrambled for the leavings.

And on the heels of his realization came an absurdly strong regret. A gut-wrenching, twisting sorrow. With one sentence, everything shifted.

He had never looked at the world through anyone's eyes other than his own. What sort of a person was he, really?

The sort of person who used others. Who cared only for his own selfish desires. Who destroyed others carelessly.

If his mother were alive, what would she think about what he did, about the life he lived?

"Elisa, I'm sorry," he whispered. What could he say to convince her? "You're right. I've never had a relationship before, and I'm finding this is new ground for me."

Elisa crossed her arms over her chest. "You're not telling me I'm your first. I know you've been with lots of women."

"Sex, yes." He turned the wheel and they rounded a curve in the road. "But Elisa, you are the first person I've ever felt something for." He wanted to say something stronger, but he was afraid she wouldn't believe him. How could she believe that someone like him could love anyone?

"Is it so strange that I've never had feelings for anyone before? I actually thought I was incapable of emotion—until I met you."

"The problem is you've lied to me so often, Adrian, that I don't know if you're lying now."

"I've never regretted my past lies to you as much as I do now."

"You lie all the time." Her voice tightened. "And you're good at it. I've caught myself believing you even when I *know* you're lying. So where does that leave us?"

"There's no way I can prove what I'm saying is the truth." His expression exuded sincerity, but he knew she had seen it many times before. Would she believe him this time? "All I can ask is that you look at my actions and not just my words. All I can do is tell you exactly how I feel, and let you draw your own conclusions. I've never felt this way before, and frankly, it scares me. I wait for every word you say; I hang on every expression on your face. When we're apart, you fill my thoughts. I question everything I do and wonder 'What will Elisa think?' It's overwhelming sometimes." He let his voice fade.

"But you're still involved with that gang."

He was silent for a moment. "It's not that easy to leave."

"What do you mean?" she said. "Can't you just tell them you're going to quit?"

He had to smile at her naïveté. "Surely you know there would be—consequences if I did."

"I thought you said Tenebras wasn't as violent as the rumors said."

"I never said they were completely non-violent. In fact, there would be some major risks."

"What do you mean by that?"

He thought about his last meeting with Schwartz, the delicate balance he was maintaining. He was aware of the impression he had left behind, with Rory, with Cesar, with Mario. So much was going on in his absence. Would it all work out the way he planned? There were so many potential risks.

He sighed. It had been easier when he didn't have to worry about a conscience. When he just took what he wanted.

Emotion—was painful.

"I've already begun plans to… retire." He didn't want to tell her about Schwartz's threat to her, the threat he himself was responsible for. There was so much he had to do to make sure that both he and Elisa could walk away from Tenebras and live. He would have to deal with Schwartz and Holman. Traitors in his own organization would have to be handled. It would not be easy, especially if he planned to avoid bloodshed.

"Would you really be willing to give up all the money?"

Adrian changed lanes smoothly, and accelerated up the onramp to a highway. "Believe me, there are plenty of lawful ways to become extremely wealthy." It was true that his best strategy at this point was to acquire assets legally. Beyond a certain point, the risk-reward structure no longer favored illicit activity. "I always planned to become a legitimate businessman as soon as possible."

He merged into the flow of traffic. "Let me make you a promise. Give me just a few more months to extricate myself from Tenebras. After that, I promise to tell you everything, let you be the judge of what I've done. And even more, I promise to let you be my conscience. I will never do anything that will go against your morals."

She stared at him, saying nothing.

"Could that be enough?" he murmured.

There was terrible conflict in her eyes. He had no idea what she was thinking. All he knew was that she held the weight of his life in the balance. He felt strange; was he incredibly weightless or unbearably heavy? He had become detached from gravity, like a planet hurtling through the void of space, waiting to be caught by the gravitational well of a new sun.

And then she placed her hand on his arm, and everything fell into place. His orbit stabilized and centered itself.

It was the end of everything, and the beginning.

For some reason, he found himself remembering a long-ago day. His mother had dressed him in a new coat and told him to run and look at himself in the mirror. He dragged her much larger coat from the closet and handed it to her.

"Now you look at yourself in the mirror, Mommy!"

She gave him a big hug. "Looks like we match, Adrian."

"I love you, Mommy."

"I love you too, Adrian."

His hand brushed over Elisa's. She reached out one finger to stroke his cheek, and when she drew back, a single teardrop glistened on her fingertip.

 ## Ben

"You're a cop!"

"Not so loud!" Keisha said. "Principal Robson was the only one who knew, up until yesterday. Now it's just you and Adrian Salas."

Ben's face darkened. "Salas? Why him?"

"He's an intern at Schwartz Pharmaceuticals, so he could be helpful. Besides, it's obvious he's not a gang member."

"How is it obvious? It's not obvious to me." Ben crossed his arms and resumed walking.

Keisha rolled her eyes, so exactly like a high school student that Ben almost laughed. "Oh, please. He's a complete nerd, Ben. Besides, Robson vouches for him."

He made a sarcastic grimace. "Yeah, he must be okay if Robson says so." He took her by the arm. "Keisha, Salas is one of the people I've been suspicious of for months."

Keisha pulled away from him. "And Robson was suspicious of you. Everyone is suspicious of everyone else in this school."

"But listen, Keisha. Mario is involved for sure. I know he's a member of Tenebras. I suspect he's one of their leaders, one of the Blades. He may even be their Captain. I spotted Cesar Peralta, who doesn't sneeze unless Salas gives him permission, talking secretly with Mario in a back corridor, and passing him something."

"So?"

"Don't you see, that must mean Salas is involved with Tenebras."

She shook her head. "Ben, that's the weakest chain of supposition I've ever heard."

"But—"

"Listen to me. Tenebras has been flooding the neighborhood with false rumors. If I were to listen to every single hot tip, I'd be busy for the next five years, and guess what? I wouldn't get anywhere." She tightened her lips. "We already made one big misstep. We've got to start moving on this case."

"Listen—"

"No, you listen to me. We're going after Schwartz Pharmaceuticals and for that we need Adrian's help. I don't want you bad-mouthing him. Now as for you, I need you to help me gain entrance into Tenebras."

Ben's jaw dropped. "You—want to become a member of the gang?"

"It's the only way to find out what's going on."

"But it's dangerous! You've heard the rumors about kids going missing, right?" He snorted. "Well, I suppose you could ask Mario."

"No. I have a plan for that. But yeah, it'll involve Mario—and you."

"Me?" asked Ben, eyebrows climbing his forehead. "You are totally out of your mind. There's no way I can help you get membership in Tenebras."

"Wait till you hear my plan."

 ## *Rory*

Rory moved silently down the hall toward the corner where he heard a murmured conversation. Mario Fonseca and Ron Hundley were speaking together, their voices low.

"My, my," he said. They guiltily jumped apart. "What're you two talking about, hmmm?"

Mario scowled. "Just the next shipment, Fong. What's it to you?" He stuck out his chin.

"Oh, nothing," Rory lowered his voice. "I was just thinking that it was too bad the Captain chose to go on a luxury tropical vacation for the weekend. Especially when there's so much going on right here." He watched their faces closely.

Hundley scratched his crotch and frowned. "Yeah, so what? Captain does whatever he wants, doesn't he?"

"Didn't you hear the news last night about Lindley and Washington?"

"What?" Mario pretended disinterest.

Rory examined his fingernails. "You know they were guarding the Twenty-Second Street warehouse, right? It seems they were ambushed by some of our rivals from Eastside."

Ron and Mario exchanged glances. Then Ron snarled, "So? They were careless. They blew it. What's that to us?"

Rory lifted one shoulder in a shrug. "So you don't think it's a problem that he's off fooling around with his little piece while we're all risking our lives for him here?"

Mario growled, "That almost sounds like insubordination, Fong."

Rory said, grinning, "Don't trip over the big words, Mario. I'm just saying while he's gone anything could happen. And I might suggest that you two think about where that would leave you."

Mario hesitated. "So… what are you suggesting?"

The wind had died down, but a leaden sky capped the thin layer of snow that had fallen overnight. The sun had barely risen, but in one of the asphalt yards in back of the school, Cesar Peralta was moving through an intricate martial-arts dance.

Rory watched silently as he went through his moves. Only Cesar would be practicing tai chi outside on such a cold and miserable day. The kid was insanely self-disciplined, and never seemed to need any fun to lighten up his life.

He waited until Cesar had completed his routine, and walked over as he began his post-workout stretching.

"Hey, Cesar, how's it going?"

Cesar only grunted in response. Rory knew Cesar despised him, but that just added to his amusement. He had learned long ago from Adrian that hatred was one of the most easily manipulated emotions.

"Have you gotten the reports on the weekend activity yet?" He knew that Cesar already had the reports, but he wanted to see how he'd react.

"Of course, Fong." Cesar's voice was clipped with annoyance. "What do you want?" He communicated with Rory as little as possible, exchanging only information that was necessary. Rory knew that he would be irritated by being sought out like this, outside of regular channels, and he grinned.

"I was just noticing that there's been a significant drop in revenue over the weekend since the Captain's been gone."

"So?" Cesar bent to stretch over his left leg.

"Ever since he's been... distracted... by this woman, there's been a downward trend." Rory waited as Cesar deepened his stretch. "You've got to have seen it."

"Your point being?" Cesar snapped.

"I was just thinking that she hasn't really been good for the organization. Don't you agree?"

Cesar straightened. "I see where you're going with this, Fong, and it's not going to work. You're trying to manipulate me into doing something about this woman."

Rory backed away in mock surprise, raising his hands. "Oh, no, I never said anything like that."

"He would know. He always knows."

"No, no." Rory's smile grew. "I was thinking about something more subtle. Something no one could object to. Or trace back to us."

23

 *Elisa*

ELISA WALKED TO SCHOOL singing. Some days the cold bothered her, but not today. It was a brilliantly clear winter day, shards of sunlight glinting off icicles on the eaves of the buildings. It had snowed over the weekend, and although the streets were already cleared and cars rushed by, spattering dirty brine on the sidewalks, the city still appeared white and clean.

Sumiko greeted her at the school entrance. "Hey, Elisa! How was your weekend? Tell me what happened!" She linked arms with Elisa as they walked up the stairs to their lockers.

"What's to tell?" Elisa said, suddenly cautious. "We had a good time together. We talked a lot."

Sumiko gave her a once-over. "You can't have spent much time indoors. Your face looks tanned."

"Tanned?" Elisa put her hands to her cheeks. "Why, that's strange."

"How can you get tanned on a camping trip in the winter?"

She frantically cast around for a plausible story. "We were out in the snow! The sun must have reflected off the snow and given me a bit of a burn. I should have used more sunscreen, but who would have thought that you need sunscreen in the winter?" She burst into a high-pitched laugh that sounded extremely artificial to her own ears.

Sumiko scratched her chin. "You went hiking in the snow?"

"That's right. It was fun!"

"I heard there was nearly a foot of snow in the mountains. Didn't that make hiking difficult?" Sumiko cocked her head.

Elisa twisted her combination lock. "Right—we didn't just go hiking. We went—snowshoeing!" She grinned suddenly at her idea. "We walked around all day in snowshoes, and it was really hard to get used to them, so it was difficult to get back to the camper at the end of the day." She laughed. "So that's why we were out so long in the snow, and why I got burned!"

Sumiko gave her a strange look, but shrugged.

"Elisa! How was the big weekend?" Chloe came up from behind and threw her arms around Elisa. She yelped.

"It was fine." Sliding out of Chloe's grasp, Elisa picked up her math book from the bottom of the locker.

Chloe waggled her eyebrows at Elisa. "You look like you've had some sun! Where did you say you went for the weekend?"

"She went snowshoeing," Sumiko said. She gave Elisa a sidelong glance. "Isn't that right?"

"Yeah! We went snowshoeing in the mountains on our camping trip." Elisa put a hand behind her head and laughed again, shrilly. Her face flushed with embarrassment.

"Snowshoeing?" Chloe's mouth hung open. "Where did you go?"

Elisa bit her lip. This lie was getting way too complicated. She cast about desperately for help, and spotted Adrian at the end of the hall, coming up the stairs with Rory Fong. Rory had an uncharacteristically serious expression on his face.

She waved wildly. "Good morning, Adrian!"

His head came up, and Elisa could feel the warmth of his smile all the way across the hall. It sparked an answering heat in her, a ripple like light passing through water, and her knees weakened. He walked away from Rory without a backward glance, leaving him staring, lips pressed together tightly.

"Good morning." His eyes focused on Elisa.

"I hear you introduced Elisa to a new sport," Sumiko said.

Adrian glanced at her, his face as unruffled as usual.

Elisa shook herself mentally and jumped in. "I was just telling them that we went snowshoeing in the mountains on our camping trip this weekend."

He picked up the thread effortlessly, without even a flicker of surprise in his expression. "Yes, Elisa did very well for her first time on snowshoes." He smiled at her with just a hint of pride on his face. Once again, she marveled at how smoothly he lied.

"Where did you go?" asked Chloe again.

"Past the river and into the wilderness area at the east end of the national park." Adrian bent forward, eyes focused on Sumiko's face. "What happened to you, Sumiko?"

"Me?" asked Sumiko. "What do you mean?"

Adrian traced her cheek with a finger. "You have a bruise here; what happened?"

She put her hand up to her face. "I was sparring in karate practice and one of my opponents got past my guard, that's all. He wasn't able to pull his punch in time."

"I wouldn't have thought there was anyone who could get past your guard at this point."

Sumiko shrugged. "It happens. I messed up this time. I—"

Chloe interrupted. "You don't look tanned, Adrian."

"Tanned?" He lifted one eyebrow.

"From the snow," she said. "From being out in the snow all weekend, like Elisa here."

"She does look a little rosy from all that healthy outdoor activity." He tapped his binder. "By the way, Elisa, did you do problem seventeen on the calculus homework due today? I had a question about what the teacher was asking us." He pulled Elisa aside and she gratefully dug in her backpack for her math notebook. When he touched her arm, her unease about lying to her friends was completely forgotten.

The crowded, noisy hall faded away, and she could see nothing but his eyes, feel nothing but his touch, knew only the two of them together.

Then the bell rang, and Elisa hurried off to class. She had gotten away with another lie. But how long, she wondered, until Sumiko or Chloe caught her out? What would she do then?

 ## Adrian

That night, Adrian gazed into the fire in his study. Returning to his organization after only three days away had been, in some ways, entertaining. In other ways—not so much. It had all begun to seem a little tedious.

A piece of the log glowed, dropped off a larger block of wood, and fell through the grate to the stone hearth beneath.

It used to be that every time he had a spare moment, he would ponder his latest plans, contemplate new schemes, and work out little details on existing operations. But now, all those spare moments went to thinking about Elisa. The hours he used to spend scheming about new ways to increase his power and wealth now went to reminiscing about time spent in her company or planning how to make their next date even more spectacular.

It was hard to sit here, alone in his study, when he knew she was only five minutes away, in her apartment, also alone. He rose, paced to the back of the room, returned.

He had grown unaccustomed to denying himself anything. He wanted her, now. He wanted to breathe in the scent of her, to feel her long hair trailing over his bare skin, to take her under his hands, overcome her stammered resistance, and drive her to shattering pleasure.

He closed his eyes.

In the early days, he had spent long periods of time denying himself, waiting, planning. He had waited for years: a very long portion of his life. Patience was his strong suit. He reminded himself of that, took a series of deep breaths.

It was vital that he focus. He had to admit it: she *was* a distraction, a dangerous distraction from the many critical and sensitive operations he was running, ventures that all needed his adroit handling. It was ironic that he had held Rory's own secret attachment over his head.

Of course, even Rory and Cesar didn't know the true extent of the risk. He was keeping Schwartz at bay for now by stepping up Rapture distribution, but it was becoming more and more disturbing that he was responsible for so much addiction and suffering.

He had to stop.

But as soon as Schwartz got even a hint that he was planning to leave the gang, what would happen to Elisa? Adrian lowered himself into the armchair, lifted the glass of brandy on the end table and took a long, slow sip.

"Snowshoes." He had to laugh at her bizarre imagination. It was quite clear that Elisa Gallardo was not merely a weakness or a liability. She was a great big hole in his security. A major risk to his careful plans. She could not lie to save her life; it was only a matter of time before her friends—and Ben Lancaster and Keisha Huston—figured out exactly what was going on.

What was he going to do about her?

He had been deluding himself in Nassau. When he was far from his day-to-day operations, it had been easier to imagine that a normal life with Elisa was possible. But it couldn't be.

He set down the glass. A chunk fell off the log in the fireplace and the flames abruptly faded. His skin chilled.

 *Mario*

The spot between Mario's shoulder blades prickled. Cesar Peralta was right behind him on the stairs. When they reached the top floor, Cesar ushered him into a small room, where Adrian Salas sat behind a desk, working on a tablet computer.

"Hello, Mario," Adrian said very softly. Mario sat down, swallowing. What was all this about? Had Adrian finally figured it out? Was he pretending not to know to amuse himself before he ordered Cesar to bury his knife in his back? "Thank you for coming."

Mario growled to himself, but made sure to keep quiet. Why was Salas always so freaking polite? Mario preferred straight shooters, even if they hated you. Salas could talk like you were his best friend and stab you a moment later. At least with Ben Lancaster, you always knew where you stood. He saw amusement in Salas's eyes and tried not to squirm. Salas's amusement was never a good thing.

"Cesar. Play the recording."

The voice of Ben Lancaster burst from a small speaker in the center of the desk, unexpectedly loud. "Why are we meeting in a *supply closet*? This is ridiculous, Keisha."

Cesar adjusted the volume. Adrian leaned back in his chair, watching Mario's reactions.

"No, it's good security," came a sharp rejoinder. "What I have to say to you is highly sensitive, not to be discussed outside this room."

"What's so special about this closet?"

"This room has been swept for bugs and is secured. We don't know who might be a spy for Tenebras."

"I'm not used to all this cloak and dagger crap."

"Do you want to stop Tenebras or not?" Mario pictured her standing up and placing her fists on her hips.

"Hey, chill out. Tell me what your big plan is."

Papers shuffled.

"The best strategy is for me to try to infiltrate Tenebras itself."

"How the hell do you expect to get in? Half the school wants to join that damn gang." Ben's voice swelled with outrage.

Mario sniggered. "Hell, even Lancaster is lusting after us." He reclined in the seat and grinned widely. Cesar frowned and motioned for him to be quiet.

Ben continued, "They've got some kind of initiation rite you want to stay the hell away from."

"Will you be quiet and let me explain?"

A pen scratched on paper.

"Here. This is the second floor of the east wing. During third period, Mario has class here. You've got class here."

"Right, so what's the point?"

"I'm getting to it, so shut up. Tomorrow after third period, after the bell rings, I want you in this corridor, where I'll be waiting."

Ben gave a muffled snort of laughter. "What are you drawing there?"

"I want you to make a scene, pick a fight with me. Then we'll—"

There was a louder noise of derision from Ben. "What the—? Why are you drawing a bunch of cats?"

"You idiot! I'm trying to draw a diagram so simple even a bonehead like you can understand the plan!" Her voice was sharp. "Besides, what's wrong with cats? Now, I want you here, and we'll fight in front of Mario's classroom. I want him to come out and see us. Mario hates you, and if he sees us fighting, he'll be more open to me. He knows what a good fighter I am; I could be useful to him. I'm going to drop some hints about needing money. I already told him a sob story about going to detention school." There was a short pause. "Any questions so far?"

"Yeah. I want to know why your drawings suck." Ben's voice sounded angry, but he was laughing at the same time.

There was the sound of a loud smack.

"Ow!" cried Ben.

"Now, are you going to shut up and listen or not?"

"You just told me to ask questions!"

"I meant questions about the plan, idiot!"

"Your plan sucks big time! Why the hell would Mario think that just because you're fighting me you'd be a good recruit? Mario may look like a brain-dead goon, but he's not a complete dumbass. He's not going to fall for it."

Mario muttered, "Call me a brain-dead goon..." He fell silent at Cesar's sharp glance.

"Got a better plan?" Keisha's voice was hard.

There was silence.

"Ben, Rapture is spreading like crazy. We've got to do something *now*."

Ben lowered his voice. "Yeah. But it's dangerous."

"Idiot." But Keisha's voice sounded affectionate. "Of course it is. But that's my job. This plan may not be perfect. But at least it'll soften Mario towards me. Anyone who can't stand his worst enemy can't be all bad."

Adrian gestured to Cesar, who stopped the recording.

Mario crossed his arms over his chest. "They're right. I'm not so dumb to fall for that trick."

Adrian tilted his head. "Of course you wouldn't, Mario. But in this case..."

"You want me to pretend to fall for it, recruit her into the gang." Mario's mind was working furiously. What would Schwartz think about this latest move? And what about Rory?

"Exactly," Adrian said. "Don't make it too easy, but allow her to pique your interest. Hint that you might be willing to recruit her. Draw her out."

"You want any information out of her?"

"There's nothing we need from her. She's pretty much gone rogue, and this bogus idea is just part of it." Adrian waved a dismissive hand. "Just let her think—eventually—you'll be recommending her. Let her believe that her *plan*"—Adrian's lip twitched—"is going to succeed."

The metal door to the abandoned parking garage clanged open, and Mario entered, holding Lonnie by the scruff of his neck. He tried not to wrinkle his nose; the air reeked of gasoline tainted with an acrid undercurrent that bit into his throat. He gave the kid a vicious shove, and he staggered and fell to his knees. Lonnie was gaunt and pale. Deep shadows lay under his bloodshot eyes, and his body shook with tremors.

Schwartz, the lab owner, stood in the shadows at the other end of the low-ceilinged chamber, half-hidden behind a stack of corroding oil drums. Dark fingers of oil spread outward from his feet, staining the crumbling concrete floor of the garage. He watched as Mario hauled Lonnie up again, shoved him forward, and then kicked the backs of his knees so he fell to the ground again.

"Mario, who's this?" Schwartz's voice, shrill and cold, reminded Mario of an oil slick on an arctic sea.

Lonnie crawled forward on his hands and knees, whimpering. Approaching Schwartz, he groveled on the dirty concrete before him. "Sir," he whined, prostrating himself. "Please—"

Mario huffed out a breath. "Like you wanted, someone who got on the Captain's bad side. No more slip for Lonnie, Captain's orders."

Lonnie inhaled raggedly and pushed himself halfway up on his hands and knees, angling his face up toward Schwartz. His mouth twisted into a distorted grimace that might have passed for an attempt at a smile. "Please, sir, let me help you." His voice broke. "I'll do anything."

Schwartz regarded him thoughtfully. "Lonnie. I'm wondering how far you might be willing to go for me."

"Anything." Lonnie's voice shook.

"Hmm." Schwartz bent, dipped two fingers in the slimy, rainbow-hued pool of liquid in front of him, and held his greasy dark fingers to Lonnie's mouth.

The kid's Adam's apple bobbed and for a moment he froze. Then, slowly, he parted his lips. His tongue emerged, swollen and coated with white. With a jerky, awkward motion, he bent forward and licked the sludge off Schwartz's fingers.

He doubled over, retching and gagging.

Schwartz's thin lips stretched in a rictus of a smile.

Lonnie coughed a few more times and stopped. "Like I said before, I'll do anything for you," he whimpered hoarsely. "Only, please, can't I have just one hit…" He trailed off as Schwartz's face darkened.

"Oh no. You don't get your reward until after the job is done, and done well. It displeases me that you're asking even before I've told you what I want you to do. It makes me think that you're not sufficiently eager to please me."

"Oh, no, no, sir, all I want is to please you," he moaned. "Please, tell me what you want me to do."

Schwartz's eyes glittered. "Excellent." He leaned against the rusty side of one of the barrels. "I take it you have no objections to bringing down Adrian Salas."

24

♆ Keisha

THE USUAL LUNCHTIME RUSH crowded the halls; the air was damp, redolent with sweaty teenagers and moldy paper products, and through it all threaded a slightly burnt odor from the cafeteria. Keisha pushed her way through a crowd of students. "Adrian, I'd like to speak with you in private, if you please."

"Sure, Keisha." He gave her a deferential nod and followed her up the stairs. He stared around the supply closet in amazement. "This is your base of operations?"

Keisha scowled. "Don't ask questions. This is a secured room, so we can discuss matters pertinent to the case here but nowhere else."

Adrian nodded. "I see. How can I help you?"

"First, I wanted to let you know that I was very pleased with the evidence you gathered in the report you submitted yesterday."

He offered her a humble smile. "I'm glad you found it useful. I'm very concerned about illegal drug activity in our community."

"I think it justifies upping the ante on the operation against Schwartz Pharmaceuticals. Based on what you said in your report, I've decided to set up a sting. The first thing I want to know is— how good are you at acting?"

There was a pause, and then Adrian smiled modestly. "Well, I *am* president of the drama club. Although I have to admit we don't have the budget to put on any plays, so I've never gone onstage."

"For this to work, it's critical that you be convincing in your role. If you don't think you can handle it, I'll get another cop to come in on this. What do you think? Be honest now."

"I think I can do it."

Keisha weighed his response. He had done an excellent job so far gathering incriminating circumstantial evidence against Schwartz and Holman. It pointed to the manufacture of Rapture in their lab, and linked them with a known drug kingpin. Vince had been following up on all the leads and had told her Adrian's information had been crucial. "You realize there is substantial risk involved, don't you?" she asked. "If Schwartz or his underlings suspect something is going on, they could do anything. Drug manufacturers are seldom pacifists."

"I understand. But I'm willing to take that risk."

 *Adrian*

Adrian let himself into Elisa's apartment with his key. She had invited him over for dinner, and he was going to eat with her, discuss strategy, and leave immediately after. He was only coming over because he was hungry, not because he wanted to see her. It was... efficient, to share a meal while they discussed what would happen next.

Elisa hummed to herself in the kitchen, and a large pot of spaghetti sauce simmered on the stove, filling her apartment with the scent of tomatoes and spice. Adrian set a grocery bag on the counter. She turned a page of her cookbook, hands covered with flour.

He brushed her hair aside with one hand, and touched his lips to her neck. Her skin was flushed from the heat of the kitchen, and her pores had opened, allowing her scent to escape into his nostrils. He breathed in, a shock of excitement traveling from his head to his toes.

She relaxed in his arms, and he felt the urge to sweep her up, take all that softness and those lovely curves into the bedroom, run his hands over her until she trembled. Until she wanted nothing but him.

With his iron will he put aside his longings, kept his embrace neutral, dropped his hands from her body.

"Adrian, it's great to see you! Wait till you see what I'm making for dinner. Spaghetti and spinach soufflé!"

"Sounds... original," he said. "I brought some bananas and chocolate ice cream for dessert."

"Chocolate, thank you! I knew I'd forgotten something."

He took the groceries out of the bag and put them away in her refrigerator.

"So how was your job today?" She switched on a burner, put a pat of butter in a skillet, and waited for it to melt. "You went to your internship, right?" Her fingers tensed on the handle. She was avoiding his eyes; it must have occurred to her that he was lying to her about his job too.

His voice remained calm. "It went quite well." He glanced at the stove. The pot was boiling so vigorously that red sauce was splattering over the white ceramic stovetop. He reached around her to turn down the burner. "The heat needs to be a little lower."

"The recipe said to simmer. Do you know how to set the burner?"

"You set the knob about halfway." He showed her. "The flames should be about that high, see?"

"How come you know so much about cooking, Adrian?" She fell silent; she must have been aware of the unintended double entendre in her words. Would she speak of it today, question him as to the purpose to which he put his knowledge of chemistry?

He shrugged, not responding, got a spoon out of her drawer and dipped it in the sauce, took a nibble. "Mmm. Tastes good. Although I think it could use a little more garlic." He cut a clove from the braid hanging on the wall, found her garlic press, and squeezed the juice into the simmering red liquid.

She watched his hand as he swirled the wooden spoon in the thick liquid, not meeting his eyes. He tossed the spoon onto the stovetop and pivoted to face her. The red sauce stained the utensil's handle, turning the pale wood crimson. "Elisa," he said. "Don't look so troubled."

"I—" she whispered, her hands against his chest.

Without breaking eye contact, he reached behind him to dip a finger in the sauce.

"Don't!" she cried. "You'll get burned."

He laughed and bent his head to hers. "I never get burned," he whispered. He held up his finger, now dripping with thick red liquid, and ran his tongue from the base to the tip. "Delicious," he murmured. He brought his fingers to her lips. "Open up," he commanded softly.

She opened her mouth, taking his fingers between her lips, licking them quietly, her tongue curling around his fingers. Slowly, he lowered his mouth to hers, teasing her with his tongue, a sleek invasion he knew she would not resist.

They had much to talk about—but he would be less distracted if they addressed physical needs first. He turned off the burner and carried her into the bedroom. When he released her, he tumbled her down onto the bed and leaned over her. He ran his hands through the luxurious array of her hair fanned out beneath her.

"Elisa. You are so beautiful," he whispered. It still astonished him how much she could affect him. When he was with her, he could forget, for a while, all the pressing, dangerous concerns that surrounded him.

And yet, as he kissed her again, he knew that he was indulging himself recklessly in her. She was an addictive drug, taking his mind away from what he needed to do to survive. He should spend less time here, more time making sure his plans came to fruition.

And yet—he could not tear himself away. Not tonight, at least. He would stay with her tonight. Tomorrow—tomorrow would be soon enough to do what he needed to do.

 ## Kim

Kim crouched behind a leaking oil drum in the old parking garage, her heart pounding. When she had decided to follow Mario and Lonnie, she had no clue what was really going on. She had snuck in and watched their meeting with the creepy old guy—Schwartz, they had called him—and overheard just enough of their plans to make her shake with terror.

Long after they had left, she remained curled into a small ball on the bare concrete floor, arms wrapped around her knees, rocking back and forth. The gasoline fumes burned her nose, but she made no move to leave.

This was it. Her chance to finally get revenge on Adrian and that girl. She could tell Mario she wanted in. She could help them with their plan to destroy Adrian.

Even by doing nothing, she could get her revenge. She could allow the plotters to go forward and benefit from the bloody destruction.

That was probably best. It sounded like the old guy's plan was going to succeed, but you never knew around Adrian. You never wanted to get on his bad side, just in case. It wouldn't be smart for her to take sides in this battle. All she'd have to do is say nothing and let it happen.

She hated Adrian with all her heart. She wanted to see him bloody and dead on the ground. She'd look at his body and laugh. She'd spit on his cold flesh. She'd kick his gorgeous face, see those beautiful eyes closed forever, that velvet voice stilled for eternity.

Why did her eyes feel wet? She hated him.

She wanted nothing more than to bring him down. She angrily wiped the tears from her face.

Adrian thought less than nothing of her. If the tables were turned, he'd let her die. He'd use her or kill her if it pleased him.

Kim bent her head to her knees and closed her eyes. She rocked back and forth for a long time, until her tears finally dried up.

She couldn't let it happen.

Her lips twisted into a sardonic smirk in the darkness. She had it bad. It was crazy, stupid.

Slowly she got to her feet. There was nothing for it. Her course was clear. She slunk out of the parking garage, and once out on the icy, dark street broke into a run.

There was somewhere she had to go.

She had to warn Adrian, but she knew she couldn't get in to see him. He was still furious at her and had refused to have any contact with her since the incident with the slip in Elisa's apartment.

But she could go to his best friend and second-in-command. The kid who knew more secrets than anyone, who had been Adrian's trusted lieutenant since middle school.

She was going to find Rory.

 Mario

Mario swaggered down the main hall past clusters of kids at their lockers. Shouts echoed from up the hall. He was going to enjoy seeing Ben Lancaster and Keisha Huston going head-to-head. They were both good fighters, fun to watch, and he couldn't wait for a rematch with either of them. He was itching to fight Huston again after she'd taken him off-guard a few months ago. Hopefully his chance would come soon. There was no way someone would be let into his gang without demonstrating their fighting skills.

Kids were gathered in a tight ring around the combatants. Mario pushed his way through the crowd. Most of them were cheering Keisha on as she delivered a sharp right uppercut to her much larger opponent. It was obvious to Mario's experienced eye that Ben was pulling his punches. He was much bigger than her and just as fast, although she appeared to be better trained. Ben was a natural fighter, of course. The two of them shouted insults as though they hated each other, and Mario gave them kudos for doing that part of the show exceedingly well. Down the hall, Vince Devore leaned against a locker, pretending disinterest. Another good actor.

Mario admired the grace and elegance of Ben's style as he sidestepped, spun, and punched. His muscles bunched and flowed, his fine-featured, scowling face flushed red, and his shock of bright hair bobbed and shook. Now, there was an opponent worthy of Mario himself, as so few opponents were. He paused a moment longer just to enjoy the show before wading in to stop the fight.

"Hey, Lancaster! Shouldn't you be ashamed of beating up on someone half your size?" he called out, and had the pleasure of seeing Ben's face flush even further with embarrassment.

"Shut up, Fonseca." Breathing hard, Ben spun so fast Mario almost didn't block his first blow. Mario grinned with fierce joy and returned a volley of punches. Keisha gasped for breath, hands on her thighs, watching from the sidelines.

Mario's grin widened. Ben would soon have to pretend to be defeated and slink away. He'd be damned if he let the guy pretend. He was going to enjoy pounding his rival into the ground. He moved into a near clinch and delivered a powerful jab to Ben's lower abdomen. Ben's breath was knocked out of him, but he still managed to jump back, raising his fists immediately to block the next blow.

"Stop!"

Mario looked up. A teacher was coming at them from the other end of the hall.

"Knock it off!" he yelled. "No fighting!"

Shit. That was way too quick. You'd think Ben and Keisha could have planned it better.

Both he and Ben stopped immediately with the ease of long practice avoiding school staff. Ben melted into the crowd in one direction, and Mario faded back in the other, carefully timing it so that he would be shoved close to Keisha.

"Nice moves, Fonseca." She rubbed the back of her hand over her face and grinned through a split lip.

"Thanks," he said with a swagger. "That asshole giving you trouble, Huston?"

"Nothing I can't handle," she said. "The dickhead was accusing me of trying to deal drugs, can you believe it?"

Mario's jaw dropped in mock dismay. "Really? Lancaster's such an uptight dumbass. He should know better than that." He grinned wickedly at her. "Only Tenebras has the right to deal on this campus. And that ain't you."

She glanced over her shoulder and lowered her voice. "Not that I wouldn't mind getting into some of that action. I could use the dough."

"Fuck, I dunno anything about that."

At his locker, he twirled his combination. Keisha followed him and stood at his elbow, large dark eyes cocky. "Hey, big guy," she began.

He spun and grabbed her by the collar. "Shut up, dumbass. You don't wanna call me that."

Her eyes widened and he was gratified to see her swallow. It was good to be feared. That was how it was gonna be from now on. Satisfaction bubbled in his chest. "Sorry! I'm sorry, Fonseca!" He let her go and she staggered. Her voice humbled. "I just—well, everyone says you're the man to see if someone wants anything around this school."

"What's that supposed to mean, bitch?" he said, slamming his locker shut.

Keisha drew closer, lowered her voice further. "Everyone says you're a member."

Mario snorted and chugged down the hall. Keisha tagged along behind. "You look too smart to believe what everyone says."

"Fonseca," Keisha pleaded, "I really need money. Couldn't I get in on it? I'd make a good courier because of my size—no one suspects a little girl. And you know I can fight."

"Yeah," he admitted. "You can fight." His face split in a grin. "You sure stomped that son of a bitch Lancaster."

She grinned back. "Bet he didn't like his ass getting kicked by a girl half his size."

He pretended to consider. "All right, Huston. I'll think about it."

"Thanks! You won't regret it, I swear."

Mario walked away, thinking of what he would report later that afternoon.

Yeah, I won't regret it. But you will. Schwartz will be ready. Adrian's left himself wide open with this one, thinking I'm playing his game to lure you in. He's going down hard. And you, Keisha the cop, are just going to be collateral damage.

 *Elisa*

Elisa placed the glassine star on top of her small Christmas tree and stood back to eye it critically, for a moment caught by the glittering, blurred reflections of light through its wavy panes. She always decorated a miniature tree every year, just as she and Carlos used to do back when he was still around. It always made her sad, and this year was worse than usual.

She would be alone again this year, as she almost always was at Christmas. Her mother was rarely home during the season, and Elisa had become accustomed to celebrating the holiday alone. But this year she had hoped, for once, that she would be able to spend it with someone she loved.

"I'm terribly sorry to have to appear to distance myself from you, Elisa," Adrian had said. "But you yourself asked me to leave Tenebras. If I don't plan my departure carefully, they will kill me."

Yes. It was her fault. She had asked him to leave the gang, and in her heart she knew it would be dangerous. Should she have asked him to risk his life?

She firmed her lips. Yes. She couldn't live with the activities he was involved in. Even though she hadn't dared to ask him point-blank if Tenebras was paying him for drug synthesis, it was clear he was doing terrible things.

He had to stop.

But the thought of what they might do to him—it was the most horrible thing she could imagine.

Part of her wanted to grab him and say, "I don't care what you do, as long as you stay safe. As long as you do whatever it takes to stay alive. Because more than anything else, I couldn't live if you were dead."

This must be the shadow the fortuneteller had warned her about. The terrible dilemma.

"I'll have to spend the winter vacation laying the groundwork for my retirement from Tenebras," Adrian had continued. "I'm sorry I won't be with you, but it's the best opportunity to finish things up cleanly and safely."

She nodded, biting her lip. He took her hand. "But don't worry. When this is all over we'll be together again, and I'll be free, just as you wished."

"Yes," she whispered. "I understand, Adrian. It's for the best. But—" She raised her eyes to his. "Please be careful."

"Don't worry. I have everything all planned out. We'll both be safe, as long as you stick with the precautions I've laid out for you."

With his words, her heart chilled further. It hadn't even occurred to her that she herself might be in danger from the gang. But of course there was risk, now that everyone in Tenebras knew about her.

So she was spending most of the holiday holed up in her small apartment. What would Carlos say if he knew she was in hiding because she was dating a gang member? He would shake his head.

"I'm so disappointed in you, Elisa. How low can you go?"

"But I thought he was the kind of person you'd want for me. A model citizen, straight-A student."

Carlos scolded, "No, you found that dark side of him thrilling. You must've known, from your very first date at the fair, that something wasn't right. But you kept on. Just like Mother. You even slept with him! And after everything you promised me."

"I'm sorry, Carlos. I'm sorry I couldn't keep my promises."

"You're going to be even sorrier."

The branches of the little pine left long red scratches on her arms as she pulled away, and all the lights on the tree blurred as she blinked away tears.

25

 *Holman*

HOLMAN WHISTLED TUNELESSLY between his teeth as he pipetted liquid into a large test tube clamped over a Bunsen burner. He made a notation in the dog-eared lab notebook on the bench beside him. The latest experiment was yielding excellent results. If it continued on this way, he was definitely going to be making a name for himself in the world of biochemistry. He made another observation of the liquid in the test tube and noted it.

He yawned, rubbed the back of his neck, and glanced at his watch. It was quite late. The development of Rapture had ended up being extremely lucrative, but the long hours required for his extra-legal activities on top of his job as chief scientist at Schwartz Pharmaceuticals were exhausting. But his work was vital to Schwartz, providing desperately needed funds to the company.

The drug had all sorts of fascinating effects on the human body. He was opening up an entirely new line of biochemistry research. Certain parts of the earlier work in the development of Rapture looked as if they might lead to the discovery of a new type of anti-depressant. If only he had time to delve more deeply into that area of research. Luckily, his student intern, Adrian, was surprisingly good. Still, Holman didn't want to let him know how important his results actually were, because then the kid might start getting the idea that *he* was the genius.

And that wouldn't do. No, that wouldn't do at all. The revolution in anti-depressants would be led by the brilliant, the famous Eric Holman.

Soon he would publish certain whitewashed results with himself as first author. Then all those snotty universities that had turned down his job applications, saying his work was "too business-oriented," would listen. At last, they would appoint him to that distinguished faculty position he had long coveted. Finally, he would get the respect he deserved.

But there were still obstacles in his path to greatness. Holman frowned. He needed more human subjects. Animal experiments just hadn't provided the results he required. It was regrettable that the last group of human subjects hadn't survived long. He hadn't been able to observe the changes in brain chemistry he needed. It was too bad he couldn't involve the student interns in that work; he could have used Adrian's insight. He would tell Schwartz soon that they needed to send Fonseca out on another collection run.

The soundproofed lab in the back had already been emptied of the previously failed subjects. Fonseca had been quite helpful there too.

He would need at least a dozen. Fonseca charged an exorbitant amount to round up a few homeless people cluttering the downtown Rockton alleys. Hopefully Schwartz wouldn't balk at the expense.

But he also needed subjects undamaged by drink, drugs, or exposure. Fonseca had hinted he could help there too, mentioning he had his eye on a couple of healthy young specimens he could bring in soon, teenagers from the local high school. Holman had jumped at the chance, despite the much higher price tag.

Schwartz shouldn't complain about the cost. Not only was Holman synthesizing a powerful drug that was making them all rich, but he was also advancing science and helping to clean up the homeless problem. Who would miss a few impoverished teenagers in this overpopulated world? They would probably die as a result of gang violence anyway. Really, Holman was doing a service to society. He puffed out his chest.

A knock sounded on the lab door. The night security guard let his visitor into the room. Fonseca's lackey was slight and pallid, the signs of advanced Rapture addiction visible to Holman's expert eye. Bloodshot eyes, tremors, extreme pallor. Shaggy, shoulder-length, light brown hair fell in an unruly tangle over a dirty shirt collar as the kid sidled into the room, teeth bared in a rictus of a grin.

"Got a truck full of 'volunteers' out in the back parking lot for you," the kid said.

"Good." Holman looked down his nose at him. Such lack of discipline, addicting himself to such a dangerous drug. He and all the others deserved what they got. "Have them brought to loading dock C."

Time for more scientific progress.

 Elisa

Despite Elisa's worries, nothing appeared to happen, and by the time the New Year rolled around, she had almost forgotten to be afraid. She was sitting alone in her apartment late one chilly January night when someone pounded on her door. Her heart lurched. Adrian had given her strict orders not to open it without checking first.

Glancing through the peephole, she stiffened, heart thudding.

It was Kim.

What could she be doing here? Adrian had been right, Elisa thought: they were coming after her.

Kim was hunched over, one hand wrapped around her upper arm, her harsh panting audible through the wooden partition.

"Elisa," she called. Her voice was reedy and weak. "Hey, can you let me in?"

Elisa said nothing. Her mother would have insisted on calling the police. Adrian would have told her not to be foolish. Both of them would have demanded she keep the door shut.

"I know you're in there, Elisa. Please—" Kim coughed. "I'm not gonna hurt you." There was a long pause. "You're one of us now; can you please help me? I've—I've been shot."

Elisa checked the peephole. Blood was seeping out from between Kim's clenched fingers, staining her sleeve. Was it a trick?

Probably. Kim had beaten her up in the girls' bathroom all those months ago. Why should Elisa think Kim was on her side now just because she was dating a member of the gang? She was "one of them"? Ha. Likely story. Adrian had warned her to watch out. Kim didn't have her best interests at heart, he'd said.

But Elisa couldn't just leave Kim to bleed out at her front door. Hadn't she decided it was time to make her own decisions?

For most of her life, she'd followed her mother's ridiculous rules. Then, in a single moment, she tossed them all aside and devoted herself to Adrian.

But his judgment was just as severely lacking as her mother's. Yes, he'd had a hard life, but that didn't justify his poor choices. And it was because Elisa had gone along with his lousy decisions that they were stuck in this mess, that she was cringing behind a locked door, not even daring to go to the grocery store.

In hiding. In a modern city in the twenty-first century. Crazy.

Well, it was too bad. A human being was bleeding out and she was done with spending her life afraid. Fuck 'em.

She opened the door.

Kim staggered in and collapsed on the couch. "Thanks," she said, trying to grin at Elisa in her old, insouciant way, but it ended up more like a grimace of pain.

Elisa was shocked at the size of the bloodstain on her clothes, leaking out around the hand Kim kept tightly wrapped around her left arm. "What happened?"

"Goddamn bastards were chasing me; one of them winged me." She sagged with weakness. "Lotsa creeps out on the street for some reason. Dunno who or why the fuck they're after me. Been hiding out, waiting till I could come here. Knew you could help me."

"You've lost a lot of blood, and you're going to lose more. You need to go to the hospital."

"No! No hospitals." Kim slumped lower on the couch. "They'd fucking arrest my ass." Her voice sharpened. "Just lemme stay for a night."

Elisa tugged at her hair. "But I can't take care of you."

"S'easy," Kim said. "You just gotta take it out." Her eyes flickered open, then shut again. "Give you instructions."

There was no way Elisa could remove a bullet from someone's arm. "Ben! You need to go to his clinic. He could help you."

Kim opened one eye, some of her old irony returning. "You gotta be fucking kidding. Ben wouldn't do shit for me."

"The Lancaster Free Clinic doesn't turn anyone away."

"Nah." Kim slumped again, eyes closing. "They'd call the cops for sure. I'd be dead meat." Her head lolled to one side. Alarmed, Elisa put her hand on Kim's forehead. She was burning up with fever.

It didn't matter what Kim said, Elisa was going to call the hospital. But Kim grabbed her shoulder before she could get up. "No! Don't tell anyone! You'd be fucking signing my death warrant!"

"You're going to die anyway without treatment."

"S'okay. You can do it. You just need a sharp knife and some boiling water."

She wanted *Elisa* to perform an operation on her, right in her living room? Was everybody in this world nuts?

"Here's all it takes." Kim's voice started out faint but strengthened as she continued. "Boil water to sterilize the knife. Then you dig it into the wound and flip out the fucking bullet. Nothing to it." She exhaled with a racking sound Elisa realized was meant to be a laugh. "Get a bowl, something to catch the bullet in, to keep all the blood from wrecking your nice couch."

Elisa heard Carlos's voice. "Aiding and abetting a gang member? Let's see, that's ten years to life. Just call 911 instead."

Her mother said, "You're not capable of doing a job that requires that much skill. You know how stupid you are."

Adrian added, "It's probably all a trick anyway. She hates you."

That made Elisa angry.

"Shut up already! I'm not gonna let her die!"

She went to the bathroom, got scissors and a washcloth down from the shelf, and ran hot water on the towel. Returning, she found Kim slumped over, unconscious. She cut away Kim's sleeve to expose the wound and hissed in dismay. The edges of the hole were jagged and inflamed. Kim's arm was swollen, angry and red around the wound, and a discoloration had appeared around the edges. Even Elisa's untrained eye could recognize the signs of infection and blood poisoning.

She went to the kitchen and set the water boiling. She gathered her equipment, tested the keenness of her best kitchen knife, and dipped it into the water.

She laid everything out on a tray and brought it back to the couch where Kim lay, now restlessly muttering to herself.

"All right," Elisa said, her voice startling her with its firmness. "I'm going to do it now, Kim. Are you ready?"

Kim steeled herself, eyes going hard. "Ready as I'll ever be."

Carefully, Elisa washed the wound. The towel soon became soaked with blood. She wrapped a strip of cloth around Kim's bicep to stave off more bleeding and gave her another washcloth. Kim clenched it between her teeth and nodded.

Pushing up her sleeves, Elisa picked up the knife. She felt a little faint, but took a firm hold and kept it steady. She brought the knife to the wound, probed quickly, and felt it hit something hard. Kim grunted into the cloth as her eyes rolled back in her head. With a movement that surprised her with its surety, Elisa shifted the angle of the knife, dug in further and with a flip of her wrist scooped out the offending slug of metal. It clanged into the bowl along with more blood, mercifully kept from spurting thanks to the tourniquet.

Kim gasped, her eyes rolled, and she passed out. Elisa cleaned the wound with hot water and rebandaged it, her hands rock steady now, as though she had tapped into some innate source of strength.

She wiped a cool cloth over Kim's forehead. Her fever was still high, but surely she would feel better the next morning.

"Tell the Captain," Kim muttered, twisting her head back and forth.

"Shhh," Elisa said. "Be quiet now and rest."

"No!" Kim's eyes opened in a moment of lucidity. "S'important. You gotta tell the Captain that Fonseca's turned traitor." Her breath came in harsh gasps and she could hardly get out the words. "And I think Hundley too. He needs to know." Her eyes closed again and she slumped back, losing consciousness.

Elisa stared down at her in dismay. Why would Kim think Elisa had any way to contact the Captain of Tenebras? Surely the Captain would see Adrian's departure as a betrayal. But what Kim was saying sounded like a warning.

She needed to talk directly with Adrian, but his instructions had been very clear.

"Don't try to contact me under any circumstances," he had cautioned. "There will be a trace on my phone. For your own protection, I'm going to pretend to lose interest in you. That way, if there's any reaction to my departure from Tenebras, it will be deflected from you."

Elisa settled back down on her heels. What was really going on? Maybe she needed to stop blindly following Adrian's instructions and think about things more carefully. It was time to get a few questions answered.

As she rubbed her hand over her face, trying to plan her next step, another knock sounded at the door.

Elisa ran to the peephole. At the sight of the person on the other side, she threw open the door.

Adrian.

His hair was disheveled and there were shadows under his eyes, but her heart leaped and she threw herself into his arms.

"Adrian! I've missed you so much!"

"There isn't enough oxygen in the air without you either, Elisa." He held her for a long moment before gently detaching himself and closing the door. When he saw Kim, his voice became cold and hard. "What's she doing here?"

"She came to my door with a bullet wound." Elisa fluttered her hands. "I don't know what's going on, but I had to help her—"

"Elisa, what have I told you about being far too trusting?" He strode to the couch and examined the unconscious Kim, checking the bandage on her upper arm.

"What story did she feed you?" His expression was icy.

"But it was true! She'd been shot."

"Did she say who did it?"

"She was kind of delirious. She started talking about Mario and Hundley being traitors."

"I see. How interesting," he remarked, glancing at the tray piled with bloody washcloths. "It seems I'll have to talk to her after all. That bullet wound might need care," he added idly, his fingers going to the bandage. Kim stirred restlessly at his touch, moaning.

"I had to take the bullet out of her arm myself."

Adrian raised his eyebrows. "You did? Impressive. I didn't think you had any medical training."

"I don't."

He carefully unwrapped the bandage and inspected the wound. "This was a good job."

"It's still infected."

"But the swelling is going down. Did you pour alcohol on it?"

Elisa nodded.

"I left a first-aid kit in your bathroom. Why don't you get her an antibiotic?"

She had taken out the antibiotic pills earlier, not too surprised to see prescription medication in Adrian's special first-aid kit. She'd thought she'd give one to Kim when she woke up, so it only took her a few seconds to grab the pills and return to the living room. Adrian had already awakened Kim. She was shaking her head weakly when Elisa returned.

"But, Captain—" Kim said.

Captain. A cold wave washed over Elisa.

She heard Kim's words again. *Tell the Captain.*

No.

"No—" she said, her hands splayed in front of her in unconscious defense.

Adrian rose to take the medicine, smiling. "Thanks for the antibiotic. Kim was just telling me some details of the Captain's latest plans," he said smoothly. "I hope you understand that this is all confidential."

He took the medication from Elisa's boneless hand.

He was so good at lying. His cover personality as a harmless nerd was so well-crafted. He'd never seemed afraid of the gang, unlike everyone else. He'd always seemed confident they would act precisely as he expected. In the back of her mind, Elisa had known that something was off. He didn't act like someone who performed tasks or ran errands for a dangerous criminal gang.

He acted like he was in command.

She had written it off as his personality and his supreme self-confidence. No. She'd lied to herself because she hadn't wanted to admit that her boyfriend could be the leader of a murderous criminal gang.

"No," she said again.

Adrian ignored the pills in his hand. His expression reflected only mild puzzlement. "What's wrong, Elisa?" he asked gently.

"No—it can't be," she whispered.

He took her in his arms. She was stiff and shaking. "Come," he said, reassuring. "Sit down on the couch. You look like you're going to faint. I know it can be rather disconcerting to have a woman with a bullet wound end up in your living room."

She sat and leaned against him. He stroked her hair. "Shall I make you something warm, Elisa?" He let her slump against the couch. "Kim, why don't you tell us what happened while I make hot chocolate?"

Obediently, Kim struggled to a semi-reclining position as Adrian headed for the kitchen. "Okay, I was on a raid for—for the Captain. Everything's been a fucking mess lately." She took a few ragged breaths. "I already reported to Rory about Mario's meeting with this creepy guy last week. So I decided to follow him last night.

"It was dark and raining and pretty hard to see where he was going. But finally, he went inside an old building on Ninth Street. Another guy was lurking around, too, and I saw him go in the side door. It was Vince Devore." She glanced sidelong at Elisa. "You know, the narc."

Adrian said nothing as he took some mugs from the cupboard.

The pot began a warbling whistle. "I saw Hundley hanging around too. Mario's a traitor." Kim's voice was harsh. "Dunno about Hundley. I was gonna wait for Mario and the narc to come out, but then—someone fucking shot me. I never saw them." She closed her eyes. "So I ducked behind some garbage in the alley. Started feeling kinda faint, thought they'd come back to finish me off, so I snuck away to hide. When I woke up, I saw I was near Elisa's apartment. I remembered it from our previous... I mean, from—anyway, I knew it was near. I thought, hey, she's a member now, maybe she'll help." She shrugged. "Didn't have anywhere else to go."

Adrian remained outwardly calm as he poured boiling water into three mugs.

"That fucking traitor Mario is planning to k—" Kim broke off and glanced at Elisa again. "He's planning some bad shit."

Adrian returned to the living room with the mugs steaming on a tray. The rich smell of chocolate filled the room. "Kim, just because Mario spends a little time talking with a narc doesn't make him a traitor."

"Fuck," Kim whispered. "Didn't you get the report from Rory?"

"There are many possible reasons why Mario could have been doing what he's doing." Adrian handed each of the girls a mug. His voice was reasonable as he ticked off points on his fingers. "He could have been on special orders from the Captain. He could have been gathering information. He could have been trying to suborn Devore." He sipped his hot chocolate. "Kim, you're jumping to conclusions. Mario's loyalty is not in question."

Kim shook her head, confused. "No..."

"Why are you so solicitous of my welfare? Haven't you and I been at odds lately?"

"You know I've always been loyal." Her eyes slid over to Elisa. "Loyal to Tenebras, that is. Uh, we both are." She lowered her mug.

Adrian took it as she slumped over and emitted a very loud snore.

Elisa would have laughed, but she had also become very sleepy. She yawned widely. Adrian watched her over the rim of his mug.

She lay back on the couch, closing her eyes. Adrian took the mug from her hand. He lifted her, carried her into the bedroom and gently tucked her into bed. Just like Carlos had done when she was very young. But she could no longer think coherently, and the last thing she remembered was the comforting touch of Adrian's hand, folding the blankets over her.

26

 *Adrian*

ADRIAN WATCHED Elisa lying peacefully asleep in her bed, her hair spread across the pillow, her face blessedly relaxed now, no longer filled with that soul-wrenching doubt and agony—doubt about *him*.

He turned away from her, his face twisting since no one could see it. Pain tore at him like a knife, as though his chest had been cut open and his blood turned to acid. It had finally become real to him: he might lose her, and it was agony.

Slipping Ambien into both of their drinks had been overkill, rather inelegant of him. But when he had seen the shock in Elisa's eyes after Kim made that clumsy slip in front of her, he had, uncharacteristically, panicked. He had only wanted to get Kim, the blundering idiot, away from Elisa by any means possible, without damaging himself in her eyes any further.

He had planned to reveal the truth to Elisa, but not so soon, and not so abruptly. Now everything involving Elisa was spinning out of control, ironically, just as his other plans were going so well. He wasn't used to having things go so far awry. He wasn't used to having to deal with… feelings. He had always thought he was a rational being.

How could he have been so wrong?

So wrong about so many things.

It was hard to believe, but Elisa had forgiven Kim—had forgiven someone who had clearly wronged her. In his world of revenge, justice, and retribution, such a thing was unthinkable. Foolish. Insanely naïve.

And yet... he could see it in Kim's eyes. Whatever hatred she had once borne in her heart toward Elisa had dissolved. She had become, against all odds, a friend.

He went back to the other room, took out his cell phone. He made a call, gave the order to have Kim taken to headquarters and kept locked up for safety. He would decide what to do with her later.

He returned to Elisa's bedroom and sat down beside her. And there, where no one could see, he dropped his head into his hands.

Elisa's lips were gently parted, her lashes brushing her cheeks. Adrian knew how she would react when she finally admitted to herself that he was the Captain of Tenebras.

If he were a good man, he thought bitterly, a decent and good man, he would let Elisa go. She clearly deserved someone far better than him. Someone who wouldn't expose her to danger, someone who wouldn't threaten her values, someone who wasn't hard and cold, and yes, evil, like him. All the love, all the goodness, all the things that mattered had been burned out of him. He was eighteen and all used up.

He had done it to himself.

She deserved a good man who could love her the way she needed to be loved.

He should walk away. For her sake. Make it utterly clear to her and everyone else that he was done with her. Make the pretend distance real.

Take up with someone else.

But even as he thought it his mind rejected the idea violently. Take up with someone else? There would never be anyone else. He couldn't even pretend with anyone else. Ever. How could he have imitation sex with anyone now that he had tasted the real thing? Now that he knew the kind of love that went bone deep. Soul deep.

The pull toward another human being that slammed into you, took you over with a force more fundamental than gravity.

If she left him, everything would shut down. The moment she was gone, there would no longer be any direction, any sense, any foundation to his life. His heart would beat a meaningless rhythm until it inevitably ground to a stop. He would spend what little time he had left making up for the evil he had done on this earth. It was a debt that was far too great to pay, but he would do what he could.

And then… he would find a way to die the death he deserved.

If he were a good man, he would accept that fate and leave Elisa to a better one.

But…

But he was not a good man.

He stretched out on the bed full-length, facing her as she slept. He ran his hands through her warm, silky hair, stroked her cheeks gently with his thumbs. She half-turned into his touch, murmuring. He thought he heard his name on her lips, and he leaned forward to kiss them gently. They were soft, soft and warm, alive and vibrant. Life-giving.

No. Giving up was not an option. He would do whatever it took to earn her love.

Even if it meant playing by her rules.

Even if it meant giving up everything for her.

He would change his plans. At least, he could count on one person who was utterly loyal.

He took out his phone. "There's something urgent I need to do at the lab. In the meantime, I have another task for you, Rory."

 *Jim*

Jim Holman stared at the open file on the lab computer, his heart thumping. He had just been playing around, pretending he was the infamous hacker Anonymous Jim, breaking into major computer systems around the globe. He'd tried a few of his uncle's old passwords, which he had found in his desk drawer, and had thought it might be fun to put one over on the old man. But as the text scrolled past his eyes, he broke into a sweat. If this was what it looked like, the old man was not the person he thought he knew.

Jim swallowed, trying to decide what to do. This was something bigger than he was used to handling. He frowned. Mr. Schwartz had been giving him a hard time about slacking off at work. Why, the hypocrite! If Jim was right about what was going on here, his uncle and Mr. Schwartz were involved in some big time criminal activity.

Jim closed his eyes. He remembered a conversation in the break room a few months ago. It now made so much more sense. Mr. Schwartz had complained that finances were bad, and had announced that he might have to "follow in DeLorean's footsteps." There had been general laughter from the other adults, including Uncle Eric.

When Jim had demanded an explanation, Uncle Eric, after much laughter, had finally said that John DeLorean was the founder of an auto manufacturer a few decades ago who had run into financial trouble while designing an innovative car he thought would take the world by storm.

"Yeah," added Mr. Schwartz, grinning. "He made a car that was so fast, it could really *suck up the white line.*" Everybody else broke up into helpless laughter. Annoyed, Jim had demanded that they share the joke.

Uncle Eric scratched his head. "They say that DeLorean entered into a drug deal, trying to move a large shipment of cocaine in order to get quick cash to shore up his floundering car company."

"You're not serious!" Jim demanded, and the adults had exchanged glances.

"No, of course not, Jim," said Mr. Schwartz. "DeLorean ended up in jail."

"And his car was a piece of shit," added Uncle Eric with a snort.

Jim had almost forgotten the discussion, writing it off as another of those old-timer in-jokes the adults seemed overly fond of. Recalling the conversation once again, his heart hammered. He stared at the chemical formulas scrolling across his screen. He needed to talk to someone. But who? Not Uncle Eric, not the cops. He didn't want to get himself or his uncle in trouble. Then he thought of his sister. He and Mira were constantly at each other's throats, but when the chips were down, there was no one he could count on more. He yanked his cell phone out of his pocket.

"Breaking news, Mira!" he stage-whispered when she answered. "Come to the second-floor computer lab. I've got a life-or-death hack I need to show you."

 ## Adrian

Adrian glanced at the lab clock. 4 AM. He rubbed the back of his hand over his forehead. His eyes were starting to blur. He'd been running tests for hours, comparing the results of his molecular simulations on the computer with the results in his test tubes. Nothing yet.

The door banged open, and Schwartz entered.

"Working late, Adrian?" Schwartz smiled with a thin veneer of benevolence. "I'm so glad to see our student interns being so enthusiastic."

"I'm just following up on that line of research you asked me to take, to enhance the addictive potential of Rapture."

Schwartz rubbed his hands together. "Good, good. Any results?"

"Not yet."

"I'd recommend hurrying up. As long as you keep doing what you're doing, you and everyone else will be safe."

Adrian clenched his fists. "I don't think so. It's worse than anything I expected. I've found signs that there's an unpredictable environmental factor that, when combined with Rapture, is more deadly than we thought. Even the slightest trace can then cause cellular degeneration at the telomere level. It means that everyone who's handled Rapture is at risk. Not just the people who've taken it internally. Trace amounts on the skin could be enough to trigger this response."

"Oh, come now, my boy. It can't be that bad. I'm sure you're exaggerating."

Adrian shot him a level glance. "Do *you* want to take that risk? You've been exposed as well."

"And I feel fine, my boy." He chuckled, revealing yellowed teeth. "Keep on with what you're doing. Soon I'll have exactly what I need."

Adrian's face twisted with curiosity and frustration. "Which is what?"

Schwartz laughed. "You have no need to know. Besides, do you really want that on your conscience? You're the one who invented Rapture, after all. Just remember, do as you're told, and you and your... associates, will prosper and profit."

Then his joviality dropped away from him like the stroke of a knife.

"Fail, and you will all die."

 ## Jim

"See?" Jim pointed out the next file to Mira. She sat beside him on a lab stool as they huddled over the computer screen. Her brows were drawn down, and she tugged absently at her pink-and-white t-shirt as she read.

"I don't know, Jim."

"Look," said Jim, much more confident now in the presence of his sister. "It's clear from this file that Uncle Eric and Mr. Schwartz are working together to make some illegal drug. And they're working with that dork Adrian. You can see all the evidence here in black and white!"

"I don't know," she repeated, twisting the end of one of her pigtails around a finger. "What are we going to do? Is Uncle going to be arrested? Do you really want to get Uncle in trouble? And Mr. Schwartz?"

"You're right," he said, pounding his fist decisively into his open palm. "We don't have enough to talk to the police or to Uncle. We need to do more research. Gather sufficient evidence. Like detectives, or private eyes," he said, warming to his subject. "Here's what we do," he said. "We tail them!" He could already see himself sneaking around behind the nefarious suspects. He just needed to get the appropriate clothing for his new career. A trenchcoat?

But Mira was aghast. "Tail them? What if we get caught?"

Jim waved one hand dismissively. "Aw, Uncle would never hurt us, Mira."

"If he's involved with a drug deal," she pointed out, "he's dealing with people who wouldn't hesitate to kill a couple of kids who poked their noses into the wrong place."

"Naw." Jim was sure of himself now. A trenchcoat wouldn't be dashing enough. How about a fedora? "Uncle would keep them under control. Look, it seems that Adrian Salas is their link to the gang at Rockton High. Now, does that guy look dangerous to you?" He put his hands on his hips, tilting his head at what he imagined would be the right angle if he had some rakish headgear.

"No," she said, pursing her lips. "He just seems like a bit of a nerd." Then her mouth firmed. "But if he's working with a gang, then he's our enemy. We've got to defeat him."

"That's the spirit," said Jim with satisfaction. A fedora it was. "We'll tail Adrian when he leaves the building after work, find out what he's up to."

 ## Elisa

Elisa pulled her books from her locker in a daze that had persisted since yesterday morning. She had awakened, groggy and sluggish, to an empty apartment and a note from Adrian saying he would make sure Kim received proper treatment. She hadn't been able to contact him since then.

She still couldn't believe it.

He couldn't be the Captain. Not Adrian. She needed to talk to him.

"Hey, Elisa!" Sumiko's voice rose over the hubbub. "What's up?"

Elisa pasted a smile on her face. "Not much. Just waiting on my early action college admissions. How's things with you?" She was getting a lot better at pretending on a moment's notice.

Sumiko shrugged. "I haven't seen Adrian around much. He's not sick, is he? Did you give him that terrible flu you got over December break?"

"He's been visiting colleges. I haven't seen him much either."

Sumiko's eyes pierced her. "There's nothing wrong between the two of you, is there?"

Damn Sumiko. She was far too perceptive. What could Elisa say? *Oh, nothing's wrong, really, other than just finding out that Adrian might be a drug lord and murderer?*

No. It couldn't be.

"Sumiko, how much of what you told me about Tenebras is really true? I mean about all the killing."

Sumiko laughed. "Aaand she changes the subject."

"I was just worried. I heard gunshots outside my apartment a couple days ago."

Her brows lowered. "I hope you've stopped doing your laundry at midnight, Elisa. You need to be more careful."

"Are you going to answer my question?"

"What question?" Chloe strolled up to them, eating a cupcake. She licked icing off her fingers.

"Did you bring any for us?" Sumiko folded her arms.

Chloe grinned and waved an Apricot Apron bag. "You're in luck."

"Ooh, our carrot raisin cupcakes are my favorite." Elisa's mouth watered. "You know, Mrs. Rojas changed the recipe to use all my suggestions."

"Mmmm," Chloe said. "Well, whatever you did, it's delicious."

Sumiko groaned. "Don't encourage her, Chloe, or she's going to start nerding out about chemistry in cooking or how eggs are an efficient binder for methyl cellulose or something."

Elisa frowned. Sumiko was talking nonsense. And she wasn't *too* much of a cooking nerd, was she? Although, at lunch the day before she *had* gone on and on about the amazing properties of eggs.

"Okay, then, what were you talking about?" Chloe asked.

"How many of those wild rumors you were spouting about Tenebras last fall were true? Are there really mass murderers in our school?"

"Oh." Chloe's lips tightened. "I don't really know. People say all sorts of things. I guess most of that stuff was kind of exaggerated." She crumpled up the paper bag and stuffed it in her backpack. "I gotta go to class." She headed off.

"See?" Sumiko said. "Chloe knows all the gossip and she's not worried."

Elisa wrinkled her forehead. It sounded a lot more like someone had been telling Chloe to keep quiet.

Was she getting too cynical and suspicious?

The bell rang, and Sumiko ran off to class. Elisa was late again, but she couldn't bring herself to care too much about her attendance record these days.

She slammed her locker shut and almost ran straight into Mario, standing right behind her.

"Sorry!" Elisa's muscles tensed, ready for flight.

He blocked her with his arm, a disturbing smile on his face. "No need to apologize, Elisa, especially since we're *such* close friends." He brought his face near to hers, and she shuddered. "I got something important to tell you." His breath reeked of cigarettes and rotten meat, and she tried not to wince.

He leaned in further and she held her breath. "There's something about your boyfriend you should know."

Elisa's heart banged against her chest. "What?"

"Nah, I won't tell you." He held up a hand to forestall her protest. "'Cause you won't believe me. Better show you directly."

She gaped at him, unable to say a word.

He leaned in again, whispering. "Go to the basement, room B13, at two o'clock. There's gonna be a meeting. You might find out something interesting." With a final careless smirk, he walked away.

She stared after him. Mario was a dangerous bastard. She knew better than to trust him. Kim had said he was a traitor, but Adrian had dismissed the suspicion. Elisa gritted her teeth. She had to admit she was terrified.

But so what if it was a trap? She could take care of herself. Hadn't Adrian himself taught her self-defense?

And where the fuck was he?

She jammed her book into her backpack and decided to follow up on Mario's tip.

 *Keisha*

Keisha paused at the dark doorway and pushed away another wave of dizziness. This was it: her chance to infiltrate Tenebras. It was all up to her and her wits now; she was going completely unarmed into the heart of gang territory.

She had asked Mario, "So what do you think? Can you get me in?"

Mario hemmed a bit. "I can get you an interview, but after that, it'll be up to you. Sure you wanna do this? Captain decides against you, you'll be killed right then and there."

"I'm sure. Just tell me when."

She strode into the shadowed room. A student was sitting in the darkness at one end, and Keisha could not see his face.

Coming closer, her jaw dropped in shock.

It was Mario.

"You!" she cried.

He lounged in the chair, sporting a wide grin that showed most of his teeth. "Yep, it was me all along. Fooled ya, didn't I?"

Keisha gritted her teeth as a wave of disgust ran through her, but she kept her face impassive. "Yes, Captain, you fooled all of us."

He sneered and cocked his head at her. "So tell me, why should I let a little girl like you join us? We value strength and power. Got no room for a girl who's gonna need to put on lipstick or fix her hair every few minutes."

Keisha glared. "I don't care who the fuck you think you are, you bastard, but I'm no *little girl*. I can fight better than most of your men and can probably lick you too," she spat. "Just give me a chance to prove it." Fists on her hips, she stared straight into his eyes, level with hers even though he was sitting.

There was a long silence. She stood her ground, defiant.

Then his grin widened. "So, the midget has spunk. Maybe you might be useful to us after all." The grin dropped away. "You got one chance. Your first assignment'll be given to you later this week. If you succeed, you move to the next step in the initiation." He grinned again. "Fail, and you'll be made a plaything for the Blades. Not that that wouldn't be fun too."

Keisha's defiant glare did not falter. "I won't fail."

"Good. We're always in need of competent members." He lifted a hand and gazed idly at his fingernails. "For some reason, too many of them keep dying on us." His sneer widened. "You're dismissed."

 Jim

"Shhh!" Jim cautioned, sidling into the company parking lot as Mira shadowed him silently. He wore an old fedora and mirrored sunglasses. "And here's the world-famous hard-boiled detective, Sneaky Jim, in 'The Case of the Deadly Nerd,'" he announced. Mira rolled her eyes.

Although all the snow had melted, the air was still chilly. A high overcast of eggshell white hung over the city. A bright yellow sports car sat by itself in one corner of the lot. Jim continued his dialogue in an undertone. "Sneaky Jim was all over the nerd's car like newsprint on day-old fish."

Mira's nostrils flared.

Jim adjusted his fedora, ducking and creeping from car to car as Mira trailed along behind him. "The criminal's sports car stood out like a sore thumb in a barrel of bad apples."

Mira choked. "You really need to work on your dialogue," she whispered. "Be serious! We could get into real trouble."

Jim tried the door handle and crowed. "Success! Jerk forgot to lock his car." He preened. "Maybe I do have a future as a private detective."

"Shhh!" It was Mira's turn to hush him.

He took a moment to glare at her before carefully sliding into the tiny slot behind the passenger seat. He grunted. "It's a good thing we're pretty small. Ouch!" he complained as Mira folded herself on top of him. It was even colder inside the car than out in the open air, and the chilled leather of the seat made him shiver. "Geez, fatso, you really need to go on a diet. And here I thought you were good at hide and seek."

The two of them waited in silence, crammed on top of each other. Adrian had been speaking with Uncle Eric about the final tasks of the day. He should get to his car any moment now.

Footsteps approached, and Jim and Mira almost stopped breathing. Someone opened the car door and slid into the driver's seat. From where Mira was lying, she could just barely catch a glimpse of thick brown hair. The driver started the car and drove off, accelerating and decelerating rapidly as he maneuvered through the city streets. Mira was thrown on top of Jim several times and barely managed to keep from grunting each time. One of his elbows poked into her ribs painfully.

Finally, after what seemed like forever, the car slowed down and pulled into a parking spot. After the driver's footsteps had faded away, Mira poked her head up, only to be yanked down by her brother. "Get down!" he hissed. Then he, too, poked up his head. "We're at school!" he whispered. "Adrian's heading to the back door. Let's go!"

 ## Keisha

In the basement room, Keisha assembled her team for a last-minute briefing. One of the bare light bulbs had burnt out, making the low-ceilinged room even gloomier. The furnace clanked in the background, casting a dull reddish glow over the faces surrounding her.

Mario had given her the room's key for her mission. It would be empty for the next two hours.

It should be enough, she calculated, for her to bring the first stage to completion. She checked out her participants.

Vince scowled, the picture of a murderous brute. Adrian stood quietly in a corner, looking exactly like the mild, ineffectual scholar he was. Hopefully, he could act the part she had assigned him. At least he had a good memory and was reliable. He didn't need to be the world's best actor to fool people. He had brought in two other students to help. Keisha had shrugged. She had already gone so far off the rulebook it didn't matter. Rory Fong leaned casually against the basement wall, fine dark hair hanging in his eyes, acting as though he belonged in this grim place.

Keisha's glance flicked to Cesar Peralta, standing in the corner, his lips pressed tightly together. He had said not a word during her explanation, appearing almost disgusted by the whole procedure. But when she had quizzed him on his lines and role in the operation, he had recited it all back to her letter-perfect.

"Right," Keisha said, "does anybody have any final questions?" There were none. She nodded. "Good, then everybody please take your places. Now we wait."

 ## Elisa

Elisa walked slowly down the long, dark hall at the far end of the school. Most of the ceiling lights in this part of the building were broken, and shattered glass piled up against the walls. The fluorescents sputtered over markings and dirt on the walls and floor. She rarely visited this part of the building. Her heart pounded as she passed the graffiti scrawled on one of the walls: three concentric diamonds, Tenebras's symbol.

She remembered Mario's warning; it now seemed so long ago. "See that mark? That means it's Tenebras territory and you should stay out. We own this school. You stay out of our way, you'll be okay. But if you cross us—" He drew his finger across his throat. "Get it?"

Was Adrian really the Captain of Tenebras, a monster who would kill people who crossed him? No, he couldn't be.

She rounded the corner. At the end of the hall, in the flickering light, Cesar stood in front of the double iron doors leading to the basement, braids hanging below his shoulders and over his powerful arms.

He stepped in front of the door, blocking her entrance. "You can't go in there."

Elisa wet her dry lips. "Please," she said. At Cesar's blank stare, she gathered up her resolve and lied again. She was doing it so often these days; she must be getting better at it. "Adrian told me to come. I'm just following his orders. You know who I am, right?" If Adrian truly had power in the gang, Cesar would let her in.

He eyed her for a few long moments, but finally swung the door open. "Go ahead," he said, eyes flicking away from her.

She nodded her thanks and slipped inside. As she made her way down the stairs, voices rose from below. She stopped short on the landing. In the room below, a few people stood in a rough semi-circle around a slight figure with her head bowed: the new girl, Keisha Huston. Rory leaned on the back wall. But Elisa's gaze was drawn to the far end of the room, where a black armchair sat upon a raised platform. Lounging in the chair, completely relaxed, sat Adrian. The faint light reflected off his glasses.

Elisa crept closer to listen.

27

⚖ Keisha

THE ONLY NOISE IN THE BASEMENT room was the slight shuffling of feet as the group took up their positions. Keisha stood in the center, near the furnace. Vince leaned against a wall, cleaning his nails with a switchblade. Adrian sat in the armchair at the end of the room, his chin propped on his knuckles. Rory waited silently at the far wall, arms folded. Cesar stood upstairs at the main entrance. The back door had been left unlocked and unguarded for Jim and Mira to sneak in.

It was crazy doing this with civilians, but Keisha didn't have any choice. With the department's budget cuts, they had been outsourcing manpower more and more. Even the department copywriter had been downsized. Keisha had had to write the dialogue herself. She wasn't much of an author, and she suspected the lines sounded kind of hackneyed, but at least the students had been downright eager to help her out. She pushed down her momentary twinge of conscience by telling herself that it was unlikely that any violence would occur at this stage of the operation.

They waited. No one spoke as the long minutes went by. Then they heard stealthy footsteps creeping up from the back entrance.

It was their cue. Keisha nodded at Vince to begin.

"Got the latest shipment from Schwartz. He said that Holman was getting sloppy and almost had an accident in the lab. He sounded angry, but then he demanded more money."

Adrian leaned forward and said, "That doesn't sound too good. Rory, have you tested the shipment yet?"

"The quality of the latest batch isn't up to par." Rory snapped his blade shut. "I think it's time we eliminated Schwartz and Holman. We have the formula, and they're not useful anymore."

Keisha said, "Now wait a minute. I agreed to work for you only because you promised there wouldn't be any killing involved. I don't want to be involved in murder."

There was another soft shuffle of footsteps, this time from the stairs leading down from the main door. The faint sound was almost drowned out by Keisha's voice.

Adrian said, "So, you no longer wish to be a courier for me, Keisha?" He shifted in his seat. "In that case, you're no longer of any use to me. Kill her, Rory."

"Aww, not my new bestie," Rory ad-libbed mockingly. He moved forward, knife ready.

 Adrian

There was a faint gasp from above, and Adrian glanced up at the sound. Silhouetted halfway down the steps, Elisa stood frozen in mid-step.

Without a second of hesitation, Adrian jumped from his chair and dashed up the stairs. "Elisa, what are you doing here?"

She stuttered, but nothing coherent came out of her mouth. Adrian steered her up the stairs, his lips in a stern line and a hand in the middle of her back. Elisa twisted and tried to see what was going on behind them, but he pushed her forward.

Before she could protest, they were out the door. Adrian's gaze fell upon Cesar.

"Cesar," he said, his voice heavy with menace, "I thought you were guarding the door."

Cesar paled. "I—I'm so sorry. Please forgive me."

Elisa flinched. "Adrian," she asked, her voice squeaking, "you weren't really ordering Rory to kill Keisha, were you?"

"Of course not. Nothing there was as it seems." He ran his hand through her hair and brought his lips close to her ear. "You surely don't think I would do anything like that, do you?"

"I—I don't know, Adrian. I mean—" She glanced sidelong at Cesar. "I've heard the rumors about the Captain. I couldn't believe they were about *you*, but…" Her pulse throbbed under the skin of her wrist, held loosely in his grip. He couldn't tear his eyes off the struggle in her face.

She was going to think he had still been lying to her.

Which of course he had been. Just not in the way she thought.

Adrian tightened his lips. "No, you don't understand." He lowered his voice. "I'm actually working with the police. This is an undercover sting to help stop the spread of Rapture."

Elisa stopped and stared at him. Emotions flashed across her face too fast for him to follow. Then she put her hands on her hips and glared. "Adrian, you're not up to your usual skill at lying. That's way too far-fetched."

Damn. He needed to explain. He could explain anything, but there was just no time now. He was already taking critical seconds away from Keisha's plans.

He would talk to Elisa after class; it was only a couple of hours more. Her opinions wouldn't harden in such a short time. He still had time to convince her.

After all, this time he had the truth on his side.

And the truth was what really mattered, wasn't it? After all his years of lying, now that he had finally come to value honesty, surely telling the truth would make everything come out right.

It had to.

"We'll talk about it later. But I need to get back to my part of the show, or the sting will be endangered. Cesar, escort Elisa back to class. And get someone else to stand guard at this door." His lips thinned. As Cesar steered her away, Adrian added in a low, intense voice, "I promise I'll explain everything as soon as I can."

He returned to the basement room, his emotions in turmoil, although nothing showed on his face. Fortunately, not much appeared to have happened while he was distracted by Elisa's arrival. As planned, Vince had stepped in and blocked Rory's knife. They were now engaged in a heated argument while Keisha begged to be reinstated, swearing she would continue to participate in the gang.

Adrian stepped calmly back into the fray. "Both of you," he commanded, "stop brawling at once." He glanced at Keisha. "She says she wants to continue; that's fine."

Rory stepped away from Keisha and his knife disappeared. "Whatever you say, Captain."

"Now," Adrian continued, keeping his face smooth despite the clichéd dialogue Keisha had written, "I agree with you, Rory. Schwartz and Holman have outlived their usefulness. I want you to find them tonight and finish them off. They always work late at the lab. Make it look like a robbery."

Rory nodded. "Yes, Captain."

They all listened for sounds from the back of the room where Jim and Mira were hiding. After a moment, they heard a stealthy patter of retreating feet. The two were rushing to warn their uncle and boss. Keisha nodded, a satisfied smile on her face. She signaled to her team. Officers had been stationed outside, ready to follow Jim and Mira. They would pick up the kids and get them to talk. Her plan was working perfectly.

All the while, Adrian's mind was spinning, only a fraction of his attention on the scene playing out before him. Instead, he was thinking about what he would say to Elisa.

He just wanted to finish this so he could get back to her and make it all better.

Where had it gone wrong?

It had seemed so amusing at first. Keisha had followed every clue, had snapped at every bit of bait. The police's interests lined up exactly with his planned revenge.

A few days ago, he had given her his report. She had glanced up at him with a big grin splitting her face. "Adrian, you've done it! This is exactly what we need."

"I thought you'd be pleased."

"Pleased doesn't begin to say how I feel." Keisha got up and paced around the small room. "It's time for us to move into the final act." There was a gleam in her eye. "Yes. This Jim and Mira will be our conduits to Holman and Schwartz. Now, we have to be careful to make sure we can rope them all in. Okay, here's what we need to do."

Adrian kept his face attentive and serious as she laid out her plan.

"You can get Jim and Mira to the school, right?"

"Well, I did find that kid checking out my car once." He shook his head. "But it would be pretty obvious if they were hiding in there."

Keisha waved a hand. "Just as long as you can pretend you don't notice them."

He rolled his eyes. "Sure. I'm good at pretending to be clueless."

She paced back and forth, mumbling to herself, and then sat down, pulled out a pad of paper and drew on it.

After a while, he chuckled. "Are those cats you're drawing there?"

Keisha glowered at him. "Why is everybody a critic? I just want to make sure that we keep all the principals straight. That's what we learned in training: it's important to be aware of all the players and all their roles in the operation."

Adrian straightened his face, but his lips were still twitching. "I understand."

Keisha continued drawing. "Now—" she began, then paused and glared at Adrian.

"What?"

"I'm waiting for you to criticize my drawing skills."

"Keisha," Adrian said, smiling, "I would never be so rude."

She snorted and resumed drawing. "At least someone in this school has some manners," she muttered under her breath. She continued aloud, "I want you, me, and a couple more of us to stage a meeting in the school basement."

"The basement? It's off-limits to students."

"Leave that to me. I'll get it arranged," she promised with a dismissive sweep of her hand.

"All right," he said. She slid the pad of paper to face him. "Who are all those, uh, people?"

"These are the gang members,'" she explained. "And over here, this is you, sitting in the chair at the end of the room."

He stared at the cat with pointy ears and square glasses and tried not to laugh. "Me? What am I supposed to be doing?"

"I want you to play the gang leader."

He appeared taken aback. "Why me?"

"You're the best choice because of your knowledge of chemistry, and because you work at Schwartz Pharmaceuticals and have connections with Schwartz and Holman."

"Are you seriously expecting me to pretend to be the 'Captain' of Tenebras?" Adrian could not stop the amusement from overflowing into his voice. Then he forced himself to keep a straight face. "The man's a bloodthirsty bastard, isn't he? How could I play someone like that?"

Keisha waved her hand airily. "Haven't you watched gangster movies? I'll have a script ready for you. All you have to do is act tough and casually order a few deaths."

"I don't know."

She folded her arms. "Come on! It's the only way I'll be able to get a warrant sworn out for Schwartz Pharmaceuticals. The district judge has been really leery of me lately for some reason." She frowned. "And remember, you're only trying to fool a couple of kids. It's not like you need to win an Academy Award."

He glanced sharply at Keisha. Could this all be a trap? Could she possibly know the truth?

No. Her face was trivially easy to read. She was just another incompetent cop in over her head. Still, better to be safe.

"But it's risky for me personally. I may end up having to do something illegal. It may look like I'm actually involved with this gang or with Rapture sales. It could hurt my admission to Harvard next year."

Keisha scowled. He could hear her thoughts as though she had spoken them aloud. *What a nerd, worrying about trivial things like college acceptances when so much is at stake. But he's shown himself to be a valuable asset to our team, so I'll cut him some slack.* "Don't worry. I'll write up a document detailing your role in our plans and giving you immunity from prosecution, even if you have to skirt the law at times. Will that satisfy you?"

Adrian nodded slowly. "Yes. I can accept that."

"Good. Now here's what I want you to do."

Adrian had been so amused by the plan that he had decided to go along with it, although it was poorly thought out, and relied on a number of dubious elements with a low probability of success. It was far from the type of scheme he would use. But it would be utterly entertaining. The immunity from prosecution was the icing on the cake.

But now he shook his head. He'd been stupid to let entertainment get in the way of practicality. Just another example of how distracted he'd been.

It was ironic that Elisa would falter in her belief in him the one time he was actually working on the side of the police, doing something she would have approved.

He needed to talk to her.

His cell phone buzzed. "Captain, I've got some bad news. Can we meet?"

 ## Elisa

Elisa cut class.

After all, she'd already hung out with drug dealers and murderers. What did an hour of truancy matter?

Besides, she really couldn't concentrate on Taylor polynomials today. She ran straight home, slammed her apartment door, and sank to the floor, face buried in her knees.

The whole time, the scene in the basement room was replaying in her head. She kept on hearing Adrian's calm, quiet voice saying, "Keisha, you're no longer of any use to me. Kill her, Rory."

No.

It couldn't be true.

She remembered Chloe's gossip at lunch that day so long ago. *"They say the Captain's been running the gang since he was twelve. They say that even though he's only a high school student, he's already lost count of the number of people he's ordered killed."*

No.

Adrian didn't kill people. He couldn't. He wasn't that sort of person.

"Kill her, Rory."

No.

"Kill her."

There was a roaring somewhere inside Elisa's head, pain like a block of ice lodged in her chest. She couldn't breathe, couldn't think.

She didn't want to think. Because if she started to, she would have to come to some conclusions.

And there were no good conclusions.

She needed to do something. She got up, sat at the dining table and sorted through the pile of junk mail.

One envelope stuck out—a large, thick white one from the Massachusetts Institute of Technology.

A fat envelope—a good sign. Elisa's heart was frozen, but still, it leaped up in her chest and pounded furiously as she tore open the flap.

"Congratulations!" it read. "You have been offered admission to the Massachusetts Institute of Technology." The professor she'd been hoping to work with wanted to meet her during an upcoming visit. A slow, distant excitement bubbled up within her. She clutched the paper, desperately, like a drowning person might clutch a life ring. Could she finally be getting some good news?

Maybe she could put all this behind her and start the rest of her life. Maybe she could just run away from Rockton, forget everyone she knew here. Forget everything that had happened.

Then she turned to the next page.

Her financial aid package. She read it through once, twice, and then three times, hoping in vain to find something she had missed.

They were basing her Expected Family Contribution on her father's salary—the salary of a man she hadn't seen in years, someone who had repeatedly refused to pay child support or contribute to their family's financial upkeep. The college was claiming she could afford to pay nearly twenty thousand dollars a year.

She had no money. She couldn't even afford to pay *two* thousand a year. Her parents wouldn't give her a dime. She couldn't go to the local state university, much less a private school. Even if she worked full-time at minimum wage in addition to going to school, her full salary before taxes wouldn't hit twenty thousand. Even if she worked overtime at the bakery this year, and saved every penny that didn't go to taxes and rent, it wouldn't be nearly enough. They wouldn't even give her loans for it, thanks to the tyranny of the EFC. And that wasn't even considering the question of whether it was a wise decision to go into debt so early in her life. She ground her teeth. She was trapped.

She would work minimum-wage jobs for the rest of her life.

"I could have been something!" her mother shouted. *Elisa cowered behind the dining table. Her mother had already thrown the casserole dish at her. It missed Elisa's head and lay splattered in a broken sticky mess behind her on the floor. "If I hadn't had to take care of you! Always crying, always dirty, always whining! It's all your fault. You're the reason I had to drop out of school. You're the reason why there's no money."*

Tears ran down Elisa's cheeks. There would never be any money.

There was no way she would ever become a biochemist, no way she would ever do the work she had always longed to do.

Unbidden, her mind returned to a conversation with Adrian, and the bitterness in his words that she remembered but hadn't really grasped at the time. "The only way out of poverty in this country is education, Elisa, and they took that away from me too. They always claim there's plenty of help for the poor in this country, but it's a lot rarer than people think."

It was ironic that she had asked him to give up his illegal sources of income just before she appreciated for the first time what that truly meant.

She finally understood, in the core of her belly, why Adrian might have made the choices he made.

If she wanted the one thing she had always dreamed of, her one chance to escape her terrible family life, to get away from the beaten track of her existence that stretched ahead of her like a narrow, dark tunnel—all she would have to do was smash her ethical compass to bits.

Oh, she could justify it. She could do great things for the world if she just had enough money to go to college.

She put her head in her hands. She could go to Adrian and explain the situation. Twenty thousand dollars was probably nothing for him, small change for the Captain of Tenebras. She shivered. He would help her.

Of course.

It would be easy.

It would make him happy. It would make her life so much simpler. So much more successful.

And they could be together.

For a moment, that cold hard knot in her chest dissolved just a little bit, and the darkness in her mind lifted just a tiny fraction at the thought that she might see him again. That she might hold him in her arms.

Her body yearned to feel his warmth pressed against her, to stand within his magic circle of protection, to hear his voice against her ear, quiver at his lips across her throat. To burn with him like a flame against the darkness.

Every single inch of her skin vibrated with longing.

But what would be the price?

She firmed her lips and sat up straight. Then she picked up the folder from the table and marched over to the plastic bin that held recycling. She took a deep breath, dropped the folder into the bin, and then went to the kitchen to chop tomatoes for dinner.

It was over.

It was all over.

The water ran in the sink and her tears ran down her cheeks.

She couldn't help imagining her next conversation with him.

"Adrian, Ben told me the police traced Rapture to Tenebras. That your gang is the only supplier."

He would shrug in that casual way. "Do you always believe whatever Ben says?"

"You know what I'm asking. Are you or are you not selling Rapture?"

There was a soft tap at the door.

It must be Adrian.

But Elisa had already made her decision. She couldn't let a murderer be part of her life.

28

 *Adrian*

THE DOOR OPENED, and Elisa stood in front of him, eyes rimmed with red, a dishtowel in her hand.

He was ready for her, his outline planned in his head. After all, wasn't persuasion one of his key strengths? He smiled his gentlest smile at her. "May I come in?"

She bit her lip and nodded jerkily. He closed the door behind him and enfolded her in his arms, pressing his lips to her forehead. She was stiff, and the skin of her wrists and hands was cold.

He took the dishtowel from her and steered her gently to the couch.

"What's wrong?" he asked, already knowing the answer.

She hunched her shoulders. "You're the Captain of Tenebras, aren't you."

"I won't lie to you anymore, Elisa." He took her hands. "But, please, let me explain. It's not like the rumors say. I—"

"You've never stopped lying to me, have you?"

"I'm not now. Please believe me." She wasn't even giving him a chance to lay out his carefully prepared facts. To tell the truth, as she wanted him to.

"Did you really—order Rory to kill Keisha?" Her voice fell to a whisper.

Annoyance rose in Adrian's throat. "I told you, that was a police sting. Keisha's still alive; didn't you see her in school today?" Why did Elisa keep harping on that clumsy playacting scene when there were so many other things that mattered more? Still, he kept his face smooth, his voice quiet. How many times had his life depended on maintaining his calm and emotionless façade?

"Don't lie to me again!" Her voice rose. "Why would the cops come to a gang leader to set up a sting?"

"I'm not lying," he said mildly. "Keisha's an undercover cop, and she doesn't know I'm involved with Tenebras. She thinks I'm a straight-A student and far too much of a nerd to be involved in anything shady." It was the absolute truth.

She rubbed an eyelid, shaking her head. "Come on."

He took out his laptop. "Here, I'll prove it to you." Surely, truth and logic would win her over. Of course, he could manipulate her emotions instead. He could bend her to his will. But he was different now. He would do things by her rules. He would show her how he had changed. He brought up the letter of immunity from the Rockton police department.

Elisa scrolled through the document. "You could easily have forged this."

Of course—that was the logical conclusion he would have come to as well. Telling the truth was such a straitjacket. Stating the absolute facts made it so difficult to explain. But Adrian was trying. He opened his eyes wide. "You don't believe me?"

"Adrian, you've lied to me so often and so well, I just don't know what to think. I find out you're the leader of a gang that terrifies everyone in the school, and right afterward I hear you ordering…" Her voice faded. "I just don't know."

He took hold of her hands, gazed at her with eyes wide and guileless. "Elisa, I swear to you, from the bottom of my heart, by my love for you, that I am telling the truth now." Why wouldn't she trust him? For perhaps the first time in his life, he was deliberately avoiding lies. It was infuriating.

She twisted away.

To be honest, to be fair, he shouldn't use their attraction for each other to influence her. But he couldn't help himself. He took her in his arms and kissed her, held her shaking body until her sobs stopped.

Elisa was holding back, and it both saddened and irritated him. He was giving her complete candor. Why did she stubbornly refuse to have faith in him? So what, after all, was the value of truth? It was overrated. Truth only led to trouble. Lies were much better, much smoother, more efficient.

It was too bad that love seemed to require honesty.

Love and trust—he had always assumed they were the emotions of weakness. Not as powerful as fear and intimidation.

But perhaps they were more complex than he had ever imagined. Perhaps he should have delved into them more deeply after all. Had he been wrong all these years?

If only he weren't so busy right now dealing with the police, arranging his plans around Rapture, and avoiding death threats from Schwartz, Holman, and Mario, he could put more attention into studying the art of these strange and foreign emotions. But Elisa had already distracted him so much. If he let it go further, both of their lives would be at risk.

"Have you really done all those things?" she whispered. "What they say the Captain has done? All those horrible, horrible crimes?" Her eyes were wide, hands twisted tightly in her lap.

His smile was its most reassuring. "Of course not. It's all for show, so I can keep control of the gang." He tilted his head to one side, as though inviting her in on the truth. "Do you think an overly intellectual nerd with a flair for manipulation and trickery has a chance of surviving an encounter with all those criminals? It's so much more effective to convince them that I'm an utterly evil, selfish bastard. Someone with an unpredictable murderous streak and a violent past a mile long. Someone who has all the authorities in his pocket." He lifted his eyebrows. She had to understand: in his world, fear was the only currency. He would have been dead long ago if he hadn't terrified them all. Of course, he had to hurt people. Surely she would understand that.

Elisa stared at him. He waited for her to speak, but it was as though she had been struck dumb.

Could he explain the power of fear to her? "They follow me because they're afraid. They cling to my confidence and strength. They don't know what I'm really like."

The words burst out of her like blood spurting from a wound. "What is the real you, Adrian? What is your true personality? Do you even know, after all the playacting, after all the roles?"

That wasn't such an easy question to answer. "The truth is, I have many facets to my personality, and I can choose which one to display at any time." He reached out, stroked Elisa's hair. She sat like a statue, as though she could not feel his touch. "In my deepest self, I detest taking life; it's such a waste. But to the Captain, life means nothing. He kills without thought, without compunction. And so the others follow him and obey his every whim, quaking in terror."

Adrian had only been a child when he had first designed the Captain's persona. A powerless child, completely at the mercy of those around him. He had waited in the shadows, observed quietly, watched as others interacted. He had planned everything so carefully. Over the years, he had built the character of the Captain, refined him, improved him. Enhanced his power. Achieved a string of unbroken successes with him. His eyes gleamed.

"You have no idea how compelling the threat of death can be. And so much less costly than actual murder. No bodies to dispose of, no cops to pay off—and it fits in so well with my image. The bodies must have been mysteriously disposed of by my extremely effective organization. The cops are all in my pay. No one dares cross me, and all because of these terrifying rumors about the Captain."

He had the power now. He *was* the Captain.

No one would hurt that child any longer.

Elisa shook her head. She sat rigid, her eyes wide and staring.

Wait. No.

He wasn't really that person.

Was he?

Adrian could see it in her eyes. He was losing her. Telling her the truth was destroying her love for him. Desperately, he tried to talk faster, tried to get her to understand. He could not lose her. He would not lose her.

"Elisa." He took her hands in his. "My knowledge of human nature tells me I could manipulate you into staying with me." He shook his head, his eyes intense. "But as a demonstration of good faith, I am being utterly honest with you instead. I'm doing exactly as you asked, simply telling you the truth."

Her smile was bitter. How many times had he manipulated her emotions, gotten her to believe whatever he wanted, spoken with such sincerity in his voice and eyes?

"I'm sorry, Adrian."

"Come with me," he said. "I promise you I'll leave all this behind. I can start a new life—with you."

"I can't live with all the things you've done."

"Can't you forgive me and allow me a fresh start? I admit that my conscience has been numb for many years. But you can bring it back. And in the meantime, I'll let you be my sense of right and wrong, as I promised. I will only do things you approve of." He gazed at her with utter sincerity.

"No. I can't tell what are lies or what are truths from you anymore. You've completely confused me. I don't know what is the real you. I don't even know if it exists."

Adrian held her close, but she sat stiffly in his arms. "I'm here. I'm real. This is real. I love you. Can't you just accept that? Can't you accept me?" His voice was soft, persuasive.

But it didn't matter anymore. Elisa had moved beyond his persuasion.

She pushed him aside and stood. "No. I'm sorry, Adrian. I don't want to drag this out any longer. We've all had to make hard choices. I just can't live with the choices you've made. That's all there is to it." A tear leaked out of one of her eyes and trailed down her cheek. "I'm sorry. But I think it would be best if you left now."

Adrian's lips parted, and he let out a long, long breath. "One part of me is telling me now to go back to my old ways, to threaten you." His nostrils flared. "I could do that, but I won't."

He stood and gave her a chaste kiss on the cheek.

"Goodbye, Elisa."

At the threshold, he paused, glanced at her.

He had always been a patient man. There were still so many lines of strategy yet to play out. These new rules had their challenges, but he could win under any rules. He always did.

It was time to work on the next part of his plan.

Then he walked out the door without looking back.

 *Rory*

"I've got something you need to hear, sir," Rory said.

The man standing in the shadows of the old parking garage sneered. He didn't say anything for a moment, and in the silence, the slow drip-drip of water falling on concrete was clearly audible. Rory shuffled his feet.

"Do you want me to play the recording?"

Schwartz waved his hand, irritated. "Go ahead."

Rory took a step forward and drew a small object from his pocket. Elisa's voice emerged from the device.

"No. I'm sorry, Adrian. I don't want to drag this out any longer. I just can't live with the choices you've made. I think it would be best if you left now." A choked sob emerged from the tiny speaker.

Schwartz raised a brow.

"I just thought you ought to know, sir, that you don't have leverage over him anymore."

Schwartz's lips twisted with annoyance. "Are you sure this is real? He's a tricky bastard."

Rory gave him a sly grin. "Definitely. I've been following them for a while and watching her stew. Yep, she's done with him."

"Ha. Who would have thought it?" Schwartz scratched his temple and paused for a moment in thought. "Then we'll go ahead with Plan B. Besides, I have another use for her anyway."

"Plan B?" asked Rory.

"You have no need to know. Go. I'm done with you." He made an irritated brushing-off motion with his hands.

Rory pocketed his device. "What use do you have for the girl?"

"You're far too curious for your own good."

Rory shrugged, smirking. "Isn't that what makes me useful to you?"

 ## Adrian

Rory darted out of the bushes. "Captain! I'm glad I caught you. We need to talk."

Adrian looked him up and down, bored. "What is it now? Not more of your 'bad news.' I already told you it was taken care of."

The expression on Rory's face didn't change, but he whispered, "We've got a real problem."

Adrian raised one eyebrow.

"Schwartz and Mario are making their move sooner than we thought. There's something going on that I don't know about. We have to figure it out—I think it's something big. Something scary."

"Don't worry, Rory. I've got it all under control."

Rory shook his head. "I think there're a few things even you don't know. I hear Schwartz promised Mario the Captain's slot for real—as soon as he gets rid of you."

Adrian scoffed. "If he thinks Mario can handle it, he's stupider than I thought."

"They seem to think you're no longer so useful. I don't know what they've learned."

Adrian raised a shoulder in dismissal. "They'll never be able to continue the synthesis without me. Not to mention the next steps in the plan."

"From what I heard, Schwartz thinks Holman made a breakthrough and they're all set. He mentioned a 'Plan B.' I heard him telling Mario to move ahead with it."

Adrian cocked his head. "Plan B?"

Rory shrugged. "No idea."

"All right. Meet me back at headquarters in two hours."

Rory's face twisted. "Wait. Did you find—"

Adrian put a hand on his shoulder. "Don't worry. We'll take care of it."

Rory examined his face carefully. Then he nodded slowly. "Okay."

 Keisha

"Vince!" Keisha rushed through the precinct door.

"The warrant?"

"We got it. I'm assembling a SWAT team now. From what those kids said, they've got high security at the lab and a boatload of explosive chemicals."

Vince shook his head. "How'd two kids—what, freshmen?— find out all the details on this drug operation? You sure it's for real?"

"One of them claims he hacked into Alfred Schwartz's computer account. Who the fuck cares? Something shady's going on at that company and if it's good enough for the judge, it's good enough for me."

Vince scratched the back of his head. "You rushed in a little too fast last time, didn't you?"

"Fuck that!" Keisha clenched her fists. "This is different. I've got evidence from Adrian as well."

"Evidence from a bunch of kids. You're on shaky ground."

"Hey, in this business you gotta take a few risks. I'm grabbing a conference room for the briefing. Are you in or out?"

He shrugged and bumped her shoulder gently. "You should know by now I always have your back, Keisha. Even if you're a crazy cat lady."

 ## Elisa

Elisa didn't want to go to school. She would have to see Adrian, and she didn't want to. She didn't want to have to deal with all the explanations to her friends, all the questions.

Slowly, she put on her school clothes and packed her backpack. Then, her feet dragging, she set off. She left later than usual to arrive just as the final bell rang. The last thing she wanted was to run into Sumiko and Chloe at their lockers.

She cut it a little too close, and had to run to make it to class on time. But she did, making it to her seat just as the bell rang. Out of breath and sweating, she tried to focus on the teacher's directions.

Although, what was the point anymore? She didn't need good grades to work in the bakery. She sighed and got out her book. It was hard to give up the habit of being a good student.

The day dragged on forever. She kept half looking out for Adrian. She dreaded going to math class because he would be there, and she would have to avoid making eye contact. But he wasn't in class. Puzzled, she got out her homework. He rarely missed math.

At lunch she passed by the table for two where she and Adrian usually sat and walked to her old table with Sumiko and Chloe.

The two girls looked up in surprise.

"What's this? You slumming today?" asked Chloe with a grin.

"Where's Adrian?" asked Sumiko.

Elisa slumped into the seat. Refusing to make eye contact, she muttered, "I don't know. We broke up yesterday."

Instantly, she could sense the concern and sympathy that she had so wanted to avoid.

"Oh, Elisa, I'm sorry." Sumiko hugged her.

Chloe's mouth hung open. "What happened? I thought you two were the perfect couple!"

"No, it just didn't work out for us."

"But why?" persisted Chloe.

"I guess..." Elisa said, pausing for a long time as she looked down at her sandwich. Could she ever tell them the truth, that Adrian was secretly the Captain of Tenebras, the most feared man in the school, a gang leader who reputedly had the blood of dozens of people on his hands, a man she had witnessed ordering a cold-blooded killing? No. That was too dangerous a secret to burden Sumiko and Chloe with.

But despite it all, she was not afraid of Adrian. She never had been. Even though she had heard all the rumors, now, about the Captain of Tenebras and his fearsome deeds, she still had feelings for him. She still longed for him to look at her with affection, to hear his deep voice murmuring that he loved her. Despite all his crimes, despite all the lies, he had truly loved her, in a way that no one had ever loved her before. Tears swam in her eyes at the magnitude of what she had lost, what she had given up. Even though she knew it was the only thing to do.

"We just wanted different things from the relationship," she said lamely. Then she stuffed a big bite of cheese sandwich into her mouth so she didn't have to talk.

At home that afternoon, her eyes still aching, Elisa listlessly washed her chopping board and plates. She heard a key turning in the lock. Surprised, she let a dish clatter in the sink. Adrian always knocked before he used his key; was he coming back?

But when the door swung open, she took a step back. It wasn't Adrian.

It was Mario Fonseca, his eyes bright and manic, pupils constricted to pinpricks.

He grinned widely. "Hey, princess, long time no see."

"What are you doing in my house?" she demanded, hands on her hips. "Get out at once."

He leered at her. "I don't think so, sweetheart. You see, there's been a coup in Tenebras. You're looking at the new Captain." He stuck his thumbs in his belt loops and smirked.

"What?" Her jaw dropped. "What happened to—the former Captain?" She wouldn't call him Adrian in front of this slimeball.

He shrugged. "Who cares?" He loomed over her. "Anyway, you're coming with me." He grabbed her arm and dragged her toward the door.

"What? Wait!" she cried, trying to dig in her heels and pull away from him.

With a shrug, he punched her in the face.

Pain exploded in Elisa's head. She lost her balance and fell over backward. Her head struck the corner of the coffee table, and everything went woozy.

Just before her consciousness faded, Mario picked her up and slung her over his shoulder. "Oh yeah, princess, you're mine now. You're gonna be my ticket to the big time."

29

 *Ben*

"WHAT DO YOU MEAN I can't come on the raid?" Ben folded his arms.

He and Keisha huddled against the school in a vain attempt to escape the icy wind. The bulb over the side door was broken, but in the weak light from a streetlamp, Keisha's face was grim and stern.

She glared at him. "You're a civilian and a high school student. Of course, you can't come on a police operation!"

"That hasn't stopped you before," Ben pointed out. "You've been using us all the time on your operations."

Keisha glanced away. "There's real danger here. No. Leave it to the professionals."

Ben balled his fists as she pivoted and left without another word. It was too late for her to get all officious. She'd already crossed too many lines.

He straightened and trotted home. The wind made his teeth and ears ache, but he scarcely noticed it. Ben slipped inside his house, heading to the back closet where he knew his dad kept a revolver. He was busy in the clinic as usual, and no one saw Ben sneaking into the room. He pulled the gun out of its slot, checked to make sure it was loaded, and tucked it in his waistband. Then he shrugged on a jacket and ran to catch the bus to Schwartz Pharmaceuticals.

 *Elisa*

Elisa's head pounded like the day her mother had slammed her against the toilet tank. Her vision wouldn't clear. All she could see were bright, fuzzy lights all around her. Fiery pain raged in both of her shoulders.

She gradually realized she was half lying on a dark green linoleum floor, and her arms were stretched above her head.

She couldn't pull them down.

The memory of Mario attacking in her apartment flooded back. Abruptly realizing she needed to wake up, now, she tugged at her hands again. She couldn't move them; her wrists hurt. She blinked her eyes and focused.

Her wrists had been secured with nylon zip ties to a metal bar attached to a long, waist-high counter.

Elisa smelled chemicals, and when she looked around, she recognized lab benches, a centrifuge, and racks of test tubes. She was in a large room lit by banks of fluorescent lights and crowded with lab equipment. No one was around.

Where was she? More importantly, how could she get away?

Ironic. Earlier this morning she'd been feeling as though her life was over just because she'd broken up with her boyfriend. Now, her life really was at risk.

Of course, this all probably had something to do with Adrian. Dating the Captain of Tenebras was dangerous.

But it had been her free choice. And now she had to deal with the consequences.

She pulled herself up to a sitting position. She had some freedom of movement if she twisted her wrists sideways. Could she reach her cell phone? But it was gone. Of course they would take it. She blinked several times, trying to get rid of the dizziness and pain.

A voice sounded behind her. "Is this one of the subjects I've been promised?" Adrenaline shot through Elisa's body, and she twisted to face the speaker.

"Yep, she's all yours. Clean, as requested." Mario stood in the doorway, leering at her. Elisa narrowed her eyes and glared.

He'd caught her off-guard in her apartment. She should have kept Adrian's self-defense training in mind at all times. He'd warned her that she should always be ready for an attack. But in her emotional funk, she hadn't kept her focus. Even if she never saw Adrian again, she wouldn't forget what he had taught her.

If she ever got out of this lab alive, that was.

An older man stood beside Mario, deep creases in his forehead and brown stains on all his fingers. He eyed Elisa with a blank, unsmiling stare that chilled her all the way down to her toes.

She gritted her teeth. She'd be damned if she'd give in to Mario and his allies.

She pushed herself to a more stable position, tugging surreptitiously at the zip ties around her wrists. Unfortunately, there wasn't an inch of give.

The man nodded irritably to Mario. "Go feed the subjects in the back room. You've been gone long enough." He slammed the door almost on Mario's back, and Elisa was alone in the lab with him.

She lifted her chin. "Who are you and what do you think you're doing?" she demanded. "Let me go at once." She was not going to show fear even though her heart was pounding so hard, she thought it would burst the buttons on her blouse.

The man snorted. "Let you go? I paid too much for you. But you should be grateful—your useless life will, at last, be of service to the greater good."

He slowly approached, holding something behind his back.

 ## Adrian

Adrian straightened up from where he'd been examining a stain on Elisa's coffee table. Rory had reported something suspicious happening around her building, so he'd gone to check on it personally. When he'd knocked on her apartment door, there had been no answer. He'd been furious to see the guard he'd set on the building had been missing. Clearly Schwartz—or someone else— had made his move.

Despite all his safeguards, all his efforts.

Had they killed her or just taken her? And where? He looked around the room one more time, his mind working frantically. He forced himself to breathe deeply. Logic was what he needed now, cold and clear logic, not blind emotion. His chest expanded and his clenched shoulders relaxed.

If they'd wanted to kill her, they wouldn't have bothered taking her. That meant they had some other plan. He'd thought he'd set things up so that Schwartz would learn that he and Elisa were no longer together. So what could have led them to arrange for her kidnapping?

His mind ticked over the various points of logic. It was all too likely a parting shot against him combined with something they needed. Why might they need Elisa? And for how long would they keep her alive?

His phone buzzed. "Yes, Rory?"

His lieutenant's voice was strained and breathless. "I missed them. Goddammit, they've got Sierra."

"All right. We'll find them. I'll pick you up."

Rory had gone to the homeless encampment downtown. It must have been Mario and his lackeys who were collecting people. And based on Adrian's research into Schwartz's and Holman's files and secret experiments, Mario could only have taken them to one place.

Schwartz Pharmaceuticals.

If Schwartz and Mario were collecting lab subjects for Holman, Elisa would be there as well. And according to what Adrian had discovered, their human subjects didn't last long after being injected with the drugs.

They only had hours. Maybe minutes.

 *Rory*

Only a few weeks ago, Adrian had approached Rory.

"I know where she is."

Rory forced nonchalance onto his face. "What?" He had to pretend not to care, not to know what it was all about. But inside, he was panicking. This must be about Sierra. How could Adrian have learned about her? How could he have found where she was when Rory had failed for years?

But most of all: what would he do to her now that he knew?

Because it was true that Rory had had disloyal thoughts. And his leader was unforgiving. He had seen evidence of that many times before.

Adrian smiled a thin, cool smile.

Rory swallowed and backed away. "I don't know what you're talking about."

"I've learned some interesting things these past few months," said Adrian casually.

"What do you mean?" asked Rory. He rubbed his palms on his jeans, the skin on his fingers cold.

"I'm proposing a deal. One that will end with both of us achieving our desires."

Rory's heart was beating fast, but he tried to appear calm. "Spill it then," he said flippantly.

"What would it be worth to you, for Sierra Mayes to be safe?"

"Who?" Rory's eyes were flat and hard.

In an instant, Adrian had him flat against the wall, elbow at his throat pressing against his jugular. Rory choked and his fingers scrabbled ineffectually at Adrian's iron grasp.

Adrian's eyes blazed. "I don't have time to play games," he said coldly. "This will be your one and only opportunity. I'm being generous in return for your past loyalty. Exceedingly generous, since I know what you've been planning. Are you ready to listen?"

He released the pressure slightly, and Rory's vision started to return. He coughed and rubbed his throat. "Yes, Captain," he rasped.

Adrian gave him a long, cool look, holding him in place almost effortlessly. Rory coughed again and dropped his eyes. "Sorry," he whispered.

"Very well. Here's my offer. I promise you Sierra Mayes's safety and my protection. In return, you give me absolute loyalty and obedience. I have a plan for you to follow. At the end of the year, if you follow it, I'll release you from Tenebras with a nest egg, new identities, and the chance to start a new life."

Rory swallowed, fingers still kneading his throat. "Why?" he squeaked. "You always told me attachments were weaknesses."

Adrian released him. "Let's just say... I've found what might be the greatest strength of all."

Rory ran out of the alley and wedged himself into the front seat of the Lotus. Adrian put the car in gear and they swung away from the curb.

"I was too late," Rory cried. "By the time I got to the homeless encampment, everyone was gone. Sierra was gone." He blinked rapidly and brushed his hair out of his eyes.

"Did you find out who was running the operation?" Adrian accelerated around a panel truck and cut in front of it. Rory was thrown back into the bucket seat.

"Two that fit the description of Mario and Lonnie."

Adrian tightened his lips. "As we suspected."

"I swear, I've been doing everything you ordered. To the letter. I thought they were all fooled. I was sure they believed I was betraying you."

"Maybe they did," Adrian mused. "It may just be a coincidence that they picked up Sierra today." He glanced at Rory. "I found some documentation at the company that shows they've been conducting human experiments for a while. Using them to test new variants of Rapture."

He nodded at his cell phone clamped in a dashboard holder. "There's a secured section of the lab I've been meaning to access. But there isn't a lot of time." A glowing dot shimmered on a map display.

Rory's fists clenched. "We've got to get her out."

"We're getting them all out," Adrian said. He shot through a yellow light and accelerated around a line of traffic. "I'm taking Schwartz Pharmaceuticals down."

"How can we get inside the building? I thought they had some really high tech security."

Adrian smiled tightly. "They do. But as it happens, they have a rather technologically sophisticated enemy."

The back loading dock at Schwartz Pharmaceuticals was hidden behind high walls. Adrian parked his car some distance away, and he and Rory wrapped their jackets around themselves and approached the building on foot. Adrian fiddled with a small device, fingers stiff in the icy wind. "I'm disabling the surveillance cameras on this end. We'll only have a few minutes to get in before they reactivate."

Adrian tried the knob on the back door. It clicked open, and they both paused, but no alarms sounded. They slipped inside.

This part of the lab wasn't even held to the slipshod standards of cleanliness of the front offices. Grime and dirt streaked the floors, and rusty irregular patches smudged the formerly white walls. The air stank with an old animal smell that reminded Rory of the zoo. The reek only intensified as they moved up the corridor, guns at the ready.

"About sixty more seconds until the security system reboots," Adrian murmured to Rory. He gestured toward the end of the corridor. "There's our target." Up ahead, an unmarked door with a heavy lock stood ajar.

Rory took point, his gun out, darting around the corner. Adrian followed, scanning to the rear and behind them. At Rory's intake of breath, he ran forward.

The big, low room stretching before them was dimly lit. Lopsided rows of cages were stacked to the ceiling. The animal stench intensified.

But what lay before their eyes surprised even them.

Each of the cages contained a human being.

30

 *Elisa*

THE MAN INCHED FORWARD, staring at Elisa as though she was a particularly delectable meal. She gritted her teeth and strained against the bindings.

"You'll do just fine," he said, looking her up and down. "No sign of liver damage, skin is clear, no apparent addictions. How much do you drink?"

She glared and lifted her chin. "At least eight glasses of water every day."

He threw his head back and laughed. "A sense of humor, too. What a find." He picked up a notebook, jotted down a few lines, and set it down.

He circled her, leering. "We'll see, we'll see," he said, rubbing his hands together. He vanished around a bank of equipment and came back holding a syringe.

Sweat started out on Elisa's forehead. "What's that?" she demanded.

"You'll soon find out." The man set the syringe on the table, pulled out the notebook again, and made a few quick notes. "Hmmm, how much do you weigh?"

She tossed her head. "That's one of the questions you never ask."

He chuckled. "Estimated body weight, height, age," he mumbled to himself, scribbling. "Heh heh, Alfred, so much for your Operation DeLorean. You wouldn't have gotten anywhere if it weren't for me. I am the genius here."

Alfred—that was the name of the CEO of Schwartz Pharmaceuticals. He worked with a scientist called Eric Holman. So she'd been brought to the company where Adrian had his internship. And DeLorean? What was he talking about?

She tugged again at the zip ties. She was not going to be somebody's lab experiment. Didn't fear give you unusual strength? Maybe adrenaline would help her break the straps.

Holman took the cap off the syringe and squeezed out a few drops of liquid. He approached her, baring yellowed teeth. "Now, darling, be good. It's time for your shot."

At his words, she tensed. He came closer. Her self-defense training with Adrian came back to her, crystal clear. *"Wait until they're within range, then move suddenly and precisely."*

Holman swooped in to grab her arm, and she reared back, lifting both legs, bracing herself against the lab bench, and kicked hard, straight at the hand that held the syringe.

She was slightly off target, but she hit his hand, and the needle went flying, skittering off into a corner. His face turned red with rage. "You goddamned bitch," he snarled, nursing his hand.

His tone of voice pierced her. Hadn't she been called those very same words before? They'd told her to be good, do what she was told, don't resist, be a good girl. Don't be a bitch. Girls are supposed to be good.

And by *good* they meant passive.

Someone who sat there and took whatever punishment she was given, as though she deserved it.

But she didn't deserve it. She never had.

"You stupid child," Holman spat. "Did you really think anything you do matters? I've got plenty more where that came from." He spun a table on wheels. It rattled over the floor, displaying a rack that contained several dozen hypodermics prepped and ready to go.

If she had to kick every single one of those needles out of his hand, she would.

He picked up another syringe and sidled toward her.

An alarm blared through the lab and he started. The intercom squawked, "Breach in zone 3A. Breach in zone 3A."

"Damn. That's the—" He snarled, "Don't move, bitch. I'll be back for you in less than five minutes." He dropped the needle on the table and left.

Alone in the room, Elisa frantically tugged at her restraints. It was no good.

Casting a quick glance at the door, she tugged herself a few feet along the metal bar she was lashed to. On a shelf at the far end of the lab bench stood a number of small, neatly labeled dark brown glass bottles with ground-glass stoppers. A few white plastic bottles dotted the row.

Maybe there was some acid on the shelf that could dissolve the plastic that was holding her. She deciphered the chemical formulas in her head.

HCl: hydrochloric acid. Ouch.

H_2SO_4: sulfuric acid. Double ouch.

HF: hydrofluoric acid. She shuddered. That, especially, wouldn't do any good. It could dissolve just about everything, including human flesh and bone, but not plastic. Not something she wanted to risk spilling over her wrists.

There. A polypropylene bottle at the end of the row. C_3H_6O. She read the chemical formula once, then twice, sudden hope leaping in her chest.

Acetone.

Otherwise known as nail polish remover. One of the few fluids that could dissolve plastic. And nylon zip ties.

Straining against the ties, she lifted a leg onto the bench, stretching as far as she could with her toes, aiming for the shelf. She reached toward the bottle.

It was just a little too far out of reach. She dropped her leg and leaned forward. Now her face was only a couple of inches away, but those inches might as well have been a mile for all the good it could do her. Her body just wouldn't stretch far enough. It was a physical limit, impossible to overcome.

She sagged against the bench. It was hopeless. What was she thinking?

Her mother scolded, "Look at the mess you've gotten yourself into. It's all your fault, you know. Why bother? Just sit still and let it happen to you."

Elisa bent her head and her hair fell over her face. Maybe she could just hide behind it, pretend none of this was happening.

Just like she used to do.

She sat, panting, immobile, while hopelessness and fear drenched her. There never had been any hope. She was going to die here, a victim of some crazy experiment. It was nothing more than she deserved.

Wasn't it?

The thick curtain of her hair darkened her vision and hid the room from view.

No. She didn't deserve to die. She had too much to live for.

She had a future career in biochemistry.

She had someone who loved her.

Her breath caught in her throat. Someone who loved her. While they were both alive, there was still hope.

She wasn't going to give up. She was never going to give up again.

The fluorescent lights glowed through the long auburn strands before her eyes, tracing golden lines of light from one end of her field of view to the other. It almost looked familiar.

The lines of her hair. The length of her hair.

Her hair.

She reared back as far as she could, arching her back, pulling against the ties, and then abruptly snapped her neck forward. Her long hair swung out and knocked the bottle off the shelf. It toppled over and landed with a small thunk on the laminate tabletop.

She lunged forward and captured it with her teeth. The polypropylene yielded slightly, and she tasted plastic. Twisting her head, she slowly, carefully unscrewed the top with her mouth.

The fumes hit her. She nearly gagged and dropped the bottle, but she held on until she was dizzy for lack of air and the muscles in her jaw ached. The bottle top loosened, then wobbled off.

She carefully angled her head so the bottle tipped sideways. Liquid splashed over the zip ties and across her hands, an icy cold spray over her wrists.

The acetone evaporated rapidly from her skin, chilling it further, and she tugged experimentally at the cable ties. Were they a little looser?

How many of the five minutes had gone by? It felt as if she had been there forever. How long until Holman returned?

She yanked her wrists apart with all her strength.

Yes! There was more give in the zip ties. She tried again. One piece of the plastic had softened and stretched. All that working out with weights as part of her self-defense training was paying off.

She heard a noise from the other side of one of the lab doors, and froze for a second, glancing up. Nothing. She pulled at her wrists with renewed vigor. The plastic band dug into her skin. She pulled and pulled.

It slipped free.

She took a deep breath, slid both hands out of the zip ties, and pushed herself up to standing. She rubbed her wrists.

At the far end of the lab was another door. She had no idea where it led; she only knew it was the one that Holman hadn't used to enter.

Just then, the doorknob rattled from the outside.

 ## Rory

It was the smell that hit him first. A thick, fetid, overpowering reek that was worse than animal waste. It was the most repellent mixture of feces, vomit, and human sweat Rory had ever encountered in his life.

Cages.

Rows of cages stretched out under long strips of pale fluorescents to the far end of the room. There were dozens of cages in each row.

Then he saw what lay within.

Rory had seen some pretty terrible things in his life. Hell, he'd been responsible for a few of them. But he'd never seen anything like this.

The wire-mesh confines weren't more than four feet tall and about as wide and deep. Each was padlocked shut. Inside each, a human being squatted or lay, sometimes covered by a bundle of rags.

Somewhere in the room, someone was whimpering and crying.

Rory glanced at Adrian. He was accustomed to seeing no emotion on his face; the Captain issued orders in a dead-calm voice, no matter the nature, his expression always serene and unruffled.

But now he saw Adrian's face twist with disgust and pain, for just a moment before his lips firmed.

"We're going to get them all out," he said. "You find Sierra."

There were two rings of keys hanging on a hook by the door. Adrian grabbed one and tossed the other to Rory. He walked down the row, methodically trying the keys in the padlocks until he unlocked them.

Rory hesitated only a second, then ran down another row, glancing from side to side, searching for Sierra.

The cages were coated with grime and reeked of human waste. The figures inside turned dull, hopeless eyes on him as he made his way past.

Then he caught a flash of a familiar profile.

Within one of the cages was a girl who would have been pretty if she weren't so thin and dirty. Her blonde hair hung in lank tresses on either side of a skeletal face. A torn, shapeless flannel shirt hid the lines of her body.

He stopped, curled his fingers around the wire mesh of her cage and brought his face up close to the bars. Their eyes met. Hers were vividly blue, insanely blue, a blue that pierced him so deeply he felt as though his breastbone had been split and his heart exposed to the air, pumping blood that only mattered if it could give her life.

"Sierra."

She staggered to her feet and croaked, "Rory." She offered him her unique lopsided smile.

His hands trembled as he tried to fit the key in the padlock. As though from somewhere far away, he heard shouts and screams, cage doors clanging; someone wailed long and loud. Adrian's voice rose above it all, organizing the escape, directing people to help one another. As always, Adrian possessed the mesmerizing ability to get others to fall in line before his will, the power to quiet the hysterical and steel the terrified. The battered, previously hopeless prisoners formed themselves into an escape party. They passed the keys from hand to hand, and helped carry those too ill or poisoned to move.

But Rory could not take his eyes off Sierra. Something in her eyes had always compelled him, some power deep within her restored him, made him believe he was somehow more than just a worthless criminal or a slippery survivor. More than a mere collector of nasty tricks and shady deals who simply managed to get by.

Rory no longer remembered his parents. He had grown up on the streets, been in an institution briefly, and had run away. He was good at sneaking around; good at eking out a living on the streets by begging, stealing, running odd jobs. He went to school because they gave him free food. He lied about his address and about everything else, but he got by.

He had no friends. Who needed them?

Until one day.

He had been making his usual rounds when he saw a young girl, face half-covered by tangled blonde hair, wrapped in filthy clothes, scrounging in one of "his" garbage cans. He was going to warn her away when she turned her pretty, dirty face toward him and he was caught by the intense blue of her large, wide eyes. She took a step backward, her legs buckled, and she slumped against the can.

Surprising himself, he squatted down beside her, pulling out his latest treasure: a bar of chocolate, stolen from a nearby drugstore.

"Hey," he said. Those astonishingly blue eyes opened and fixed on him.

He held the candy bar out to her. "Collapsing from hunger ain't a good thing around here."

Her eyes focused avidly on the chocolate and one hand came up to take the bar. Then she hesitated, gazing at him fearfully. "Naw, it's okay," he said, feeling an odd desire to reassure her. "You can have it."

She sat up and gobbled the chocolate, eyes fervent. He watched her in silence.

"What's your name?" he asked. He wondered at himself. Why did he care?

Her eyes darted back and forth. He saw her planning to lie, saw the moment she changed her mind. She swallowed the last bite of chocolate and lifted her chin. "Sierra." Then she tipped her head to one side. "Now you have to tell me yours."

He didn't hesitate. "Rory."

She smiled, and it lit up her thin face, like a flood of sunlight pouring through the narrow alley.

After that, Rory scavenged a cardboard refrigerator carton from a recycling truck and the two of them lived together under a rusty old fire escape in an alley. They watched out for each other when they stole food, fought back to back against the other street kids, and huddled together for warmth at night.

And they talked. She was the first person—the only person—Rory had ever opened up to, shared his feelings, fears, and dreams with.

Then one day they caught her, sent her back into the system. Rory had never understood before what it felt like to be lonely. He went back to the empty box, slept curled around himself, haunted the social services office in hopes of catching a glimpse of her. But weeks went by with no sight of her, until one morning he woke up to a hand scrabbling at the front flap of the box. He jumped up instantly, his small knife ready in his hand.

It was Sierra.

She looked wonderful. She was clean and she had new clothes. She crawled into the box beside him and for a few moments it was just like the old days, the two of them chattering away about anything and everything. Rory pressed her about her new foster family, and she was evasive. It was okay, she said, but Rory could see the lie in her eyes. But her voice trembled when she told him that she couldn't live on the streets anymore. She liked being warm and indoors.

Rory didn't like it, but what did he have to offer her? After a couple of hours, she was gone, leaving him alone once more.

Ever since then, Rory had tried to keep tabs on her as she moved from foster family to foster family. She started drinking, and he warned her about it, but she shook her head. She said it was the only thing that kept her going. Rory said nothing more.

Then one day, he lost track of her. There had been some incident with her foster family, and Social Services had moved her away to protect her.

He had no idea where she had gone.

He was alone again. Then Adrian had attracted him with his cold certainty, his utter fearlessness. Rory attached himself to him with tenacity, fought beside him, and demonstrated his loyalty over and over. He became Adrian's closest companion, his right-hand man, privy to many of his inmost secrets.

But he had never trusted him. Had never trusted anyone.

For the past few years, he had been squirreling away cash. Working for Tenebras had its advantages. When he got out of high school, and Adrian moved off to college, he hoped to stay behind, find Sierra, who would be turning eighteen soon and leaving the foster care system, and get them a real place to stay. Find a regular job. The two of them could be together, with an actual roof over both of their heads.

He had always kept his attachment to Sierra a secret, not mentioning it to anyone. Especially Adrian. For, as he well knew, attachments were a liability. A weakness.

When Adrian approached him a few months ago with his offer, asking him to play the role of traitor, it had taken a while for him to really believe it. But Adrian had never lied to him.

Rory had been the one who had faltered in his loyalty.

He'd been an idiot. When he realized the truth, he had thrown himself into his role with all his skill and ability. He was good at it. Lying was his forte. Hadn't Sierra herself told him that?

But still, he hadn't been good enough to find her. He'd never been good enough.

Rory fumbled with the key in the padlock. At last, he fitted it in the slot and swung the door open.

Sierra fell into his arms. Thin, so thin, but the shape of her body within his embrace was still familiar.

"Are you all right?"

Her eyes were bloodshot but she winked at him. "Let's get out of here so you can really be my hero." She grabbed the keys from his hand and unlocked the next cage in the row.

"Come on," she urged the boy inside. A dark purple bruise ran down one side of his face, and his eyes were wide and staring. "Get out and follow them." She pointed to a stream of people headed out the back, shuffling toward the loading dock, where a tall, skinny kid had been commandeered by Adrian to make sure that the stronger prisoners helped the weaker ones.

Sierra's wrists were almost translucent, she had lost so much weight, and her hands shook.

They had freed several of the prisoners and Rory was working on another cage door at the end of the row, when he heard a side door latch rattle behind him. He spun to face it.

Mario stood framed in the door, a Glock cradled in his arm.

His eyes flicked over the room, and his face twisted into a snarl.

Then he raised the gun in slow motion.

"No!" Rory shrieked.

Sierra began to turn, slowly, so slowly, her eyes widening.

Rory saw the gun so clearly, as though it were outlined in brilliant light. The barrel pointed directly at Sierra. The muscles in Mario's forearm were just beginning to flex as his finger curled over the trigger.

Rory reached for his own gun, but it was too late.

There was only one thing he could do.

It would go against everything he had learned on the streets, all his careful training, all his reflexes honed in a lifetime bent on survival.

The moment Mario's finger contacted the trigger, Rory bent his knees and jumped.

Directly in front of her.

An unbelievably loud gunshot split the air, and something hit him hard in the chest. It spun his body around. Losing his balance and toppling over, he glanced up and met her eyes one more time.

They were blue, blue as the sky, blue and vivid.

With a quiet sigh, he smiled and closed his eyes.

31

 Schwartz

SCHWARTZ SLAMMED DOWN his office phone. His contact in the police department had just warned him that a warrant had been issued against his company. A SWAT team was on the way.

He ground his teeth in fury.

It was too soon for the police to arrive. He had laid plans for most of the blame to fall on someone other than himself, but right now there was still too much evidence against him personally onsite.

It was time to take more extreme action. He opened the locked drawer at the bottom of his desk and pulled out the special security key. He examined it for a moment. He had planned to use this system only in the direst emergency. Was it too soon?

Off in the distance, he heard a gunshot.

Gritting his teeth, Schwartz slid the key into his pocket and left the office, locking the door carefully behind him. The central control room for the security system was just down the hall. He swiped his card through the slot and leaned close for the retina scan. He pulled the heavy reinforced door open and strode inside, slamming it shut and dropping the safety bar into place.

He sat at a bank of computers and typed furiously for a few seconds. Images popped up on the screens all around him, displaying views from external security cameras. A crowd had gathered in one of the back parking lots.

It seemed the police had already arrived. Their undercover agents looked particularly scruffy.

No time to lose. He inserted his emergency key in the special slot.

He had only recently installed this state-of-the-art security system. It was originally designed for labs located overseas in hostile territory. Some might call it overkill. Paranoid.

But now Schwartz congratulated himself on his foresight.

As the key twisted in the slot, monitors flicked on. A warning signal beeped.

With a rumble, blast doors lowered over all the exits of the building, including the windows. Schwartz's ears popped slightly as the chamber pressurized.

The entire building was now effectively sealed off. All external walls had been constructed from reinforced steel, designed to repel attacks. No one could get in or out—except through the secured exit from this control room. Of course, it was after closing time, so most of the employees had left. The remaining humans in the building were primarily people who knew too much. People who needed to be cleaned up.

Schwartz gave his reflection in the computer monitor a tight smile.

That would take care of the external threat. It would keep the police out—at least for the time he needed.

Now to deal with the internal threat. He flipped several more switches, transferring control of the entire system from the front security office to here. More alarms went off as bank after bank of monitoring devices were reassigned to his control.

Several screens lit up, and security cameras displayed empty corridors, fire doors hanging open, a row of cages unlocked with their doors hanging open. Bodies on the floor.

Schwartz narrowed his eyes. What was going on?

It didn't matter. It was time to clean up this operation and move on. He'd gotten all he needed from it, and one of his talents was knowing when it was time to cut his losses. He had everything in place for a clean getaway.

Holman had been useful, but he had become more and more unstable recently. Another loose end to snip, along with the local kids. Schwartz had been playing Mario off against Adrian, using the gang as foot soldiers. They would be left hanging so the police would have someone to scapegoat. As a bonus, it would take some of the pressure off Schwartz. Handy.

Schwartz sighed in regret. Now Adrian Salas... there was a truly promising young chemist. With a mind like that on his side, the sky would have been the limit for Schwartz's drug profits. It was too bad.

All the work he had spent establishing this cover, building up a legitimate business. Gone.

It would be a terrible accident. Too bad all those people would die. But it was necessary. It had to be a clean sweep. No witnesses.

He'd installed the high-tech chemical fire retardant system himself, after the company who sold it to him kept insisting on those annoying safety procedures. Of course, he hadn't let them know about the blast doors.

Yes, his foresight was definitely paying off.

He flipped open the clear plastic cover over a set of red switches, and pressed all three of them down.

Immediately the lights all over the lab dimmed, red and white strobes illuminated the corridors, and a voice boomed out over every speaker on the intercom system.

"Warning. Emergency fire retardant process activated. All personnel must evacuate. In thirty minutes, all oxygen will be ventilated from the building. All personnel must evacuate immediately. Please proceed to the nearest exit."

Not that the warning would do any good, now that he had lowered the blast doors. All the exits were sealed.

On the security cameras, a few people rushed for the doors, only to find them locked. He watched their panic-stricken pounding for a few minutes, and smiled.

No one could escape, and in thirty minutes, the only room in the lab that would contain sufficient breathable oxygen was this control room.

 ## *Elisa*

As the doorknob rattled, Elisa ducked behind one of the lab benches, her heart thumping. Someone shouted, and footsteps pounded away from the door, gradually fading into the distance.

Silence fell, and she waited, immobile, for what seemed like hours.

She knew she had to get out of there before Holman came back. She steeled herself, crept to the door, opened it carefully, and peered into the corridor. No one in sight. Off at the far end of the long hallway, an exit sign glowed. Elisa took a deep breath and slipped out the door. She ran as fast and as quietly as she could toward the exit sign.

Before she reached it, the lights dimmed and a loud alarm blared. A white strobe began to flash directly over her head. She jerked to a stop, crouching. Had they already detected her escape and raised the alarm?

A robotic voice emanated from a loudspeaker in the wall. The words were almost unintelligible.

"Warning. Evacuate immediately. Proceed to the nearest exit."

No problem—that was exactly what she wanted to do.

Elisa zipped down the hall and swung left at the far end into another long corridor. Up ahead was an external door, but when she opened it, a solid slab of metal blocked the exit. She pushed, but there was no give.

Strange.

Time to look for another way out. She had passed a lab door on her way, so she retraced her steps. Through a glass panel, she saw a dim room full of what looked like long rows of cages.

A green exit sign blinked at the other end of the space.

She tried the door and found it unlocked, but when she pulled it open, she was blasted by a foul stench. She gagged. This lab must have housed animal experiments. Ugh. The empty cages were filthy. Metal cage doors hung open up and down the rows. The room seemed to be completely deserted.

At the far end, under the exit sign, was a large door that looked like it led to a loading dock.

She trotted down one of the rows toward the exit.

There was a pile of clothing in the middle of her path, and she slowed to detour around it.

Then she gasped.

It was a human being.

She knelt beside him. He lay sprawled out on the floor, bleeding profusely from multiple wounds. For a moment she wasn't sure if he was alive. Then he wheezed and choked, and she recognized him.

Rory.

She fumbled for his coat, trying to apply pressure to the worst of his wounds.

"Nah," he whispered. "You don't need to do that."

"We've got to stop the bleeding," she said. "Then we've got to get you to a hospital."

"Don't bother. I just gotta know—did she get out?"

One wound was spurting, right there in his chest. It didn't look good.

Rory coughed a little, and blood bubbled out from his lips. "Tell me, did she get out? He promised he'd get her out."

"What?"

"He's a liar, I know, but one thing's for sure. He always keeps his promises."

"Shh, don't talk now."

"He said he'd get Sierra out. She's easy to spot. Beautiful... the most beautiful girl ever. Hair the color of the sun and eyes brighter than the sky."

Elisa glanced around. There was no one in the room, and at the far end she could see the large door to the loading dock was also sealed shut. Who was Sierra?

She looked back at Rory. He gazed at her, pleading.

Whoever she was, he loved her. Elisa had to give him something.

She exhaled. "Yes. Yes, he got her out."

He let out a long breath, like a bubbling sigh, and his body relaxed. "That's it. It's all okay then." He groped for her hand and she clasped his. "When you love someone, when you really love them, they're all that matters in the world. He said it, and he was right. He said he just never knew before." Rory gasped, and his voice grew weaker.

"Shhh," Elisa said. "You don't need to talk. Conserve your strength."

"No, I have to tell you," he whispered. "I have to tell you because you're the one. He said you're the only one for him and because of it he knew he had to protect my Sierra. Because of you, she's alive. I want you to know. I want you to know that—"

He sighed, a little puff of air came out of his mouth, and then he was quiet.

His wound had stopped bleeding. Frantically, she fumbled at his chest and put her ear to his lips.

No heartbeat. No breath.

"Warning. In twenty-five minutes, all oxygen will be ventilated from the building. All personnel must evacuate immediately."

Could she get him out the door, find someone who could call 911? Maybe if an ambulance could take him to the hospital, he could still be saved.

She ran to the loading dock door, tugged at it. No. It was sealed from the outside.

This room was a trap. Maybe the entire building was a trap. To get out, she'd have to find the central system management somewhere.

She went back to Rory. His eyes were glassy and he lay immobile. Tears stung her eyes. He was Adrian's best friend. He didn't deserve to die like this.

But there was nothing Elisa could do. She squatted beside him and brushed his hair back from his forehead. She straightened his jacket and folded his hands over his chest.

She sat back. There must be some words she could say for him.

"Sierra is going to do well," she told him. "Look down on her from heaven, and take care of her. I'll tell her you love her."

The loudspeaker interrupted her. "Warning. In twenty minutes, all oxygen will be ventilated from the building. All personnel must evacuate immediately."

Elisa stood up. She had to get out of there. A gun lay on the floor just beyond his outstretched hand. She hesitated, then picked it up and slid it into the waistband of her jeans.

 Keisha

Keisha loped along the dimly lit hall, trailed by Vince. She cursed her poor timing. She'd gone ahead to scout out the area and had just turned to wave the SWAT team in when all the blast doors had gone down. Now she and Vince were trapped inside while the SWAT team was stuck outside.

Low lights and flashing strobes threw shadows along the corridors and made it difficult to see. She and Vince went from door to door, checking to make sure there was no one who needed to be rescued. The last communication she'd received before her radio went dead was that a young girl had been kidnapped and was being held hostage inside the building.

They had to find any civilians still trapped inside the building and rescue them.

And oh yes, they had to find an exit.

"Warning. In twenty minutes, all oxygen will be ventilated from the building. All personnel must evacuate immediately."

Adrian

Adrian sprinted down the corridor under the flashing strobe lights, checking each of the doors he passed.

He had to find Elisa.

She was all that mattered. Every fiber of his being yearned toward her the way iron filings lined up in a magnetic field. Whether or not she chose to be with him, he would give everything for her.

Once he had thought her hopelessly naïve, the way she longed to make the world a better place.

Now all he wanted was for her to accomplish her desires.

It was so strange, and yet so wonderful.

It was irrational, but there it was.

In the big lab, he had organized the escape of the prisoners from their cages. The entire time, fear gnawed inside him, the terrifying worry that Elisa was in danger. That every minute might be the one that made the difference to whether she lived or died.

In the past, he could have walked right by those people about to die, without a care, on his way to accomplish whatever goal he chose. Surely that was the rational thing to do.

But now, he could not leave them to their fate.

There had been no time for philosophy as he organized the prisoners, identified the leaders among them, and set them to various tasks: carrying people outside, managing others, performing first aid, contacting the police.

He was getting the last of the escapees out when the side door opened on the far side of the lab, and he spotted Mario.

Mario lifted his Glock. It was clear what was going to happen. Adrian sprinted toward him, drawing his own gun as he ran.

But Rory and Sierra were within point-blank range of Mario's weapon.

Mario fired, and Rory fell. Adrian returned fire, but the distance was too great. He'd missed, and Mario darted out the door and disappeared.

When Adrian had reached Sierra, she was crouched over Rory lying on the floor bleeding out. Adrian was going to chase after Mario, but Rory gasped out a few words, making him promise to get Sierra out first before doing anything else.

Given his wounds, there was no saving Rory. But Adrian could still save Sierra.

He grabbed her hand and tugged her past the empty cages, yanking her to the exit despite her wails of protest.

"Rory wants you to get out safely," he said. "You'll do that for him, won't you?"

The blast door had started to descend. Adrian shoved her, hard, barely in time. She rolled through and was out. The door slammed down behind her with a decisive clang.

In the sudden silence, he returned to where Rory lay on the ground, eyes closed. With multiple bullet wounds he didn't have a chance. Adrian didn't even dare move him, much less try to find an exit.

Then he heard the evacuation warning. Suddenly, much more than Elisa's life was at risk. What could Schwartz be thinking? Was he truly planning to kill everyone in the building?

Adrian couldn't simply find Elisa and escape, not just yet. He was responsible for other lives now.

If the system worked the way he suspected, oxygen levels throughout the building would be dropping over the next few minutes. People would soon show the symptoms of hypoxia: decreased vision, confusion, poor judgment, or inappropriate euphoria. The symptoms were unique to the individual. He himself had once visited an altitude chamber and observed his own behavior, deeming it potentially useful should he ever be caught in an unpressurized airplane.

Usually, judgment was one of the first things to go. And losing mental control or cognitive judgment was one of the few things that frightened Adrian.

Hypoxia could be especially dangerous when combined with lethal weapons. Mario had quite an arsenal with him. And there were undoubtedly security forces roaming the building.

Adrian would need to be very careful.

He glanced one more time at Rory. He'd been the closest thing Adrian had to a friend. And in the end he had demonstrated his loyalty. Was there anything Adrian could do to save him? A pang came over him, but he pushed it away ruthlessly. He had work to do for those still living.

He let the lab door slam behind him and raced down the hall under the flashing lights. More warnings sounded. He paused briefly to check the windows into each of the labs he passed. They were all empty. Hopefully most of the employees had heard the warnings and evacuated.

He couldn't search every room. There wasn't time. He knew where he had to go.

The central control room.

He took a right at the next corridor and dashed up the hall.

The control room was ringed by a set of large, bulletproof windows through which the occupants could scan the outside hallway. Thick glass panels reflected the flashing strobes. Set into the wall beside the heavy fire door was an entry keypad, and next to it, a full security terminal for emergency access. Adrian paused, took a deep breath, and approached the nearest window.

Schwartz sat inside at a bank of monitors. He lifted his head as Adrian drew near, and smirked.

His voice emanated from the intercom. "If it isn't our dutiful intern, Adrian Salas." His mouth twisted. "But perhaps you are not quite as dutiful and loyal as you appear, Adrian."

An icy hand closed over Adrian's heart at the sight of Schwartz. At the memory of the emails and news articles he had uncovered when he hacked into the man's account. Schwartz had been dabbling in drug dealing for a long time. The scanned news clippings and handwritten notes dated from thirteen years ago.

There had been a news clipping of Adrian's family's death. Emails to a name he had recognized.

One of his family's murderers.

Schwartz had been involved in that failed home invasion robbery so long ago.

Now that Adrian stood in front of the man, the cold rage in his stomach uncoiled and spread throughout his body. This was the monster who had destroyed his life. Who had killed his innocent family.

For nothing.

Revenge had been everything Adrian had lived for over the past thirteen years. The only thing he had lived for. The cold hand on his heart squeezed more tightly.

He was ice and steel. There was no room for emotion.

It was time to play the role, once again, of the Captain, the man with ice water in his veins and a cruel streak a mile long. He would play the game for all he was worth. Schwartz had found him useful in the past. A brilliant chemist was not someone to throw away lightly. Adrian could count on that.

Schwartz said, "It has occurred to me your loyalty might be bought. And maybe… I have the coin by which I can buy it." His eyes narrowed.

Adrian tilted his head. "I'm listening."

"Soon everyone in this building will die, including you. The only safe place is this armored control room."

Adrian shrugged. "I'm quite sure I can find a way in before the oxygen levels drop too low. I've already hacked into your system once."

Schwartz glared at him. "So it was you."

Adrian smiled. "Indeed. So—do you have anything of true value to offer me?"

The muscles in Schwartz's jaw knotted, and he straightened them with a visible effort. A twisted attempt at a fatherly smile appeared on his face. "I know you want to live, Adrian. You want to be rich. I have enough evidence here to frame Holman for all criminal activity that has occurred in connection with Rapture. I also have a cache of funds and some new identities." His voice lowered, became persuasive. "Why don't you join me? I'll let you into this room. We allow the cleanup process to finish here, take care of all witnesses and evidence. You survive, we escape, we travel to a new country and set up shop. You and I resume the production of Rapture. We get rich, incredibly rich, enough to last the rest of our lives."

Adrian kept his face blank and calm as he listened. His mind raced. Should he pretend to accept the deal? Get into the room with Schwartz? Put his hands around the bastard's throat?

He cocked his head to one side. "A tempting offer," he said with a smile. "But…" He moved to one of the two keypads beside the door, and began inputting a sequence. "What guarantee do I have that you'll keep your end of the deal? You do know how much evidence I've assembled on you," he remarked casually.

Schwartz's eyes shifted from side to side. "You mean that trumped up set of documents you gave to the police? I have proof it was all a forgery. Proof that pins this entire conspiracy on you and Holman." He pointed at one of the terminals. "There is a secure, encrypted set of files that contains the real truth about Rapture. Including your role. It's all set to go out to the police. Besides, you'll never be able to decrypt the passwords for the security protocol to extract the oxygen. Everyone else in this building will die."

"Do you think I care if anyone besides me lives or dies?" Adrian's eyes were cold. "This won't take long. Once I'm in that room, I'll be safe. Soon it will all be over."

"Think of it: you could have all the money and power you've ever wanted."

Cold pooled in Adrian's belly. What good was money or power without family? "I know," he said. "I know you were involved in my family's death."

Schwartz's head jerked back. "What? What do you mean?"

"I saw the files. What did you think? What's one more home invasion robbery here or there? It's so easy to hire a couple of small-time thugs."

Schwartz broke out into harsh laughter. "Ha! Is that it? Is that why you persist in this foolish vendetta against me, when I'm the only one who can give you what you want? You don't know anything. Who was really behind it all. You don't know the full story. About your mother." His voice lowered. "Come with me, my boy. Work with me, and I'll tell you everything. Don't condemn me until you know the full truth. Did you know your mother left a journal?"

"You're lying."

"No. I'll prove it."

Adrian clenched his teeth and typed faster on the security keypad. "You're just trying to save your miserable life."

"She wrote about you and your sister. I know all sorts of things about her. She liked playing math games with you. She enjoyed music. Her favorite composer was Dvořák. Now there's no way I could know that if I hadn't read her journal."

Adrian's fingers fell still and he stared at Schwartz. The thought that this man might know something about his mother's past, might still possess some memento of her, some precious relic, when Adrian had nothing... It made him more furious than he could ever remember feeling. The desire for revenge leaped in him. It roared like a furnace, engulfed his soul like a conflagration.

Schwartz continued to babble. "I have information in a safe deposit box under an assumed name. So you see, if you work with me, everything will go well for you. Holman will go to jail for the drug synthesis. I am the only one who can give you everything you want."

Adrian said nothing. Yes, Schwartz would indeed give him everything he wanted, once Adrian had him under his hands. Schwartz would scream with pain and beg to give him anything he desired.

He worked at the keypad. It would only take a few minutes more to get into the control room; it was a relatively easy technical puzzle.

Schwartz's blond hair had turned dark with sweat. His eyes darted from side to side, and he panted, finally falling silent as Adrian continued to ignore him. All at once, he flipped a few switches on the console, leapt out of his seat, bolted to a back door in the lab and slammed it behind him.

Adrian's jaw muscles clenched. It was an elevator to the subbasement. Schwartz must have an escape route.

Damn! Adrian scanned the blinking lights in the control room. Only nineteen minutes until the oxygen was evacuated.

317

He had to chase after Schwartz. He had to take his revenge. But if he spent precious minutes pursuing Schwartz, he wouldn't be able to turn off the fire retardant system.

Everyone else in the building would die.

His eyes flicked to the second terminal on the wall beside the keypad. He could spend the next few minutes disarming the oxygen depletion system from there, without needing to get into the control room. There wasn't much time left. He could either turn the system off and save everyone's life, or he could hack into the control room, save himself, and get his revenge on Schwartz.

On the elevator readout, the numbers crept down to B, B2, B3, B4, and then stopped.

Schwartz was on subbasement level B4. Adrian could still catch him. He had to find out what Schwartz knew, force any information about his mother from him, and make the man pay. It was untenable that Schwartz would escape, and not even go to jail. That he and Holman would get away scot-free for all their crimes.

Adrian lifted a hand toward the keypad beside the door. It wouldn't take long to find the entry code.

Elisa's face flashed in front of him, the sun glinting off her hair, waves surging in the background.

He stopped.

Yes, he had lived most of his life focused on revenge. On violence and destruction. On death.

But now there was something more powerful in his life. Something that made a decade, even a lifetime, nothing more than a drop of water in the ocean. Something eternal. The link he had with Elisa would continue beyond life or death. And with that connection, his past life fell away like a sheet of paper consumed in a forest fire.

There were too many people who would die if he didn't disable the mechanism. Including Elisa.

His fingers stilled on the entry keypad.

He let out a long, long breath.

Turning to the other terminal on the wall, he rapidly typed in a series of attempts to disable the security system. He set one script going, then another. His fingers did not cease to move. He tried one idea, then another, as the minutes ticked down on the LED readout.

Nothing.

Nothing was working.

Then he noticed his fingertips.

They were showing the very slightest tinge of blue.

It was beginning. The first sign of oxygen deprivation.

Time was running out. He couldn't figure out how to disable the system. Adrian had always prided himself on his intellect, but now it had failed him. And from now on, his mental capacity would continually decline.

Until the inevitable loss of consciousness, and shortly after, death.

32

 *Elisa*

ELISA RAN DOWN THE CORRIDOR. The air was fresher here, thank goodness, but it still smelled like toxic solvents. The flashing lights gave the place a surreal atmosphere, and the warning broadcasts made her stomach churn. Hopefully everyone else had gotten out. Now it was her turn.

Turning a corner, she squinted at a sign pointing to the executive level. That had to be the best place to go if she was going to have any chance of stopping this countdown. Elisa pulled open a door and ran at top speed down the hall.

And then she skidded to a stop, panting, as she spied a glassed-in enclosure.

Adrian stood in the corridor, working at a terminal set in the wall.

She had to pause for a moment just to watch him. He was beautiful when he worked, his large eyes intent, those dark brows drawn down just a little in concentration, his features flawless and calm, his full lips smooth.

"Adrian," she called. "What are you doing?"

He spun, eyes widening, and for a moment his hand sketched a gesture toward the gun he wore in a holster under his jacket. Then his whole body softened and relief spread over his face.

"Elisa."

The sound of her name on his lips, low and vibrating, reverberated in her bones and made all her sinews pulsate. She took one step forward, then another, her eyes locked on his. She didn't realize they had reached out for each other until his fingers linked with hers, and a tingling brushfire of sparks wound its way up her arms and curled into her throat and along her cheeks. Her face flushed, and he pulled her closer, enfolding her in his arms and pressing her face against his chest. His heart was beating fast, much faster than usual.

Maybe they could just stay like this forever.

He murmured into her hair, "Elisa! At least you're safe."

Well, for the next ten minutes or so.

Slowly, reluctantly, they disengaged. His eyes went to a small keypad beside the door. "Maybe I should—" he began, and he glanced through the glass into the control room.

Then he stopped. His eyes were steel. "A lot of people are going to die unless I figure out how to turn off this system."

"Yes, go, go," she agreed, ignoring the sudden cold she felt at no longer having her body pressed closely against his.

Wait. They had broken up.

But did it matter? They might just die in a few minutes. If they were going to inevitably collapse and die from lack of oxygen, she wanted to do it in his arms.

Crazy.

He returned to the terminal and resumed typing. She peered over his shoulder. Figures flashed across the screen.

Error. Invalid entry. It was displayed again and again.

"What are you looking for?" she asked.

He exhaled sharply, glancing up again at the LED readout on the wall. Only seven minutes to go. "I'm looking for a passcode of up to eight letters and digits. I have a script that could find it, but not in only seven minutes. So I'm entering variations on guesses based on what I know about Schwartz."

He'd created a script that ran a few hundred variations of each string he entered manually. She didn't know much about computer security, but people tended to use passwords that had some personal meaning.

She remembered the strange comment Holman had made about Schwartz earlier. "Have you tried 'DeLorean'?"

His forehead wrinkled. "Why?"

"Something Holman said. Just try it."

"I'll run combinations based on that string." He typed for a moment.

Error. Invalid entry.

She held her breath.

Error. Invalid entry.

Error. Invalid entry.

Then: "You are about to exceed the number of incorrect attempts. After three more failed attempts, the system will lock out all console input for five minutes."

They both turned and looked at the readout on the wall. Six minutes and twenty-one seconds to go.

 *Ben*

Ben loped along one of the corridors. The strobe lights flashed eerily around him and he wondered once again if he had done the right thing, following the cops into this dangerous situation. Vince had given Keisha a hard time about all the kids involved in her operation.

"First, you bring in this underage yahoo," he had said, waving at Ben. "Then you rely on evidence from a couple of pre-teens who think they're Philip Marlowe." He snorted. "It's like you think you're in an action movie, Keisha. What's next? You're going to deputize Ben? Give him a badge and gun? Hey, how about a squad car and a pension?"

"Shut your mouth," Keisha snapped. She sketched rapidly in her notebook, tore the page out, and laid it on the table between them. "Now, both of you, pay attention to the plan." She glared at Ben. "Your job is to stay far away from Schwartz Pharmaceuticals. I want you to keep watch over the high school."

Ben rolled his eyes, but nodded. He had no intention of playing rear guard.

Not that he planned on telling them that.

After retrieving his father's gun, he'd caught the bus to the outskirts of town. It had been surprisingly easy to get into Schwartz Pharmaceuticals. He'd found a half-open window and shimmied inside to find himself in a small storage room.

It was only after he'd gained access to the building that things had started to go south. First, there were all the alarms and gunfire in the distance, and then those crazy warnings about oxygen. He'd seen the blast doors go down all over the building.

He shook his head. It didn't matter. Hadn't he told his father that he was going to protect everyone from that asshole Mario Fonseca? There were still people in this building who needed help. He increased his pace.

Keisha

Footsteps sounded behind Keisha in the corridor. Vince spun to cover her, raising his weapon.

Ben crouched behind them, strobes flickering over the revolver in his hand.

"What are you doing here?" Keisha cried.

Ben shrugged. "Too late now." He gestured. "The control room's this way. We've got to shut the system down."

Before Keisha could respond, a shot echoed all around them. Ben's eyes widened and his breath hissed out. Then he slumped forward and fell. His fingers opened and the gun clanged onto the floor.

Keisha whirled to face the new threat.

Mario stood there in a tight Nike t-shirt, balancing a Glock on one muscular arm. He sneered at them. "Was it you who let my prisoner out?" he asked, waving the barrel at Keisha and Vince. "Drop your guns." His voice grew harsh. "Now!"

Keisha glowered at him for a long beat. Mario's smirk didn't fade. Instead, he lifted his gun an inch, centering it on Ben's heart. Keisha's shoulders sagged. She bent slowly and laid her pistol down on the linoleum, motioning for Vince to do the same. There was a long moment of silence, and in the sudden quiet, they could hear the uneven whine of the fluorescent tubes above their heads. There was a scrabbling sound behind the ceiling tiles, fading off into the distance.

Keisha straightened and backed against the wall.

 *Adrian*

Adrian glanced up from the monitor at Elisa. "This is our last chance," he said. "We only have three more tries before we're locked out of the system."

"It has to be something based on DeLorean," Elisa said. "What else have you tried?"

Adrian shrugged. "I'll try one more combination," he said.

He entered the last few keystrokes, paused.

Then he hit enter.

He was still working when a gunshot rang out, very close by. His hand fell to his own gun as he pivoted and peered around the corner. He gestured to Elisa to stay behind, but she trotted ahead and then jerked to a stop.

At the end of the corridor stood Keisha and Vince—and Mario with a gun on them. Ben lay slumped motionless on the floor.

Mario grinned. "Well, if it isn't the Captain. Or should I say, the former Captain?" He sneered. "Drop your gun, Salas, if you don't want me to shoot your pretty little piece right here."

Adrian smiled calmly and let the pistol fall out of his fingers; he held his hands out, palms open.

His face betrayed nothing of the emotions behind it. He forced himself to gaze neutrally at Mario when all he wanted was to plunge a knife into his throat. Mario had kidnapped Elisa. Had worked with Schwartz and Holman, and risked everyone's life. Had betrayed him.

Mario's voice was hard. "Here's what I want, and what you're going to give me, Salas. I want—"

Footsteps pounded around another corner, and Eric Holman appeared. Breathing hard, eyes wild and staring, he stopped short at the tableau before him.

Mario dropped back and stood with his back against a wall. His massive handgun swung to cover both Holman and Elisa. "It looks like we're all here, don't it."

Keisha said, "So, you two are working together?"

Mario looked blank for a moment. "Huh?" He glanced at Holman. Then he grinned. "Yeah. Yeah, we are," he added, with an expansive gesture with his pistol.

"What?" said Holman. "I've never seen this kid before in my life." Mario shoved the pistol's barrel at his face. He tensed.

"Don't move, you dickhead. You stay still, or else." Mario bared his teeth at Holman. "Both of you. Down on the ground. Kneel on the floor." He spun back to face the others. Keisha had taken a small step forward, but she froze at his gesture and stood very still.

Holman knelt, shaking his head. "You're crazy. Whatever you say."

Elisa carefully lowered herself to the ground.

 *Mario*

Mario's gun swung in an arc to cover his hostages. His face split into a huge grin at the tension in the faces around him: his former leader, unarmed and unmoving; the cops standing helpless, everyone's eyes fixed on him. He savored the rush of power that surged through his body, fueled by adrenaline and Rapture. He had as much slip as he wanted now. An unlimited supply.

He was in control now. This must be what it felt like to be Salas, on top of the world with everyone else at your feet. It was finally all going Mario's way. He wondered why he had ever obeyed Salas's orders, when it was so much better to give the orders himself. It was finally time to get what he wanted.

Lonnie and Ron Hundley had come to the lab with him, armed to the teeth. Then the dipshits had managed to get themselves killed by security guards. But Mario had found the formula for Rapture and the escape plan in the computer. Now all he needed was a little nest egg and he could disappear, set up shop somewhere else and manufacture the drug himself. He'd be rich beyond his dreams, but more than that, he would give the orders. He would be the kingpin.

He waved his gun at Vince and Keisha. "You two cops. I want you to get me ten million dollars in cash, a plane, and a pilot. Or I'll start by offing this little girl here." He gestured again. "And from you too, Salas. Ten million dollars as well."

Keisha shook her head as though he had gone completely crazy. "We don't even know if we'll get out of the building alive."

Adrian's face was calm. "It'll take me some time to arrange that, Mario."

Mario sneered. "Then you better start working on it, *Salas*." He spat the name without any respect, reveling in it. "You always thought you were better than us, didn't you?" His voice dripped sarcasm. "Now you're just one of us. Less. As a matter of fact, I want you to show it." His voice rose. "I want you to kneel. Kneel to me, Salas, or I'll kill her right here as we stand."

"You'd really give up your hostage, twenty million dollars, and a chance of escape just to engage in some petty one-upmanship with me?" Adrian's voice was smooth, with a faint note of surprise. He didn't move. "I wouldn't have thought even you would get so carried away."

Mario's breathing became ragged, and he glared at Adrian. There was a faint scuffling sound off to the side. A beeping noise came from the console on the wall.

Adrian said, "You've always had a bit of an inferiority complex, haven't you? Never quite good enough, never quite strong enough."

"That's enough from you, Salas," shouted Mario. He raised the Glock and pointed it at Elisa's forehead. "I'm gonna shoot her, now."

 ## Elisa

Elisa stared at Mario, her chin up, too numb to be afraid. Behind her back, her hand brushed the smooth cylinder of the Colt tucked in her waistband. Could she take it out, cock it by feel, use it? She had fired that exact gun at the shooting range with Adrian. But targets were one thing, a human being another.

She heard her mother's voice once again. "Fighting is for men." Somewhere in the hallway, a fan turned on with a whoosh.

Adrian's voice was cool. "Do that, Mario, and you're going down for murder one. Killing in front of so many witnesses? Giving up your hostages? I thought you would know better by now."

Mario's face twitched and his muscles contorted. Adrian's expression was utterly placid.

Elisa stretched her fingers, hesitated, reached out. Her mother whispered again. "You'll never find a man if you act like one."

No.

"You need to be good," her mother whispered. She said that whenever Elisa had an opinion of her own, whenever she tried to do something her mother didn't want. Whenever she did anything.

But no one had rescued her today. She'd gotten away from that lab on her own.

Now, people would die unless she did something. She had to be the one doing the rescuing. Her mother had said that taking action was bad. Shooting someone was always wrong, right? That's what it meant to be good or evil.

But what about self-defense? What about protecting others?

Good and evil were a lot more complicated than her mother would have had her believe.

She reached out with her hand, slowly, slowly, half an inch, an inch. Behind her back, she grasped the heavy Colt.

"You're the one who should have known better," Mario hissed at Adrian. His face twisted. "You stopped doing your job, and for what?" He sneered. "For some *girl*. Everything's been falling apart while you mooned over her. People are dying because you've been careless." He took a step to the side and angled his body toward Adrian. "It's time for you to go, and for new management to take your place."

Elisa slipped her fingers into position around the trigger, fighting to keep her breathing soft and even. She moved very slowly, infinitesimally, sliding the revolver around her body.

Adrian said softly, "You're not going to be able to manage anything, on the run from the police over kidnapping charges."

Mario snarled, and twisted away from her, swinging his weapon to bear on Adrian. "You're the one who's gonna die, right now. I can kill you and keep my hostage for later." He pulled back the hammer, kept the barrel pointing at Adrian's face. The click was loud in the stillness.

Adrian simply glanced at Mario, expression calm as always, even in the face of death. As though his death wouldn't matter. He had chosen to draw Mario's attention away from Elisa. He was risking his life for her.

This man, the one she'd believed was selfish and evil, was risking his life, and not just for her. For everyone in the building.

She'd been wrong about so many things.

Adrian smiled. "Now," he murmured.

A gunshot pierced the silence, echoing and ringing against the cement floors and walls. Ben jerked where he lay, and Keisha stiffened and her fingers twitched towards her empty holster. Mario's expression was puzzled—as if he wasn't sure whether or not he'd just shot his long-time leader—and then his pistol dropped from boneless fingers and blood spurted from his arm.

Elisa squatted on her knees, the Colt heavy in her hands, a tiny stream of smoke trailing up from the barrel.

She'd done it.

Adrian ran to her side. "Are you all right?"

She wanted to sit up straight, but everything was wobbling around her. Her head was aching again. The revolver fell from her limp fingers.

Quick as a flash, Keisha scooped up the Glock Mario had dropped. "Now it's your turn not to move," she said, cocking it at him as he sucked in uneven breaths, clutching at his arm, eyes wild.

"Warning. In sixty seconds, all oxygen will be ventilated from the building. All personnel must evacuate immediately."

Adrian leaped up and ran for the terminal set in the wall. His fingers flew over the keys.

The clicking echoed loudly in the silent hall. Everyone's eyes were riveted on his actions. Elisa felt as though she was floating.

Could Adrian still think straight as the oxygen levels dropped? She'd thought her idea was so clear, but now it all seemed so vague. And how could he even put it all together when there were so few tries left?

She should get up and help him. His face was pale, and his fingers began to slow. His head drooped slightly. Was it too late?

He hit one last key and slumped against the wall.

Nothing happened.

It was over. They were all going to die, but somehow Elisa couldn't bring herself to care. She felt so tired and sleepy. Her head still ached from Mario's attack. She closed her eyes.

"Script complete," a robotic voice announced.

Her eyelids felt like lead, but she opened them. The lighted display in the lab shimmered in her vision. The red digits in the wall readout kept on clicking downwards.

10 seconds.

9.

8.

7.

Then the display froze.

"Security protocol has been terminated. Restoring normal oxygen levels. Opening blast doors."

She knew that should mean something, but everything was becoming very fuzzy. She closed her eyes again.

 *Mario*

Vince jumped forward with a pair of handcuffs and, before Mario could move, took his good arm in an arm lock and restrained him. Holman sagged against the wall, sliding down to sit on the floor.

One of the other cops emerged from a corridor. "Got all the others in restraints," he announced, waving back along the hall.

"Have you got them all taken care of here?" He eyed Mario with grim approval. "You got this one. Good."

"Yes," Adrian said softly. "I can't think of anyone who won't be pleased that you've finally got the notorious Captain of Tenebras in custody. From what he said today, it sounds like he's completely insane."

Mario's head came up at the import of Adrian's words. "No—" he wheezed. "It's not me. It's—"

Keisha snorted, her weapon still trained on him. "Don't bother lying, you bastard. We've got all the evidence on you, and with the additional charges today, you're up for the death penalty for sure."

Mario's eyes rolled in panic as he realized what was happening. With a sudden, fluid leap, he twisted away from Vince, bounded to his feet, and ran down the corridor. Keisha didn't hesitate. She lifted her pistol, took aim, and fired. Mario jerked once, and then fell to the ground and lay unmoving.

Blood welled out of his mouth, and he choked on it. Lying on the ground, he glanced up at Keisha, standing over him. Her face swam in and out of his vision. Mario's face split in a grin one last time. It was how he always imagined he would die, drowning in his own blood. How his mama had always said he would end up. Far preferable to rotting in prison, under the heel of weak idiots and bureaucrats jabbering about the *law*. He choked one more time, and his eyes closed.

Keisha

"Shot trying to escape. Too bad." Keisha shrugged. "Saves the taxpayers money on the trial." She spotted Holman, and her eyes narrowed. "What's this one still doing without cuffs?"

Vince slapped handcuffs onto Holman's wrists. The man lifted his bound hands, outraged. "Hey, what's this?" he demanded. "I'm one of the good guys. I was just trying to rescue the hostages."

Keisha snorted. "Tell it to the judge. You have the right to remain silent."

Vince leaned over Ben, examining his leg. "It's all right," he assured him. "It's just a flesh wound, as they say. The bullet passed right through. You're going to be okay." He clapped him on the back and grinned. "Great job. Maybe we'll even make you a deputy. You could earn a pension one of these days, given all the work you've been doing for the force." He cast a sidelong glance at Keisha. She wasn't amused.

Adrian, bending over Elisa's unconscious body, interrupted. "I need to get Elisa to a hospital, now."

Ben glanced up and said to his one-time adversary, "Bring her to my dad's clinic. It's closer."

33

Keisha

THE PRECINCT HUMMED with excitement and satisfaction. Vince tipped his chair all the way back, feet on his desk, idly tossing a golf ball up in the air and catching it. He grinned at Keisha. "The report's all written up," he said. "Thought you'd like to see the draft before I send it in."

She flipped through the pages. "Great job, Vince." A smile tugged at her cheeks. She'd taken some big chances, but she'd gotten away with it. They had nailed the Captain and broken Tenebras. Holman was in custody, his synthesis operation shutdown. Schwartz had disappeared, but there was no evidence against him anyway. Jim and Mira had been released to the care of their parents.

"I don't think anybody's going to look into the shooting death of Mario Fonseca, the notorious Captain of Tenebras," Vince said. "Trying to escape from police custody, wasn't he?"

"I had too many encounters with Fonseca. The guy was an absolute creep." Keisha picked up a stack of notes. "The world's better off without him."

"Damn straight. And all the other simultaneous busts were successful. They got dozens of gang members dealing Rapture. I think we've got most of Tenebras in custody."

Keisha snatched the ball out of the air and held it away from Vince when he made a grab for it. "Congratulations to us, then. It's good when it goes the right way for once, isn't it?"

 *Elisa*

Elisa opened her eyes, surprised for a moment she wasn't in her apartment. The tang of antiseptic filled her nostrils, and a heart monitor beeped in the distance. She lay in a hospital bed, surrounded by the cheerful and brightly-painted walls of the Lancaster Free Clinic. Everything came rushing back. Mario attacking her, being taken to that lab, being held as a hostage.

"Hey." Ben walked in the door, a bandage around his leg. His frown was so familiar, so *normal* that Elisa couldn't help grinning. Her life hadn't felt normal for a long time.

"How's your leg, Ben?" It surprised her that her voice sounded calm and cheerful.

He sat on an orange molded plastic chair by the side of the bed and pulled at his collar, embarrassed. "It's nothing. Just a flesh wound. Not a big deal. But what about you?"

She forced a casual laugh. "I'm sure I can go home soon and give this bed to someone who needs it more."

"You're not going anywhere until my dad's checked out that nasty concussion."

She touched her forehead, but the pain was—mostly—gone. "I'm fine. Your dad's kind to have me here." She needed to get up as soon as she could; there were so many things she had to do. And one person, in particular, she needed to see.

Ben rubbed a hand over the back of his neck. "Don't worry about it, Elisa. It's the least we could do."

"I was more worried about you taking a bullet for the cause."

"Oh," said Ben, fidgeting, "I didn't do anything." He looked away for a moment. "Adrian was the one who got him to take the gun off of you." He scratched his ear and scowled down at the floor. Then the words all tumbled out in a rush. "He risked his life. Mario could easily have shot him. I'd never have thought he'd do that. He really loves you, Elisa." He stopped, turning red. "I—I guess I was wrong about him. Keisha told me he'd been helping her out with the sting, but I just thought—well, it doesn't matter what I thought. I kind of made an ass of myself. I—I wish you lots of happiness with him."

"So he really was working with the police?" Elisa's heart flip-flopped. That whole 'ordering a cold-blooded killing' was just a show after all. In the rush of getting everyone out of the lab and then recovering from oxygen deprivation, she'd never had a chance to talk alone with Adrian.

"Oh, ho, ho, the sleeping princess is awake!" Dr. Lancaster's booming voice cut across their conversation. "How's your head feeling today, Elisa?"

Behind him crowded Sumiko and Chloe, grinning widely.

"Hey," said Sumiko, "We heard you'd figured out a way to score a legitimate excuse for senioritis." She shook her head. "Gotta give you credit for imagination. I mean, getting kidnapped to avoid homework? Who thinks of that?"

Chloe dumped a stack of books on the bed. "So like the good friends we are, we decided that misery loves company."

Elisa snorted and pushed the books away. "I'm feeling fine, Dr. Lancaster. And I'm grateful to you for taking care of me."

"Eh," he muttered. "We're happy to do it. Actually, I'd rather have you as a patient than all those Rapture addicts." He wrinkled his brow. "I don't know what's going to happen to them now that they've shut down the supply."

Elisa's heartbeat accelerated. "But isn't it good news?"

"Well, of course, there won't be any new addicts now. But these poor kids." He gestured in the direction of the larger public ward. "They have a rough time ahead of them. They're addicted to a substance that isn't being made anymore. I'm doing the best I can to make them comfortable, but they're all going to be going through some very painful withdrawals. Some of them, I'm afraid, might not pull through."

Her mouth went dry. "You mean, they might die?" Her voice almost cracked on the final syllable. She needed to talk to Adrian, and soon.

He was going to need her help.

Dr. Lancaster cleared his throat. "Rapture is a nasty, nasty drug. Once you get it into you, it doesn't let go of you easily." He scowled, and for a moment, the resemblance to his son was striking. "The pisser is, the goddamn city has refused to give me any funding for Rapture addicts. They say, 'the city's resources should be allocated to ongoing problems.'" He lowered his brows in a hard sneer. "Bastards. We've got people here who're at risk of dying because the cops were too slow to shut down the dealers, and the goddamn city is crying poor. The police chief is just their mouthpiece."

"Hey!" said Ben, matching his father's scowl. "The cops did as good a job as they could. It wasn't their fault it was a tough case to crack. That Eric Holman turned out to be a pretty slick guy."

"Hah!" said Dr. Lancaster. "My son, the police officer! I'm proud of him, but of course, that's what you'd expect since he has such a fine, upstanding father." He threw Ben one of his idiot grins. "On the other hand, he still has a lot to learn. I mean, getting shot on a routine mission?"

Ben balled his fists, but a voice spoke from the doorway before he could say anything. "You really should stop getting into fights with that bullet wound." It was Keisha, her black hair gleaming, wearing a neatly pressed police uniform. "I came to thank you for your help, Ben." She nodded to Dr. Lancaster. "You must be very proud of your son. He did some outstanding police work as a volunteer. As a matter of fact, the mayor's going to give him a medal."

Ben scowled. "Just what I need, some pompous ass shaking my hand and giving me a piece of pot metal."

"Whose ass is shaking?" Adrian appeared at the threshold. The room felt suddenly lighter, as though all at once it was easier for Elisa to breathe. She couldn't tear her eyes away from him. He wore a cream silk shirt over elegant black slacks. She couldn't help noticing how his clothes flattered the lines of his body. Wow. Even in a hospital bed her hormones wouldn't shut up. Maybe she really was feeling better.

Dr. Lancaster snorted. "Come on, son. We've got more patients to see." The two left the room as Adrian entered.

Adrian's gaze sought out Elisa's. "I'm sorry I didn't get here earlier." His voice was soft and composed, but dark circles ringed his eyes. "Work in the lab has really kept me busy." So he'd been working while she lay around in a hospital bed. His jaw was covered with a faint shadow of stubble, but of course, on him, it looked sexy. His eyes appeared larger and more vulnerable than usual, and it took a moment for her to notice that he wasn't wearing his glasses.

That's right. He'd told her he never really needed them. Something about dropping a mask.

"Yeah," said Sumiko. She glared at Adrian and jammed her fists onto her hips. "Real friends who don't dump her just before she gets kidnapped."

Chloe folded her arms and stepped in front of him. "She doesn't want to see you, jerk. Go away and let her recover in peace."

"I think," Elisa said, abruptly worried that he might believe them and go away, "you have it backwards."

Adrian raised an eyebrow. "I'm not going anywhere." He pulled out a chair and sat down next to the bed, reaching out a hand.

Elisa's fingers curled around his, and all the fine hairs on the back of her neck began to sizzle. Like when she stepped into a warm shower on a cold day, her entire body relaxed and opened. It was as though she had been short of oxygen all her life and now, for the first time, she could fill her lungs completely. She was going to hold his hand and never let it go. Whatever he had done, whatever he had been in the past was over. There was so much more he could do now. So much more they could do together.

Chloe and Sumiko both raised their brows.

Keisha broke the awkward silence. "Adrian! I was just telling Ben he was getting a medal from the mayor. You're getting one too." She smiled broadly at him. "Thanks to your hard work, we've shut down a big-time drug operation, and arrested a whole slew of gangbangers. Don't worry about that accusation against you. The DA's given you immunity from prosecution. The city of Rockton thanks you."

Adrian's expression remained neutral. "I didn't do much. You arranged everything and ran the whole operation. It was a highly efficient sting. Very intelligently planned."

Keisha gestured dismissively. "No, I want to give credit where credit is due. You guys all did a wonderful job. Adrian, you exceeded my expectations."

But Adrian focused on Elisa as she listened to Keisha, his face pale and drawn. "Elisa. How are you feeling today?"

She registered the double meaning of his words. He still didn't know. "Thank you for saving not just my life, but everyone's, last night."

He squeezed her hand more tightly. "You were the one that really did it. You came up with the phrase to stop the countdown, and you stopped Mario from killing anyone."

"We did it together. I'm sorry for not believing you earlier about the sting."

"Hush," he said, bringing her hand to his lips and kissing her fingers, his gaze not leaving hers. "I completely understand why you might have felt that way. It was my fault, and it's been my fault all along. I only hope I can begin to earn your trust in the future."

Elisa shook her head, her eyes smarting. "I've always trusted everyone else. I don't know why I stopped trusting you."

"Please," he said softly, "don't be upset. I don't want you to ever be upset again, Elisa."

It was as though no one else was in the room. "Adrian," she whispered, "I love you. My life won't be upset if we can be together." Yes, there was still an enormous amount of work to do, taking care of those Rapture patients—if the city wouldn't do it, they had to. Together.

Together—that single word caused all her tangled emotions to lift and smooth themselves. A deep knowledge pierced her. Yes. Together they would do whatever needed to be done.

His eyes widened and brightened, and the dark circles under his eyes faded like dawn lighting the night sky. "Elisa, I love you too."

Elisa perched on an orange vinyl chair in the shabby waiting room of the Lancaster Free Clinic, a clear plastic bag containing her meager belongings at her side. Dr. Lancaster had finally discharged her, and Adrian had offered to take her home. But when he pushed open the clinic door, his face was gray and shadowed, and his usually carefully chosen outfit was rumpled. He picked up her hospital bag and they walked out into pale spring sunshine. A breeze lifted Elisa's hair off her neck as he opened the passenger door of his Lotus.

She slid into the tiny car, and in a strange way, it felt like coming home. But the scent of leather mingled with gasoline brought back uncomfortable memories.

"Why do you look so worried?" She glanced at him sidelong. "From what I heard, you got away with everything. The newspaper said they found all the drug sources, and all the dealers are in jail." She narrowed her eyes. "Time for the complete truth," she insisted.

He sighed. "For you, always."

"So?" she prompted as he pulled away from the curb.

His fingers trembled slightly on the steering wheel. "You heard what Ben's dad said about the Rapture addicts. They're all at risk now. I've been in the lab working on some ideas I had before, trying to come up with a way to get them off the drug, to reverse both the poisoning and the addiction." He ran a hand through his hair. "But I'm stuck. I can't figure it out."

She noted the pallor of his skin, the bags under his eyes. "When was the last time you slept?"

"I think it was the night before we got locked in the lab."

"Seems like going to bed might get you unstuck." Okay, she really didn't intend that double entendre.

Really.

But Adrian was too ragged and exhausted to pick up on it. "Elisa, you don't understand," he said in a low voice. "I'm the one who's responsible for all the Rapture addicts. Just because I'm not in jail doesn't mean I don't deserve it."

All she wanted to do was take him in her arms and comfort him. On the other hand, he was right. "Well, maybe you don't deserve to sleep. But you'd be more effective if you did."

"I'll take a nap in the lab. I want to get you home first, though."

She crossed her arms over her chest. "If you don't go home and go to sleep, I'm going with you."

He leaned his head against the back of the seat. "Right now, I don't really have a home."

"Then we go to the lab."

"Don't *you* need to rest?" Concern suffused his face, momentarily washing out all his tiredness.

She placed her hand over his on the stick shift. Warmth and strength flowed over her entire body. "Adrian, I've spent the last three days doing nothing but lying in bed. Let's go."

He drove so calmly and gently on the way to the lab she had to remark on it. "Aren't you wasting all of this car's excess horsepower? Not that I'm complaining."

He smiled. "I don't need to drive like that anymore."

"Hmmm. Maybe Mario did something good for us after all?" she teased.

"It's more like something about you seems to have filled a part of me I didn't even know was missing."

She squeezed his hand more tightly. "We're a good team."

He signaled a left turn. "Mmm. I've never been on a team before."

Her eyebrows climbed up her forehead. This was the guy who never used to go anywhere, even the school cafeteria, without his entourage. "Um … didn't you run a criminal organization?"

"That wasn't a team. It was an extension of my will."

She cocked a brow at his arrogance, and he shrugged. "I have a lot to learn. This is a whole new world, and I hope you'll teach me."

He turned his palm upward and their fingers linked. No matter what, she was looking forward to it.

The lab appeared surprisingly peaceful compared with the last time Elisa had seen it. No flashing lights, no alarms blaring, just a few people in white lab coats scurrying around, their voices hushed. She wasn't surprised Adrian had no trouble getting her a visitor pass. The security guard seemed positively deferential.

The lab where he'd been working was cluttered with chemicals, open laptops, and scribbled-in lab notebooks. She wandered over to check his progress. "What are you working on?"

"Do you know how addiction works?"

Easy question. After all, she was planning to be a chemistry major. "When dopamine floods the brain and shortcuts its reward system."

He beamed. "Exactly. Rapture is even worse than most opiates because it activates both the amygdala and the hippocampus. Worse, in some cases, it causes a cascade reaction within the brain that essentially poisons you, even if you've only been exposed to a minute dose. Your synapses lose cohesion, and you can revert to childhood. Your brain ends up with fewer neurons and much sparser connections."

"Ugh." She wrinkled her nose. "Doesn't sound good at all."

He rubbed an eyebrow. "I'm trying to develop a chemical analog to methadone that focuses on breaking the glutamate bonds within neurotransmitters and returns the amygdala to normal."

"Doesn't methadone just lessen the physical symptoms of withdrawal?"

"Rapture works differently than heroin, and this analog I'm creating is much more than merely an agonist. It's more like an antidote."

Her skin began to tingle. "That would be fantastic," she said. "You could actually heal all those addicts permanently."

He shook his head. "I'm not quite there. I'm close. I'm so close! I thought I had it yesterday, but then it all went wrong. I had to start over completely."

"What happened?"

"I created a molecular simulation on the computer, but when I tried it for real, it got stuck in the middle of the synthesis. The precursors I'm using have a tendency to explode."

Elisa scanned the room. "You're being careful, right?" A few char marks streaked the sides and top of one of the benches.

He shot her a brief smile. "When have you known me not to be?"

She rolled her eyes. "Only when you're breathing."

He laughed, but his expression immediately became earnest. "The reaction has to occur at a low temperature to keep it from exploding. I'm using an antipyretic gel. But it's below the gel's freezing point."

"So the problem is that your substrate melts?"

"If I freeze the gel, the reaction stops. If I allow the gel to turn to a liquid, well…" He rubbed his chin, and she noticed for the first time that his stubble looked a little singed.

He swiveled the laptop so she could see his calculations. "I need new precursors, but none of them are effective to get to the final synthesis."

She frowned. "Have you considered using a different substrate? Like some kind of cellulose?"

"What good would that do?"

"Sounds like you need a reversal in the physical properties of your base. Normal chemicals become liquid at higher temperatures and turn solid at lower temperatures, right? Ice melts at 32°F as it gets warmer, and if you take chocolate or butter out of the refrigerator, they get softer and more liquefied as they get warmer."

He shrugged. "So?"

"Some carboxymethyl cellulose compounds behave like eggs."

He raised an eyebrow. "Eggs?"

"You know, when eggs sit in the refrigerator, or at room temperature, they're liquid. But they're unusual. Eggs are one of the few substances that turn solid at higher temperatures."

He looked thoughtful. "But that's actually a chemical change, isn't it?"

"Yes, but some of these compounds behave similarly. They melt at cooler temperatures. If you heat them up, they turn solid." She waved her arms, getting excited. "That way, if your chemical reaction becomes exothermic and gets ready to explode, this stuff would solidify and shut it down."

Adrian rubbed his chin, pensive. He opened his laptop and typed furiously. She peered over his shoulder. He scanned rapidly through a series of articles in an online chemistry journal, reading at his usual blinding speed.

Then he slammed the lid shut. His eyes were bright. "That's it!" He put both hands around her waist, his fingers and thumbs girdling her midriff. A current zipped through her from one of his palms to the other, as though her own body was becoming exothermic, boiling like a reaction gone wild.

He lifted her effortlessly into the air, and spun her around in a dizzying circle, round and round, laughing. She had never seen his face so carefree before, his eyes gleaming with pure delight, all the calculation and playacting gone from his expression. His muscles flexed under her hands and they flowed together like perfect dancers, hand to shoulder, fingertip to fingertip, soul to soul.

The lab whirled around them. Sunlight winked through the half-open blinds as they spun, a glittering tracery of gold like a whirling kaleidoscope that seemed half-familiar. His beautiful features filled her vision as all the shadows faded away.

Their faces were only inches apart. She licked her lips and the grin on his face suddenly became more feral. She wound the fingers of one hand through his warm and messy hair. His long lashes dipped. She leaned into him and pressed her lips to his.

His lips were warm satin and toasted almonds; that slightly burnt aftertaste from his singed stubble only rendered him more savory. She smiled against his mouth. He was delicious. Tasting him felt like risking a conflagration. But what was life without risk?

If she was playing with fire by choosing Adrian, so be it.

Let it burn.

Fire could be dangerous, but... it gave lifesaving warmth. Roasting over a cook fire made food nourishing — and delicious. Baking, heating, burning could change the very structure of a substance, transmuting it from poison into elixir. The subtle chemistry of sustenance was nothing without fire.

Every cook knew that.

She combed both hands through his hair, and enfolded his head in her arms. She wrapped her legs around his torso, her inner thighs molding to his hips, and the sun swathed them in golden light.

34

 *Elisa*

ALL THE WINDOWS in the school cafeteria had been thrown open. The sweet smell of wisteria sprawling over the south wall mingled with an aroma of freshly cut grass from the field and wafted into the room full of chattering students.

Chloe dropped her tray on the table. "Elisa, you're back! Are you doing okay?" Her eyes glittered with excitement.

Sumiko rolled her eyes. "Nothing makes you more popular than being a kidnap victim," she commented dryly.

Elisa managed a sarcastic grimace. "Well, I'm fine now. No problems." She dug into her lasagna.

"So," Chloe said, leaning close. "You have to tell us. Every. Single. Detail."

Elisa shrugged. She'd been practicing the shorthand version. She wouldn't lie, but she sure wasn't going to reveal everything. "What's there to tell? I got kidnapped by a dealer who got shot by the police. A SWAT team shut down the drug manufacturing plant and freed all the people they were using for experiments. And the gang responsible got apprehended. End of story."

Chloe frowned. "It's a good thing you're going into chemistry and not journalism, because storytelling is definitely not your forte. I've read juicier reports in the local paper."

"I'm just glad they kept our names out of it." Elisa bent her head to her food. Deflection. That was going to be her new skill. "I don't want to spend the rest of my senior year fighting off reporters."

"You've got more important things to do," Sumiko said, waving a fork. "Like how did your college applications go?"

She'd hoped they wouldn't ask that. "I got accepted to MIT, but they didn't give me enough financial aid, so I guess I'm not going."

Sumiko dropped her fork. "You're what? Girl, you are so going. Congratulations!"

"My parents aren't going to help me, and my EFC's too high."

"Call up the MIT office of financial aid. Tell them your situation."

"I know about the internet, Sumiko." Elisa ticked off the conditions on her fingers. "I don't count as an emancipated minor, there's no documented abuse in my family, I'm not in the military, and I'm neither twenty-four nor married." She shrugged. "It's no big deal. I'll keep working at the bakery, save money, and when I turn twenty-four, I'll apply again. It's only about five years."

"What's only about five years?" Adrian squeezed into the seat and wrapped an arm around her.

"She got into MIT but won't go. She's got the most pathetic excuse ever: no money," Chloe said, rolling her eyes.

Adrian smiled. "You know, there are quite a few private foundations that offer scholarships to students that meet their criteria."

"I've got no problem waiting." She'd come to peace with her decisions.

He eyed her and tipped his head to one side with an all-too-familiar smirk. "I believe we need more fairness and justice in the world. That's what these philanthropic foundations aim for."

Elisa shoveled in more lasagna and spoke around a mouthful of pasta. "A laudable goal, but nothing to do with me."

He leaned into her and whispered. "We've got a few key tasks for our team. Bring Schwartz to trial and get you into MIT—all legally and ethically." His eyes glinted. "I love a challenge."

She shook her head, but she had a feeling there were going to be more than a few challenges ahead for them to face together. But interestingly enough, they no longer filled her with dread.

Her dread had usually come from wondering what those voices in her head would say about her life. She hadn't heard any of them since that day they were trapped in the lab.

Maybe the oxygen deprivation had suffocated them.

Her mother had called—she was going on another extended retreat. She told Elisa not to expect her back for at least another year. Elisa told her she was moving out, and she seemed supremely uninterested.

Good. She didn't want to talk with her mother about her new life. Sleeping with a former gang leader after all those times her mother had insisted on dressing Elisa in white because it 'symbolized purity'? Ugh. Elisa wasn't sad to be moving on and away from her.

Adrian held out a small wrapped box. "I've got a present for you."

"What's this?" Elisa asked, turning it over in her hands.

"Don't just sit there, open it, silly," said Sumiko.

She unwrapped it. Inside was a pair of brand-new glasses, very similar to the pair she had lost so long ago and couldn't afford to replace. Slowly, almost reverently, she unfolded them and placed them on her nose. Instantly, the world sprung into crystalline focus.

Scalloped wisteria clusters dangled over the windows, magnolias swelled with pure white blossoms, and new green buds enveloped the birch trees at the far end of the field. In the further distance, fine lines of branches pierced the pale blue sky, all the tiny details of the vast world suddenly clear and rich and full of promise.

Could she tell Adrian how vivid and beautiful and alive the world was now?

"I donated my own glasses to charity," he said softly. "Now that I'm with you, I'll never hide again." His words had the ring of a solemn promise. He took her fingers in his, and slowly, with his eyes never leaving hers, he brushed his lips over the back of her hand, launching an array of sparks up her arm that warmed her as though she stood before a blazing fire.

He gazed at her with such intensity she couldn't tear her eyes away. Without his glasses, his face was intensely vulnerable. A thrilling rush swept her from head to toe, and she laced her fingers more deeply through his, wanting only to press herself against him, skin to skin, heart to beating heart.

This man had opened himself fully to her. Trusted her completely. Loved her.

She almost couldn't breathe, overwhelmed with the magnitude of his trust. She would protect him with her life.

And she knew, as surely as gravity held twin stars in each other's orbit, that he felt the same.

A couple of weeks later, Elisa visited Ben at the clinic. She peeked into one of the rooms and saw a healthy-looking boy lying asleep in the hospital bed. He looked familiar.

"Is that Pete?" she asked, astonished at the change in his appearance.

"Yeah," Ben huffed. He rolled his eyes. "What a jerk."

"What's wrong with him?"

"He wasn't so bad when he was really sick," Ben groused. "Hell, when I thought he was going to die I almost felt sorry for him. Now he's just been making a nuisance of himself, harassing all the female patients and nurses."

"He looks kind of peaceful," she began.

"Heh," Ben snorted. He put a hand behind his head and gazed off into the distance. "I may have put a sedative in his IV." He eyed her sidelong, but she only shrugged. Her slavish, rule-following days were over.

"I heard that you're also treating Kim Lugo."

Ben jumped up, finger to his lips. "Shhh! She's here anonymously." He lowered his voice. "The clinic could get in trouble for not reporting bullet wounds to the police, but my dad, well, you know what he's like."

Elisa mimed zipping her lips shut. "No one'll hear anything from me. But I saw your other ward was practically empty. How'd you get the treatment for Rapture? I thought the mayor had shut down your funding."

Ben grinned. "It was the damnedest thing. This private foundation actually reached out to us. There's a new development in Rapture treatment, and they got fast-track approval for clinical trials. They offered to pay for all our medication and treatment for our patients."

She raised her eyebrows. "A foundation? Do you happen to know the name?"

"My dad knows, but they wanted to remain anonymous. But who cares? Whoever they are, they're brilliant. The treatment works. Everyone's going to make a full recovery."

Rory's funeral was held on an early morning at the Sunset View Cemetery. The line of cars and hearse wound slowly up the hill toward the A-frame mortuary. The air smelled cool and fresh, sweet as cut flowers. It was a long walk across the wet grass to a stand of white lilies and blue ribbons, where a man in a black suit stood holding a leather-bound book, greeting people in hushed tones.

Adrian and Elisa stood at the back of the crowd of mourners, holding hands. Sierra sobbed in the front row, and a crowd made up of mostly high school students, uneasy in rented finery, shuffled from foot to foot. A few adults were also in attendance, those who had heard the tragic love story on the news. Rory was being hailed as a hero for helping rescue all the homeless people who'd been victimized by Eric Holman, now in jail pending multiple counts of murder, kidnapping, and various other crimes. Sierra's story had gone viral on social media, and a college fund had been set up for her. Donations were still pouring in.

"He would've liked that," Elisa said.

Adrian raised an eyebrow. "Only his heroic deeds remembered? Of course."

"That Sierra's future has been taken care of."

He squeezed her hand. "I'll watch over her."

The funeral director wrapped up the ceremony, and news cameras whirred as the mayor stood up to make a speech. Adrian's lips tightened. "Will you come with me?"

"Anywhere," she said.

He pointed around the back side of the hill. "Let's go to Area D."

They walked through damp grass studded with brass plaques set flush with the earth. Clusters of lilies, peonies, roses, and other multi-colored flowers dotted the ground.

Adrian's hand enfolded hers. They neared the crest of the hill, the wet grass swishing against their shoes. Reaching the top, she inhaled sharply. The dewy earth fell away from them; trees coated in the pale lime-green of spring splayed irregularly into the bright sky. Beyond, hazy in the distance, the city spread out like a vanishing checkerboard, downtown windows gleaming like diamonds in the morning light.

Adrian scanned the ground nearby. "Here," he said, stopping at a row of plaques beneath a bower of wisteria. Mounds of lilies draped the ground, and Elisa dropped to her knees to read the names.

Armando Salas, 1964-2003
Elizabeth Salas, 1969-2003
Emma Salas, 1995-2003

Adrian stood, hands in his pockets, looking down the hill and out at the city.

"She would have liked this," he murmured almost to himself. Elisa joined him and gazed out over the vista. "My mother loved views."

Elisa reached for his hand and shaded her eyes with the other. She imagined a young, dark-haired woman in a bright red dress dancing over the long slope of the lawn, laughing, flinging her hair up to the sun. "She's happy here."

Then Elisa hesitated, inhaled, and pointed to the other side of the small stream. "My brother's over there."

He followed her gaze. "Carlos?"

The words she had never said aloud before tumbled out. "He was shot by the police during a robbery seven years ago. He was seventeen."

Adrian took her in his arms. Hot tears stung her eyes, but she swiped them away.

"My dad left and my mom kept saying that Carlos had just moved out and would be back at any time."

Adrian squeezed her more tightly.

"He always wanted me to be good," she said.

"You are good." Adrian kissed her softly on the forehead. "No one better."

Elisa fished a tissue out of her pocket and wiped her nose, then tipped her head back, meeting his eyes. "You know what? You are too."

He raised his eyebrows skeptically. "Good?"

"What matters is what you do from now on. The past is over."

He stared out over the city, at the street pattern extending into the haze below, and became still. One finger flicked at his slacks. "Does anyone really know?"

"We're going to be together, and you're going to do work that makes the world a better place," she predicted. "I know you'll be a good person."

The diamond-like glitter on the myriad windows below softened and merged into the amber glow of morning. Adrian shifted, and sunlight flashed across his features. He took her in his arms, and his breath stroked her cheek. His voice, deep and low, resonated in her ears like a benediction. "Then it's decided. What *you* believe is all that matters."

The morning sun warmed her bare shoulders; the sky glowed with honeyed light. A small breeze rippled the clusters of lavender blooms dangling from the pergola. The fragrance of wisteria mingled with Adrian's clean scent. She lifted her face to his, and their lips met with the sweet familiarity of coming home.

Epilogue

ADRIAN TOOK A GAP YEAR to clean up some of the mess around Rockton before going to Harvard. Elisa worked at the bakery full-time, and they both volunteered in drug treatment and anti-gang programs. They moved into an apartment together.

On the one-year anniversary of their first date, Adrian proposed.

They were married soon after, and when Elisa resubmitted her application to MIT, she was considered an independent adult and received full financial aid.

Ben won a pre-med scholarship, and Kim, inspired by her experience at the clinic, became a medical technician and eventually a nurse. Cesar gave up his gang life and went into private security. He continued to secretly enjoy poetry.

Keisha and Vince both received promotions and never again had to work undercover in a high school. After a few more years of bickering on the job, they got married so they could argue 24/7. They've never owned more than six cats.

As the fortuneteller had predicted, Elisa and Adrian eventually had four children and lived a long, loving, and happy life together.

The only shadow in their bright life occurred about ten years after the events in this story when Alfred Schwartz unexpectedly returned with the journal that belonged to Adrian's mother.

But that's a story for another time.

Acknowledgments

So much is owed to the many people who helped with this book at various points in its creation that I can't possibly begin to thank you enough:

Bonny Becker, Karen Finneyfrock, Allison Augustyn, Toni Littlestone, Jason Strayer, Kim Ross, Rita, Ara, Ken, Diana, Flarie, AC, MS, LWW, TFM, and many others all read earlier drafts of this novel and provided valuable feedback. Forgive me for not mentioning every single one of you by name, but please know that you all have my deepest thanks.

Special thanks to Kimberly Ito for her amazing editing skills, to Fran Walsh, kick-ass beta extraordinaire, and to Christian Fuenfhausen for the fantastic cover.

Sophia Amador
October 2016

About Alford Marr Press

Alford Marr is a Seattle-based publisher
of memoirs and fiction.

Find print and ebook editions and
sign up to receive notice of new books:
www.alfordmarr.com